THE DREAM MAKER

KIERA NIXON

Nixe

To my sister, who helped build this dream.

———

'Follow your dreams,' everyone says.
But where to find one worth following?

For Maatje Finkel, it was four years ago.
The first night without her sister.

The night she discovered the hotel . . .

———

THEN: MAATJE

Maatje knew she was dreaming because the window had been closed when she'd fallen asleep. Now the sash gaped wide and the bedsheet acting as a makeshift curtain flapped in the breeze. Down below, in the moonlit paddock that Mum and Aunt Marjorie planned to turn into a vegetable garden, stood a shaggy chestnut horse.

"Elinor?"

Had her sister missed her so much she'd ridden all the way to Maatje's dream from her new boarding school? Finally they could gallop through wildflower meadows again, and churn sand and salty spray along the beach. Elinor always had the best horse dreams.

Maatje ran as fast as she could outside. The horse raised his head and considered her through a mouthful of grass, but Elinor was nowhere to be seen.

Of course she wasn't. Elinor was too far away to dream with. Besides, her horse dreams had stopped when the divorce came; Mum and Dad's arguing had scared them away. Scared Elinor away too.

"Baggy," she named the pony, scratching behind his

withers and swallowing back her disappointment. "What happened to the rest of your herd?"

Looking back at the new house, Maatje decided it looked a lot better in the dark, without the grey and the rain. Beyond, the empty moors beckoned. Somewhere out there her sister dreamt without her.

She heaved the paddock gate open. "Come on, let's go and look for them."

Like Elinor's dream horses, Baggy loved to run. Maatje lay straddled across his back, tucked close to his arching, straining neck, and together they flew. Leaping over brooks, dodging ghostly boulders and squelching through bog. The moor yawned dark and endless as she ripped through the starless, soggy space on her equine rocket.

Lonely space, without the thunder of accompanying hooves. Without her sister's laughter.

But there was another sound. A violin. Carrying through the night as if the raspy grass and mud-clogged streams themselves were singing. Calling. *Come and play, because life is beautiful.*

And they followed its tune up a hill shaped like an overgrown tortoise, where a boy stood atop, playing his fiddle, moonlight spilling through his fingers.

Maatje slid off Baggy's back and watched the music twist and dance around her. Downhill it swept, quavers stacking themselves like bricks, swirling treble clef turrets and triangular crescendo rooves slated with sharps. A solid crotchet driveway cobbled with semibreves stretched out from the big bass doors and harmony twinkled in every window.

A mansion, made entirely out of music. Yet as solid as anything she'd ever seen before.

The boy played on until rhythm pumped from the chimney and the door knobs sparkled with staccato shine, then he lowered his violin and offered Maatje a grin.

8

"Hello."

Maatje's jaw swung like a gate without a latch. "How'd you do that?"

He was a little older than her – fifteen or sixteen – with vibrant blue eyes that reflected the lights of the mansion like magic. "The Manager likes the hotel to be built afresh every night. Easier than washing the sheets."

"It's amazing." Maatje became embarrassingly aware she was dressed in her pyjamas and covered in mud. "A strange place to build a hotel though, in the middle of nowhere."

The boy gave a small acknowledging bow. "On the contrary, nowhere can be found by everyone."

As he spoke, cars began drawing up the driveway, emptying pyjama-clad passengers into the hotel. A man riding in a little toy train dodged in and out of the arriving legs and someone parachuted onto the roof. Six wild ponies wandered around the side of the hotel. Baggy gave an excited whinny and galloped down the hill to greet them.

Maatje giggled. "Baggy found his herd!" What she'd give to see Elinor amongst all the crowding faces. "May I take a look? I've never seen a hotel made of music before."

The boy threw his fiddle into the air where it flew off on silent tawny wings. "It would be my pleasure."

Partway down the hill, Maatje felt as she always did before stepping into her sister's dreams – that often invisible, but ever-present, barrier between minds.

This wasn't her dream. The hotel and boy belonged to somebody else. A stranger.

She stopped walking.

It definitely wasn't Mum's or Aunt Marjorie's. Their minds didn't feel like this. But who else's could it be? The new house was miles from anywhere.

The boy must have seen her apprehension. He turned and cocked his head, as though the wind whispered its secrets in his ear. "This is the Manager's hotel for the tired and lonely dreamer. Everyone is welcome."

Maatje wrinkled her nose. "That's impossible."

No one could fit everyone in their dream. Mum had once tried to invite both Maatje and her sister into hers. She'd had a headache for days.

"There's only one impossible thing in all the world." The boy brought a carefully closed fist out of his pocket. "Want to see?"

Maatje nodded.

He opened his fingers. His palm was empty.

"Nothing?" Maatje frowned.

"Exactly." The boy gave a smile to embarrass the stars. He still had the violin bow in his other hand and shook it out like a rolled up carpet. It spilt down the hillside, becoming a long slippery slide. "So, you coming?"

Both Mum and school had drilled into Maatje her entire life to never enter a stranger's dream, and really, apart from Elinor's, no one's dreams had ever appealed before. She'd asked why it was so bad, but the reply had always been either, "Don't get clever," or, "Because it is." Those weren't reasons. If she entered a stranger's dream and something bad happened, Maatje could always wake up, back in her room, safe. She was an expert at waking up on command.

She also itched to see inside this Manager's impossible hotel.

Maatje took a deep breath and launched herself down the slide.

THEN: MAATJE

"I'm Will by the way," said the boy, taking Maatje around the side of the hotel to avoid the bustling entrance.

"Maatje."

They arrived at a small open door at the side of the hotel, which belched orange light and the sounds of clattering crockery. Inside was a hubbling, bubbling mass of heat and noise and purpose. A steaming pit of tomato soup in the centre hissed and whooshed up like a geyser, splattering into the mosaic of bowls arranged around it. Brave chefs rushed to retrieve filled bowls and replace them with empty ones before the soup erupted again. Clouds of flour drifted high above the mayhem, and chefs with machetes hacked to contain celery the size of bamboo that sprouted from a countertop forest of carrot orange trunks and plumy lettuce leaves. Maatje ducked as a fairy cake whizzed over her head on stubby sponge wings, while a chef with a net on a stick chased after it.

Oh, if Elinor could have seen this!

A hollowed-out watermelon the size of a small room sat serenely to one side in a garden of fanned strawberries, peeling orange lilies and plump buds of grape. Inside, the walls were carved with frilly flowers of red, white and green and the floor tiled with shiny black seeds. A dark-haired lady worked amidst bouquets of pineapple, kiwi and mango, her sharp knife unravelling an apple like a long red ribbon.

She made a half bow in Maatje's direction and held out another apple. "Today we make apple rose."

Maatje turned, thinking she was talking to Will, but he had disappeared. "You mean me?"

The lady nodded.

Eagerly, Maatje picked up a knife and tried to copy. A large triangular chunk of apple landed on the counter.

"Have you got a peeler?"

"No, no." The lady's eyes grew wide. "A knife is more precise. Please . . ." She reached an elegant hand around Maatje's and moved her fingers into the right position. Together, carefully, they began to unwrap the apple.

When they both had long strips of skin, the lady showed Maatje how to roll it so it fanned out to form a rose. Beautiful, and so simple, Maatje instantly began to work on her own. Tight on one side, loose on the other . . .

There!

It looked like a deformed turnip. She resisted the urge to squish it up in frustration and unrolled it to try again. This time she listened carefully to the lady's instructions, and to her delight a sort of squashed rose blossomed between her fingers.

"I did it!"

The lady smiled. "Very good. Another."

They placed their apple roses amongst the grape buds and orange lilies and each picked up another apple. By the time Will reappeared, red-cheeked and with the renegade fairy cake in one hand, Maatje had made four roses, each better than the last.

"If you're looking to get a job, you'd better have a bath first," he said.

Maatje flushed. She'd forgotten how she looked.

Will passed her the fairy cake as they left the kitchen. It was delicious. Dinner had been half a can of cold baked beans after no one could find any gas canisters for the hob.

Out in the lobby, guests milled about, some dressed in their best suits and others padding about in their pyjamas like Maatje. The clerk at the main desk nodded to each as they passed and disappeared through the many doors that were labelled things like: dining room, library, vanishing room . . .

Maatje licked the icing sugar from her fingers. "What's in the vanishing room?"

Will stared at her. "You can see that?"

Maatje nodded. "Is it private?"

Will winced and led her to a great wooden vine in the centre of the lobby. Its twisted trunk was formed of shallow steps, spiralling up through the heart of the hotel. The plant's tendrils wound across the lobby ceiling, dropping bunches of glowing crystal flowers like chandeliers, then all the way up into the darkness of the floors above until it looked like starlight.

"May I?" Will offered Maatje a gentlemanly palm.

Her breath caught. No one had ever treated her like this before. She pushed her questions about the vanishing room aside and eagerly placed her sticky fingers in his. Each step hummed under her footsteps, reminding her of the music from which it was made.

"Hold tight." Will squeezed her fingers and began to climb faster, up, up and up.

The humming stairs built to a chorus, the sparkling light from the chandelier flowers swarmed like fireflies around them, and before she knew it, Maatje wasn't climbing at all. She was floating.

"Oh!" She grabbed Will's other hand in surprise as they drifted between the branches. "Wow."

Will laughed. "Best way to travel."

"I love it!" Maatje tried a somersault. Then another. Her elbow caught a flower and it tinkled like wind chimes.

Will glided onto a landing and steadied her when she attempted a graceful touchdown that turned out to be harder than he made it look.

Maatje didn't want him to let go. She wanted to fly forever. She wanted Elinor to fly with them.

"What's the bathroom like?"

Will heaved open a heavy door that poured purple curling steam.

Maatje grinned.

'Follow your dreams,' everyone said.

But Maatje was happy playing in this one.

NOW: MAATJE

The fine misty rain had deceived Maatje yet again as she marched umbrella-less to work from the bus station. No more than a six-minute walk and she was soaked through – from her gloves and thick woollen coat right down to her underwear. One day, when she was a top dream therapist and earnt lots of money, she'd learn to drive. Then she'd have a nice parking bay at the SDRC and a glove compartment where an umbrella would always live for the short hop from the front seat to those big, gleaming automatic doors. But for now, here she was, with a floppy, soggy bus pass tucked into her wallet, and a squelch to her shoes. Nothing to do but enjoy it.

She rounded the corner and the enormous glassy hulk of the SDRC loomed in the haze above the rest of the buildings in town.

The Shared Dreaming Research Centre.

Maatje had plenty of dreams to follow nowadays. Dreams to revolutionise the world of dream therapy with her incredible discoveries. Dreams of fixing her sister. And realising them all started here.

Outside the building were the usual rabble of protesters. Maatje had been surprised how many people were against shared dreaming when she'd first seen a protest, and saddened by the number who simply didn't have enough trust in their fellow humans to let anyone in.

There was quite a large crowd this morning. Maatje glanced at their signs as she skirted round them.

Man's mind for himself

Keep sleep sacred

She quickly ducked her head in fear of being heckled and ploughed through the front doors into the warmth.

Inside was calm and clean. Maatje pretended to wring herself out to Camille on reception, who shook her perfectly dry, glossy head in exasperation. Good. She'd probably lend her an umbrella if the rain didn't stop in time for the party that evening. There were always one or two in the lost property. Maatje continually added to the collection.

She squelched past the massive twinkling Christmas tree over to the lifts, her squeaking shoes echoing loudly in the vast atrium. A floor polishing machine followed, sucking up the stream that trickled from her feet.

"Oh my god, Maatje Finkel, did you swim here?!" Hanna, her colleague and effortlessly glamorous SDRC data analyst heralded her arrival in the office.

Their boss, Paul, didn't even lift his head from his work as he said, "Maatje, we're in the labs all day today. I've got three new blockers for you to try."

The labs were her favourite place. It hadn't been long into her apprenticeship when Paul had discovered Maatje was very good at entering other people's dreams, even without an invitation. Since it was his job to devise mechanisms dreamers could put in place to stop intruders, Maatje had instantly become his antihero guinea pig. All she had to do was break into the dreams of blocker scientists who created his carefully thought-out barriers. It was a welcome escape from her usual role of report typist and paperwork filer. Now she got to work with the pros. Even if they had so far dismissed all her thoughts on dreaming.

"No one can control their dreams like that, Maatje," sighed Ulf, a tall, silver-haired blocker who liked handing out sherbets. She'd just given him her suggestions for how he could have stopped her wheedling her way through his block that evening. "We can only guide the metaphor."

Sitting up on the bed in the stark white lab, Maatje closed her mouth. She'd been careful not to mention the hotel this time.

"And on that note we're done," Paul said, glancing at his watch. "Off to the party with you all – good job."

Maatje peeled the probes off her head and yawned. Her first work Christmas party. A fancy affair held in the grand manor house of the SDRC's biggest shareholder, Hubert Kröte. Hanna was giving her a lift.

"Maatje, put this into the system quickly, would you?" Paul handed her a scribbled table full of numbers he'd been filling in all day. It made very little sense, but was easy enough to copy out. Paul hated typing. She shook the sleep from her brain and sat down at the computer.

"I'll see you at Hubert's later, yeah?" He pointed to her expectantly.

Maatje raised a finger in the air in confirmation, still too tired to speak, and started typing.

She'd succeeded with two out of three blockers, which wasn't bad. Though it meant more work for Paul every time she got through their barriers. He and the blockers were clever men who understood a lot about dreams, but wouldn't stand for any notion that dreams might actually be a little more impossible than even they knew.

"You can't share dreams with anyone further than the room next door," Ulf had said.

"You can't fit more than a few people in your head at the same time," agreed Hans.

"You can't choose what you dream about," Walter added.

These were boring, fundamental absolutes that rigidified their expectations so much that Maatje slipped around them unnoticed, and they continued to be stumped by it. Weren't scientists supposed to be open to anything? How was she supposed to help Elinor if they wouldn't even consider her ideas? If they thought the hotel was some childish fantasy? She wasn't a kid anymore. She'd be nineteen in a few months.

An anguished cry echoed in the corridor outside, jolting Maatje fully awake. Her heart pounded in her chest even as her brain tried to make sense of what she'd heard. She chided herself and chuckled. Dreams lingered down here. Either that or someone else was running late to the party.

When she returned to the office, Hanna was in a long cream gown with sequins in all the right places, fixing little pearls into her hair.

"There you are," she said, handing Maatje the shimmering purple dress she promised she'd lend her. "We have to leave in fifteen minutes. I don't want to miss the welcoming drinks."

Maatje felt like a movie star by the time they made their way to the front doors of the SDRC. Heels clacked on the shiny floor; feathers of dark auburn hair tickled her neck. She drew her coat tighter as the cold breeze outside hit. The left-over puddles from the morning's rain shone with silver stillness in the light pouring from the SDRC.

"Oh my goodness!" Hanna cried.

Striped police tape surrounded the place where people

had been protesting earlier, and three white tents had been erected within its perimeter.

Maatje's heart did a somersault. But they only did that when people died. What had happened?

"Protestors." Hanna's shock disappeared behind a disapproving tut. "They're a different breed."

NOW: FRIEDRICH

Earlier that same day, as Maatje came around the corner in the rain to see the protest outside the SDRC, Friedrich was holding his sign: *Privacy is a RIGHT*. The rain didn't bother him, as his was an important task: to outlaw shared dreaming. It pained him that society couldn't see how wrong it all was. Just because it was possible, didn't mean people should do it. And the SDRC aided and encouraged their participation.

A SDRC worker lifted his middle finger to the crowd as he went from his car into the building. A couple of protestors reciprocated the gesture. Friedrich rose above it – but only because his wife was standing next to him. His beautiful black-eyed Brenda. Not only did she believe in the cause, but she was walking proof of it. As a child she'd been a weak dreamer, and her neighbour and his friends had frequently broken into her dreams to abuse her and the things she dreamt about. She'd never told anyone about it because they'd threatened to do it all in real life if she did. Nowadays she was stronger. She had learnt to block people. Friedrich had helped.

He'd accumulated many tactics to keep people out of his dreams over years of flitting from foster home to foster home. Well-meaning and not so well-meaning foster parents, and their snobby kids. A gang at the children's home had been the worst; they'd been the last people to ever get inside his head. That had been thirteen years ago when he'd been twelve.

No more.

Two protestors went over to the car of the SDRC worker who'd sworn at them and dragged their keys along the side of it. A security guard ran out of the building and hailed them angrily.

Brenda sighed. "This is why no one takes us seriously, because of idiots like them."

Friedrich put his arm around her and kissed her cheek. "Want me to offer to pay for damages?"

Brenda nudged him with a fond smile. He loved her smile. It was ever so slightly wonky and made her look like she was teasing him. "Do you want your children to eat for the rest of the week?"

Friedrich looked away. He'd taken a couple of hours off work to attend the protest this morning. Computers could wait, but the top scientists on the continent meeting the CEO of the SDRC couldn't.

Brenda worked weekends when Friedrich was at home to look after the kids. This protest was a rare moment the two of them had together. Anja, their eldest, had just started school, and Milo was in playgroup for a couple of hours, so Brenda had been able to accompany him.

A number of security guards gathered around the car and some protestors followed. A few of the guards pushed them towards the entrance of the car park, while others wrestled with the two who'd scratched the car.

"Come on, all of you, get out of here. You ain't wanted."

"This is a peaceful protest," shouted one protester, as a guard shoved her back.

"Didn't you hear what he said? Get out. This is private property."

"So are our dreams!"

The pushing quickly turned to kicking and the protestors kicked back. A few picked up stones from the flower beds and launched them at the guards. They deserved it, but Friedrich didn't want any trouble. He waved his sign furiously over his head. If they were going to get kicked out before any of the SDRC's guests came, he would make sure at least the security staff saw his message.

Brenda hissed when a stone hit her in the back of the head. "Come on, Freddie, let's get out of here."

But they couldn't. They were surrounded by what was fast becoming an angry mob, squeezing them towards the doors to the SDRC.

"Stay back!" a guard yelled, unsheathing his gun and aiming it into the crowd.

Friedrich felt Brenda's hand in his. They were still being shoved forward. More guards pulled out their guns.

"Hold it right there!"

"You're not going to use that!" someone yelled.

A large stone struck one of the guards in the temple, knocking him out cold.

"Stop!"

A shot ran out. Then two more.

People ran in all directions, screaming.

Brenda?! He'd lost her hand in the fray and dived back to find her.

People punched, scratched and even bit him as they fought their way past.

Another gunshot.

There was blood on his clothes, on their clothes . . .

22

Friedrich could hear nothing over the roar of terrified people and the blood rushing in his ears.

"Brenda!"

He found her lying on the concrete, her beautiful black eyes unseeing. A bullet in the middle of her forehead.

Time blurred around him. He touched her cheek gently, then harder. As feet kicked at them, he covered her with his body to protect her from their trampling. Even when they'd gone, he still lay there. He couldn't look at her. It wasn't real. None of this was real.

"Oy, you!"

Rough hands grabbed Friedrich and pulled him away.

"Get off me!" He ripped and swung and screamed like a wild animal. Some of them were touching her. "Get off her! Brenda!"

He wrenched himself free and threw himself to her side, scooping her into his arms.

But the hands grabbed again and the world lost focus. He tried to headbutt the guard who had pinned his arms to his side, but his head rolled uselessly. What was happening?

Then he saw the needle.

"Whatdidyoudotome?" Friedrich slurred.

"We just need you to relax," the man with the needle said. He was wearing a white lab coat.

"Youkilledmywife."

"Take him inside," the lab coat man ordered.

"Brenda!" He couldn't see. Was he going blind? The world rippled and his cheeks tickled with the dampness of rain.

They lay him on a trolley, starting to roll him away, and there was nothing he could do about it. Brenda got smaller and smaller, and someone else knelt at her side instead of him.

No, no, no! The words couldn't leave his brain any more

23

than his movements could. In his head, he cursed them all and thrashed out until he was free from the trolley and back with Brenda, but all he could really do was twitch a hand.

People bid the guards and the man in the lab coat a good morning as they passed, giving Friedrich concerned looks.

Help. Help me, he wanted to call to them. But the only noise he made was a deep guttural moan.

By the time they stopped rolling him, sleep beckoned heavy. They were in some sort of laboratory, white and metal everywhere. Computers and wires. He couldn't make sense of any of it. He had to stay awake. He had to get away.

"Just relax." The lab coat man leant over him and smiled.

This was really bad.

NOW: MAATJE

With a deep clang, the towering wrought-iron gates to Hubert's manor opened to admit them. Beyond, flickering lanterns marked the long, winding driveway down to the light-strung house at the bottom. The front steps were iced in red carpet and guarded by two enormous Christmas trees. The butlers at the top bowed as they passed, and pushed the doors open. It was all very grand.

Inside was a feast of festive cheer. The smell of something quite delicious wafted through the air. Maatje's stomach gurgled in glee. Food would be her first stop after the formalities were over.

"Hello, welcome," said a beefy-lipped man with a red face and floppy hair. He grasped Hanna by the arms and kissed her on both cheeks, then moved to Maatje, lingering on her a little longer, his cologne completely masking the smell of food.

"My, you are a pretty one," he told her. "I think I would have remembered seeing you here before."

"Maatje. I only started three and a half months ago." She tried to smile, but he was standing far too close.

"I'm Hubert," he said. "Proud to be part of the SDRC ever since it began almost twenty years ago."

Maatje blushed bright red. This was the famous Hubert. Without him, the SDRC would still be a couple of intrepid scientists working in someone's bedroom. They had a lot to thank him and his money for. "Then I've got quite a bit of catching up to do."

Hubert chuckled. "If there's anything my staff can't get you tonight, come and see me." He gave her a wink then looked over her shoulder. "Ah, Mrs Steen, how marvellous of you to come."

Maatje and Hanna walked into the grand hall, closer to the glorious aromas. The buffet tables were still empty, but waiters with white gloves offered trays of champagne to the guests.

"Thank you." Maatje almost spilt the contents of her glass everywhere when Hanna gave her a sharp nudge.

"There he is."

Robbie. Hanna's crush. She'd been deliberating over the best ways of addressing him at the party for most of the month. He was chatting with their boss, Paul.

"Well, go on then," Maatje encouraged, licking a drop of champagne off the back of her hand as discreetly as possible.

"Oh, I don't know," Hanna squirmed. "Do you think he'll even be interested? Why don't we walk past him and I'll laugh loudly at something you say?"

"Hey, Han, Maatje!" Paul waved them over.

Hanna squeaked in Maatje's ear.

"Robbie, these are my two colleagues, Hanna and Maat-je," Paul introduced them. "Ladies, this is Robbie from the calibrations department."

There was a tremendous amount of cheek kissing again, before Hanna timidly asked what part of calibrations Robbie

26

was involved in. And that was it. The pair had eyes for no one else.

Paul excused Maatje and himself and whispered, "She can thank me later," as they walked away.

Paul was great. He'd known when he'd accepted Maatje onto the apprenticeship that dream therapy was her major interest, and – after warning her not to mention the impossible hotel from her childhood if she wanted to be taken seriously – hooked her up with Doctor Becker, a knowledgeable scientist who not only inspired Maatje, but was as lured to the buffet tables as she was when the food eventually arrived.

The evening passed in a blur of formality and frivolity. All the top dogs of the SDRC gave speeches, including the CEO Rufus Sterne and Hubert, and a large bunch of flowers was given to a scientist who was retiring. Food and drink flowed as endless as the band's ability to belt out Christmas tunes.

At about one in the morning, Maatje decided she'd had enough. Battling blockers in the labs all day had exhausted her and their torment hadn't ended there; that night all three had twirled her across the dance floor too.

She sank into a chair with an ice-cold drink and kicked off her shoes. Hanna was nowhere to be seen. According to Camille, she'd slipped out with Robbie about an hour ago. Maatje decided to give her lift home twenty more minutes, otherwise she'd call a taxi instead. She stretched back and closed her eyes . . .

She found herself in front of a chipped red door. The door to someone else's dream. It was thick with the pulpy, invisible barrier that always sent thrilling shivers down the back of her neck – somewhere new and exciting.

Maatje wondered who else had fallen asleep at the party as she knocked. There was no answer, so she jiggled the handle and pushed the door open.

Inside was the town square. She recognised the big stone fountain in the middle of the cobbles with its half-naked statue. Except, rather than water pouring out of the jug in the statue's arms, when the jug filled, this statue leapt to life and threw the entire contents onto the group of children laughing and splashing in its basin.

The houses around the square were also missing. Instead, the space had become a gigantic playground. Slides the size of electric pylons, a forest of monkey bars and roundabouts that pinned its riders to the edges like a centrifuge. There was a glimmer of impossibility to the air, as though any moment something wonderfully unexpected would happen. For a heart-stopping second, Maatje thought she could hear Will's violin, but it was only a blackbird singing its lungs out in the trees.

It was, however, exactly the sort of eye-popping, toe-itching place the hotel had been. Who in the SDRC had dreams like this?

That was when she noticed there were no other adults about. Just children, all frolicking on the attractions.

"Hello!" she hollered to a group clambering on what looked like a giant lime jelly. "This is an amazing dream. Whose is it?"

As soon as they saw Maatje making her way towards them, they all bounced so hard they ended up inside the gummy blob, floating wide-eyed like fearful bits of fruit cocktail. Maatje prodded the jelly. Cold and smooth, just like the dessert. She put a foot on it and immediately the world began to wobble. The sensation was so peculiar, she started laughing. A couple of the kids giggled too, but then the wobbling

28

began to feel increasingly as if someone was shaking her by the shoulders . . .

———

"Was my dancing that unimpressive?" Paul let go of her shoulder as Maatje opened her eyes.

"I was waiting for my ride home." She blinked around the hall to see if Hanna had returned, but she was still absent. As was Robbie.

"You want a lift with me? I've just about had it too. My feet are half a size too big for these shoes."

Maatje nodded and thanked him, but her head was still half in the dream playground. She checked around the hall again to see if she could spot who'd been napping with her, but everyone was either laughing, dancing or saying their goodbyes.

"Paul?" she asked as they made their way down the front steps. "Does Hubert have any children – or grandchildren?"

"No, but he lets half the manor out as a children's home. It's a wonder the man has any time for himself with all his causes."

"I didn't know that."

Paul smiled. "He doesn't publicise it. Why do you ask?"

Maatje scolded her heart for racing. So long had she been looking for a dream like the hotel, it had immediately jumped to the conclusion that this dream was shared by all the children in the home. But that was impossible. No mind had space for so many. Not any mind the SDRC had come across.

That was what Paul would say anyway. *Had* said many times already.

"Oh, no reason."

But Paul had never met the Manager.

THEN: MAATJE

Maatje rode to the hotel every night afterwards.

At first she'd been afraid it wouldn't be there any more, or that she'd be unable to find it. Her dreams had never been as steady as Elinor's. But the giddy beauty of the lone violin beckoned Maatje and her horse across the moors, to where Will, with a final flourish of his bow, would grin and say, "I've got something to show you."

And every night became more wonderful than the last. They explored vast underwater caverns in the basement, full of colourful fish and wild tentacled creatures; they bounced over the clouds from the topmost turret, soft as cotton and infinitely mouldable. Maatje gave herself a thick plumy moustache, and Will made a pair of wings on which he flew so fast he whipped the clouds into delicious spun sugar, flavoured raspberry in the rising sun.

Maatje didn't only explore. She helped Taeng, the fruit lady, in the kitchen too, perfecting the apple roses and grape buds. But her orange lotuses still looked more like half-eaten sunflowers. Head chef Giovanni had a soft spot for her stomach and insisted she taste every new recipe for guest quality control, a task very much to her liking.

But Will was her favourite person to spend time with. As the Manager's assistant, truly anything could happen when he was around. No one at home nor school took Maatje seriously; they either put up with or dismissed her fanciful, childish ways. Will didn't. He listened to her chat and chat, with his big blue eyes and dark lashes like a girl. On the odd occasion when she saw a door or a corner the other guests couldn't, he looked at her as if she was the only one who could see him too. Then back came the grin and he'd take her hand. Off again, to discover something new.

One night, Maatje arrived at the hotel to a buzz in the air. A couple of honeymooning guests had turned up and since they'd neither had the family nor the finances for a wedding bigger than a ten-minute visit to the registry office, the Manager had proposed a full-out party to celebrate. Maatje went straight to the kitchens to assist Taeng with the fruit platters, then helped a couple of chefs wheel them out to the dining room, which tonight was a giant marquee formed entirely out of the trunks and branches of twisting tropical trees, their smooth, polished roots knotting the floor. Fat leaves flapped gently in the breeze from outside. Maatje peeked through them, toes sinking deep into the hot sand of a vast golden beach, framed with a lapping sea as clear as a swimming pool. She'd never been abroad before. The air bloomed hot and new in her lungs and the sun painted everything with joy. It felt as if she'd stepped into an advert at the travel agents.

Will rushed into the marquee behind her with an armful

of cutlery and a couple of balloons tied to the back of his trousers.

"Do you play volleyball?" she asked, poking a balloon.

Will grinned. "Absolutely."

He untied the balloons and threw one to Maatje. It was heavier than she'd expected, more like a beach-ball. Which of course it now was. There was suddenly a volleyball net outside too. Maatje felt a stab of envy. How she longed to be able to control her dreams like this.

They played long enough to get sweaty, sandy and sea-soaked. Lying in the shallows to cool down after Maatje's narrow victory, their hair and fingers drifted in the gentle pull of the water.

"Are you real?" she asked Will.

He hesitated. "Does it matter?"

"Yes." Maatje sat up with a splosh. "Because if you live near me, maybe we could meet up. All the kids at school are just into computer games or make-up, and Elinor hasn't written yet . . ." She swallowed against a hard knobble in her throat. Elinor was probably too busy having horsey dreams with her new school friends to care about Maatje. Maybe she wanted to be there. She hadn't made a fuss about going, not like Maatje had. Maybe it wasn't just Mum and Dad who Elinor was relieved to get away from.

Will sat up too, rubbing water from his face. "We already meet up."

That didn't answer the question. A bead of water trembled on the top of his lip and she had the craziest urge to wipe it away for him. She quickly ducked her head and busied herself sloshing water through her fingers.

"Here." Will handed Maatje a pale peach flower and a pin. "I'd better get back to work. Got to give all these flowers out, and I can't forget to blow up the rest of the balloons.

Here's a flower for Taeng too." He splashed to his feet and scooped up the volleyball. "I'll beat you next time."

Maatje made a rude noise. "Hah, you wish!"

It didn't take her long to dry off in the hot sun. Soon the entire hotel were lined up along the shore, welcoming the beaming couple with flower petals. One day, Maatje would be like them. She'd absolutely have her wedding here. Her cheeks reddened as she wondered briefly what Will would look like in a suit and tie, his arm through hers.

She sampled every single dish at the buffet, each better than the last. The fruit display was commended more than once, and she swelled with pride.

Will remembered the balloons. They floated up in the leafy canopy all night until the couple danced alone together to a band of chirping, chattering, whistling birds and insects hidden amongst the foliage. Then the balloons all lit up, a tiny butterfly visible inside each one, flapping and fluttering as the balloons drifted down to the floor. Everyone went to take a closer look at the creatures trapped inside. Maatje took the pin holding the flower to her clothes and popped a balloon. The butterfly flew out and landed in the palm of her hand. It wasn't a butterfly at all, but a piece of paper, flopping life-lessly as soon as she closed her fingers around it.

She heard a couple of other pops as others used their pins to free the paper butterflies, and soon the marquee was full of popping. Maatje unfolded her paper.

Mrs Juli Franz.

That was all it said. She knew Mrs Franz. She was the frail old lady Maatje had helped down the stairs once. She looked around the room. Yes, there she was, sitting in a leafy armchair, watching the proceedings intently.

"That's your dance partner for the next song," whispered Roberto, one of the waiters, in response to her confusion, his armful of empty plates teetering.

"Mrs Franz? Really? I'll break her."

He laughed.

Maatje went over to say hello to the lady as the music started – a quick chittering jig.

"Maatje, dear. How are you enjoying the party?"

"Very well, Mrs Franz." She showed her the paper. "Apparently, we're supposed to have this dance together, but don't worry if you don't want to."

"No, of course I will." Mrs Franz creaked as she struggled to her feet. Maatje whipped out a steadying hand. "Thank you dear. I haven't danced in ages."

And it showed. The two of them rocked and creaked at about half the speed of the music, but Mrs Franz didn't seem to care; her face had wrinkled into one gigantic smile.

"Oops-a, sorry." Head chef Giovanni wobbled past with his partner – a very tall, grey-haired gentleman who Maatje thought wouldn't look out of place wearing a monocle. They were standing on each other's toes and almost took Maatje along with them.

The song finished with a flourishing tweet and Mrs Franz almost collapsed onto Maatje in exhausted delight.

"Oh, I think that's me done for the night," she gasped.

Maatje led Mrs Franz back to her chair and brought her a glass of water.

"Thank you, dear. What a party."

Maatje sat next to her, fanning herself with a nearby leaf.

"It reminds me of the one the Manager put on for me when I first came here."

Where was the Manager? He'd gone to all the effort of arranging this evening, but not shown his face. But then Maatje had never met him, so how would she know what he looked like?

"My son had just died," Mrs Franz continued. "It was an awful time. But he asked me to tell him all about Frank, how he loved skiing and renovating old motorbikes. And before I knew it, he'd got the whole hotel doing the things Frank loved." Mrs Franz laughed. "He put a ski run out in the moors. And there were all these old bikes for people to ride. Oh, and all his favourite food was cooked. I don't know how they managed to make my knödel soup. It tasted identical. They played Frank's awful loud music, and people spent the evening pulling crackers with little stories about his life in them."

A tear ran down Mrs Franz's cheek. Maatje wasn't sure what to do.

"When I woke up, I went and fulfilled his lifelong dream." She pointed up at the chirping marquee canopy. "To fly in a spitfire."

She laughed again and Maatje did too.

"You went in a spitfire? In real life?"

Mrs Franz nodded. "Took Frank's ashes up with me." She sniffed. "He's a good man, that Manager. A good man."

Maatje nodded, then jumped up and grabbed Will. He and Roberto had just finished carrying in a huge cake. "Your turn to dance with me."

NOW: FRIEDRICH

The white-coated nightmares sat on the top of his firewall like vultures ready to swoop. Friedrich felt around in the fragments of letters and numbers at his feet and grasped a code that was mostly brick. Thanks to his job in network security, his dreams were often strewn with useful materials he could build defences from. He launched the brick up at the nearest white-coat. The man leant back, dodging the brick as it skimmed past, but tipped too far and toppled off the wall out of sight.

One down; two to go.

Wham! The next brick was on target. Right in the chest. Another white-coat down. Friedrich hoped it hurt.

But the third was fast; he cut through the spiky, wiry code strung across the top of Friedrich's wall and abseiled down into his mind. The man's consciousness pressed against his own.

No! The violation made him feel sick.

Friedrich hounded towards him, and when he was close enough, grabbed the white-coat by his dangling leg and hurled him against the wall as hard as he could. The man's head cracked against the glowing brickwork like a wet stone. Blood poured and he disappeared. Blinked out of existence.

Friedrich stepped back. Had he killed him? He'd never killed anything before, apart from a few swallowed flies on his daily run to work.

The man's consciousness vanished along with his body. The relief was so intense, Friedrich stumbled. So it was true what they said: kill someone in your dream and they return to their own mind. *Ha!*

He felt strange though. Dream or not, he'd just chosen to hurt a man so badly that he died. Oh, but he was so angry. And it wasn't as if he'd really died, like Brenda had. That so-called scientist had got off lightly.

"That's the closest anyone is going to get!" he yelled to the two he still sensed on the other side of his wall. "Make one move further and you won't even have time to regret it!"

Friedrich turned with a snarl, like a tiger pacing its cage. He had to wake up. It was the only way to stop these ever-intensifying attacks. What did they want from his head that was so important to them? Or were they just enjoying the challenge of hacking their way in?

Wake up; wake up.

Anja and Milo were waiting for him. What had happened to them? Friedrich had no idea how long he'd been asleep for. Who would have picked them up from school and playgroup? He could only imagine how scared and confused they were.

"They are being looked after."

Friedrich swung round. A voice, a white-coat, on his side of the firewall. Someone had got in, and they were reading his thoughts.

"GET OUT!" Friedrich thundered towards the man, head down like a charging bull. The white-coat stood there pathetically, ankle deep in bits of code – Friedrich's code,

Friedrich's head – holding up one of the many bricks he had used to so carefully build his wall.

Friedrich bowled into the white-coat and the brick went flying. He seized him by his white collar and ran with him until he slammed against the wall. Then he grabbed him around the neck and squeezed.

"How do you like it in here?" Friedrich delighted in the sweet malice that coated the words on his tongue, watching the watery eyes widen in panic as the white-coat tried to breathe. "Relax, it's all in my mind." Friedrich nodded to his strangling hands. "Would you rather you weren't?"

It was too easy. The man gave up in moments, dropping all of his puny weight onto Friedrich and disappearing.

It didn't feel as bad that time – killing. He could get used to it. At least he still had some sort of control left.

THEN: MAATJE

"This is the last one, I promise."

"Mum, the other shoes were fine," Maatje groaned as she was dragged along the street.

"They were far too wide for your feet."

"They were comfortable."

"They would have given you blisters. Come on, it won't take a minute."

They had already spent three hours in two shoe shops hunting for new school shoes. Maatje had needed a new pair long ago, but hid them over the summer to avoid exactly this situation.

She had each foot measured in both shops – to get a second opinion, Mum said – and Mum had examined every possible shoe for sale, with Maatje having to try on about two thirds of them. All of them felt okay, but Mum had found fault with every single pair.

Luckily, this was the last shop in town that sold shoes. Mum would have to settle for something in here, though the chances were she'd decide the second pair Maatje tried on half a lifetime ago were the best option after all.

"Hey, cracking fruit," said a middle aged man to Maatje, nodding as they passed on the pavement. It was Mr Kirn, a guest at the hotel. He had been really grumpy when he first came, but now liked initiating karaoke rock concerts. It was a shock seeing him in real life, but she managed to squeak, "Hello," before he walked out of earshot.

Mum turned pale. "How do you know that man?"

If she told the truth, Mum would throw a fit, so Maatje shrugged and lied. "He taught us still life at school. I drew a pineapple."

The colour returned to Mum's face and she smiled. "I didn't know you liked drawing. Can I see this pineapple? We could hang it up in the dining room."

"Oh, erm . . . no, he took it," Maatje spluttered. "For an exhibition."

"Wow, it was that good?"

"No, he took everyone's."

The shoe shop lingered close on the left now.

"After this, do you want to get some crafty stuff for you and Elinor to do in the half term?"

Maatje stopped. "Elinor's coming?"

"Of course."

Maatje's heart bubbled up into her throat. She missed her sister madly. "Yes, yes – let's get some nice thread and beads to make friendship bracelets."

Mum nodded and marched into the shoe shop. Maatje didn't mind any more. Elinor was coming! Tonight she'd ask Will to see the Manager. She needed to know if he'd do something to welcome Elinor, like he had for the honeymooning couple and Mrs Franz. Something so spectacular she'd never want to go back to school.

Maatje was almost singing when she got home, a box of new shoes under one arm and a bag of thread and tiny glass beads in the other. She kicked off her old shoes and started upstairs with her booty.

"Maatje, can you peel some apples for me? They're coming out of my ears," Aunt Marjorie called from the kitchen.

Maatje groaned. The apple tree in the garden was bursting with fruit and her aunt had given up experimenting with different ways to use them, taking instead to stewing huge vats and freezing them. Aunt Marjorie was quite aggressive in the kitchen, and so far Maatje had been able to steer clear of her apple battle. Her joy today, however, made her generous.

She skipped back downstairs and over the tiled floor towards the counter.

"Peeler's over there." Aunt Marjorie motioned to the drawer below the cutlery.

Maatje picked out a knife instead and skinned the apple in one thick ribbon. She was on her third when she realised Aunt Marjorie was watching her.

"Where on earth did you learn to peel like that?"

Maatje shrugged. "A friend taught me."

"You'll have to teach me sometime. I could save myself years in the kitchen."

Maatje finished peeling the apples, then chopped them into cubes and tipped them into the stock pot.

She was sliding over the tiles and out of the kitchen when Aunt Marjorie's last demand came: "The compost bin for the peelings is . . ." She went quiet and Maatje smiled to herself. She must have discovered the little roses on the worktop.

THEN: MAATJE

Will wasn't there to greet her that evening. Maatje followed the violin's call, but when she arrived atop the hill, he was gone.

No slide, no zip wire; nothing but her own two feet to plod on down to the hotel.

Maybe his list of jobs was extra-long tonight and he didn't have time to wait for her?

Everyone in the kitchen was unusually quiet – mixing, chopping, stirring with intense concentration. Even the soup geyser – tonight a creamy potato and leek – seemed to be behaving itself with a near perfect aim in every bowl.

"What's going on?" Maatje asked Taeng. She was arranging porcupine-shaped apples around three giant swirling cantaloupe tortoises.

"I glad you here." Taeng barely looked up from her work. "You make pear fans?"

Maatje nodded and picked up her knife. "But what's happening?"

Taeng didn't reply until she saw Maatje peeling the first pear, then she leant towards her, eyes wide and sparkling.

"The Manager come downstairs," she squeaked. "He make an inspection."

Oh. Maatje's heart thudded. Finally she was going to meet the Manager. This was her chance to ask him to do something special for Elinor. Though now the opportunity was so apparent she didn't know if she had the guts to even talk to him, let alone ask a favour.

Her knife slipped and she took a big slice out of the pear. *Damnit.* She picked up a new one and started again.

But she had to ask. She was already jealous of the other boarding school girls who probably were running with Elinor's horses. She was *her* sister, she didn't want anyone else becoming more important. She needed the hotel to make a big impact.

Ugh, another pear ruined. Maatje threw the knife down.

Taeng placed a cool hand on her arm. "You not have mind for carving tonight. Go where you must be."

Maatje winced that it was so obvious, but thanked Taeng and ran off into the hotel.

"Ricardo, have you seen Will or the Manager?" she asked the clerk at the main desk.

"Both in the games room," Ricardo sang, twirling room keys around his fingers.

The games room was next to the vanishing room. Will still hadn't shown her inside it.

"But what's in there?" she had pressed him.

"Nothing."

Will was wrong if he thought she'd lose interest with a dull, adult explanation like that. Maybe she could take a quick peek now whilst he was busy . . .

"The games room is on your left," Ricardo called behind her.

Maatje pulled back from the handle as if she'd been burnt. "I just wanted to have a look."

Ricardo cocked his head. "At the wallpaper?"

"No, the—" She frowned. Was she really the only one other than Will who could see this door? "Never mind."

Tonight the games room looked like the garishly carpeted side room of a pub, with a packed crowd around a pool table where two men chalked their cues.

"What a run, Erik!" someone cheered.

"Come on, Mr Manager. Show him who's boss around here," another countered.

Mr Manager? A tall, thin, dark-haired man blew across the top of his cue and stretched across the table.

Pop, click. The red ball rolled into a pocket.

The room erupted. Will beamed behind the Manager's shoulder. He'd never looked so proud.

The Manager high-fived a guest before leaning down to aim another shot. He finished off the balls one after the other, before finally pocketing the black to whoops and cheers.

"Amazing!"

"Well, it is his dream."

"Hard luck, Erik."

Maatje felt a little underwhelmed. It had been an ordinary pool game. No oddly shaped balls or obstacles or unexpected explosions showering the cheering spectators with confetti. Maybe even the Manager liked to have normal days sometimes.

She wiggled through the crowd over to him. Better just to ask about doing something for Elinor before she thought too much about it. The Manager was shaking hands with Erik.

"Oy, watch where you're treading!"

"Sorry, Gunter." She quickly removed her foot from the guest's trailing dressing-gown tie.

"It's Maatje." Gunter broke into a smile and nudged the lady next to him. "Ma, this is the girl who does the fruit."

"Ooh," a wisp of an old woman reached for Maatje's

hand. "Dear, they are all so wonderful. I can hardly bear to eat them."

"I just help out," Maatje admitted, watching the Manager grip Will's shoulder as they disappeared through a door at the other end of the room. "But thank you."

She excused herself, and after tripping over Erik's discarded pool cue, stumbled through the door too.

The corridor outside was empty. Just numbered rooms with polished wooden doors and old-fashioned lamps along the striped walls. She'd never seen the hotel look so plain before.

Then, as she watched, the light bulbs began to swell and break away from their lamps like bubbles, until the air was full of spheres of light. Maatje opened her hand towards one and it burst with the tinkle of breaking glass, but the softness of soap.

She laughed. "Couldn't stay serious for long, could you?"

Maatje ran up the corridor to tuneful popping as she brushed past the floating spheres, following the bubble-blowing lamps into another corridor where the spectacular pinged and ponged out of the walls everywhere she looked. The polished doors warped her reflection like mirrors at the funfair, and the wallpaper stripes strummed like guitar strings as she ran her hand along them. It was as if the hotel had been behaving itself for the inspection, but as soon as the Manager had passed, it wanted to sneeze sparkling dust from every swept corner.

Maatje thought this would help her find the Manager. The more ordinary the hotel looked, the closer she was to him.

Yet she never found him.

Nor Will.

They must have gone to his office on the top floor. She

didn't have the courage to go there, especially if they were busy discussing business.

Disappointed, Maatje told herself there was always tomorrow. In fact, tomorrow would probably be better if the Manager's mind was full of inspection and winning at pool tonight.

But that wasn't the only reason she felt low. Will had completely ignored her. He hadn't even noticed she was there. They were supposed to be friends. Will spent so much time with her, she'd thought maybe he liked her a bit more than that too. Or hoped.

Of course the Manager was more important to Will. He was Will's boss.

She was determined to make him feel bad about it tomorrow.

NOW: MAATJE

"Happy Christmas!" Aunt Marjorie wrapped her wobbly arms around Maatje as she came through the door.

"Happy Christmas!" Maatje kissed her cheek, kicking off her shoes and putting her suitcase next to them.

"Oh, you're all cold, come in and warm yourself at the aga."

Maatje followed her into the kitchen and accepted a hot mug of tea.

"How's your apprenticeship going?"

"It's great. I'm helping out in experiments now. Paul is working on ways to protect the minds of high government officials. I have to play the terrorist and try to break in. He's made some very interesting progress."

"Have they managed to keep you out?"

"Once." Maatje took a sip of tea and sighed as its warmth spread through her. "I have to write up all the paperwork on it when I get back next week." She looked round the kitchen. Since she'd left home, Mum and Aunt Marjorie had turned the house into a B&B. The dresser sagged under the weight of all the extra crockery. "How's the new business going?"

"Slow this time of year, so I've got into knitting nativity sets for the church."

"Darling!" Mum ran into the room, arms outstretched and a Christmas pudding shaped hat on her head. "Merry Christmas!"

Mum's hug smelt of cinnamon. When Maatje pulled away, she saw it was coming from the tiny cinnamon sticks she'd made into earrings.

"Is Elinor here yet?" Maatje asked.

"No, not yet." Mum handed Maatje a Father Christmas hat. "Put this on."

"Maatje, I'm doing melon starters again this year," Aunt Marjorie called over her shoulder as she scoured potatoes with a fork. "Would you mind lending your magic on them again?"

"Of course, how'd you like them?"

Maatje rolled up her sleeves and began carving, ears peeled for Elinor's arrival. She hadn't seen her for almost two years now. At every family celebration, she had made some excuse not to come: her studies, sickness, prior engagements. Last Christmas she'd been with Dad, so this year Mum had been adamant Elinor had to be with them.

The doorbell rang and Maatje ran to answer it, melon juice dripping from her fingers.

"El!"

"Happy Christmas."

Maatje hugged her – and her bulging bags of presents – tightly. "It's so good to see you."

As Mum and Aunt Marjorie took their turns to greet Elinor, Maatje made a quick note of her sister's appearance. She looked good actually. She'd dyed her hair white-blonde, which suited her well, and she didn't look anywhere near as tired as the last time Maatje had seen her. She even accepted the silly elf hat Mum offered.

Things went well whilst they prepared then ate lunch. Everyone stuck to safe subjects: the weather, the B&B, politics . . . Maatje longed to inject a bit of life into them all. She'd come armed with topics for charades and word games and quizzes, but Aunt Marjorie would have something to say if she brought any of them out whilst they were eating.

"So, Elinor, where are you doing your placement?" Mum was the first to step into dangerous waters.

Elinor shrugged. "The university hospital, probably."

"You could move closer to here for a bit." Mum's eyes shone. "There's a lovely community hospital near Maatje. Or if you wanted to train as a GP, you could live here and work in the village surgery."

"I'd rather make my own way," Elinor replied.

"What's wrong with here?"

"Mum," Maatje warned.

"But she'd be closer to family. I can't bear the thought of you all alone in that big city. Do you have a boyfriend yet?"

"And Dad isn't family?" Elinor's voice was sharp.

"Well, he has Lila to look after him now." Mum pulled the same face of disgust she used every time she mentioned Dad's girlfriend.

"And you have your sister and Maatje." Elinor stood up, fingers pressed white against the tabletop. "Just because you don't like him, doesn't mean the rest of us have to think likewise."

"Okay." Mum put her hands up in surrender. "I'm just saying, it would be nice to see more of you. And I just want you to do well, not waste your talents being an overlooked doctor in a hospital. A GP is such an important part of the community and the hours are a lot more sensible."

"I don't want to be a GP, okay?"

49

"Well, maybe in the future, darling. You can keep your options open."

Maatje closed her eyes in disbelief. Why did Mum wonder why Elinor never visited if she did this every time she came? Mum had always pushed Elinor. She was far smarter than Maatje. Always excelled in school, getting a scholarship, then a bursary for university. She'd always been the golden child. The one Mum would chat about to her friends in the village. Maatje wished Mum took her a little more seriously, though she'd hate to be in Elinor's shoes, constantly having to be better and do better. She knew Mum loved her too. She just didn't have any expectations from her. "You're like me," she always said. "You're not an academic. You'll go wherever life takes you." Apparently Elinor had potential she couldn't let go to waste.

"I'm going to get some fresh air." Elinor marched out of the room.

"What about dessert?" Aunt Marjorie called after her.

Maatje stood up too. "I'll go with her."

Elinor was halfway down the lane when she caught her up. The afternoon air was sharp with frost, but the clear blue sky showed no sign of a white Christmas.

"Can I join you?" Maatje puffed.

Elinor shrugged.

"I like your hair. How long have you had it like that?"

Elinor ran her hand through it. "About six months. I was bored of it being such a miserable colour."

"You look like a Barbie."

"Hey!"

"It's a compliment!"

Elinor gave her a little push off the road into the half-frozen boggy grass. "Your melon starter looked really good by the way. Where did you learn to do that?"

Maatje hesitated. At work her colleagues only laughed

when she mentioned the hotel; with family it always ended in a shouting match. Maatje had never completely forgiven Elinor for telling Mum about it.

"Oh." Elinor turned away and didn't ask any more questions.

Maatje was glad.

They walked in a companionable silence over the moors for a while until Elinor grabbed her arm.

"Look!" she whispered.

A herd of wild ponies grazed on the brow of the next hill.

"Oh, aren't they gorgeous?"

The tiny creatures looked like cuddly toys with their thick woolly winter coats and cartoonish faces.

Elinor moved towards them. One brave pony took a couple of steps forward.

"Watch he doesn't bite you." Maatje stayed back. She had never been as sure of horses in real life as she was in dreams.

"Oh, no, he won't," Elinor crooned, dipping her hand in her pocket and unwrapping a mint. She held it out to the pony.

"Hey, you could have offered me one," Maatje complained. "I've got a chronic case of Brussels-sprout breath."

Elinor scratched the creature behind his ear as he crunched. A couple of others came sniffing round her, batting her with their heads for a mint too.

"Save one for me!" Maatje called as three more ponies munched their sweets.

"You'd better come and get one then."

Maatje wasn't going to risk it. The ponies were eying her up warily, even though they were the ones with the power to stomp her to death.

"They don't like me. I think you're the horse whisperer here."

"I'm cheating with the mints," Elinor admitted. All the tension lines from lunch disappeared from her face as she tickled the ponies under their chins.

"I don't suppose you get many horses in the city?"

Elinor sighed, as though resigned to a miserable horseless fate. "Wouldn't have time for them anyway."

They continued on their way, and back came the lines.

The day ended better than it had started. Maatje's games, when she and Elinor returned, loosened everyone up, and a glass of apricot gin helped even more. To top it off, Elinor even hesitantly invited Maatje to visit her in the city sometime. This made Maatje so convinced of the day's success, she decided to peek inside Elinor's dream that night. Her own involved a Jack-in-the-box that kept spitting melon seeds at her, so she was eager to leave it to its business.

She found her sister working at the checkout of a supermarket. The queue was long and the conveyor belt rolled too fast for her to keep up.

"Ay, hurry up," a customer hailed Elinor as she tried to explain to another with a pony in their trolley that it couldn't be for sale because it didn't have a barcode. The customer put it on the conveyer belt anyway.

Maatje joined the queue with a packet of mints, and was soon shoved forward by more customers squeezing in line behind her.

"Just go away, everyone!" Elinor slammed her hands down on the till. "I'm fed up with dealing with all this useless crap. Leave me alone."

There was gasping.

"So rude."

Elinor's manager came out and disciplined her until she

went back to scanning with a scowl. She didn't look up again. Not even when she picked up the mints and Maatje tried to get her attention. She was too absorbed in her dream. The mints went on top of the overflowing pile at the end of the till, joined by the items from the customers behind. Faster and faster the conveyor belt went. Maatje couldn't bear to watch any more. She left the shop and went back to the Jack-in-the-box. This was the same sort of dream Elinor had been having since the day the horse dreams stopped. Always rushing around, working hard at things she didn't want to do.

No matter how much better Elinor had looked on the surface, she hadn't changed inside. Now she was just better at hiding it.

They'd never hidden anything from each other as kids. Not until Elinor left Maatje with a scholarship to the new school.

Not since they fell out over the hotel.

What could be eating away at her sister? She had such a great future ahead of her.

"Don't worry, El," Maatje muttered to herself, flicking the melon seeds back at the Jack-in-the-box. "One day, I'll bring you a dream that'll fix you up no problem."

THEN: MAATJE

"Where's Will?"

Ricardo at the hotel reception peered down his long, straight nose back at Maatje as though he might like to disappear beneath his desk. "What did he do to affront you?"

"Sorry, Ricardo, I'm not angry really." Maatje tried to smile. "I'm just . . . Will hasn't said hello for two nights now. How can anyone be so busy, they can't even say hello?"

"Well, Master Willem is the Manager's right-hand man. He's got a lot on his plate making sure the hotel runs smoothly."

"It never stopped him before." This time, Maatje needed a good reason why Will hadn't waited for her on the hill. Had she done something to offend him?

"Well, if you see him, let him know I'm looking for him."

"Erm . . ." Ricardo looked pointedly over her shoulder.

Maatje whirled round and there was Will, waltzing through the front doors with another girl on his arm.

She couldn't help it. Jealousy flared through her bones, even though the girl couldn't have been more than eleven years old. Perhaps it was because she had the most glorious, thick, golden hair, or perhaps it was that Will looked even happier with her than he had with the Manager yesterday. The pair were enraptured with the whirl of autumnal leaves that blew in with them: bright reds and crispy browns, every shape and size, fluttering like butterflies and landing upon their delighted fingers. They danced straight past Maatje and the reception desk without noticing her at all.

Ricardo's merry chuckle fuelled Maatje's bubbling fury. "You've gone the colour of my father's gazpacho."

She scowled and flounced off in Will's direction. How dare he ignore her.

She rapped Will on the shoulder and he spun round before reaching the door to the lounge.

"Maatje!" He beamed as if nothing was amiss, which just made her angrier. He waved a butterfly leaf off his nose and stepped aside so the annoyingly pretty girl was in view. She wore a huge, burnt-orange leaf like a cloak. "This is Rachel. I was just telling her about the octopus you carved from a watermelon last week. Rachel, this is Maatje, our newest kitchen associate."

"I'm not just a kitchen associate." Maatje glowered.

"No, she's also our fun inspector and current volleyball champion."

The girl laughed. Ugh, such a pretty laugh too. Maatje had hoped at least her voice would be ugly so this jealousy would stop eating away at her. Nobody could be pretty in every way.

"Which reminds me – I've got something to show you."

Maatje flinched. That had always been Will's line to her. Now it was directed at Rachel. If she'd been a kettle she'd have boiled over.

"Are you okay?" Will gave her a concerned look. Finally, he'd noticed.

"Yes," Maatje replied, determined to play it cool.

"Great." The grin came back in an instant. "We'll see you around." He pushed the door to the lounge open and he and perfect Rachel walked through in their cloud of leaves.

Maatje played her next, unspoken lines in her head to the door instead. *Yes, I'd love to come too, but I was wondering if you could take me to see the Manager? There's something I'd like to ask him. No? Okay. I'll find him myself.*

Maatje humphed and glowered at Ricardo, who was still watching with some amusement, then stamped up the twisted, glowing stairs.

The Manager's office was on the top floor; this much Maatje knew, but without Will, floating up and down was a random event, and tonight the hotel seemed to be ignoring her as well. Maatje told herself she didn't care. Walking was quicker.

The first floor glowed with the magenta coals of an endless sunset, the second creaked oiled timber and tasted of sea, and the third stretched with emerald grass and taut tent canvas. The fourth floor was a scorching desert and the fifth and final floor a freezing tundra. Maatje rubbed her arms and tested her bare feet in the snow.

Cold. Very not fun cold.

"Hello?" Her breath clouded the air. Surely no one would want to sleep up here.

The rooms were doors set into the twinkling snow sculptures of handsome men and women. Giants caught in the ice by their endless waves of beard and silken tresses, desperation in their frozen eyes.

Maatje shivered. No, she didn't like this floor at all.

A scratching and a thud came from inside one of the snow statues: a woman shaped with cruelty so dazzling it looked like loveliness.

Maatje jumped back. "I-I'm looking for the Manager."

A *tap, tap, tap* was her only reply. A finger on the door in the snow woman's ravenous, gaping mouth.

"Are you okay in there?"

Tap, tap, tap.

Maatje sucked in her courage and tried the handle. It was locked.

Tap, tap, tap.

"Do you need some help?"

Tap.

Maatje swallowed. "Hang on a second. I'll go and get the key."

Room number fifty-two. She memorised it and sprinted back down the stairs.

"Ricardo!" she gasped, skidding to a stop at the reception desk. "Do you have the spare key for room fifty-two? I think a guest is locked in."

Ricardo narrowed his eyes. "There is no room fifty-two."

"No, on the top floor in a scary statue . . ."

Ricardo raised a hand to stop her, pointing behind him at the board of keys. The numbers stopped at fifty-one. "See."

Had she remembered it wrong?

"Here." Ricardo fumbled about behind the desk. "Try the emergency skeleton key instead." He held out a screwdriver. "Some doors can be quite stiff; you just have to be firm with them. I'd lend you a hand, but I can't leave the desk."

"Thanks – this'll be great." Maatje raced back up the stairs with the screwdriver, dripping sweat by the time she reached the top floor again. The freezing air was now a welcome relief.

Tap, tap, tap.

Maatje knelt in front of the door. Fifty-two. Maybe it was another of the things only she could see.

"Don't worry. I couldn't find the key, but I've got a screw-driver – that should do the trick."

Dad always said this when something needed fixing. Maatje had never even used a screwdriver before, but she felt like an expert as she slotted it neatly into the dent on the first of four screws holding the handle in place.

Ricardo had been right: the screw was stiff. The screwdriver slipped again and again before it reluctantly loosened.

Clink. The screw fell to the slab of blue ice under her knees and rolled around in a circle.

"One down." Three more.

Clink, clink, clink. One by one, all the screws fell out and Maatje pulled the handle from the door. The door swung out and knocked her on the head as she bent down to retrieve the escaping screws. Success!

She clambered to her poor purpling feet and pulled the door open fully.

A blast of wind – even colder than the corridor – struck Maatje in the face, brutal and sharp, knocking all the breath from her lungs. The shape of a lady, pale and outlined in blue, glided towards her. The same lady as the sculpture, but so much more terribly beautiful.

A thunder of feet on the stairs and – *SLAM!* – a gasping Will threw all his weight against the door to shut it. It rattled against him, but he didn't let up.

"The lock!" Will nodded to the handle in Maatje's hands.

Heart thudding, she slotted the handle into the door again and screwed it back in place. The ice lady on the other side put up a fierce fight, slamming into the door so the screwdriver slipped and a screw clattered to the floor. But at last, Maatje got them all in, and after one last battering from the other side, there came only silence.

Will sighed and leant away from the door, his dark hair damp. "It's best if this guest stays in their room."

Maatje was still too shocked to reply. She didn't like the fear on Will's face; she'd never seen him scared before. She wanted to ask who this lady was – why she was locked inside a freezing snow statue – but his wide eyes begged her not to.

She nodded. "Okay." Goodness, how her heart pounded. She was surprised she hadn't woken herself up.

A small tentative face appeared from the stairwell, as pale as the ice lady. Maatje could have added her own and Will's fear together and it wouldn't have even come close to little leaf-wrapped Rachel's terrified expression. Will went over and wrapped her tightly in his arms.

Maatje didn't like how the girl buried her head into his chest. She told herself he was only hugging her because she was so frightened. Nothing else.

Tap, tap, tap.

Rachel shrivelled at the sound. Will locked eyes with Maatje and tilted his head towards the stairs.

Relieved she wasn't in trouble for poking about in rooms she shouldn't, Maatje fled down them, determined to put as much distance between herself and room fifty-two. Will's and Rachel's footsteps followed, so she put on an extra burst of speed. Right now, she needed just as much distance from them.

NOW: MAATJE

"You're not going as well, are you?" Mum turned her guilt-inducing voice on as Maatje dumped her bag by the front door.

"Well, yes, actually." Maatje had woken up in a bad mood after spending time in her sister's dream last night. Elinor had left straight after breakfast and Maatje was attempting to do so an hour later.

"But what about our Boxing Day walk?"

"Yes, the Moors Museum has just opened." Aunt Marjorie leant round the doorframe to the kitchen. "Do you remember I told you that man came round asking for old items we no longer use? I gave him the old mangle from the garage. It's on display now. I'd like to go and see it."

Maatje couldn't think of anything duller than going to see a boring old, rusted up mangle. What she wanted to do was go back to her apartment and write up her latest thoughts on Elinor. She had a sister to fix.

"Oh, that'll be nice," Mum agreed. "Come on, Maatje, just for a couple of hours. We'll drop you off at the train station afterwards."

The guilt voice was working. Mum and Aunt Marjorie just wanted to spend some time with her. She could give them two hours, couldn't she?

Argh! Why was she such a pushover?

"Okay, let's go and see your mangle."

Mum gave a squeak and squeezed her arm.

"Let me pack some leftovers for lunch." Aunt Marjorie retracted her head back into the kitchen.

Maatje sighed. Of course they were going to be longer than two hours.

———

The Moors Museum was in the old woollen mill. A big grey building just like the B&B, which looked just as miserable. Inside, every nook and cranny was filled with equally unimpressive exhibits. No wonder they had been so keen to take the mangle from Aunt Marjorie. It fitted in perfectly with all its drab counterparts.

"I love how they've recreated the old laundry room," Aunt Marjorie crooned. "Doesn't it look good there?"

The old mangle stood in a room made entirely out of chipboard and painted garish colours. There was even a chipboard person, her wooden arm outstretched as if using the mangle. Piles of moth-eaten clothes surrounded it, along with an iron that looked like a cannonball.

Maatje left Aunt Marjorie and Mum admiring the display and wandered around, only half looking at any of the things on show. Why did a shrivelled old shoe deserve to be placed in a glass case? The label next to it explained it had been fished out of a nearby bog and was thought to be over two hundred years old. Maatje nominated this piece for The Most Pointless Artefact Ever Award and moved on.

In one corner stood a large case of newspapers below a

projected slideshow of some of the local front pages throughout the years.

Farmer claims woolliest sheep title in national competition

Controversial new town route – one way reversed

These ridiculous headlines were accompanied by equally ridiculous photos: a man who was more beard than face beaming as he knelt by a sheep with the same predicament; and another showing two – what would now be considered – classic cars stuck nose to nose on a single lane street.

Maatje was just turning away when a third headline and photo caught her attention.

Instantly, her insides shrivelled like the two-hundred-year-old shoe.

Looking back at her from under the most horrific headline was the face of the person she had spent the last four years hoping to find again.

The Manager.

THEN: MAATJE

As Will fiddled a clef of alto ridges to the roof of the hotel, Maatje tossed up whether or not it would be a good idea to continue to be mad at him. He certainly deserved it; he didn't even look sorry.

But his smile was so beautiful and he rubbed Baggy's nose in such a warm welcome that Maatje felt all her bitter words dissolve on her tongue.

"There's a new game that needs your expertise tonight," he told her. He placed his violin on the ground and rolled it back and forth, testing the wheels of the go-kart it had turned into. He offered the back seat to Maatje.

"I thought you'd never ask." Maatje grinned back. "Though I've been meaning to ask you . . . would be possible to speak to the Manager first? My sister's visiting from boarding school next week and I was wondering if he would make an attraction for her with some horses, as a sort of welcome thing?"

"Of course." Will coughed as he tried to smother a laugh. "Don't worry – he won't eat you."

Maatje realised her face had curled into a nervous

grimace. With red cheeks and defiant, folded arms, she slipped into the go-kart seat. "I'm not scared."

"No?" Will sat down in front then pushed the kart down the hill. It rumbled and bumped over the tufty grass, faster and faster, until Maatje's teeth rattled in her skull and her brain became soup. She clung to the back of Will's seat until they rolled to a stop by the kitchen door, her stomach jumping with excitement from the ride.

Will gave her a teasing look over his shoulder. "How about now?"

"You'll have to try harder than that."

It was floating up towards the fifth floor that got her in the end. She didn't want to face those sinister snow statues again. Her fingers tightened around Will's, but he took her gliding over the chandelier branches away from the landing.

"No guests up here tonight," he said.

Though the stairs ended, the final twisting tendrils of vine continued up into the rafters. And they floated up with them. The flowers grew smaller and dimmer, wisps of fog curling around their delicate petals.

Will coughed again.

"I think you're coming down with something."

"Just a tickle." Will weaved through the pale green branches to land them on a set of narrow steps, beginning in mid-air and ending at a tiny attic door in the beamed roof. Without a banister, Maatje wavered above the dizzying drop, determined to resist crawling onto her hands and knees for balance. She was grateful when Will kept hold of her hand.

Fog coiled through the cracks in the door, thick and grey. It looked more like smoke, though it couldn't be. She'd have smelt it.

But as they climbed closer to the door, the fog caught in her lungs and she coughed too.

It *was* smoke. Smoke she couldn't smell, because you couldn't smell anything in dreams. She hadn't even realised.

She tightened her hold on Will's hand. "I'm not sure this is a good—"

CRASH!

A red-hot scaly tail lashed through the door, tearing through the rafters, billowing smoke and flames. The stairs splintered, and suddenly there was nothing but rushing air under Maatje's feet . . .

"Will!"

They ripped through branches as they dropped, tearing them from the walls in a clattering, jingling mash of light and wood. It slowed their descent, but hitting the fifth-floor landing still punched the air from Maatje's lungs. She lay there for a swirling eternity, mouth agape for air that wouldn't come, staring up at a giant red dragon clawing burning chunks off the hotel's roof.

"Maatje?" The black of Will's silhouetted head above hers cooled the red fire. He coughed again. "Maatje, breathe." His voice whispered the cool breeze of spring, reminding her lungs how to draw life.

She gasped. Gasped and shuddered and thought . . . "Dragon?"

He nodded, looking stunned. "I'm sorry. You need to leave the hotel immediately."

"What about everyone else?"

The chandelier flowers still jangled. A trembling alarm that rang all through the hotel.

"They're being evacuated." Will yanked Maatje to her feet and pulled her down the stairs behind him until sense came back to her legs. At the fourth floor, he nudged her onwards alone.

"Aren't you coming?"

"I need to make sure everyone gets out."

"I can help."

"No." Will dashed across the landing, today folded out of thick multicoloured origami paper. Bad news with a dragon about.

An ear-rattling roar and belching flame flared in the rafters above. Maatje swallowed and raced after Will.

A man dressed only in a very small white towel poked his head out of a paper bedroom. "What's going on?"

"There's a dragon in the hotel. Everyone has to leave right away," Maatje told him.

The man's eyes grew wide and he retreated from the doorway, returning with a lady who was wrapping a blanket around herself. They headed straight for the stairs, a little squashed-faced dog at their heels.

Maatje knocked at the next paper door and accidentally drove her fist right through. She slapped her palms on each of the doors after that, trying to rouse anyone sleeping through the commotion. Though she didn't know what they could possibly be dreaming about when they were in a dream already.

She was about halfway down the line of rooms when she bumped into Will again, a confused gentleman with a walking stick on his arm.

"What are you still doing here?"

"I'm helping."

"The Manager needs to end the dream. He can't do that until everyone is out. You have to go."

She gave him a sarcastic grin. *"Thank you, Maatje, for getting guests out for you.* Oh, you're very welcome."

Will wasn't impressed. "Mr Schneider, this is Maatje. She's going to take you down to the lobby."

Maatje smiled as she accepted the man's arm, but inside she was scowling. She'd kind of hoped Will would like how brave she was being.

Heat from the dragon's flames seared the back of her neck on her return to the stairs with Mr Schneider. Ash fell like snow, alongside plummeting slivers of wood and slabs of plaster, twanging and plinking as if the raging dragon was tearing violin strings loose.

Mr Schneider was slow. Watching him negotiate the stairs was like watching a sloth amble its way obliviously across a branch when there was a giant python behind it. She wanted to ask him why he had asked for a room upstairs when he could barely move.

"Out you go; thank you for your custom. Apologies for the inconvenience." Ricardo shepherded guests through the front door. Maatje handed Mr Schneider over to him before dashing back up the stairs.

"You too, Miss Finkel," called Ricardo.

"Will still needs help," Maatje yelled back.

The fourth floor was nothing but flame by the time she returned, coughing on the acidic smoke in the third floor stairwell. Her eyes stung and streamed. Maybe she was being stupid, but it all felt very real.

Glowing shreds of blackened paper wafted through the air. The dragon snarled and ripped and snorted fire above her, unfurling its wings like leathery sails as it dug razor claws into the burning stair vine. Will fell out of the smoke and down the last steps onto the third floor. He rolled onto his side, coughing and drawing noisy panicked breaths.

"God, Will, are you okay?"

"One. More. Guest," he gasped. "Go. I'm fine."

He looked anything but fine, with singed sleeves, soot-smeared face and bloodshot eyes. He could barely make it to his feet, he was coughing so much.

Maatje pulled him up and dragged him into the nearest bathroom – a thundering waterfall – and shoved him under. She grabbed two towels and jumped in too, soaking herself and the towels in the warm bubbling water before tying one around her face and the other around Will's.

"Okay?"

He coughed and nodded.

"Let's get the last guest out."

Maatje followed Will back into the thick smoke in the corridor outside, crawling along the floor where it was thinnest. Even then, Maatje could barely see the bottom of Will's shoes. Roars, crashes and crackling pops drowned out the hideous guttural groaning of the hotel's agony.

"Are. You. Still. There?" Will coughed back to her.

"Yes."

Crawling only a few doors down the corridor felt like miles. Will knocked politely against a door and stumbled inside. Maatje scrambled after.

"Close the door, quick," croaked a familiar voice from the other end of the room.

Maatje slammed it shut and rubbed her streaming eyes.

Mrs Franz smiled at them from the open window of an airy Georgian bedroom, her forehead etched with deep lines. "I thought I'd be able to wake myself up. I don't think I'll be able to handle the stairs."

"Then please let me carry you, Mrs Franz." Will offered her his sooty hand.

"Oh, Master Willem, you are kind." Mrs Franz got up from the windowsill, joints as stiff as a rusted gate. Her knees groaned threateningly, but Will held her steady.

Maatje dampened another towel in the sink and tied it above Mrs Franz's nose, then Will carefully lifted her up and over his shoulder.

"Let's go."

Maatje took a deep breath and hurled the door open. Will staggered out and she followed close. Flames licked the ceiling beams like they were chocolate bars.

A sudden rush from behind propelled Maatje forward onto her face. Wood and flames rained down on her. The ceiling of Mrs Franz's hotel room had caved in. A swishing red tail churned the room into shrapnel.

Fear crushed Maatje's throat. If they had waited a second longer . . .

"Maatje!" came Will's voice, but he had vanished into the dust and smoke and fire.

She ploughed towards the sound of him, blind and suffocating, her skin blistering in the heat.

And then there was his hand. Tight, sweaty and safe around hers. They half slid down the bubbling, hissing stairs towards the second floor.

Maatje couldn't remember what it felt like to be able to breathe. Her lungs weren't filling and emptying as they should; she felt as if she was pulling on empty muscle. She missed a step for the umpteenth time and careered into the back of Will. He fell forward too, but saved himself by throwing out an arm to grab the spiralling banister. Maatje hit her chin on his elbow and bumped down the last steps to the second floor landing.

Will's hand took hers once more. No time to fall now. The building heaved and crashed like collapsing lungs above them. Smoke bellowed down the staircase.

First floor.

The final flight was easier. Maatje could just about see her feet, swirling in a hazy sea of smoke and dizziness. Mrs Franz's white knuckles clutched Will's shirt, her eyes screwed shut.

They reached the lobby. Ricardo and the other guests were gone. Will staggered to the door, pulling Maatje with him.

Air! Oh, the most wonderful thing in the world! Fresh, cool and delicious. She pulled off the towel and gasped and coughed until all that acrid smoke was replaced by sweet, wholesome oxygen.

Will wouldn't let her pause to recover. He tugged her across the moor until a taxi drew up on the grass beside them, then lowered Mrs Franz to her feet, holding her arms until she found her balance again.

"I'm terribly sorry about this entire affair, Mrs Franz. I do hope you'll be okay."

Mrs Franz wheezed as if her internal organs plotted to escape, and wobbled towards the taxi, where the driver held the door open for her. "I'll be fine as soon as I wake up. Thank you for your help, the pair of you. That was quite an adventure."

The taxi drove off and Maatje's eyes widened. "Baggy!" She'd forgotten all about him.

The pony ran up on thudding hooves, tossing his head, the whites of his eyes rolling in their sockets. The other horses were gone.

"It's okay, Baggy. Let's go, shall we?" Maatje rubbed his neck soothingly as she slipped her leg over his back. Once mounted, she nodded to the space behind her. "Will, do you want to come with me? How are you leaving?"

"Don't worry about me—" He broke off with a fit of coughs. "Go and give your terrified horse some peace."

Maatje grinned. They'd survived. But she could celebrate with Will tomorrow. "Okay, well, see you around."

Baggy needed no encouragement. As soon as she wound her fingers into his mane, he shot across the moors. The heat of the hotel faded into cool night and Maatje dared look back. The dragon had grown into a humungous, raging serpent, wrapped around the flaming building, its scythe-like claws dug deep into the sides. Great jaws opened like a knifed chasm, wide enough to fit the entire hotel. And Will – dear

Will – strode back towards it, straight through the burning front door.

"No!" Maatje cried.

The dragon's teeth snapped shut upon the hotel, in a crushing flash of blinding orange.

Then nothing.

It was gone. The dragon. The hotel.

Will.

NOW: MAATJE

Maatje threw the photocopy of the newspaper article onto Hanna's desk.

"I found him," she announced glumly.

"Found who?" Hanna turned away from the computer and picked up the article. "And Happy New Year, by the way."

"Happy New Year," Maatje replied, sounding as if she was wishing her colleague anything but. She didn't care. The year had already been ruined. Her life's work had been ruined.

"This article is four years old." Hanna frowned. "Who is this dude, anyway?"

"Read it. He's the Manager of that hotel I told you about."

"The dream one?" Hanna's eyes flicked over the page. "Where did you find him?"

"At the local museum back home."

"Oh gosh – he set his house on fire!"

Maatje wasn't sure she wanted to hear the details again, but Hanna was already reading aloud.

"'Georg Macher, the renowned violinist turned alcoholic and recluse since the consecutive deaths of both wives, is believed to have fallen asleep in his office in front of an open fire. His two children were rescued from the blaze, but Mr Macher was pronounced dead at the scene . . .' He died?"

Maatje nodded.

"Well, what do you expect, drinking so much? He probably never even woke up as he was burnt alive."

"That's a horrible thing to say."

"He nearly killed his kids, Maatje!"

"But . . ." Maatje squirmed, anxious to defend the man she had looked up to for all these years. "I think he couldn't wake up because we were in his head still – all the guests at the hotel, I mean. There was a fire there too. He'd dreamt up this assistant who was trying to get us all out of his head so he could end the dream. I had no idea it was a real fire or I wouldn't have wasted so much time."

Hanna blinked. "There is no way on earth you can blame yourself for this guy dying."

"But he really wanted me out of the hotel, Han. I was just being silly and stubborn."

"Nothing's changed then."

Maatje scowled. "This isn't a joke."

"No." Hanna swung around in her chair and levelled her gaze at Maatje. "This hotel of yours. It's all very . . . fanciful."

"It was real—"

Hanna raised a hand to cut Maatje off. "But you have to remember, you were a kid back then. And if this guy really did invite you into his dream, then on no level was it okay, yeah?"

This was like Elinor and Mum all over again.

"It wasn't just me—"

Hanna's palm lifted higher. "Doesn't matter. If he died,

73

he got off lucky. And so did you. This is not the kind of guy who could have helped revitalise shared dreaming – or whatever you wanted to find him for. He was a groomer and a drunk and the world is better off without him."

"But he didn't . . ." Maatje picked up the article and stared at the beaming face of the Manager, violin at his hip. After the fire, when the hotel hadn't appeared again and she'd spent night after night running with Baggy over the empty moors, Maatje had tried to turn her own dreams into a replica of the hotel. She'd only think happy things before going to sleep and practised her hardest to take control – just something small to start with, like making a leaf fall from a tree. But her dreams would do what they always did – what everyone's always did – their own thing. Eventually, even Baggy disappeared.

Elinor had visited and there'd been no hotel to take her to, though she'd needed it. Her sister was miserable. She barely spoke, barely ate, barely did anything but sit in her room, do homework and have her usual exhausting, frantic dreams in which Maatje couldn't reach her. Maatje tried telling Elinor about the hotel instead. And Will. Every detail, just in case some of it rubbed off on her sister and made her smile again.

But instead, Elinor told Mum. Told her that Will had held Maatje's hand, and of the embarrassing wriggly feelings she got when he listened to her so intently. Mum told the police and the police searched the overgrown garden for signs of anyone camping there. No one believed that the Manager might have been dreaming from miles away. Maatje was glad they'd never find him. She'd told Elinor before she went back to school that she never wanted to see her again.

She hadn't meant it. But Elinor took Maatje's anger seriously. She stayed with Dad every holiday after that. Now she was at university and had her own place in the city.

Christmas was the most they'd spoken in four years.

Maatje had eventually come to terms with Will not being real, but never lost hope that one day she would meet the Manager again. That he'd help Elinor the way he'd helped everyone in his hotel, and Elinor would know Maatje cared.

Now it meant nothing. The Manager had died the day the hotel disappeared and any chance Maatje had of getting her sister back had died along with him.

"He didn't . . ." she tried again. "And even if he did, his dreams really helped people. He understood how to make people better."

"Then now it's up to you," Hanna said. "Now you have to take what you saw and apply it to the real world. The world where people can't drag hundreds of others into their dreams and control what happens there. Apply it to us."

"I can't."

"Then it can't have meant much to you. Stop blubbing and do something else with your life."

Oh, but it did. Hanna was right. She couldn't quit now. Dream support machines were getting increasingly powerful, as well as knowledge about sleep and the brain. Besides, if there had been one person with the Manager's abilities, surely another must exist too? Just the other day, she had stumbled into that dream at Hubert's manor where it seemed the children were all sharing a dream together . . .

Maatje froze.

The rush of heading home for Christmas – of wondering if Elinor was coming and how she'd be – had pushed it clean out of her mind.

Was it possible? Did Hubert know a dreamer like the Manager?

Her heart began to thud and she started shaking. "Hanna, Hanna, I have to speak to Hubert!"

"What? Why?"

"I . . ." Maatje thought she might burst. "Do we have his number?"

Hanna began scrolling through her spreadsheets.

"No, don't worry," Maatje stopped her. "It's best if I speak to him face to face."

NOW: MAATJE

"Kröte residence. Do you have an appointment?" a polite voice buzzed from the box outside the locked gate to Hubert's manor.

Maatje leant further out the taxi window. "Erm, well, no, but I'm here to speak with Mr Kröte about some groundbreaking new research I think he could help with. Can I come in?"

The line went dead and for a moment Maatje thought she'd been refused entry, then slowly the gates swung open and the taxi took the long drive down to the house. It looked different in the day. Rolling green lawns and ancient trees perfectly aligned along the edge of the road. Maatje felt very scruffy in her jeans.

"Want me to wait for you?" the taxi driver asked.

"Great, thanks. I won't be long." Maatje leapt out of the taxi and strode up the rounded stone stairs to the front door. A stout gentleman bowed her in and led her to a small panelled office that smelt of rich mahogany and varnish.

A small bespectacled lady with deep red lips and tightly

pinned-back hair frowned at her from behind a large desk. "He's a very busy man, Miss . . ."

"Finkel, Maatje. I'm from the SDRC." She unzipped her coat to show her badge.

The secretary flicked through the heavy diary in front of her, humming pointedly. "You're going to have to make an appointment."

"I'll only be five minutes. I know how much the SDRC's projects mean to him; that's why I know he'll be interested in what I have to say."

The secretary hummed again. "Well, his lunch meeting's just been cancelled, so you might be in luck. I'll call up to him now and see."

"Very grateful."

The secretary's long red nails tapped a number into the phone then continued to tap on the desk as she held the phone up to her ear.

"Mr Kröte, a Miss Maatje Finkel from the SDRC is here to see you. She says five minutes – are you free?"

Maatje heard Hubert's bellowing voice through the receiver, though it was too muffled to make out the words. When it stopped, the secretary covered up the mouthpiece to address Maatje again.

"He asks if you are the pretty one, from the party?"

Maatje's eyebrows shot up into her hair. "Er, yes?"

The secretary took her hand away from the receiver. "She says yes." A moment later, she placed it back on the hook. "He'll be down in a minute. Please take a seat." She pointed at a brown leather sofa behind Maatje and returned to her work.

Maatje's backside had barely touched the seat when Hubert burst into the room.

"Ah, I remember you," he said, wagging his finger.

"Couldn't keep away." He shook her hand in a firm but sweaty grip. "Come, let's go somewhere quiet."

He led her down a hallway, panelled just like the secretary's office had been, and into another little room which was empty save for a couple of chairs and a heavy mahogany table. Hubert moved the chairs closer together and sat down, stretching out so their knees almost touched when Maatje sat opposite.

"So what may I help you with today, young lady?"

Maatje instantly forgot her discomfort and launched into voicing the whirlwind of thoughts in her mind. "Well, you see, I accidentally fell asleep at your Christmas party – not because it was boring, it was a lovely night, but I was tired from being in the labs all day – and I stumbled across a fascinating dream that I think belonged to the children who are in your care. I'm hoping you can tell me who was making that dream for them."

Hubert's eyebrows shot up and his jaw twitched. When he didn't speak, Maatje took this as a good sign and continued.

"There's a project I'd like to develop as part of my apprenticeship; one that uses dreamers with lucid control to develop new forms of psychotherapeutic treatments. I was wondering how much control this dreamer of yours had and whether they'd be interested in getting involved with my project."

Hubert was turning the colour of his secretary's nail polish. His gritted teeth started to hiss and Maatje realised with a jolt that he wasn't excited – he was angry.

"How dare you!" he erupted. "How dare you enter the dreams of the children in my guardianship without permission!"

Maatje's jaw fell slack. She hadn't thought about that.

"Those children are some of the most vulnerable people in our society. They are in my house under my protection.

You have no right to go barging into their sleep. Who's your superior? I'll call them at once."

"Oh no, please don't do that!" Maatje leapt to her feet. "I'm sorry. I didn't think. I just found myself there and had a look around. I was part of a similar dream as a child myself. A hotel. The Manager there could share dreams with hundreds of people at the same time and control exactly what went on in the dream. I've never seen anything like it before or since. This dream was so like the one from my youth that I forgot I was trespassing."

"Your superior's name . . ." Hubert demanded.

"Please, I'm sorry. Let me make it up to you."

"Now!"

Maatje felt like a bug being squashed under a boot. "Paul Weber."

"Department?"

"Dream defence."

Hubert pulled out a pad and jotted this down. He stabbed his pen in Maatje's direction. "You disgust me, Miss Finkel. You are a disgrace to the name of shared dream research. Mark my words: you will never work in this area again."

"Mr Kröte, I'm truly sorry—"

"And that's the last of it." He cut her off. "Now get out of my sight before I call the police."

THEN: RACHEL

The hall fell silent the moment Matron stepped through the door. A hundred faces turned her way, some in mid-chew, others with forks dangling forgotten by their mouths. Then they noticed Rachel standing by Matron's side and a hundred pairs of eyes flicked down to her. She tried to wriggle behind Matron's hulk, but Matron's hand was still clamped around hers and pulled her back into sight.

The silence broke. Chairs scraped, spoons clanked and everyone got to their feet.

"Good afternoon, Matron," they chanted as one.

Matron raised a beefy finger at a girl near the front. Rachel guessed she was about twelve years old – the same age as herself. The girl ran to stand in front of Matron, looking at her feet. She wore black plimsolls, identical to the pair Rachel had just been given.

"Eva, this is Rachel," Matron barked. "Show her the ropes."

Eva nodded and offered Rachel a hand, still staring at her feet. Timidly, Rachel followed her back to her table.

Matron pursed her lips as she scanned the rest of the

room. "Stefan, you can sweep the entire dining hall once everyone's left, you filthy wretch."

A ginger boy's face turned the colour of his hair. Rachel spotted a sprinkling of roast dinner under his seat and his white sleeves were stained gravy-brown.

Matron nodded to the two aproned ladies standing behind a counter full of metal pans before striding out again.

The whole hall let out a breath and the clatter of cutlery began once more.

Eva turned to Rachel. She had light brown pigtails and more than her fair share of freckles. "What you in for?"

"My dad died." Her throat grew hard and sore.

A hum of sympathy arose from around the table and a couple of kids said, "Mine too."

"What about your mum?"

"She died when I was born," Rachel said.

"Mine ran off with a sailor," a boy put in.

"Mine had cancer."

"Are you going to get anything to eat?" Eva nudged Rachel.

"I'm not hungry." She wasn't sure she'd ever be hungry again. Everything had been flipped upside down. Only two days ago, she'd been running around at home, collecting leaves to show her brother. And then *poof*: flames, hospital, a kind lady with a pink scarf and Matron yanking her down the panelled hallways of an orphanage. No one would tell her, but she'd guessed it by now: Papa was dead, and her brother? No one would say anything about him either. She just wanted to go home.

"Don't cry." A boy on her right leant towards her. He had a shock of crazy black curls, skin the colour of a treasure map and the biggest, brownest eyes she had ever seen.

"Sorry," Rachel gulped. "Everything's just . . ." She couldn't continue. She'd cry again if she did.

"Going too fast?" the boy finished for her.

Rachel nodded.

"Yeah, it does at first. But you get used to it. The main thing to remember is: if you can survive Matron, you can survive anything."

"When I first came here, I cried for two weeks straight," Eva announced.

"How long have you been here for?"

"Two years," said Eva.

"Five," the boy added.

Rachel's eyes grew wide.

"Some of us don't stay long," Eva said. "They let you go when you're sixteen, or if other family members come and rescue you."

"You got any family?" asked the boy.

"My brother. He'll come," Rachel decided. He was sixteen; that was why he wasn't here with her. Not because he was dead too.

Her throat tightened. *No.* No more crying. She had cried enough.

"I have a sister at university," a girl across the table said, one front tooth bigger than the other. "She's going to get me out when she's graduated. Is your brother at university?"

Rachel shook her head. "He's at school. But he won't wait until he's finished. As soon as he knows I'm here, he'll get me."

The curly haired boy winced. "He can't get you out then. You gotta be eighteen to be a guardian. Hard luck."

Rachel shook her head adamantly. Two years was too long to wait.

A lady with tight lips walked into the hall ringing a hand-bell. She stood in the doorway long enough for the noise to make Rachel's head start to ring too before she walked back out again without a word.

Chairs clattered and children began to get to their feet.

"Back to class," the curly haired boy announced.

Rachel followed them to a wooden-panelled room tall enough to house a giant, though he'd have to have been a thin one as it wasn't very wide. About ten children came in with them, all of them heading straight to their desks. Rachel hovered by the door, not sure where to go.

The curly haired boy saw and went back to her. "Have my desk," he said, pointing it out to her. "It's next to Eva – and Matron did tell her to look after you."

"Where will you sit?"

"At the back." The boy grinned. "Where I oughta be."

Rachel cracked a smile too. "Thank you."

"Nah, thank you." The boy swaggered off. "Hey, Mathieu, watch your back!"

When the teacher came in, she didn't seem to mind the new arrangements. In fact, she made no sign of having noticed Rachel was new and in the boy's seat. She trotted straight up to the whiteboard in a skirt so tight she was forced to take mouse-sized steps, and started writing.

Paper rustled and pen lids dropped to the desktops. Rachel spun wildly around until Eva passed her a sheet of paper and a pen.

"Just write whatever she writes," she whispered.

The other lessons that afternoon went similarly to the first. The teacher came in and wrote on the whiteboard, and everyone copied out what she was writing. Sometimes the teacher would get a couple of students to say some of the sentences aloud, but most of the lessons were conducted in silence.

Another handbell rang in the corridor, just as the light outside the window turned golden. Rachel collected her sheets of paper, stretched her aching wrist, and followed Eva to a dormitory full of bunkbeds. Eva pointed out a top bunk that was free and an empty drawer where she could put her things. Rachel didn't have much. Just her school notes and a toothbrush the kind lady with the pink scarf had given her.

She followed Eva down to the common room: a vast space with dusty shelves holding ripped board games. Most of the children sprawled on mats on the floor playing hand games or making little birds out of paper. A few sat at the big table in the corner, frowning with concentration over textbooks and notepads.

"This is where we go before supper," Eva explained. "You can relax or do your homework here. The older kids have a better room on the other side of the dining hall. But you have to be fourteen to go there. They have a radio!"

Rachel followed Eva about for the rest of the evening, not really processing much, but going through the motions. She ate very little at supper, something the rest of the children at her table took advantage of, helping themselves to her spaghetti. Then she showered and changed into a pair of pyjamas the bathroom attendant found for her. They smelt as if they'd been in the back of a cupboard for years. Finally, she copied everyone else and stood by her bed whilst Matron strode up and down the dormitory like an army sergeant – watching, scrutinising – then, like a crocodile, seized a girl by her arm and marched her out of the room.

The same thing happened the next night, and the night after. A different child each time. Sometimes from her dormitory and sometimes from the boys'. They weren't seen again until the next morning, picking at their breakfast, curled over and quiet. Rachel was too scared to ask where they'd been. The other kids exchanged only sympathetic glances.

NOW: MAATJE

B ack at the office after her disastrous visit to Hubert, Maatje spent the rest of the day clicking her thumbnails together. Every time there was a knock at the door she almost fell off her chair.

Hanna pretended not to notice her behaviour, and Maatje tried to act as normally as possible so Hanna wouldn't crack and ask her what was up.

A lot was up. She had been a complete and utter idiot. Why hadn't she thought about how wrong it was to go inside the head of a child she didn't know before she blurted it out to the child's guardian?

But was it actually illegal? Would the police really get involved? They'd come when Mum had told them about the Manager.

After work, Maatje spent the entire evening dreading the buzzer on the door of her tiny apartment or a late phone call advising her not to come into work tomorrow. One sleepless night later, she summoned the courage to go back to the SDRC and act as if everything was fine.

Stupid, stupid.

The knock finally came sometime around mid-morning, after Hanna had handed out the biscuits. Maatje had taken one as to not arouse suspicion, but the crumbs tasted like sawdust in her mouth.

It was more like half a knock, as the hand making it stopped abruptly and Paul's head appeared on the other side of the frosted glass window. The red-face topped with floppy hair next to his was unmistakably Hubert's.

Maatje's heart stopped beating and she went rigid in her chair. Hubert himself had come to kick her out.

"What's going on?" It seemed Hanna could bear no more of the tension and looked between the frosted glass and Maatje expectantly. "Is that Hubert?"

Paul came into the office first, looking as though he'd been knocked on the head by a large branch. He gaped a bit, clutching the edge of the door before saying, "Maatje, Mr Kröte is here."

Saying sorry would have been a good start. "I wasn't thinking" a close second, but both of them were excuses, and besides, she couldn't speak a word. She rose to her feet automatically, her body knowing it had to remove itself from the building.

"He'd like to speak with you in private," Paul continued. "Take him to meeting room three if it's free. They have the comfiest seats."

Maatje baulked. So Hubert hadn't told him? Or had he? Nothing about Paul's face looked cross, he just appeared stunned, as someone might after being visited by one of their heroes.

"Okay," she said finally, and walked dazedly out into the corridor.

"Miss Finkel!" Hubert boomed, a beaming smile on his face.

Did the man have amnesia? Yesterday he'd promised to

have her sacked.

"Mr Kröte," Maatje squeaked.

"Oh no – it's Hubert to my friends, please. And may I call you Maatje?"

"If you like." Maatje was still waiting for the fury to return. "This way."

Meeting room three was a cluster of squishy armchairs set around a gleaming glass table. Hubert fell into one with a sigh.

"Would you like a drink?" Maatje went over to the tiny kitchenette in the corner – basically a sink and a kettle in a cupboard.

Hubert waved a plummy hand. "No, no, just sit. I'm here on business."

Maatje chose a chair as far away from the man as she could get without offending him and perched on the edge.

"Listen, about the other day. I shouldn't have lost my temper like that," he said.

"You had every right to," Maatje replied. "I was completely in the wrong. I was excited and . . . yeah."

"I recall you saying you were excited because you hadn't seen a dream like it since you were a child."

"Yes." Maatje nodded. "Though I wasn't there long enough to know for sure. It just had this feel—"

"Would you mind telling me about this dream from your childhood?"

"Of course." And with careful relief, Maatje told him all about the hotel, the Manager, Taeng, Will and Baggy. She told him about the floating, flowering staircase, the theme-shifting floors, the fruit carving . . . and the dragon that put an end to it all. She finished with her recent discovery that the Manager was a man called Georg Macher who had died in a fire the same night the hotel dream ended.

"But it wasn't just fun-filled nights. The hotel really

helped people too. The Manager gave everyone there exactly what they needed. I wish I could have talked to him about it."

She waited for Hubert to laugh and dismiss her story, or get angry again for wasting his time with fantasies, but instead he hummed. "I must attest something similar. The dream you stumbled upon in my orphanage has been happening for nearly four years now, and the children are a lot happier for it."

Maatje blinked. Hubert believed her? Not only that, but he'd had the same experience? "I knew he couldn't be the only one!" she crowed. "I've been reading into how therapists use metaphor all the time to help treat their patients. But what if they could use entire dreamscapes? Something they could control and mould to meet their patient's needs? No one seems to think it's possible, but with a dreamer like the Manager, it could be, couldn't it? Who is your dreamer? Have they ever been part of any research like that?"

"Alas, I have never even met him," Hubert sighed. "He keeps me out. He keeps all adults out. I would have called the police if he hadn't had such a profound effect on the children's wellbeing."

"He's a he?"

Hubert shrugged. "I've been calling him my dream maker, but to be truthful I know nothing else about him. The kids have told me there's nobody else in the dream but them. I've recently thought about bringing the police in just to find out more, but I don't want him to catch wind and run. He's too precious for that."

Maatje nodded. "The Manager at the hotel liked to stay just as anonymous. He only came down once when I was there, to check on things. He created fake hotel staff in his place."

Actually Will was the only fake staff member she knew

about. She wondered how many more were as well. Ricardo? Giovanni? Taeng? She hoped not.

"But this brings me on to you," Hubert said. "When my anger finally abated and I could think clearly about what you had told me, I needed to know: how did you get in? Like I said, no adult has ever entered the dream maker's dream. It's a place strictly for the children."

She shrugged. "Well, I'm quite good at getting into dreams. Too nosy for my own good, my mum says. Paul uses me against his blockers."

Hubert's face cracked a smile, showing every one of his gleaming white teeth. "Well, that's it then. How would you like to become partners, you and I? I could do with such talent and enthusiasm. Come to the manor this evening; we'll contact this dream maker and together bring dream therapy into the new century." He held out his hand.

What a question! This was supposed to be Maatje's life's work. She'd envisaged years of struggling through the ranks and car park at the SDRC before she could finally stand in front of the investors and ask for the funding to help her chase some childhood memory. Now Hubert was handing it to her on a platter.

She reached out and gave him the firmest handshake she could muster.

THEN: RACHEL

Rachel went to bed early that night. She'd found a book on the top shelf in the common room, and though the first chapter had been ripped out and most others nibbled by woodlice, she threw herself into it: a world far, far away from this horrible new reality.

She didn't notice when the rest of her dorm came to bed, and not even when they all snapped to attention for Matron. Leila, the girl who slept below her, almost pulled her arm out of its socket as she yanked her out of bed. Rachel landed with a loud thud, loose pages of the book wafting towards the neighbouring beds.

"Ow!" Her ankles throbbed and she glared at Leila rather than thanking her for the warning.

Matron heard the racket and marched their way. Rachel shoved the majority of the book under the duvet, hoping to be able to recover the rest later, and looked at her feet.

Please let her pass us . . .

Thick, heavy black shoes stopped in front of them.

Don't look up; don't look up.

The temptation was too great. Rachel lifted her head, and

Matron's massive hand clamped to her shoulder and piloted her out of the room.

She'd been chosen.

Rachel's heart hammered wildly. She still hadn't asked the others where they were taken each night. And now it was her turn.

She tried to reason with herself. It couldn't be that bad; they all came back in the morning, even if they looked rather grim.

Keeping her head down, Rachel watched as wooden floor after wooden floor, stairs, carpet, and more wooden floor rushed past her feet. She half ran to keep up with Matron's pace. Going slower meant sharp fingers digging deep into her skin.

Eventually they came to a stop. Rachel peeked up out of the corner of her eye, but didn't recognise this part of the orphanage. It looked a lot grander than the main building. Naked white statues ogled her with pupilless eyes.

Matron rapped on a door, half opened it and pushed Rachel inside.

A man sat splodged in a magnificent gilded armchair. Rachel snapped her head down again and heard the door slam behind her, Matron's thudding footsteps fading away.

"It's okay," the man said. He had a warm voice, and sounded as if he was sucking a toffee. "You've been specially selected tonight."

Rachel peered up at him between curtains of her golden hair. He had a face like a tomato and pouting lips like a supermodel. His hair might have been her colour, or perhaps whiter, but the room's light was too orange to make it out. He was smiling at least, and talking to her – unlike the other teachers who just ignored her.

"That's better. Now I can see your pretty little face. You're new here aren't you?"

Rachel nodded.

The man shook his head, tutting. "So sad; so sad."

Rachel just stood there. What was sad? Did he know Papa?

"My name is Hubert. I run this orphanage," the man continued. "And who do I have the pleasure of meeting?"

"Rachel."

"A beautiful name," Hubert commented. "Don't look so nervous. You don't know why you're here, do you?"

Rachel shook her head.

"Well, as a treat I like to let one of you children sleep in the main manor each night – in a more private and comfortable bed than those crowded, noisy dormitories. See, nothing to worry about. Here, have a hot chocolate."

Hubert leant over and picked up a silver teapot from a silver tray on the table next to him. He poured a steaming thick liquid into a mug before dipping a pair of tiny silver tongs into a silver sugar bowl and dropping a cluster of pink and white marshmallows on top. Rachel took the offered mug without question.

"Now, you must be tired." Hubert stood up. "Let me show you to your quarters."

He took her into a room panelled in rich-smelling wood. In the centre, upon a huge, patterned rug, stood the biggest bed she had ever seen, with four posters and a canopy and curtains around the sides.

"Yes, it's nice isn't it? Finish up your hot chocolate and pop into bed, there's a good girl. Matron will take you back in the morning."

Rachel sipped her drink. It was still far too hot, but she had to show Hubert she was being obedient.

"Goodnight then – sweet dreams." Hubert walked back to the door and left the room, blowing her a kiss as he did so.

The moment she was alone, the bedroom seemed to grow

three times bigger. Rachel tiptoed as fast as she could to the bed, setting the hot chocolate down on the bedside table. She climbed up onto the mattress and gave a little bounce. It was amazingly soft, like a giant pillow.

She wriggled between the covers and sipped more hot chocolate. This didn't seem so bad. What had all the others been so scared of? She didn't like being alone though. She'd always shared a bedroom with her brother, and the other children seemed very far away . . .

She drained the last extra-chocolaty dregs from the mug and snuggled down into the bed. It hugged her back, warm and fresh. Luxurious, but the smell was still foreign. So, just like every other of the seven whole awful nights that had passed since she'd arrived in the orphanage, she fell asleep wishing she was back at home.

———

"Eva told me," said Louis the next day as she slipped into a seat next to him with her bowl of watery porridge. He was the boy with the curly hair she'd met on the first day and had become a good friend. "Sorry."

"About what?" Rachel asked.

"About getting chosen last night. It sucks."

"It wasn't so bad." Rachel shrugged. "A bit weird, but the bed was lovely. I've never seen one with curtains before."

Louis frowned. "What happened in your dream?"

Rachel stopped. She couldn't tell him. Not about that. Not yet. Probably not ever.

"I don't really dream." It was truthful . . . enough.

"How'd you mean?"

"I sort of go to sleep and then wake up in the morning and nothing happens in between."

Louis laughed and slammed the table with his hand. All

the bowls on it jumped three centimetres into the air, sloshing porridge and clinking spoons.

"Careful," grunted Ted, the boy with the thick glasses.

"What's so funny?" Rachel asked.

Louis looked as though he'd just been told he had the day off lessons. "Hubert must've had an awful night then, you jammy spanner."

"What, why?"

"Hubert's a useless dreamer. His dreams are super-boring, so every night he picks one of us to dream for him. And he don't play nice either. You gotta do what he wants, and if not . . ." Louis broke off and pulled a face that wasn't funny. "It's fun when you have a nightmare though. Hubert don't stay long. But sometimes it'll mean he'll make sure you miss breakfast, or get the teachers to give you extra homework as punishment. I stayed up all night once. Refused to sleep. I didn't eat the whole day because of it, but he don't use me much any more."

Rachel stared at him.

"Don't worry." He nudged her. "You're a lucky one. You don't dream. He won't call you again."

His words brought little comfort. The thought of Hubert wandering through people's dreams as if he owned them made her feel sick.

"I think everyone who goes in the room should refuse to sleep," Rachel said.

"Like a rebellion?"

"Yeah. He'd soon stop if no one dreamt for him."

"We tried that," Louis countered. "Hubert just used the same person for three days straight until he gave in and fell asleep."

"Have you told anybody?" Rachel asked. "From outside?"

Louis shrugged. "No one listens. We're just kids."

"What about those with family like Ella? Her sister's at university, right?"

"Ella's sister has been at university for eight years," Louis replied.

"That's a long time. What is she studying?"

Louis raised an eyebrow and said nothing.

Rachel sighed. "But there has to be something we can do."

"Like I said." Louis shrugged. "You're fine. Hubert don't want you."

That night Matron took Rachel to the comfortable room again.

THEN: RACHEL

"Hello again, young lady." Hubert grinned and pressed his fingers together as Rachel was pushed through his door. She decided it was safer to say nothing.

"Why the glum face?" Hubert frowned. "Did you not enjoy your visit last night?"

"I don't think it's very nice of you to go into other people's dreams like that."

Hubert looked surprised. "No? But that was exactly what I was going to ask you about: your dream." He dropped his hands to his lap and continued. "Just who was that glorious lady who met me in your mind last night? She looked like you, but a lot more . . . shall we say, mature?"

Rachel felt her heart freeze. No. She wouldn't tell him. Couldn't tell him.

"She was most amenable. It was nice to have some adult company for once." Hubert's eyes went hazy. "So tell me, where did she come from? A memory? If so, it's very well formed for someone of your age."

Rachel shook her head.

"Now come on." Hubert leant towards her. "I'll meet her again tonight, won't I? Do you think she'd tell me if I asked?"

"She's a liar," Rachel blurted.

"A liar?" Hubert hummed thoughtfully. "What does she lie about?"

"Everything. To get her way. Don't trust anything she says."

"Now that's a bit harsh. I thought she was lovely. I've met a lot of dishonest people in my time and she's certainly not like any of them."

"She's worse."

Hubert raised his eyebrows. "And how would you know this?"

Rachel clamped her mouth shut. She'd said too much already.

"She's not breaking into your mind, is she? We can call the police if someone is giving you grief."

"No." Rachel shook her head again. "She's always there."

"How long?"

"Since I was born."

"So she's some sort of extra personality of yours, who only shows herself in your dreams?"

"They're not my dreams," Rachel said. "I mean they are, but she won't let me dream them."

"Sounds like she's doing you a favour," Hubert said. "Dreams can be frightfully tedious."

"They're *my* dreams and *I* want to dream them."

"Then why do you let her take over?"

"I don't have a choice. She doesn't want me there. She doesn't like me. I killed her." Rachel stepped backwards. Hubert was leaning so far forward she could touch his nose. Not that she wanted to.

"Killed her?"

"She's my mum." The truth was out. She couldn't stop it.

"She died giving birth to me, but a bit of her must have grabbed hold of my mind. Now she lives in my dreams instead."

"Fascinating," Hubert breathed. "But you can't blame her for it. Why not let her have your sleep if she can't have her life? I certainly enjoyed her company."

Rachel shook her head. Hubert didn't know what he was getting himself into. "She picks on my brother and haunted my dad until he locked himself away all night and all day. I wouldn't mind if she was nice, but she hurts people. She'll hurt you."

Hubert laughed. "I think you're just too young to understand the implications of her unfortunate situation. And I for one would like to get to know her better. Would you like another hot chocolate?"

Rachel's face burnt. Why couldn't he see what she was telling him? Why had she told him about Esther in the first place?

Well then, maybe he deserved to be played and discarded by Esther. She'd warned him.

She thrust her chin forward in response to Hubert's question and marched through the door into the comfortable room.

NOW: MAATJE

There was the red door again. Just as it had been during the Christmas party. The door that led out into the town square and the children's shared dream.

Maatje tried knocking, but just as before, there was no answer. Twisting the handle, she pushed the door inwards.

It didn't move.

She turned the handle round further, but still the door didn't budge.

She tried the other way, but again, nothing.

The door was locked.

Damn. They didn't want her in. Surely there was another way . . .

There were no walls attached to the door; it stood alone in inky blackness. Maatje felt the air to the sides for any weaknesses.

Nothing.

She walked right around, but it remained a chipped red door – no more.

"Hello? Is anyone there?"

Laughter echoed through the wood. Maatje pressed her ear against it.

"Hello?" She knocked again. "Would it be possible to speak to the dream maker here?"

Nothing.

And then, a blackbird fluttered up and landed on top of the frame. It peered down at her with one beady eye, head cocked. "Please leave," it sang.

Maatje pulled back. She had not expected it to speak.

"This place is not for you."

"Are you the dream maker?" Maatje wasn't perturbed. "Please, I'd like to speak to whoever is making this dream. I need their help."

The blackbird straightened its head and fluttered down, behind the door.

"No, come back!" Maatje ran behind the door, but there was only the blackness.

Right. Time for action. If the blackbird could get in and out of the dream without opening the door, then maybe she needed to become a bird herself.

She placed her hand against the door, as close to the dream as she could get. If this dream maker was anything like the Manager, she'd have a chance of success. It was mind over matter, literally.

Feathers sprouted out of her fingers and the door shot up in front of her, becoming an epic red skyscraper as she shrank. Quickly, she flapped her new wings and tweeted in delight. It had worked! She sang loudly in the voice of a finch and flew up and over the door.

Beyond it wasn't the town centre playground, but an ash tree, standing as still as death in the windless vacuum between dreams.

There was the blackbird again, perched delicately on a twig. Maatje flew over to it.

"Will you talk to me?" she asked.

The blackbird hopped further along to the end of the twig, away from Maatje. Then it chirped and flew away.

The debrief with Hubert at breakfast went well considering his excited expectation the night before. He'd given her one of his opulent rooms to stay in, as close to the orphanage as she could get without having to step inside. Maatje had hoped to have returned to him with more successful news.

Hubert nodded grimly when she mentioned the black-bird. The creature had been the bane of his life. But he was reassured when Maatje told him she had some ideas to convince the bird to let her in. As she sat in the private car Hubert had arranged to take her to work that morning, she wasn't entirely sure what those ideas would be, but she couldn't very well admit that she was stumped after the first attempt. He'd call off the whole project and it was too important for that. She just had to get past the red door . . .

"Excuse me, hi." Maatje leant forward to address the driver, neatly dressed in a navy blue uniform. It all felt a bit pretentious.

"Ma'am," he replied.

"I was wondering if you could drop me off in the old town square."

"Certainly, ma'am." The driver nodded.

The car pulled up beside the fountain – covered in plastic to protect it during the winter months – and Maatje sat down on the edge, blowing into her hands to keep them warm. Crammed together in a big block around the fountain were sandy-coloured town houses, taller than they were wide, their brightly coloured doors like pegs on a line.

Doors.

Maatje jumped to her feet, her pulse racing. There were three red ones, but only one was the same shabby scarlet as the door in the dream.

It's probably nothing. Just a coincidence because the dream maker liked the look of the door, or absorbed it unconsciously. There's no reason to get excited . . .

But she was already standing in front of it, hand up ready to knock. Before she could make a move, it opened.

"No, no, I go shopping." A lady with a thick accent emerged armed with a large basket of sheets and some hessian sacks. "You want a room?"

"Well, actually, I—"

"No, no, I can't now. You talk to my colleague – Guillermo!" She turned and shouted up the stairs before Maatje could even take a breath.

"He come. He sort you out. I go now."

The lady left.

Maatje supposed she could leave with her, but her colleague was already coming down the stairs into the hallway.

Will.

It was Will.

He stopped at the door's threshold right in front of her, breath in his lungs, a hole in his sock.

She stared. Could it even be possible?

"You're real."

Not the best opening line to a conversation.

"Hello," he replied.

"Hello – yes, hello," Maatje gushed. Then she couldn't think what else to say.

"I take it you're not really looking for a room?"

Maatje laughed. A little too hard. "No. Actually, I . . ." Damn, why was it so hard to talk to him? "Do you want to get a coffee?"

Will looked behind him. "I have to—"

"Please?"

A shadow of a smile creased the corner of his mouth, perhaps more of a grimace. "Okay."

"Thank you!" Maatje bounced back to let him out. He slipped into some scuffed shoes and a coat, squinting in the bright, crisp morning light.

Maatje couldn't help but sneak a look at him again and again as she led him to her favourite coffee shop. He was real. He was real. He looked the same and yet so different. Older, like her, by four years, and though he had been pale in the hotel he was more so now. The sort of pale that came with not sleeping, or lack of sunlight, or being ill. Before he had been quite a bit taller than her, and now they were almost the same height, but his hair was still dark and messy, and those magical blue eyes considered her just as carefully.

"Anything wrong?" he asked.

Maatje jumped back into the present. "No . . . just . . . I can't believe it's you."

Will gave another hesitant smile.

"Here we are. What would you like?" Maatje pushed open the door to the shop and stepped into its warm, fragrant interior.

"A glass of water would be great."

"Nothing else?" Maatje pressed.

"No, thank you." Will bobbed his head.

"Okay, find us a table. I'll be over in a minute."

The queue couldn't have lasted longer if it tried. There were only three people to be served in front of her, but Maatje was desperate to get back to Will. She kept glancing over at the little round table by the window where he sat, scared he might disappear.

Eventually she placed the water in front of him and a

black coffee for herself. She pulled up a chair and asked, "So, how have you been?"

"Good, thank you." Will nodded. "Yourself?"

"Yes, very well. I'm working at the SDRC now. Well, doing an apprenticeship."

"Congratulations."

Maatje nodded, feeling the conversation falling flat already. She'd just have to cut straight to it. She put down her cup. "I'm sorry."

Will tilted his head. "What for?"

"The fire."

Will just stared at her.

Say something, Maatje. Something else.

"Were you the Manager all along?"

He nodded.

"You inspired me to study dreams, you know. To help people."

"That's good." Will looked distant.

"But I really am sorry. If I had known the fire was real, I'd have left sooner. You weren't hurt, were you? And Georg Macher . . ."

He flinched. "Maatje, you're good. Really. Nothing happened that night that wouldn't have happened anyway."

"He was your father?"

Will shrunk into his chair.

Maatje quickly changed the subject. "You're making the dream for the kids at the orphanage too, aren't you?"

Will looked intently at his glass, knuckles whitening around it. Goodness, what was wrong with him?

"Yes."

Maatje breathed a sigh of relief. "Can I talk to you about it?"

"There's not much to say."

"Well, I have to go to work in a minute, but I've started

this new project, looking at shared dreaming the way you make it. Bringing wonder and joy to so many people, and being there for kids who have nothing else. It's amazing. What you can do is amazing. You could help revolutionise the way we study dreams, if you'd let us run a few tests, learn what you can do. We'd compensate you for your time of course."

"I'd rather not, if that's all right by you."

"It can just be me and you . . . if you prefer."

"Adella asked me to clean the hostel."

"Then you can come tonight. Actually that would work better for me too – give me a chance to prepare. Very few people will be around then."

Those blue eyes begged her to release him, to let him vanish back into the hole he'd been hiding in all these years. But she couldn't. This was too important. He didn't realise it yet.

"You're not allowed to say no."

Will frowned then gave another half-smile. "Still as stubborn as ever."

Maatje gave him a wicked grin. "So you'll come?"

Will gave the slowest, most hesitant nod in the history of the world. "Okay."

Maatje threw her hands in the air. It was lucky the table was between them or she might have given him a hug. "Thank you so much; you're a star."

She drained the last dregs of her coffee and leapt to her feet. "I have to run, but I'll see you later. Thank you!"

She ran out of the shop, pulling her coat around her as she was welcomed by the icy breeze.

Thinking twice, she ran back in and scribbled her mobile on a napkin.

"My number, in case you need it." She pushed it in Will's direction and ran out again.

Wait until she told everyone in the office! She gave Will one last glance, just to check she hadn't imagined it all.

He hadn't moved, staring at her vacant chair as though she were still sitting there. She stopped walking. He looked lost. It wasn't the Will she remembered.

She rapped on the glass. Will lurched as if she'd woken him from sleep. She drew a smile on her face with her fingers, and tapped her cheeks encouragingly.

Will cracked one of his grins. A proper grin. Back at the hotel, that grin had invited adventure and wiped away worries.

Content, Maatje crossed the road.

THEN: RACHEL

From then on, Rachel was summoned to the comfortable room almost every night, and became a hero throughout the orphanage. She received high fives down the corridor when the adults weren't looking, and words of thanks and slaps on the back from people she'd never spoken to before.

For the last three nights in a row, Hubert had ignored her and gone back to using some of the other children, but they'd all come back with beaming smiles on their face. Leila – Rachel's bunk buddy – had been summoned last night and a crowd of people sat around her at breakfast, chattering excitedly.

"The playdoh was giant, right?"

"You wimped out on the tree swing though, Bruno."

"Shhhh!" Eva elbowed Ted as Rachel sat down, knocking his glasses off into his plate of toast. "Hi, Rach!"

"Morning. What you talking about?"

"Just stuff." Bruno shrugged.

"How was Hubert last night, Leila?"

"Oh, I dunno." Leila looked over at Eva. "Okay?"

They were trying to keep something from her. It had been like this all week and she was tired of it. They weren't trying to avoid her, but she was beginning to feel left out.

Everyone rushed down their breakfast and jumped to their feet as soon as the bell went. Rachel grabbed Louis.

"What's going on?"

Louis looked as if she'd just knocked him on the head with a football. "What d'you mean? I'm going to class."

"Not now – just then. You're all not telling me something."

"No, we're not." He widened his big brown eyes and gave her his best hurt expression.

"Stop it. I don't believe you. Everyone keeps changing the conversation whenever I come near."

"Nah, just your imagination."

"Louis . . ." She looked at him hard.

He frowned. "Okay, I'll tell you. But first you've gotta tell me why Hubert keeps wanting you back in the room when you don't even dream."

Rachel wracked her brains for an excuse. "Maybe I do dream, but I'm not there, so Hubert has them all to himself?"

Louis raised an eyebrow. "Really?"

"Well, how would I know, if I'm not there?"

"True."

"So tell me . . ."

"Okay, but it's only because we didn't want you to feel left out, so don't get cross."

Rachel nodded when he paused to give her his most serious look.

"Last week, someone started making a dream for us. All of us, except the adults." Louis lowered his voice and pulled Rachel out of the dining hall and down the corridor. "It's huge. Everyone goes there now. I never knew a dream could hold so many people. And we can do what we like. There're giant swings, treehouses and rope bridges, a beach with surf-boards and slides and all this amazing food and a huge boulder where you can see for miles and miles at the top . . ." he trailed off and grimaced. "But we didn't want to say, because you can't dream, so you can't go there with us. And it didn't seem fair, because you were saving us from Hubert."

"I'm not saving you from Hubert," Rachel scoffed, but already her heart began to flutter at the things Louis had told her.

"Well, you don't have to any more because . . . guess what? The dream don't just stop adults getting in, but Leila and the others who were sent to the room – Hubert can't get inside their dreams neither, cos there's this blackbird that keeps him away."

"Will." His name passed her lips before she could stop it. She had tried her best not to think of him, in case he was dead too, but the dream was his. He was alive!

She threw herself around Louis and hugged him as tightly as she could. Oh, she was so happy!

"You're not cross then?" Louis's muffled voice came from underneath her arm. She let him go.

"No, no." Rachel beamed. "It's for me. The dream's for me. The blackbird's my brother. He's trying to make contact."

"Your brother? But you don't dream."

"When he was there, sometimes I could. He's trying to reach me. You have to give him a message."

"Whoa! Okay, so what's the message?"

What could she say? They were standing outside the classroom door now. Everyone else was already inside and the teacher would arrive soon. But there was so much to tell Will. He was going to get her out of the orphanage!

"Tell him that I'm here. I can't get there, but I'm here," she said. "And . . . I love him."

Louis turned red. "That could be awkward coming from me."

"Don't be such a wimp – he'll know it's not you who loves him. Please, will you tell that to the blackbird?"

"Okay," Louis promised and pushed open the classroom door.

Rachel marched alongside Matron to Hubert that evening with her head held high. Nothing could bring her down now she knew her brother was alive. She would demand that Hubert allow him to visit her. A month was already too long.

She walked in before Matron could push her. Even the sight of Hubert couldn't remove Rachel's smile. She listened to Matron's feet clump away before she opened her mouth.

"You look very happy tonight," Hubert began, getting there first.

"Yes, I had some good news."

"Would that about your brother, by any chance?"

He knew?

"Yes."

Hubert nodded thoughtfully. "Your mother was telling me about him. He's caused me a spot of bother. I thought I could overcome him, but he's a pretty strong dreamer, isn't he?"

Rachel jutted out her chin. "You shouldn't go into people's dreams when they don't want you to."

"Miss Rachel, respect for your elders was not something your late father was very successful at teaching you, was it?"

Rachel glared.

"But I can see, under the circumstances, you are just excited to hear news about your brother's whereabouts. So I'll let it slide for now. Has he always been able to dream like this?"

"Like what?"

"So big. So many people in it. I gather he can control his dreams fully."

"Yes." Rachel swelled up. "And if he doesn't want you coming in, you won't be able to."

"A pity," Hubert hummed. "I'd like to marvel at his abilities first hand. You couldn't arrange for me to have a private visit?"

Rachel jerked back in revulsion. "No way."

Hubert narrowed his eyes. "You know what Master Willem's doing is illegal. I could get him locked away for a long time. Is that what you want?"

"No!" Rachel gasped.

"If I didn't like Esther so much, you would have a lot more to answer to, young missy. I want you to tell your brother to let me see this so-called amazing dream world first hand. I need to check that it's suitable for the children under my care. He'll listen to his little sister, won't he?"

"I can't go into my dreams. She won't let me."

"I'll ask her nicely."

Rachel shook her head. She had the most horrible feeling she had to keep Will as far away from Hubert as possible.

"You know, if I can't inspect this dream, I'll have no choice but to call the police. You do understand that don't you?"

"Yes, but—"

"Then be a good girl and get to bed. I'll have a word with your mother. You can ask him tomorrow night."

Rachel raced down to breakfast the next morning and hijacked Louis at the counter.

"Whoa, watch the porridge!" he yelled as it sloshed over the rim of his bowl.

"Louis, can I trust you?"

"Trust me?" Louis frowned. "Yeah, why?"

"Hubert knows about Will. But it's not good; I know it's not good."

How could she impress the severity of the situation without telling him about Esther? She was more worried about her than anyone. Her mother had made some sort of team with Hubert, telling him all about her brother. Esther was always planning and scheming ways to hurt Will.

"You need to tell the blackbird to leave. He has to go far away from here. Hubert wants to arrest him."

Louis splattered more porridge on the floor. "What? Why? It wasn't me. I didn't say anything to anyone, I swear."

"I know, but Hubert said it's illegal for Will to make the dream. Please . . . you'll tell him, right?"

"How would Hubert know where to find him?"

Rachel rolled her eyes. "How long do you think Will was trying to visit me before he resorted to the dream? Of course Hubert knows where he is. He has to run away."

Louis made a noise like a cat with stomach ache. "But it's such a good dream."

"Louis!" she begged.

"Oy." One of the canteen ladies jabbed a ladle in Rachel's direction. "You eatin'?"

"Yes, yes, thanks." She took a bowl and looked back at Louis.

"Move along – you're holdin' everyone up," the canteen lady barked.

Rachel and Louis went to their usual table. Mathieu, one of Louis's best friends, tried to pull him into a conversation about elastic-band missiles, but Rachel wasn't finished with him yet.

"Louis?"

"Okay, okay," he agreed through gritted teeth. "But on your head be the happiness of everyone here."

"I'm sorry." And she was. She really was.

"Yeah, well. It was good while it lasted."

NOW: MAATJE

The last bus home came at half past eleven and it was almost eleven o'clock now. Maatje couldn't wait much longer. Where was Will? Had he got cold feet? She should have got his number as well; she was completely bound by him without it.

She groaned and dropped her head into her arms. Was it time to make another cup of coffee? What would that be – her third?

The phone let out a shrill ring. Maatje jumped halfway across the room in shock, her chair rolling back until she hit the stud wall. Racing to the phone, she snatched it off the receiver.

"Hello, Dream Defence, Maatje speaking."

The only response was the sound of dead tone and the ringing continued.

Her mobile! *Idiot.* Where was it?

She found it at the bottom of her bag. The number was from reception.

"Hello?" she gasped.

"Hi, Maatje . . . I'm here."

Will.

"Great, great. I'll come down and meet you. You need a pass to get anywhere."

"Okay."

Maatje hung up and raced to the lift.

When she arrived, Will was staring up at the vast atrium that was the main entrance of the SDRC.

"Hi!" She shook his hand, immediately realising that it felt very odd and told herself never to do it again. "We'll go and set ourselves up in the labs, if that's okay?"

Will nodded carefully. "It's huge, this place."

"Yup." Maatje looked up too. "And it's all to study dreaming."

"Big business."

"Important area to research." Maatje led him towards a lift and they stepped inside.

A few seconds later, the lift pinged and opened its doors, a cool voice announcing their arrival in the basement. Maatje led Will to the lab they used most often and ushered him inside.

"This is the machine that takes all the readings whilst you sleep." She patted a crisp bed surrounded by wires and monitors. "It looks scarier than it is."

"Very white," Will said.

Maatje grinned. "To make sure we keep it clean. But we'll start off next door, with a few questions. Would you like a drink?" She took him through a pair of adjoining glass doors to the surveillance room and went over to the kitchenette.

"No, I'm fine, thank you," Will replied. He sat on the edge of one of the sofas, picking at his palm.

Maatje settled for a herbal tea in an effort to ween herself off the caffeine and sat down opposite.

"Thanks for coming," she said. "It really means a lot to me."

She ran through the list of consent questions, pausing only briefly when Will answered that his emergency contact was Adella at the hostel, who'd wonder where he was if he didn't turn up to clean the rooms tomorrow.

"Do you live there?"

Will nodded. "She's very generous. I get food and board if I clean the rooms for her."

For a moment, Maatje's insides echoed like an empty cave. Did he have no one else in the world who cared about him?

"What sort of readings do you take?" Will asked when the questions were done and they went back into the main lab.

Maatje switched on and calibrated the meters with the monitors. "I'll measure how your sleep cycle works, and at what point you start dreaming. Also brain activity – which parts of your brain are working whilst you dream and how. I won't be able to get a reading of what you're actually dreaming about, so remember what you get up to so I can match it up with the data later."

"Okay."

"Just make your dream for the orphanage as you always do."

Will bobbed his head, then chuckled and rubbed his face when she pointed at him to lie on the bed. "Sorry, a bit nervous."

"Would you like some Tranquil? It helps you relax to get to sleep."

"No, I'll be fine. I'm good at falling asleep." He sat down on the mattress.

Maatje placed probes on his head and stuck a couple to his neck. Her breath caught for a moment as his hair tickled her fingers and she felt warm skin beneath the pads. He was real. She could still scarcely believe it. "You good?"

"Yes."

"Right then . . ." She scanned the monitors. Everything was working fine. "Whenever you're ready."

Will really wasn't exaggerating when he said he was good at getting to sleep. He let go of the waking world as if he was glad to be rid of it. His heartrate slowed and balanced out and his breaths came in even waves. Maatje watched his temperature dip as his body prepared for deep sleep. Perhaps she should have another coffee. It might be an hour before he started dreaming; the first stage was when the body did all its patching up and repairing.

Hang on . . .

The monitors began to buzz with activity. Will had hit REM sleep even though he'd been down less than five minutes. She scribbled the time on her pad and leant over Will. His eyes flickered fast underneath their lids, a sure sign the computer wasn't lying. He was dreaming already.

Scratch the coffee; this was going to be an interesting night.

But his heart rate and temperature began increasing again. The monitor activity died down and he stirred.

"Will?"

Blue eyes flew open and he sat bolt upright. Maatje only just pulled back in time to avoid hitting heads.

He reached up and yanked the probes from his head.

"Careful." Maatje lowered them to the stand, then did the same with the neck probes as his fingers peeled those off too. "What happened? Is everything okay?"

Will shook his head and slid off the bed. "Someone's in trouble."

He was out of the door before Maatje could blink. She raced after him.

"Will!"

Along the corridor he ran, brushing his hand across the long line of lab doors as if searching a half-forgotten memory.

At the far end, he sprinted down a short flight of steps that led to more labs. Maatje had never been this far into the basement before. Some of the strip lights had blown bulbs, and others flickered, giving her the sense she'd stepped into a horror movie.

"In here." Will rested a palm on a door near the far end of the building.

Maatje flopped against the wall next to him. "What's in here?"

"Someone inside needs help. Can you . . . *blip-blip*?" He waved his hand in front of the key card reader.

Maatje hesitated. If she used her card, others would know she'd gone unauthorised into someone else's experiment and there could be heavy disciplinary action. "Are you sure? What's wrong in there?"

"There's a man being kept against his will."

"What? Don't be silly," Maatje scoffed. "This is a research centre, not a prison."

"He's not seeing it that way."

"He thinks he's being held prisoner in this lab?"

"Can we go in and ask him?" Will pleaded.

Oh god – she hoped she wouldn't regret this. Maatje pulled out her card and held it in front of the reader.

Bleep. It turned red.

She tried again.

Bleep. Red.

"I don't have authorisation to go in there," she said, pocketing her card.

"Is there another way?"

"We could get in serious trouble for poking around in other experiments."

"Maatje." Will turned to meet her gaze. "I swear to you, this is important. There is a man trapped behind this door who is afraid and hurting. I heard him calling out in his dreams. Please?"

Maatje nodded, feeling ashamed for her reluctance. "Maybe it's an experiment gone wrong?" she proposed. "I can make a key at reception. Wait here."

Maatje ran back up the stairs and down the corridor to the lift. If she wrote Camille a note to explain her actions and left it with the returned key card, maybe she'd get away with it.

Will was leaning against the wall when she returned, his head bowed, clearly lost in thought.

"Got it!" Maatje waved the card by the lock.

Bleep. Green. The lock clunked and she pushed the door open.

Inside was a lab identical to all the others: two machines with beds surrounded by monitors and wires, and a smaller observation room to the side. She peeked through the glass as she came in. No one was there. No one at the computers to monitor the stats and data, though the information poured in. The only person in the room was a dishevelled young man with ashy-brown hair lying on one of the beds, plugged in and fast asleep.

Will rushed to his side. "How's best to wake him?"

Maatje wandered over to the screens. "It's best if he wakes himself. But he might need a little prompting."

Will touched the man's shoulder. "Hello?"

Wow! The monitors showed waves of dramatically heightened activity. Maatje didn't know enough to decipher what it all meant, but the man was very busy in his sleep.

Will shook him, and then again, and harder when there was no response.

"He's deep asleep." Maatje nodded at the readings on the computer.

"Okay." Will climbed onto the other bed. "I'll give him a proper nudge."

"You're going into his dream?"

"Shouldn't be long." And with that, Will lay back and closed his eyes.

NOW: WILL

A giant, glowing wall, at least twenty feet tall, encircled the man's mind, with razor-sharp wire coiled along the top. A prison built by the prisoner. He clearly didn't want anybody stepping inside his dreams.

The man still hummed the low moaning song that had originally caught Will's attention. A distraction from the terror and the pain. Will wondered if the man realised how much of himself leeched through his walls.

Will swallowed hard as he approached. The bricks were formed from tightly packed numbers and letters, glowing hot as embers. Fire didn't listen to Will any more. It knew he feared its insatiable appetite.

There was a crack where the cementing letters had crumbled and the man's voice originated. Will took a long poker and gave the loose brick a firm shove. Out it fell.

A shadow, crouched over itself on the other side of the wall, stopped humming.

Will inched closer. "Hello, are you okay in there?"

Another burning brick slammed into the hole.

Will leapt back, dropping the poker. Ebony feathers spilt from his fingers. The blackbird was braver than him.

He fluttered high above the heat radiating from the top of the wall. "You look as if you could do with some help down there, my friend."

"LEAVE ME ALONE!" a roar came back. "THIS IS MY HEAD! MY PRIVATE HEAD!"

Will couldn't help it, but with the man's voice came his thoughts. His name was Friedrich. He'd just watched his wife get shot.

Will reeled at the sight of her staring eyes.

"Friedrich," he gasped. "May I call you that? You shouldn't be alone in here, my friend. Not like this."

A hot brick hurtled towards Will and he flew out of the way.

"I understand. You don't like people in your head. Please, if you like, come into mine and we can talk there, or better still wake—"

Friedrich threw another brick at him. This time it narrowly missed searing the feathers off his wing and buffeted him into the man's mind.

Friedrich's thoughts hit him like a train.

Trapped.

Dead wife.

Children.

He didn't know where they were.

Will fluttered quickly back out of Friedrich's mind. He recognised those children. Anja and Milo. They were the newest additions to the orphanage. They'd been visiting his dream for two weeks now. He cocked his head.

"How long have you been in this laboratory for?"

The shadow stood up and stared at him. Or at least it looked like it; darkness shadowed his eyes.

"Don't worry about your children. They're safe. If you wake up—"

A fourth brick sailed past Will, then a fifth, then a sixth.

"I WILL CLAW MYSELF AWAKE, AND IF I FIND YOU'VE EVEN TOUCHED THEM, I WILL DESTROY YOU! I. WILL. DESTROY. YOU."

Trapped!

Trapped!

Thoughts, fire, fury. It was too much. Even for the blackbird. Will glided away from the smouldering wall and landed in a sprawl back in his own head; little bird heart pounding. Friedrich's mind gave even his father's tempers a run for their money.

But the man's words worried him beyond the threats and the malice. Friedrich wasn't just trapped in the lab. Worse. He was trapped in his own head.

Will woke himself to Maatje's concerned face.

"You okay?" she asked. "His heart rate rocketed just now."

Will sat up. "I think I upset him."

"He's not waking up."

"He can't."

"What do you mean, he can't?"

Will shrugged. "I don't think he can wake up."

"So we'll have to wait until morning then," Maatje sighed. "My mum is really bad at waking up too. I can switch the machine off if he likes?"

Will shook his head. "I didn't mean it like that."

Maatje's hands hovered over the keyboard. "You mean . . . he's being kept asleep?" Her hazel eyes grew greener as they widened. "No." She marched over to Friedrich and studied the wires. "See, it's just the . . ." She trailed off, tracing a tube from his arm back to the main machine. "My god, he's being kept asleep with Tranquil!"

"Is it hurting him?"

"No, but no wonder he can't wake up. I'm surprised he can even dream." She switched off the feed and gently pulled the needle out of Friedrich's arm. "Okay. Give him some time. He'll be back with us shortly."

She removed the rest of the wires before sitting down on the stool in front of the monitors with an *oof*. "I can't believe it. Who would do something like that?" She raised a finger at Will. "You wait until I find out."

A small smile pulled at the corner of his mouth. This was exactly the same Maatje he'd known as a teenager.

He turned from the way the familiarity pulled at his chest too, and watched the sleeping Friedrich, so serene despite the turmoil inside his head. Could he really have been here for over two weeks?

There was nothing left to do but wait until he woke.

NOW: FRIEDRICH

Friedrich had the world's worst hangover. The room spun like a merry-go-round – worse, because it was as if he was turning in the opposite direction. He snapped his eyes shut.

But he was awake.

Awake?

He opened his eyes again. The room drifted hazy and distant, as if it wasn't quite real. But it was. He was sure it was. If only his head would stop pounding like a sledge-hammer so he could make sense of it . . .

A grinning face hovered above him. The same grinning face that had peered through his firewall only moments ago and treated it like Lego. He'd soon wipe the smile off it.

Friedrich sprang up and grabbed the man's neck, squeezing tightly.

The smile vanished and the man gaped. From somewhere else came a woman's scream.

"Brenda?" Friedrich hands dropped from the man's neck and he whirled around. The room lurched, the woman's features blurring. But it wasn't Brenda. Brenda was dead. They had killed her.

"It's okay," rasped the no-longer-grinning man. "Take a moment to orientate yourself."

Friedrich blinked. He was sitting on the edge of a stark white bed in a stark white lab, surrounded by machinery. There were only two people. He could handle them easily . . .

Or could he? Where was that lean physique he'd worked so hard to maintain? His legs were rails on which his trousers hung like curtains. He pressed his feet slowly against the floor, testing his weight.

"That's it," the man encouraged.

The room swayed. Friedrich swayed. And he took a tentative step.

A hand grasped his elbow. What was the man trying to do – pretend to help? Or was he trying to keep him by the bed? Keep him trapped?

Friedrich rammed his elbow as hard as he could into the man's stomach – skinny elbows were good for something at least – and as he doubled over, caught him by the throat again. He pushed him back, back . . . until he winded him a second time against the wall.

"Where are they? What have you done with my kids?" Friedrich rumbled, tilting the man's head up so he could look nowhere else but him.

The man's hands clawed at his own and he rasped something unintelligible.

Friedrich loosened his hold ever so slightly. "Tell me!"

Out of the corner of his eye, he saw the woman who wasn't Brenda approach. She had a needle.

Not again!

He let go of the man and hurled all his weight on top of her instead. She went down like a skittle, the needle flying.

Friedrich crawled over to where it landed and snatched it off the floor.

Time for her to have a taste of her own medicine.

"Stop, my friend." The man's swollen throat grated as he talked. "We're here to help you."

"Help me? You're trying to drug me again," Friedrich snarled back.

The man leant against the wall, far too calm for someone who'd just been throttled. Did he still think he had control of Friedrich? But the man's composure wasn't arrogance – more tentativeness, as if he was worried about hurting his feelings.

Friedrich straightened.

"I saw your children a few times," the man continued. "I can take you to them. You don't have to fight us, please."

Friedrich had no time to consider this further as a sharp crack came behind him and a siren blared throughout the room. He spun around to see the woman staring straight at him, chin high and elbow wedged into a box on the wall, shattered glass at her feet.

She'd set off an alarm.

No. He had to escape.

But he needed Anja and Milo.

He grabbed the man and ran for the door.

Which way?

To the right were a couple of doors then the solid white wall of the end of the corridor. One of the doors opened and out came a security guard. The moment he saw Friedrich, he fumbled for his gun.

Rage coursed through Friedrich's blood. Brenda's murderers. Were they all so trigger-happy?

"Freeze!"

Yes, Friedrich could freeze, or he could ignore the guard. His gun wasn't out yet. He ran left, dragging the man with him. But then another guard darted into his path, gun already up and aimed right at him.

"Don't move!" this guard barked, huffing and red.

But Friedrich was running too fast to stop.

The guard's hands shook.

BANG!

The noise split his head open, and the man pulled him to the floor.

THEN: WILL

Louis had reluctantly delivered Rachel's message last night, and after pondering it all day, Will elected to ignore it. His dream was the only thing stopping this Hubert chap from forcing himself inside those children's dreams. Will couldn't just leave them to his mercy. Besides, he was only sixteen; how could he be arrested for making a dream for children when technically he was still a child himself?

And they didn't know where to find him. Whilst he'd been to the orphanage many times to see Rachel, he'd never had an address or a phone number to give when they told him they'd let him know when his sister was settled and could accept visitors. He'd been living rough until a couple of weeks ago, sleeping in a woodshed out of town and picking in supermarket bins for food. A kind landlady called Adella had let him stay in one of her rooms when she'd caught him rummaging through her bin one evening, and promised to feed him for as long as he needed if he cleaned the other rooms for her after the guests left. He thanked her under his breath every night as he climbed into his warm, soft bed. Twigs and straw were nothing like a mattress.

So, no address. He figured he could push his luck.

But the main reason for staying was Rachel. By the third week of trying to see his sister the lady at the orphanage reception had simply said visiting wouldn't be possible, and after a month had passed, they wouldn't even let him through the front gate. There was something up with that. So he'd created a dream, and discovered through the children who joined it how very few of them ever had visitors, or had even stepped outside the manor's walls since arriving. It sounded more like a prison than an orphanage, their sleep hijacked by the man who was supposed to be looking after them.

Will offered them the only freedom he could. Only Rachel was never there.

"Knock, knock," a familiar icy voice chimed.

Will had only just closed his eyes. Esther must have been waiting for him to start the dream. She leant against the red door leading to it.

Nothing good ever happened when Esther turned up, but for the first time he couldn't help but smile when he saw her. As much as he appreciated Louis's messages, this was the closest he'd got to Rachel in over a month.

"Sweetie, it's been so long," Esther purred, her voice like metal filings sparking off a grindstone. She'd never before looked so solid and strong. "Though I must confess this to be mostly my doing." She chuckled to herself and stepped towards Will, long blonde hair flowing over her shoulders, her white dress rippling like water. "Darling, you know I really needed the break from you. Can't you see how good I look for it?" She opened her arms to be admired – a shining angel from a Christmas card – but Will could only feel her coldness.

"It's a lovely place, this. I've found myself a man who appreciates and nurtures me and in return he's very kindly kept you away. I told him how bad you were for my health."

Before the fire, he and Rachel had been making progress with Esther, stopping her from taking over Rachel's dreams. Lying side by side, together they had pushed her into a dark corner of either Rachel's mind or his. Apart, Esther was running riot.

"I'm afraid to tell you, sugar, I don't see how I can let Rachel leave this place. You really should just leave us be—"

Will seized the moment: the tiniest wrinkle behind Esther, the way into Rachel's mind.

"Rachel, where are you?" He shot through the wrinkle like a javelin. "Don't worry, you can fig—"

An invisible fist ploughed into his middle and he flew back out again, crashing into the red door.

Esther emerged from the wrinkle chuckling. "What a waste of time. You know she can't hear you. Are you planning on spending the rest of your life making this dream for those wretched kids, trying to rescue someone who may not even want to be rescued?"

"If you'd let me speak to her . . ."

"Ah, ah, ah," Esther tutted. "Sweetie, we all know how you'll just go and poison her thoughts with your deluded ideas about freedom. I'm her mother – surely I know what's best for her?"

"Esther, I just want to see my sister."

"Half-sister," Esther corrected him. "I don't believe we have all that much in common." She chuckled again. "Oh, sugar, you just need a new spark in your life, something else to focus on. In fact . . ." She tapped him on the nose. "I have the perfect idea."

Will turned away to go through the door. He'd had enough of Esther and the children were waiting for their dream.

"Oh, Willem, I really think you'd like to hear this. It is such a good idea, honey." She smiled, her teeth gleaming white. "I'm off to do a bit of travelling. You know how lucky I am in that respect, hopping from dream to dream until I find one I like. What a privilege it is to see all these delicate processes going on in people's minds. I've always wondered what would happen if I tweaked the filing of a couple of those memories. I'm sure a little boy who's lost his teddy bear won't mind me telling him that his sister stole it, or an ugly spouse that her husband is cheating on her. I mean, if she already has her suspicions . . ."

Will stopped, his mouth falling slack. "Listen to what you're saying," he gaped. "You can't do that."

"Oh, sweetie, you know I can. I think the word you are looking for is 'shouldn't'." She chuckled. "But, wait, you haven't heard the best bit. What if I could reach the president?" She gave a delighted gasp. "How do you think it would make him feel if every night he dwelt on how much the country next door hates and disrespects him?"

"The president's mind is too well protected for that," Will said.

"Tried, have you?" Esther smiled. "And who will they come looking for when I do? A dead woman?" she chucked. "They're not going to find her anywhere."

"They might find Rachel."

"Then they'll find Rachel, honey," Esther repeated. "They can tie her down, maybe they'll even experiment on her." She grimaced. "But they can't catch me."

Esther had always played havoc with people she knew. Will's father was a prime example of this. She became the ghost in his dreams, haunting him for letting her die, for forgetting about her, for not loving her enough. But Will never thought she'd go so far as to assault strangers. She was more dream now than person and had no trouble jumping through minds as long as they were close enough together, like a bad thought. Too often Will's father had woken up hating Rachel and him, infected by Esther's meddling. It's hard to rationalise away a feeling.

"Oh, honey, you look so ponderous," Esther crooned. "Would you like that then – for Rachel to pay for all my misdemeanours?"

Will refused to rise to the bait.

Esther chuckled and walked backwards into the wrinkle. "Then you'd better leave your little kiddies' dream and come and stop me."

NOW: FRIEDRICH

"*The news tonight*," the radio announced to no one in particular. Friedrich paced the same path up and down the hostel bedroom that belonged to the man from the SDRC. It was a small room: three paces to the window, three paces back to the door. His wasted legs shook with exhaustion, but he couldn't settle. The man was in the bathroom across the hall. He had brought Friedrich here after the guards at the SDRC had given chase. No one had seen them come in, but it wouldn't be long before the police became involved and then nowhere would be safe.

"*Tax on all vehicles registered more than five years previously will be going up in April,*" the radio droned.

Friedrich needed a plan – and quickly. Once he got this man to tell him where his kids were and they were back safely with him, he'd find somewhere nice and quiet for them to live, away from any SDRC crap. Brenda had always wanted to move out of town, into the countryside, but Friedrich's work had always kept them here. Now he didn't care. He'd be a farmer, if that was what it took to keep his family away from those bastards.

"Here." The man returned with a glass of water.

Friedrich stopped pacing and accepted the glass, sniffing it suspiciously.

"It's not vodka, if that's what you're hoping."

Friedrich lowered the glass from his nose and tried to smile. "I'm not feeling all that trusting at the moment."

The man nodded, eyes brimming with understanding. But how could he understand? Friedrich snorted in disgust, took a large swig of water and slumped down on the bed.

"I'm Will, by the way," the man said.

"I'm not here for niceties. Tell me where my kids are."

Will opened his mouth, but at that moment the radio caught his attention.

"This news just in: a break-in at the Shared Dreaming Research Centre just hours ago. The culprit took an associate hostage, shooting dead a security guard . . ."

"WHAT?" roared Friedrich.

Will turned up the volume.

"The suspect is thought to be local activist Friedrich Reinhardt – six foot, of slim build, light-brown hair and grey eyes. He is currently on the run and people are warned not to approach him, but to call the police—"

"What the hell are people on nowadays? I didn't shoot anyone!"

"They've just got their information mixed up."

"Are you insane?" Friedrich turned on him. "You were there! You saw that guard shoot at us. I wasn't going to hang around to see if the bullet hit his pal on the other side or not."

Will turned white. "I didn't look back."

"Good. You wouldn't have liked what you saw." Images of Brenda flashed before his eyes and he swiped them away, spilling water over the duvet.

"We need to go to the police right now and straighten this up," Will said.

Friedrich thought about throwing what was left of his water at him. The man was still living in a dream. "Twice already you've seen me screwed over – first by the people you work for at the SDRC, experimenting on me, taking my children, killing . . ." He swallowed. "And now the police are framing me for murder!"

"You don't know that." Will was still too calm. "It wasn't the police experimenting on you. Tell them the truth and you'll soon get your children back."

"Since when have the police ever cared about truth? It's about how much money you have. I'd never win in court against the SDRC. They'd make sure I go to jail and I'd never see my kids again. I have to leave the country. Start afresh where nobody cares about who I am."

"That's not the answer, my friend." Will shook his head a fraction.

"It's my answer, and I'm not your friend," Friedrich growled. "Tell me where they are."

"If the police know who you are, they're going to have your children under close watch. You won't be able to get anywhere near them."

Friedrich got to his feet and bore down on the smaller man, snarling between gritted teeth, whilst careful to annunciate clearly, "I. Don't. Care."

And really he didn't. He couldn't leave them another minute. They needed him. He was their father.

"Okay." Will swallowed, though to Friedrich's disappointment not through fear, but reluctance. "There is a way you can see them tonight. Just see them, not take them with you. Would that be okay for now?"

"Are they being experimented on too?"

Will shook his head. "They're fine. You'll see them and they'll see you."

Friedrich sighed and pulled back. "Okay . . ." He hated

agreeing, but it was one step closer to his kids, and Will didn't have to know he'd be taking them with him anyway. He was too puny to stop him.

Will grabbed a rucksack and started stuffing things inside.

"What are you doing?" Friedrich stiffened.

"We can't stay here. They know I'm your hostage."

"You're not my hostage."

Will stopped and raised an eyebrow. "Whatever the case, they'll be coming here. And you're going to be living rough for a bit, so stick anything you think might be useful in the bag."

This man was helping him? After everything he'd done? Shaking off the surprise, Friedrich pulled open the chest of drawers and grabbed the three pairs of socks inside.

THEN: RACHEL

The common room was livelier than it had ever been that morning before lunch. Rachel hadn't known a Saturday like it. After breakfast, they had all been marched outside, shivering in shorts and T-shirts, to spend two hours playing cricket. Rachel had never heard of cricket before, let alone played it. The bat looked like an oversized ice-lolly stick and was so heavy she'd tipped backwards when she tried to swing it. But the running was good; everyone enjoyed the running. Even Ted, whose face had seen the grass more times than the soles of his shoes and was now hovering his bent glasses over a tea light at the table in an effort to straighten them again.

Everyone else chattered like birds in spring, jumping around the room after paper aeroplanes. Rachel grabbed the Connect 4 off the shelf, wiped the dust on her sweaty T-shirt and rattled it in front of Louis.

"Rematch."

Louis grinned, stuffed his aeroplane down Mathieu's top and followed Rachel to the table.

"Can't get enough of losing, eh, Macher?"

Rachel shrugged innocently. "I'm feeling good about it today."

Louis swung the game around so he was playing with the yellow pieces. "Ladies first."

Rachel shoved a red counter right in the middle of the rack. Louis put one next to it.

"I don't know if you heard," he said. "But there was no dream last night. I guess he listened to your message." Louis pouted to make sure she felt guilty. And she did, but the relief was stronger.

"Good."

Will was safe. For now.

And then she burst into tears.

"Oy, oy, what's all this about?" Louis slid the game aside.

"Sorry. Don't worry – I'm happy," Rachel sniffed. "Thank you for telling him."

"Y'know I'm just teasing you, right, about being angry and stuff?"

Rachel nodded. "I think . . . I just miss him so much."

Louis got up, walked round to the other side of the table and hugged her. She hadn't been hugged since she'd last seen her brother. It felt strange, but nice.

"Well, you've won the consolation prize instead," he said.

Rachel lifted her head. "What's that?"

"You get me!"

It didn't stop the tears, but she had to laugh. "That's a pretty good consolation prize."

"What on earth are you all doing?!" Matron stood in the doorway, the beginnings of a storm on her face. "Lunch is in ten minutes and not one of you is showered."

Ted blew out the tea light.

"I guess no one wants anything to eat. Such a shame Cook is not appreciated." Her top lip twitched and she left.

After a moment, everyone swarmed to the door. There

weren't nearly enough showers for everybody, and anyone more than five minutes late for a meal wouldn't be allowed into the dining hall.

Rachel lingered back, wiping her eyes. She needed to learn to dream. She'd done it before with Will, so she could do it again. She had to find a way to lock Esther away. Whatever she was doing with Hubert couldn't be good.

Besides, dreaming might be the only way to see her brother again.

NOW: FRIEDRICH

"**N**o."

After borrowing a couple of bikes from his landlady, Will had brought Friedrich out of town to an old barn stuffed with sweet-smelling hay. In the middle of summer, it might have been nice, but this was January and the wind found every hole in the dark, wooden walls.

They spent some time rearranging the bales into makeshift mattresses, pulling out hay to act as duvets. It was hard work with only bicycle lights to see by, but the exercise kept them warm and the barn was the perfect place in which to hide out. Anja and Milo would love it.

"Why not?" Will turned a questioning gaze Friedrich's way as he tucked himself into a hay cocoon.

Friedrich snorted. He wasn't sure the question deserved a reply. Will was the same as everyone else, unquestioning of the status quo. Why could nobody see just how wrong it all was?

Will had just finished telling Friedrich how he would be able to see his children that night – in his dreams. Apparently, Will could reach his kids' minds from all the way out here and invite them into his head. Friedrich would come in too and this was where their emotional family reunion could take place. Did Will realise how ridiculous he sounded?

He tried to stay calm and rubbed his goose-pimpled arms. "Because – even if it were possible to reach them from this barn – going into someone else's mind, or even near it, is intruding on their privacy and abusing their vulnerability. Knocking doesn't make it any more civilised. It's wrong. No deal. You leave our minds alone."

Will sighed and sat up. "Then I can't help you, I'm afraid." He got to his feet.

He was leaving?

Friedrich lunged forward and pulled one of his legs from under him, tipping Will back into the hay. He grabbed a bike light and shone it into the man's bewildered face, holding him down by the scruff of his neck.

"Where. Are. My. Children?"

Will shook his head as much as was possible under Friedrich's hold, eyes screwed up against the glare of the light. "Telling you would be a really bad idea I think."

"It would be more foolish not to," Friedrich warned, tightening his grip.

"Then I fear you would charge in, no restraint. People would get hurt and no one more than you."

"That's a risk I'll take."

"And if you get caught? You'll be sent to jail for sure. How would that do your children any good?"

Will was completely ignoring the fact Friedrich had him at his mercy. They might have been discussing politics over a pint. Suddenly paranoia blared.

"Are your colleagues nearby? Is this a trap? Getting me to sleep and then you'll bundle me back to that godforsaken lab?"

Will slumped back as if Friedrich's words had loosened

the string holding him together. "No." He flinched as though he'd been struck. "No."

Anger and distrust throbbed through Friedrich, but it was aimed wrongly. This man wasn't a threat. He lowered the light and let Will go.

He sat up cautiously, probing his throat with careful fingers.

"Please?" Friedrich begged. "Please, just tell me."

There was a long silence. The wind whistled merrily through the knots in the walls.

"Promise you won't do anything tonight?"

Friedrich couldn't. Tonight would be his best chance. He stayed silent.

Will sighed. "They're in Hubert's orphanage. The big manor house by the lake."

Friedrich leapt to his feet the instant the words were out of his mouth. He grabbed a bike, threw it out of the door and pedalled furiously off into the icy night.

Don't worry, Papa's coming . . .

NOW: MAATJE

I t was pushing three o'clock in the morning by the time the police let Maatje go. Her head not only spun from a panic pitch fear for Will and the horror of walking past a dead body, but also from hours of fierce questioning and an excruciating need to curl up in bed.

She wandered through the atrium towards the exit in a daze, trying to remember if she had called a taxi yet or not. A security guard at the door swung his arm out to block her.

"It's okay," she murmured. "I'm breaking out, not in . . ."

"Miss Finkel?" asked the guard.

Maatje sighed and looked up. He had a pleasant round face. She'd seen him about, always saying hello as people passed.

"Yes."

"You are wanted on the top floor."

"The top?" That was where the CEO had his office. Why on earth would they want her up there? And more importantly, why now? Couldn't it wait until she'd had some sleep?

"Do you need an escort or are you okay to make your own way?"

Maatje dismissed him with a wave of her hand, turning back on herself like a slug. "I'll be fine, thanks."

Back to the lifts.

She rested her head against the cool glass wall of the lift as it shot up to the fifteenth floor. She wished she could be more excited about getting to see the top boss's pad, but the world had become a hazy blur of irrelevance.

The doors pinged and slid open.

"Miss Finkel?" She was greeted by a small balding man with a head the shape of a rugby ball.

"Yes." Hopefully the questions would stay around this level of difficulty.

"Follow me."

The man pattered off down a pristine white corridor that was strung with colourful photographs of smiling people, and knocked on the glass door at the far end. Through the panes, the lights of town twinkled far below, overlooked by a man in his spacious office, who typed furiously into his keyboard. He looked up as they came in.

Maatje recognised him from the Christmas party and from countless photos all over the SDRC. This was the CEO himself, Rufus Sterne.

"Thank you, Bern," Rufus said and the balding man stepped out, leaving Maatje swamped in all the space that separated them. "Miss Finkel, I'm going to cut straight to the chase as there are places both of us would rather be."

Rufus looked younger up close – probably in his mid-thirties. As if to torment Bern, he sported a full head of thick, wavy brown hair. Not a strand was out of place. Even at three o'clock in the morning.

"A very serious incident has occurred at the centre tonight, as I'm sure you'll be aware. I've had some people trawling through our CCTV to try to discover exactly what went wrong and I was shocked to see this clip . . ." He turned his computer screen around and Maatje's heart stopped. It was showing her making the key for the lab.

"Sir, I'm sorry. I was going to return it and write a note to explain, but I never had a chance. It was an emergency. Someone needed help in there – I had to get in."

Rufus leant forward and rubbed an imaginary beard. "And on what basis was this conclusion drawn?"

"Whilst my associate and I were carrying out an experiment, he picked up on another man's distress in that room. We didn't know he was so dangerous. I wouldn't have done anything if I'd known."

"Miss Finkel, as I understand, you were in lab four and this gentleman was all the way down in lab thirty-four. So unless you're telling me that your associate – who I'll come to in a minute – has a super-human range, then—"

"He does," interrupted Maatje.

"He does?"

"That's one of the reasons we were doing the experiments. He can do some amazing things with dreams."

Rufus's eyebrows disappeared into his hair. "Like what?"

"Like take complete control of what he dreams about, create entire worlds from scratch and hold hundreds of people in his head at once . . ." Maatje trailed off. She needed to stop talking. This was Will's private business; she didn't want everyone pestering him about it. But if she could get Rufus interested, perhaps he'd step up the search to rescue him from that violent man. So she continued, "Thirty labs away is nothing; he can reach—"

At that moment, the glass door crashed open and Hubert waltzed in. Bern tottered behind him, hands outstretched as if he'd tried and failed to keep the man from entering.

"Apologies for the interruption, Rufus, old pal," Hubert boomed, coming to stand next to Maatje and slapping his hands down onto her shoulders.

"Hubert, to what do I owe this great late-night pleasure?" Pleased was the last thing Rufus looked.

"No, no, the pleasure is for Maatje here, not you," Hubert laughed and turned to her. "The hostage – is it him? Is it the dream maker?"

Maatje glanced over at Rufus, who immediately busied himself, polishing with his sleeve a golden statue of three arched stars that stood next to his computer.

Maatje gave Hubert a nod.

"Well, I never. I knew you'd find him – good job." He slapped her shoulders again, jolting her poor tired brain terribly.

"Rufus, old pal, I'm sorry about all this. You see Maatje and I have just started some new experiments, to see how far shared dreaming can be pushed. I can see it's going to be an issue doing them here with all these distractions, so I've asked her boss if she can spend some time working off-site in the laboratories at my place for a bit. Until the experiment is complete. We'll need to be going right away." Hubert flapped Maatje towards the door. "Chop, chop, girl – no time to lose."

She resisted him at first. Rufus did not look as if he was ready for her to leave yet, but Hubert guided her out like he was a sheepdog.

"I'll fill you in later, old pal," he promised and let the door close.

"Where are we going?" Maatje blinked.

"My house. Oh, this is brilliant!"

Maatje couldn't think of a single thing brilliant about anything that had happened that night, but Hubert near enough skipped to the lift.

"They were keeping a man hostage down there," she told him, once the lift doors had shut. "The man who took Will was being kept there, dosed up on Tranquil."

"You told the police this?" asked Hubert.

"Yes."

Hubert nodded. "It was a very silly thing you did, poking about in there. That man, as you found out, is very unstable and dangerous."

"He was a prisoner. He said something about wanting his kids back too."

"Yes." Hubert nodded. "But as I understand it, he was down there at his own request. He has a long history of phobias and social disorders that eventually led to his children being taken into care. He wanted them back, so he asked the SDRC to help cure him. He's been suffering terrible relapses recently, wanting to give up, because it's hard work reforming yourself, you know? But if we gave in to every druggie in rehab who wanted one more fix when things got tough, we wouldn't be doing our jobs, would we?"

That made sense. *Damn.* Why had she gone poking her nose into other people's business?

"I'm sorry," she said. "I was foolish."

Hubert laughed. "Foolish, but noble. Just don't do it again."

"Thanks for saving me from Rufus."

"I need you," replied Hubert. "You're my only connection to the dream maker."

"But that man has him." Fear for Will bubbled in her throat.

"And guess what I have." Hubert winked.

"What?"

"His children. They've been staying at my orphanage. I'm almost certain he'll be paying me a visit soon."

"Then we need to get the police over there quickly!" Maatje gasped.

Hubert held up a hand. "Already in order. All we have to worry about is our dreaming friend."

"Okay."

"I need you to come over and guard the dreaming side of things. See if the children are having the dream maker's dream again, or if he's dreaming for help. That's if he's found a moment to sleep, wherever he is. Can you do that?"

Maatje nodded. Absolutely she could. It was mostly her fault Will was in this mess in the first place. She just prayed the man hadn't decided to murder him too.

They stepped outside the SDRC. Hubert's car was parked directly in front, his driver holding open the rear door for them. Shaking herself back to awareness, she climbed inside.

NOW: FRIEDRICH

Friedrich made his way to the far end of the estate and scaled the back wall. The stonework was easy enough to climb, but he hadn't expected the glass shards cemented into the top. He wrapped his bleeding finger in a tissue, stuffed it back inside his ripped and bloodied glove, and carefully made his way down the other side.

The dark manor loomed across a vast, open expanse of grass. If anyone was looking, he'd be spotted at once. But there was no alternative.

The moment the moon slid behind a cloud, Friedrich ran for it. The grass crunched footprints in the frost. Hopefully they would only be discovered tomorrow – when he and his kids were long gone.

Friedrich leapt into the shadow of the building as the grass gave way to crashing gravel. His breath plumed thick and white. But nobody came.

A window, low to the ground by his feet, looked to be his most likely entry point. He gave it an experimental pull and push.

Locked.

No matter. The beauty of these old houses was that the windows were old too. A small single pane would be no match for his penknife.

He ran the blade around the edge of the frame again and again, cutting deeper each time. He'd taken the knife from Will's landlady, and it wasn't a particularly sharp one, scraping loudly in the silent country night. He pushed the glass and grinned as it shifted under the pressure. He ran the knife around the pane again and this time the glass cracked. *Damn.* Not what he'd been hoping for, but he could work with it. He pulled off one of his gloves and slipped it back to front over the top of the other one, so he had a double layer of protection, and pushed the glass again.

It splintered, the silence shattered by raining shards inside the building.

Damn! He'd have to work fast.

Reaching his hand through the frame, he lifted the latch, pulled the window open and slid inside. He landed in a stone room – bare but for a rickety chair and a hat stand – and slipped through the not-quite-shut door, up the stairs into the main house.

Nobody came.

He crept down corridor after empty corridor, stone turning to plush carpet and polished wood. He stuck to the carpet where he could.

Where might Anja and Milo be?

Friedrich turned a corner and jumped backwards, flipping his penknife out. But it was only a portrait, illuminated by the moon through the tall window. The painting showed a man with beefy lips and light floppy hair. He wore the expression of someone who knew he was the only person for miles around who could afford to be immortalised in this way.

Jerk.

"I was certainly slimmer back then," came a voice behind him.

Friedrich whirled round, knife at the ready. The same man from the portrait stood – more than a few pounds heavier than his oil counterpart – flanked by two even heavier men. Though there were three of them, none looked to be armed, so Friedrich had the advantage, especially as the middle man didn't look the sort to get his hands dirty.

"I'm here for my children," Friedrich snarled. "Anja and Milo Reinhardt. Bring them to me and no one will get hurt."

"Hurt?" scoffed the man. "Nobody's going to get hurt. Though it would have been more convenient if you'd made an appointment."

"No games," Friedrich warned him. "My children – now."

"Mr Reinhardt." The beefy-lipped man grew serious. "Or can I call you Friedrich? Yes, we've been expecting you . . . I'm afraid, Friedrich, we can't just let a wanted person access children under my care – parent or otherwise. Besides, there is far too much paperwork to go through in one sitting, and I'm assuming you don't have any proof of relationship with you?"

Friedrich took a step forward, knife winking. "This is all the proof I need; now take me to them!"

The two men flanking the beefy-lipped man puffed out their chests. How considerate – they'd increased the size of the target.

"However." The beefy-lipped man raised a finger, smirking. "I'm sure we could come to some arrangement. I have something you want and you have something I want."

"I have nothing."

"You took a friend of mine hostage this evening. I might accept a trade if you give me no further reason to call the police right now."

Friedrich stilled. "He's your friend?"

"We were in the middle of some quite important experiments. Being a man of science, I can't very well leave them unfinished."

This man worked for the SDRC too? Friedrich hated him even more.

"You should leave people's minds alone."

The man blinked. "And you should leave people alone. Murder; kidnap. I'm afraid the moral high ground is mine."

"I didn't kill anyone."

"That's not what the police are saying."

"They're liars."

"Then prove it to me. Bring me Willem Macher unharmed and I'll let you have your kids."

Friedrich shook his head. "I don't believe you."

Another person came into the corridor at that moment: a mousy woman, dressed in a nightgown and looking very frightened. Friedrich could just about make out what she was squeaking.

"Mr Kröte, sorry, but the kids are all crying for you."

He turned to her in surprise. "Me?"

"Yes. Matron called and said they all woke and started shouting for you." The woman shrank away under his gaze.

"Don't be so ridiculous . . ." His eyes grew round. "Is she back? Take me to them." He motioned to the two men as he went. "Watch him for me until I get back. He tries anything, call the police. One chance is enough."

Friedrich needed to follow this Kröte. He was going to see the children. But how would he get rid of these two lumps? He was a whisper of his former self, half-starved and suffering from weeks of muscle wastage. He couldn't rely on his strength to defeat them. He pocketed the knife and held out his hands to show they were empty.

"I need to see that my children are okay. Take me to them and I'll bring your boss his friend."

The men looked at each other and strode up to Friedrich, one grabbing the rope that held a curtain back.

Friedrich tensed, but held his ground.

"Hands behind your back," he grunted.

Friedrich obeyed and in seconds they had the rope tied fast around his wrists, silk tassels tickling his palms.

Hard boots kicked behind each of his knees and he crumpled to the floor. One of the men stepped on his ankle and pushed down with all his weight, grinding his shoe as if putting out a cigarette.

Friedrich yelled in agony.

"Shut up and lie still. You're going nowhere."

Idiot, Friedrich! What the hell had he been thinking? Had he been so drunk on the idea of seeing Anja and Milo again? He should have caught the men whilst they were tying his hands up. He could have knocked their heads together and wrapped the rope around their thick rubber necks. *Idiot.*

His ankle seared. Was it broken? *Damn, damn, damn.* He wouldn't be seeing his kids again today, that was for sure. He was at Mr Kröte's mercy. He buried his face in the carpet to keep from crying out again. God, he missed them so much.

But he still had one trick up his sleeve.

Will.

Kröte thought Friedrich had Will prisoner. That gave him some leverage.

"Quick, quick!" Yet another woman ran up the corridor. "Hubert needs you in dormitory one!"

All Friedrich could see was the bottom of the woman's long pale nightdress and her feet stuffed into a pair of shoes that looked to be three sizes too small.

"One of us needs to stay here."

"No, both of you – please, now. There's a fight."

The men began to mutter. "Hang on."

Friedrich heard the sound of another curtain tie being unhooked and then his legs were being tied together. His first instinct was to kick out hard, but the moment they lifted his injured ankle, he roared with pain and couldn't move at all.

"Watch the intruder for us," one of the men said. "He shouldn't be a problem."

The woman stepped back, and two lots of dark boots ran past. Once their footsteps had died away, the woman knelt next to him.

Friedrich snapped his head up and snarled at her.

"Calm yourself." Her voice lowered familiarly and she leant over to untie his wrists.

What the . . . ? Friedrich tried to catch her face. But he recognised the voice. Her lipstick was a shocking pink, her dark hair stuffed inside a hairnet. Long lashes hid her eyes as she worked. As she pulled the curtain tie away, she glanced up at his face and grinned.

Friedrich's mouth dropped. It was Will.

"What the hell?"

"Shh." Will fumbled with the knot around his feet.

Friedrich hissed in discomfort, but Will was far gentler than the men had been.

"Can you stand?"

Friedrich rolled onto his back and let Will pull him to his feet. He couldn't put any weight on his ankle at all.

Will wrapped an arm around him and together they hobbled down the corridor, ears straining for any sound of Kröte or the men returning. Will snatched up his coat, which was draped over the basement chair, and pulled Friedrich through the little window he'd smashed earlier. They hopped together for an agonising eternity across the open grass, but no one shouted and no one stopped them.

Climbing the wall was horrific. Twelve foot of one leg

climbing. Will clambered up first, smashed a path through the glass on top with a loose stone and spread his coat over it.

"Just roll when you get to the top," he said, and leant over to grab Friedrich by the back of his jacket as he searched for a hold.

And then, finally, came the shouts, accompanied by a sweep of torchlight searching the grounds for their frosty footprints. Friedrich dropped down the other side of the wall, and by some miracle managed to land and roll without jarring his ankle too badly. Will snatched his coat, shaking tiny fragments of glass from it, and ran over to where not only Friedrich's bike lay, but Will's too.

"God, was I that easy to follow?"

Will didn't reply, wheeling a bike over to Friedrich and standing him up against it. Friedrich realised with dismay he wouldn't be able to ride.

"I'll pull you." Will rolled up his coat, tying one arm around his saddle, and handed Friedrich the other.

Voices raced towards the wall behind them, torches flashing. Will waved a frantic hand and Friedrich swung his throbbing leg over the saddle.

They rumbled slowly over grass and snagging brambles, Friedrich nothing but a useless dragging weight. Boots thudded down their side of the wall and pounded after them.

Fast enough to catch.

But then they hit smooth road, and Will powered into the dark, his nightdress flapping, pulling the white-knuckled Friedrich behind him.

THEN: RACHEL

W ill returned after two nights not making the dream. It seemed that was the longest he could stay away for. Louis tried not to look too happy when he told Rachel the news.

He tried to get her out of the orphanage too.

The first time, Louis told her about Will's plan to sneak in through the old servant's corridors. For weeks, she turned every corner expecting to see his grinning face, then ride out on his back to freedom. But he never showed.

The second time he arranged an escape in the rubbish truck and the third he got a job at the local museum and invited the orphans to visit. But every time, Hubert seemed to know about the plan and stopped it in its tracks.

Still, Will kept trying.

As she neared a year in the orphanage, Rachel heard rumours that her brother had applied to become a teacher there. He'd gone through all the training, only to be told Hubert liked his staff curvier. The police paid Hubert a visit around that time. The following night, Rachel found a note on the pillow of the comfortable bed.

No one knows you are here. No one knows you exist.

After a year and a half, Rachel began to accept she wouldn't be leaving before her time. She could only think of one reason Hubert wanted to keep her so much.

Esther.

By the look of things, Esther wanted to keep Hubert too.

Rachel tried harder to block her. If Esther couldn't come out, Hubert had no reason to hold onto her.

Slowly, slowly, Rachel started getting fragmented glimpses into her dreams – just enough time to see Esther and Hubert together, hand in hand and chatting an awful lot.

As time went by, she was able to pick up snippets of their conversations. To her horror, they mostly involved Will. Hubert hadn't mentioned her brother since that night, but Rachel should have known he hadn't forgotten about him. Not only did Hubert still remember him, he was actively seeking him out, getting Esther to test him almost every night by leading him on wild chases across the country, seeing just how far his dreaming could go and what he could do. The conversations Rachel heard were Esther giving Hubert feedback, as if Will was some sort of experiment. Hubert suggested new ideas for next time and revealed to Esther details some of the children had told him recently about the dream Will was creating for them.

Rachel never listened for long, as to not alert Esther or Hubert to her presence. And though she tried, she was never able to peer into her dreams when Esther was with Will. If she could just reach him and let him know she was fighting back . . . Did Will know Esther and Hubert were using him, or did he think Esther was playing her games out of spite? She tried to get Louis to tell him to leave again, but the blackbird ignored the messages Louis passed on.

Deep down, she was thankful he was still there.

After two years had passed, she discovered the truth.

"A machine to push the limits of dream science does not come without its trials," Hubert told Esther one night, as they sat side by side on the riverbank where Rachel and Will used to play. "But I assure you: when it is working it will be the greatest accomplishment of our century, without a doubt."

Rachel peered out of the reeds, shoes soaking in water.

"I do not doubt it, honey," Esther replied. "All I'm saying is, perhaps the migraines were because we need *him* to power it, not some half-brained scientist. We designed it specifically for him."

"My dear, I know, I know." Hubert raised his hands passively. "But this is a prototype; I have to take it one step at a time. Don't forget, we're taking massive technological leaps here."

"Sweetie, you need to get him in."

"And risk him refusing to dream for us?" Hubert was aghast. "No, no – he is better for now as he is, in ignorance. We still have much to learn."

"I think you'll find I can be pretty persuasive." Esther leant closer to Hubert.

He squeezed her knee. "That's why I can trust you not to lose him before we're ready." He leant in towards her with a look of such adoration he might as well have been a drooling dog. "Then he will have no choice but to submit to his queen." He kissed her hand. "And you'll have the beautiful kingdom you deserve."

Esther's pearly teeth shone in response to Hubert's promises. "A beautiful queendom," she corrected, then turned to shine those perfect teeth at Rachel. "I deserve that, don't I, sweetie?"

Rachel jerked back, and not just from the shock of being discovered. An invisible force blasted her away, the pleasant light of day shrinking to a pinprick as she fell, before disappearing altogether. She landed on something neither hard nor soft, just very, very black – walls, ceiling, everywhere was suffocating darkness.

"Oh, honey, I must congratulate you on the progress you've made." Esther stood next to Rachel, shimmering a painful white in the emptiness. "Though the time it took you to start dreaming again was beginning to play on me. I was almost tempted to lend a hand."

Esther had been aware of her the whole time? Teasing her with the hope of seeing her brother? "You made the machine up?"

"Made it up?" Esther pulled a face. "Sugar, it's our destiny. I thought you might like a little preview after all the effort you've put in."

"You're going to force Will to make a dream for you?"

"Oh, sweetie, far better than that. Do you know how tiring it is to be bound to you, having to sort out all your petty arousals from the day and then submit to whatever boring, childish dream your mind has created for me? Sure, I can hop around a bit if anyone is close by, but it's freedom I crave, and this machine will give me a world in which I can move around without obstruction. It will give me complete control. You think your brother is a powerful dreamer, but this machine will increase his dreams a hundred fold. Thousands of miles; millions of minds. A whole world at my feet. Don't you think it would be wonderful?"

Rachel trembled. "He won't help you."

Esther scoffed. "He'll have no choice. Unless he wants all those minds to drive him insane."

It was horrible. How could someone be so horrible? "I'll find the machine then," Rachel said. "And I'll smash it into tiny little pieces."

"Oh do, sweetie, do," Esther purred. "And do you know what I'll be doing? I'll be finding a way to make sure that one day you don't ever have to wake up again."

Rachel was too angry to care. "Try your best."

"I will, and when you're done with the feeble fighting-talk, sugar, a thank you wouldn't go amiss. I've got you a present."

Rachel didn't want anything from her. Hateful woman.

Esther gave a dazzling smile and lifted her palms to the blackness. "It's here."

Rachel looked about. "Where's here?" The question left her lips before she could stop it.

"In your head, honey. But a very boring part where nothing ever happens. I don't think you appreciated the blessing I've performed for you all these years: going to sleep and waking up unaware. But seeing as you want to dream again so badly . . ." Esther turned her back. "Good luck finding that machine."

And she was gone.

The darkness pressed in and Rachel closed her eyes for some relief. Silence was the loudest sound in the world.

NOW: WILL

"You stupid . . ." In a blur of auburn hair, Maatje stopped millimetres short of wrapping herself around his neck. "What were you thinking? Most people don't display symptoms of Stockholm Syndrome the same night they're abducted!"

Will stepped away from her waving arms. He'd just wanted to check on her dreams to see if she was okay after the night's events. "What do you mean?"

"I'm at the manor you broke into. Hubert's the one funding my project. He just told me you got all the kids to shout for him and helped this Friedrich escape." She frowned. "Why?"

Will stared. She was at Hubert's manor? Of all the people Maatje could be working for, why him?

"Will?"

He ducked away from her gaze, then changed his mind.

"Friedrich had a right to know where his kids were. So I told him. He was scared and confused, trapped asleep for weeks on end. So when he rushed off to get them, I had to

163

stop him. He can't go to prison; he hasn't done anything wrong—"

"Except kidnap and murder."

Will closed his eyes. This was how quickly fear spread lies. "He didn't kill anyone."

"He didn't? But I saw . . ."

Will's stomach dropped. She saw? He hadn't even considered the man behind them. Everything had happened so fast. And now someone was dead.

He slid to the grass at her feet.

"There was a security guard," he recalled, throat tightening. "He fired at us. There was another directly behind. I didn't see, but Friedrich never touched a gun."

Maatje shook her head. "That's not the story the guard's telling."

"I swear I'm telling the truth."

Maatje crossed her legs and sat down opposite him, so close he could make out the faint constellation of freckles across her nose. He'd tried to count them once, but it had been like counting stars.

"Will, of course I believe you, but he still attacked us. He has you prisoner. They're not going to let anyone that volatile near children."

"I'm not his prisoner."

She baulked. "Well, why on earth are you helping him? What's he holding you to?"

"Nothing. He only took me because I knew where to find his children. As soon as he had that, he didn't care."

"Then why did you . . . Will, he throttled you."

He lifted a shoulder. He'd met worse tempers. "None of those children should be locked away in a place like that, and Friedrich's still have a father who loves them." He broke off and picked at the grass. "That's more important."

Maatje's voice grew soft. "Maybe we should let the courts decide what's best, eh?"

"Courts?" Will hadn't thought about that either. He could advocate for Friedrich, but . . . He buried his face in his hands. "I just made myself a wanted criminal too."

Maatje placed her palm on his knee. "You didn't."

"I don't think the police will see it that way."

"The police don't need to know," she said. "Hubert won't tell them you broke in."

Will lifted his head. "Why not?"

"Didn't you hear what I said earlier? Hubert is funding my experiments with you. You really don't realise how vital you are to the understanding of dream science. He's prepared to let you off, as long as you're happy to continue the experiments, of course."

"And Friedrich?"

Maatje pursed her lips. "He'll do the same. But only in regards to breaking into his house. If he lets you go unharmed," – she pulled a face – "Hubert will offer his best lawyers to get him out of the trouble he's in with the SDRC."

Will blinked. This was incredible. But why Hubert? Always Hubert.

His apprehension must have spread over his face because Maatje frowned. "This was the only solution we could think of to get you away from him with as little risk as possible. Hubert wanted you both to come to tea at three o'clock tomorrow afternoon – to talk to Friedrich about his predicament and to 'rescue' you." She stuck out her chin. "I'd prefer it if you came alone."

Will wondered if it was just because he'd been on edge for the last seven hours, but he didn't like the sound of this offer. Nevertheless, there was no denying it was the best option for Friedrich. The hope of getting his children back seemed a remote possibility. "I'll work with you if Friedrich gets the help he needs. He goes to jail and the deal's off."

Maatje winced. "The lawyers can do their best, but I can't promise that."

Will got to his feet. "I'll ask him in the morning."

Maatje stood up too, hand twitching as if to reach for him, but faltering, worry etched into her brow. He didn't like that he had put it there.

He stretched out his fingers and out zipped a little fizzle of light, whizzing with life around her head. It settled on her nose with the other stars, and she reached up to touch it with a smile.

"Please be careful, Will," she said.

NOW: FRIEDRICH

F riedrich woke the next day to Will sitting up in the hay looking like a horror story: pink lipstick smeared across his cheek and the back of his hand, face pale as death as he rubbed his toes between his hands. The borrowed shoes certainly had been too small.

The sun peered through slats in the wooden barn, and despite having not seen it for two weeks, Friedrich wanted nothing more than to roll over and go back to sleep. That had been the first peaceful night he could remember in a long time.

Will gave Friedrich a hideous pink grin and crawled over. "How's the ankle?"

Oh. Friedrich had forgotten all about it. With the memory, all the horror of last night came back. He closed his eyes, wishing to return to those peaceful ten seconds of just being.

"Okay, I guess," he mumbled, giving it a tentative flex. It was stiff and barely moved with the stick splints Will had tied around it last night, but the pain was nowhere near as intense. "I don't think it's broken."

"May I take a look?"

"If you get rid of that lipstick you can."

Will licked his lips and wiped pink up his sleeve. "Better?"

It wasn't, but Friedrich shrugged. "It'll do."

Will untied the sticks, revealing his ankle swollen all shades of red and blue. "You should probably rest it for as long as possible."

Friedrich sat himself up and tested his ankle again. Sore, but not unbearably so. Good. The faster he got out of here the better.

Will was considering him.

"What?"

"You're actually going to go back there, aren't you?"

Friedrich shrugged. "What else can I do?"

Will twirled the stick splints between his fingers. "I spoke to Maatje last night – the lady who was in the lab with me when you woke—"

"When did you do that?"

Will tapped his head. "Just in a dream. Don't worry. They don't know where we are."

Didn't they? Was Friedrich really supposed to believe Will had this amazing range and not that the SDRC were waiting with needles outside? But then if so, why had he saved his skin last night?

He ground his teeth. "Why are you still here?"

"Maatje has a proposal for you."

"A trap."

"You haven't even heard what it is yet."

Friedrich pulled a face. "Don't need to. But please yourself." He motioned for Will to continue.

"Hubert Kröte is offering us amnesty from the events in the manor. He's one of the major presences in not just this town, but the country. He's offering lawyers to help fight your case at the SDRC."

Friedrich laughed. "And why on earth would he do that?"

"Because the police think I'm your hostage and they want me back safely."

"But you're not," Friedrich scoffed. "Or do you want to be? Is that what all of this is? Some sort of victim fantasy? Because if so, I want a direct trade. Last night Kröte offered me my kids for you. Tell your friend that it's that or nothing."

Will shook his head. "Hubert won't do anything illegal. Not with the police watching. He's invited us round for tea today, where he'll explain how he can assist. I told Maatje I'll work with them only if they keep you out of jail. It's in their interest to do the best they can for you. They'll have to give you your children back."

Friedrich's lip curled. "How noble of you." Still, he was inclined to believe Will meant what he said. He was just incredibly naive. "But one measly SDRC employee making a stand won't make a difference. There's plenty more idiots to take your place."

"I'm not an employee. Last night was my first at the SDRC. But I think they value my cooperation enough to help you."

Friedrich gave a loud snort. "Because you're so special, are you? Is this because of your so-called amazing range? Then you're a lab rat like me. Just wait until they lock you up too."

But the fickle part of him was pleased Will wasn't part of the SDRC – even though he supported them.

"I trust Maatje. She wants to help."

Friedrich pulled himself to his feet, applying just a small weight at first to his injured ankle. It held. "Well, I don't need her help. I'm not ready to be screwed over a third time and lose the little I have left to live for because of it." He lowered himself off the bales of hay and hobbled towards the door, listening for Will to tell him to stop, or ask where he was going. He needed someone to lash out at. But Will said nothing and Friedrich limped out of the door.

THEN: RACHEL

"I need your help." Rachel flumped with her homework to the common room floor where Louis and his best friends Mathieu and Lawrence were practising knots on the wire of a table lamp. She usually avoided Louis when he was with them. Just because they were able to evade the wrath of Matron with their silly jokes and games, didn't mean she could. But today it was exactly their years of experience of midnight kitchen raids that she needed.

"Lou, your girlfriend's here," Lawrence teased, pushing the knot tight and punching Mathieu's arm. "And now you've strangled yourself."

Mathieu groaned. "But I did it just as you said."

"Second loop, not first."

"I did . . . Oh."

They were always the first to finish their homework. Mathieu was a bit of a genius, a good thing too since he wanted to become a doctor. Louis and Lawrence copied from him, getting just enough wrong so it wouldn't be obvious. Lawrence especially didn't care about academia. He once got himself locked in the sports shed purposely and was found later that evening in a hammock made of ball bags, all the condensation licked from the windows.

"Ignore them." Louis grinned at Rachel. "What's up? You wanna use my notes?"

"*My* notes," corrected Mathieu. "And I charge three potato waffles per subject."

"Especially ignore him." Louis Frisbeed his exercise book over to her.

"Louis, I'm trying to run a business!"

Rachel put the book aside. "You can have all my waffles for a week if any of you can tell me what you know about a dreaming machine here at the manor."

Three vacant faces blinked at her.

"What's one of those?" asked Lawrence.

"I don't know, but Hubert's making one. He wants to be able to create dreams like Will. Dreams he can control and pull everyone inside. He's watching how Will does it and he's going to force him to power it once it's finished."

Silence.

"Shit," said Louis.

"I have to destroy it," continued Rachel. "So if you've heard of anything, or if you know where he might build something like this, you have to tell me."

Mathieu bit his lip. "Hubert's a patron of the Shared Dreaming Research Centre. Maybe it's there? I can guarantee Hubert doesn't have the brains to build a machine like that himself."

"But he'd wanna keep it hidden," countered Louis. "So wouldn't he have people working on it here?"

"Easy enough to check," Lawrence said. "We can sneak a peek at the sign-in book in his receptionist's office."

"Yes," crowed Mathieu. "See who keeps coming back and why. That summer ball he hosts is in a couple of months.

Once we find out who's a frequent visitor, we can gatecrash the party, get them drunk and interrogate them."

"I've never been to a party before," enthused Louis.

Rachel shook her head. "This can't wait two months. I have to do something now. Teach me how to sneak out. I'll search every room in the manor if I have to."

Louis squeezed her arm. "We don't survive that way, Rach. We gotta stay unpredictable to remain uncatchable. A machine like this would take years to build. We have time."

"But I've already been here for years." How could Rachel express the severity of the situation without mentioning Esther? It was only a matter of time before she convinced Hubert to bring Will in. What else might she get Hubert to do to him to spite her? Would the machine really drive him insane?

"In the meantime, we'll find out what we can. The ball is something solid to aim for at least, yeah?" Louis's practicality gently skimmed the bubbling panic from her throat. "Don't worry; we all want to protect our dream maker."

Rachel drew a deep breath and nodded. "Thank you."

"And you can keep your waffles," added Mathieu.

NOW: FRIEDRICH

F riedrich limped back into the barn. Going out had been a bad idea; his ankle throbbed like hell and the wind had chilled him to the core. He flopped back onto the hay. Will was still there, fast asleep. Exhausted from the previous night or hanging out with one of his dream buddies? But who would be asleep in the middle of the day?

Friedrich spied a water bottle propped on a bale next to Will and took a swig. He shivered as he swallowed the icy water, but was thankful they'd brought some. His stomach growled. They should have brought food too. He couldn't remember the last time he'd eaten. It hadn't been more than two weeks ago, had it? He looked down at his knuckles – protruding like spines through the skin of his hands. Maybe it had. Breakfast with his family had been his last meal. A sharp pang of grief rippled through him and he rubbed his face with his hands to try and remove it. Now was not the time to remi-nisce; it was time for action.

He took another deep gulp of water and rested the bottle next to Will again. Maybe the guy was right. Listening to

Kröte's offer of help would be his only chance to bring his wife's murderers to justice, if indeed Hubert was offering what he promised. Friedrich had pondered all other options for getting his children back, and though he hated to admit it, meeting Kröte would at least get him into the place, and if it all went wrong, he could revert to his original, more reckless plan.

Will stirred and shivered, rolling deeper into his coat. Like Friedrich's own, his breaths came in visible puffs. It was getting colder. The grey clouds piling up outside threatened snow. He couldn't ask his children to endure this. Not if there was another way.

"You're back." Will roused.

Friedrich made an undecided noise.

"Milo's your son, isn't he?"

Friedrich stiffened. He'd never asked Will how he'd known where his children were.

"It was naptime at the orphanage just now. He looks like you."

The anger as he comprehended Will's statement came low and deadly. "Get out of my son's head. Get out of all their heads. What the hell are you doing in them anyway?"

Will sat up. "They come to mine," he said, either ignoring or oblivious to Friedrich's warning. "It's safer that way. Some of them have the most horrible nightmares. How can children of only a few years have such terrible dreams?"

"And you think you're helping them by taking them away from their own heads? How else are they supposed to deal with them? The dreams will only be waiting when they get back. And what if *you* have nightmares?"

"I wouldn't give them a nightmare. Only a space to play them away."

Friedrich swallowed his rising anger. Will meant nothing

malicious by what he did. He was just too naive about the consequences. Like so many were. Naive and dangerous.

"You need to stop this shared dreaming, corrupting the younger generation with all your issues and neuroses. A dream – no matter how innocent you think it is – is saturated with bits of you. You have no right to burden children with your problems, and you can't decide to just not have a nightmare."

"Sure I can," Will disagreed.

Friedrich slammed a fist onto the hay. "How? Tell me – go on. Do you live in some magical utopia where your life has been nothing but bliss and purity?"

Will shook his head. "The dreams the children bring with them nudge mine into the shapes they need. A park. Nightmares turned into fear they can play with. Your Milo went straight to the climbing frames when he first arrived and now he's scrambling up mini mountains. He's quite a climber."

For a moment, Friedrich's insides warmed with something other than anger. Brenda had loved rock climbing. She'd be so proud. "Hang on – you're talking like you can control your dreams too?"

"Not quite. Dreams talk to one another; you can hear them if you listen closely. They build around everyone who shares in them. So it's less about control, and more that they've invited me into the conversation."

Friedrich hadn't ever considered such a thing. Listening to dreams was prying in his book, and he should have scoffed at the idea of having a conversation with a dream, or ridiculed Will for thinking he could make dreams out of nightmares for those who didn't have parents to kiss their dreams sweet. Instead, his eyes moistened.

He quickly lay back in the hay before Will could see, taking guilty comfort that someone was watching out for his children when he couldn't.

"I'll go and meet Hubert," he conceded. "But just to talk, no more."

Will deflated in seeming relief and lifted a thumb with a shiver of a nod.

Friedrich closed his eyes. "It's still wrong though, what you're doing." But his voice had lost its bite.

THEN: RACHEL

"Professor D. Lautner, Gretel Schneider, Tomas Reich and Doctor V. West." Louis pointed at Lawrence, Mathieu, Rachel and himself as he said each name. These were the four most frequent names in the sign-in book. Two Saturdays ago, he'd been punished for doodling on his schoolwork by having to clean the receptionist's office whilst everyone else had a rare music class. Rachel couldn't believe their history teacher had fallen for the mournful look he'd given her as he accepted his punishment. He'd looked like a guilty dog still wagging its tail.

Hubert's summer ball was tonight. They could only hope these four people would be there, and that at least one of them knew about the machine. All other avenues of investigation had turned up empty.

Lawrence had stolen the spare keys to their dormitories. Rachel shoved hers up her pyjama sleeve and it pressed anticipation against her skin as she lay in bed, waiting for the adults to go to sleep and the light under the door to disappear. This was when she would meet up with the boys. They'd borrow waiters' outfits from the kitchen staff room then slip out to the party.

Rachel ran through how she would approach Tomas Reich in her head no less than twenty times before the slit under the door vanished. She waited a couple of minutes longer, heart pounding in her chest. Fear and excitement as one. Leaving her room after lights out. Breaking the rules. Such a rush.

There was also a contentment knowing that, whilst Rachel was awake, Esther couldn't be. She was in control. And she had no desire to go back to that empty dark prison of her mind any time soon.

Esther had kept her promise. Every night, Rachel had found herself in the nowhere place. Black. Silent. Empty. Hours of nothing torture. No matter what she'd tried, she hadn't be able to get out.

Okay, time to get up.

The bed creaked as her weight left it. Leila stirred below her, but did not wake. Rachel slid down the ladder, listening intently, but the rest of the room slept on.

Tiptoeing to the door, she let the key slide into her cupped palm. Feeling the lock between her fingers, she eased the key inside.

Click.

Unlocked. Free. Rachel waited a moment in case the noise had aroused anybody, then turned the handle and slipped outside.

"Hey!" came a whisper. Louis, Lawrence and Mathieu were at the other end of the corridor, beckoning her over. She crept towards them and matched their giant smiles.

"We should do this more often," she whispered.

"Welcome to the gang," Louis breathed back.

"Ready?" asked Mathieu.

Rachel nodded and followed Lawrence down the stairs.

"Follow my steps exactly," he mouthed.

Rachel nodded again. "Wh—"

"Squeaking floorboards," Louis whispered in her ear.

The stairs and corridors went on for a lifetime. Lawrence knew all the old servant's passageways. Ones where they'd be less likely to run into people.

As they drew closer, music from the ball drifted up through the polished floorboards. Violins fiddled merrily, the brass *oompahed* away. Louis caught Rachel's wafting fingers and gave her a twirl.

The door at the end of the corridor was all that separated them from the main manor. Rachel knew it well from her visits to the comfortable room, and the fear and excitement rushed back.

Lawrence stopped in front of the door. Instead of opening it, he stared.

"Oh, hello," said Mathieu.

A piece of paper was taped to the back of the door. They gathered around it, squinting to make out the words in the semi-darkness.

Lawrence pulled out a torch.

Dear Rachel,

I would highly recommend returning to your bed. Proceeding through this door will entail consequences I've not had to dish out for many years. You should have figured out long ago, dear child, that your mind is not your own. I've enjoyed hearing stories of your plans from our beautiful friend. I trust you not to implement any of them tonight.

Best wishes, Hubert

"Beautiful friend?" That was Mathieu again. He was looking at her. But Rachel couldn't move.

Esther.

Esther had told Hubert their plans for tonight. But how had she known? How could she have known?

As the music beyond the door reached a crescendo, so did the realisation in Rachel. Esther had access to everything. All Rachel knew, Esther knew, and had known since the beginning. They were being played. Esther had let them get this far just to rub it in their faces. Rachel was truly and utterly a prisoner, awake or asleep. Whatever Rachel thought, Esther heard and relayed to Hubert. No wonder none of Will's plans to get her out had worked. She might as well have offered to spy for Hubert; at least then she'd have got some perks.

"We have to go back," she said, unable to tear her eyes from the notice. "They know everything."

"How . . . What's going on?" Mathieu's head bounced between the notice and Rachel like a ping-pong ball.

"She said Hubert knows everything," Lawrence repeated slowly and sarcastically at him. "We have to retreat."

"We're gonna give up now? Just because of a bit of paper?" Louis's hand reached for the door handle.

"No!" Rachel stopped him. "They know. I don't want you getting into trouble."

"If they know, we're already in trouble." Louis shrugged.

Rachel shook her head.

"Then how'll we find out where that machine's being built?" Louis pressed.

"Shh!" Rachel whipped her hand up to her head. Was Esther listening now? Or could she only access her thoughts once she had fallen asleep?

"Come on, Lou." Mathieu turned his back on the door. "We'll make a new plan tomorrow.

"Live to fight another day," Lawrence added.

Louis huffed in frustration. "Okay, okay."

The boys began to trudge back up the corridor. Rachel tried to follow, but her legs felt like jelly. Trapped in her head and trapped in the orphanage. Whatever she did, Hubert knew about it.

She tripped and stumbled against the panelled wall with a thud. Louis, Mathieu and Lawrence spun around.

Rachel hadn't the energy to keep her feet. She let herself slide down the wall and sat crumpled in a pile at the bottom.

"You guys go on – we'll catch you up," Louis whispered to the others. He crouched in front of Rachel and took both her hands in his. "You doing okay?"

Tears welled behind her eyes, but she didn't care if he saw. "I want to get out of here," she gasped. "I'm tired of being used."

"Tell me what's going on. Why does Hubert know what we're doing?"

Rachel shook her head hard, hoping Esther would fall out.

"What does he mean by your mind is not your own?"

Rachel had to tell him. It didn't matter anymore. And if she didn't, she'd burst. "You know how I told you my mother died when I was born?"

"Yeah." Louis sat down properly, but didn't let go of her hands. She held them tighter.

Rachel took a deep breath. Only Will and Hubert knew about Esther. "Well, she managed to survive . . . in my head."

"In your head?" Louis frowned.

"I told you I can't dream. It's because my mother takes over my mind at night. She lives in my dreams."

"Okay . . ." Louis's brow furrowed like the bark of an old gnarled tree as he puzzled over Rachel's words. But how could she explain it better? "Okay," he said again. "So she's the beautiful friend . . . ? Wait, that's why you go to the room

182

every night, isn't it, because she's made friends with Hubert?!"

She nodded. "And now they're making this machine together because she wants to live in a dream like Will's. She's going to use that machine to do to him what she's done to me." She realised her knuckles were white around Louis's fingers and loosened them. "I have to get out of here. I have to take Will far away from Esther and Hubert. I want them to leave us alone."

Louis's doe eyes shone as he nodded along with her. But she didn't want him to nod. It was impossible. She'd never be free of Esther.

"She knows everything," Rachel told him. "Everything I do; everything I think. I'm trapped here forever."

"Not forever," Louis replied.

"But she's relaying everything to Hubert. And Hubert wants Esther here. They both want this machine. I can't let it happen, but I can't stop it." Rachel had never felt more hopeless in all her life.

Louis straightened. "You can and you will," he said. "Know why?"

She shook her head.

"Because for as long as you want me, I'll be here too. I'll look out for you. I'll help you." He held her gaze. "Okay?"

Rachel let go of Louis's hands and hugged him to her. They hugged a lot nowadays, but this time as he wrapped his arms around her too, it felt different. It felt safe.

THEN: RACHEL

Louis wasn't at breakfast the next day. Mathieu and Lawrence shrugged when Rachel asked them about him.

"He got back all right last night," Mathieu said. "Probably got up early to finish off some homework."

"Well, where is he now?"

"Why are you so worried? He's missed breakfast before," Mathieu reminded her.

"That's because he still had Miss Grünwald's alarm clock super-glued to his hand." Lawrence sprayed crumbs of toast all over Mathieu's face as he spoke.

Mathieu closed his eyes and took a deep breath. "Thanks, mate."

Rachel hadn't stopped worrying since they'd seen Hubert's note last night. Sleep had been nearly impossible to find, and when she eventually did, she'd spent the remainder of the night in her dark, silent prison, screaming for Esther.

She never came.

Rachel woke up exhausted and desperate to understand why her mother was doing this to her. She needed to vent her anger, take back some sort of control. Louis's hug last night had a wonderful calming effect, but now he wasn't here, that serenity was ripping to tatters. He was the only one who knew the truth, her only link to her brother and her best friend in this hell-hole. She needed him more than ever.

Breakfast finished with a teacher ringing the bell and everyone trooping off to their first lessons of the day. Rachel took a breath. It'd be okay. She'd see Louis in class.

But he wasn't there either.

After three lessons, lunch, two more lessons, prep in the common room and dinner, there was still no sign of Louis. Mathieu and Lawrence exchanged looks at her across the table. They were worried now too.

By the time they were all showered and standing in front of their beds whilst Matron did the rounds, Rachel's heart was in a permanent state of uneasy fluttering. Matron seized her arm and marched her out of the dorm. Hubert wanted her again. Good. She had a few things to say to him . . .

"Evening." Hubert didn't look up from his paperwork as she was pushed into the room with him.

"Where's Louis?"

Hubert raised his head slowly. "I said, 'Evening.'"

Rachel wasn't in the mood to play his games. "I noticed," she snapped. "Where's Louis?"

A wide toady smile spread across his big red face. "That boy is bad for you."

"I'll be the judge of that. Tell me where he is."

Hubert continued writing. "Learning his lesson," he mumbled. "Better someone takes it for the team."

"Then better I take it," Rachel retorted. "It was me who told them about your machine."

Hubert looked up again. This time he put down his pen. "Yes, and what a foolish thing to do. You'll never get near it."

"Then I'll tell everyone about it – and about your plan. Someone will find a way to stop you."

Hubert shook his head, tutting. "Who would believe you? Most can only fantasise of such a machine being built in their lifetime, given the technology is so advanced. And even if they did, why wouldn't you want to be a part of such a thing? A future where you can control your dreams and hug family and friends halfway around the world? This machine is the first step in achieving that."

"No – your machine is so you and Esther can control other people. You don't care about anyone other than—"

"Another reason you might want to leave well enough alone," Hubert raised his voice to drown her out, "is that unlike you, who are protected by my affection for your mother and my requirements for your brother, your Master Louis has absolutely no one in the world who would miss him. Not a soul. There might be a few difficulties with paper-work, but I tell you now: he and your other friends could quite easily go missing permanently. You wouldn't want that now, would you?"

Rachel's mouth dropped. "You're not serious?"

"Try me."

"You vile and twisted bastard." Rachel spun on her heel and reached for the door to leave.

"Uh, uh," Hubert tutted. "Only your complete compliance will ensure your friends' safety."

Rachel pursed her lips so tightly they began to disappear behind her teeth. She turned.

"There really is no reason for me to be here," she told him. "I can guarantee your affection for my mother is not reciprocated. She's using you, just like you think you're using me. Will dreams in a way you'll never be able to master – machine or otherwise. It can never be a success. And as for me: pathetic, trapped, reckless Rachel . . ." She strode up to him, taking delight in her height advantage over the seated man. "You mark my words – the longer you keep me here, the higher I shall make sure you fall."

She turned again and this time marched into the comfortable room, slamming the door behind her before he could see her tears. Empty words. She really was just pathetic, trapped, reckless Rachel who was digging holes increasingly deeper for herself and the people she cared about. Now the most important thing was to get Louis back safely. Until then she had to tread more carefully.

It was three awful days before Rachel saw Louis again. Breakfast. He came in and sat at a table away from everyone else, where the preschool kids were flapping about. Immediately, Mathieu and Lawrence picked up their trays and went over to him. Rachel hurried after.

Mathieu took a seat on Louis's right, Lawrence opposite. A toddler offered them a spoonful of his slobbery porridge and Lawrence redirected it back towards the child's mouth.

Rachel smiled gently at Louis. "May I join you?"

Instantly, he stood up, chair scraping backwards, and walked out of the dining hall. Rachel stared. What had she done?

It was like this the rest of the day; Louis avoided her like an infectious disease. It was little comfort to see him generally avoiding everyone, but in the evening he quietly sat with Mathieu and Lawrence in the common room, seemingly content to be in their company.

Just not hers.

What had Hubert told Louis? What had Hubert done? Why wouldn't he speak to her? Her heart felt like a fragile egg, cracking in half over the frying pan, insides glooping all over the place.

Hubert had taken her only friend away from her.

Days passed with no change in Louis's evasion. His witty comments from the back of class had shrivelled into silence. Mathieu and Lawrence stopped joking around too, perhaps out of respect for their miserable comrade, and the whole affair was rubbing off on everyone. Rachel couldn't ignore it any longer. She had to get him to talk to her.

One balmy afternoon, the kind where the sun shone so pleasantly even the teachers couldn't bear to keep them indoors, the older kids were out playing a game of rounders. Rachel's team were losing horrifically and Louis fielded so deep she could only tell it was him by the black mane of curls atop his head. She repositioned herself closer to him, trying to look as if her attention was rapt upon the ball, but he immediately noticed and began walking away.

"Louis, wait, please!"

His footsteps faltered for a fraction of a wobble, then continued.

"Please, just one minute. Talk to me."

Louis stopped, shoulders rigid. "I don't wanna talk."

"But . . . was it something I did?"

Silence, then he shook his head. "I-I met your mother."

A seam of ice cracked through Rachel. She swayed. "Oh, Louis, I'm so sorry."

Louis scuffed the grass with his feet. "Perhaps we best don't talk for a while."

Rachel nodded, though it broke her heart to do so. Was this one of Esther's terms? What would she gain from keeping them apart? Did she want to make Rachel's life hell – as well as her dreams?

Alone. Forever.

But if that was the only way to keep Esther away from him . . .

She turned to rejoin the game, then stopped. "I know I can't stop her from pursuing you. But if you need anything at all, just ask the blackbird. He's stronger than her. He can help."

Louis half turned and the corner of his mouth twitched in an attempt to smile.

"Thank you."

NOW: MAATJE

The first flakes of the snow that had been threatening to fall for days drifted through the sky. Maatje watched them dance from one of the giant windows at Hubert's manor as she tried to take her mind off her nerves.

They were late.

Tea was already laid out on the table. A plump Victoria sponge dusted white like the grass outside and triangular sandwiches with the crusts cut off, oozing cream cheese, salmon and cucumber. The cutlery shone like mirrors, reflecting the twinkling chandelier and the flickering warmth from the open fire.

Maybe Will hadn't been able to convince Friedrich to come. Maybe he'd changed his mind.

Hubert seemed unfussed, draped across the leather sofa, idly flicking the pages of a newspaper so large it could easily double as a parachute.

Maatje rested her head against the pane. Why was she so edgy? Okay, so a criminal was coming to visit. Someone who attacked her only last night. But Hubert had his security guards strategically positioned; they'd arrive at a moment's notice. Maybe she couldn't quite believe that, after a little hitch, her life's goal was about to be put back on track? Hubert was going to offer Will a place to stay at the manor whilst they conducted their experiments. Maatje would stay too. Her cheeks burnt. Maybe she was just nervous about seeing Will again? She had to remain professional.

Then she saw them: two huddled figures on bicycles rolling towards the house. Her heart began to race and she pulled away from the window.

Hubert looked over his paper. "They're here?"

Maatje nodded.

"Good." He folded his paper away and leant back. "You can relax now. A job well done."

Maatje couldn't relax. Her job was only just getting started.

A butler ushered the pair in. Will and Friedrich, side by side – as though they'd always been together. Both had a slight bluish tinge to their lips and Will rubbed his hands as he came through the door. Friedrich hobbled in, leaning heavily on one leg. He eyed Maatje, Hubert and the table set for tea as though each were plotting something behind his back.

Maatje stepped forward, determined to play it cool, but an involuntary smile was already stretching across her face. Will was okay. That was the main thing. She shook his hand. It was like a block of ice. Her professionalism vanished.

"Oh my god – you're freezing! Where have you been? Come and warm yourself by the fire." She wrapped both hands around his purple fingers and pulled him towards the hearth. Will stiffened. What was wrong? Did he not want to leave his violent new friend's side now?

Yellow flame flickered in his wide eyes.

Oh. Idiot.

She let his hand go. "Here's good enough. Healthier to defrost slowly."

She turned, not wanting to dwell on her mistake, and tentatively shook Friedrich's hand too. He was just as cold, full of the knobbles of bone. She looked at his sunken face. Piercing grey eyes, with just a hint of orange, and once he'd pulled back his hood, thick light-brown hair. He'd be handsome, if he hadn't been giving her a look of total animosity, and with a couple of pounds of muscle added onto him.

"You both look as if you could do with a decent meal." She quickly let go and offered up the table, stepping as far back from Friedrich as possible and stumbling into Hubert.

"Not so fast." Hubert beamed. "I do believe it polite to introduce myself first."

Friedrich ignored him, limping over to the table and swallowing a sandwich.

"You have anything hot?" he grunted in Maatje's direction.

"Tea is on its way," Hubert replied for her, vaguely, for he was preoccupied with shaking Will's hand as if pumping for water. "We meet at last."

A tray with a teapot the size of a microwave was brought in and placed on the table. Hubert reoffered everyone a seat and a butler poured them tea into delicate china cups. Will and Friedrich hovered their hands around their cups, basking in the warmth. Had they slept out in the open last night?

"It has got a bit chilly, hasn't it," Hubert laughed. "Seems like winter's finally kicked in. Have a sandwich." He lifted the plate up to Will, who held up a palm.

"No, thanks."

Friedrich wasn't so restrained, taking another four and demolishing them before the plate had even reached Maatje.

"No, thank you." If Will wasn't eating, neither would she.

"You don't know how many years I've been longing to

192

make your acquaintance," Hubert told Will as he delicately plucked a sandwich off the plate as if it were the petal of a flower. "There is much I'd like to ask you, but for the moment I must thank Mr Reinhardt here for returning you to us in one piece."

Friedrich grunted and picked up the cake slice. Maatje was thankful Hubert had thought not to provide a knife. She didn't like the way he wielded it. He shovelled a large chunk of cake onto his plate.

"Do help yourself to the sponge," Hubert said. "A favourite of mine. It has strawberry jam in the middle."

The cake was already on Friedrich's fork. Maatje couldn't really blame him. It looked as though he hadn't eaten in weeks.

"So what business are you in, Friedrich? I can call you Friedrich, yes?"

"Computer Sciences," mumbled Friedrich through a mouthful of cake. He nudged Will. "Pass the sandwiches."

Hubert lifted the plate over to Friedrich before Will's arm had so much as twitched.

"So what's the deal?" Friedrich asked.

"You've already upheld your end. You brought me my dreamer, and so in return I will help you fight your case. Maatje was telling me all about it."

Ugh, he had to drag her into it. Now Friedrich's piercing gaze was on her, so hungry he might have been eying her up to eat too.

"What about my kids?"

"No rush; no rush," smiled Hubert. "All in good time."

"I need to see them today."

Hubert sighed as though deep in thought, but Maatje knew he had everything already planned out.

"I'll see what I can do, but you have to understand, Friedrich, if I am to help you, I can't be seen harbouring a

193

fugitive. I'm going to have to call the police, tell them you turned yourself in, returned Will unharmed, and that you are innocent of the crimes put to you. We'll let my lawyers take care of the rest."

"You'll send me to jail." It wasn't a question. It might have been a threat.

"Only until we can prove your innocence." Hubert's cheeks puffed in and out like a carp's. "If your story is to be believed."

"I was held prisoner. I want justice."

Hubert laughed loudly and held up a hand to stop him. "Before we get into the nitty-gritty details, why don't we let Miss Finkel and Master Willem take their leave. We don't need to bore them here." He turned to Maatje, who leapt to her feet. "You could show our guest his room – Master Willem, you are welcome to stay here whilst Maatje runs her experiments, if that is to your convenience?"

Will and Friedrich exchanged an apprehensive look.

"Oh, don't worry." Hubert laughed at their faces. "Maatje told me you also have terms. We'll have dinner all together before we say goodbye to our new friend here. It's the least I can do before he's forced to suffer prison food. Go on; off you go."

Maatje smiled encouragingly at Will. He slowly lowered his untouched cup of tea back to its saucer and even more slowly got to his feet.

He didn't want to leave Friedrich. The man's eyes glared, daring Will to abandon him. For the first time, Maatje was able to see the human in him. How vulnerable he really felt. But then the moment was gone. His eyes left Will's and he leant back in his chair.

"Thank you for tea." Will nodded.

Maatje tried not to skip as she left the room with him.

NOW: FRIEDRICH

"Where were we?" Hubert said, jolting Friedrich's attention away from Will's retreating figure and back to the man's froggy gaze. "Ah yes: what to do once you are at the police station. Luckily, you don't have to say anything until your lawyer arrives, but if it helps, here's your cover story—"

"I know my story," Friedrich interrupted.

Hubert raised his eyebrows. "You are innocent. You didn't kill the guard. You were in the SDRC voluntarily to recover from social problems that caused you to lose custody of your children. You were having dream therapy, reacted badly under the stress and tried to make a run for it. In the confusion, the guards shot at you, accidently killing one of their own. Obviously, what would a sane man do but take a hostage to protect himself—?"

"What the hell is this?" Friedrich slammed his hand on the table, making all the crockery clatter. "You want me to lie? You want me to cover your arse? I was being held prisoner. They killed my wife and forced themselves inside my dreams. My private dreams—"

"In the name of science," Hubert told him. "You were helping open up the world to people who can't share dreams. Better there than prison for rioting and murder, eh?"

Friedrich shook his head so furiously it looked as if Hubert was trembling. "No. This is wrong. You are wrong. I will not tell any made-up story to protect the SDRC from the law."

Hubert smiled his froggy smile. "Ah, Mr Reinhardt, this is where you will run into difficulties. I have to protect my assets and what I believe in first and foremost. Here I was thinking I'd help out someone who's aided us in our research, but if you're not willing to play along, I'm afraid we're going to have to terminate our agreement."

"So your new experiments with Will can't be that important then."

Hubert blinked slowly. "Quite the opposite. This could be my most important work to date."

"Well, you won't have a subject if you don't help me."

Hubert laughed. "I think you'll find I can be most compelling. With or without you he'll comply, though it would be much easier if you'd work with me too, just for a bit. If your pride can take it . . ."

"This has nothing to do with my pride," Friedrich growled.

"Good." Hubert took a sip of tea. "So which will it be? A jail cell alone or with a lawyer?" He held up the plate of sandwiches. "Another?"

NOW: WILL

Will smiled to himself as Maatje chatted at seventy miles an hour about his over-the-top manor bedroom, the experiments, and whether his landlady would mind him staying. She was walking at seventy miles an hour too, and with his feet squashed into tiny shoes, he couldn't quite keep to her pace.

"Hang on."

Maatje's concerned face whipped round. That made him smile even more. Everything was either perfect or a calamity in Maatje's world. Nothing in between.

He wrenched his feet from the shoes and showed them to Maatje to put her mind at rest. "Not my size."

"Oh." Maatje's face lit up again. "I've got something for you. In your room . . . well, if you do decide to stay – which you must."

Will padded after her in his socks, skidding over the wooden floors. She took him to a bedroom the size of a small country, gilded with gold and hung with velvet green curtains. A four-poster bed large enough to sleep a small family yawned into the room's expanse, and each of the twenty-something varnished drawers of the dresser were large enough to hold all of Will's worldly possessions.

"Is this what you meant by over the top?"

Maatje winced. "Yeah. Hubert insisted you had the best. Take it as a compliment."

It was actually a bit scary.

"Here!" Maatje waved a pair of shoes at him; the pair he'd left at the manor last night. And she picked up his jumper from the dresser.

"I could do with those, thanks." Will unzipped his coat and pulled the scratchy but very toasty jumper over his head. He bent down to tie his shoes.

Maatje nodded to the fire in a marble grate at the other end of the room.

"I'll put that out for you if you like. I'm sure Hubert has some hot water bottles around."

Will felt giddy with the lightness she exuded. Like the first gasp of a breath he'd forgotten he'd been holding. His toes tingled as if they weren't sure where the floor had gone. It was probably just the blood returning to his feet.

"How did you get mixed up in all this? With Hubert, I mean?"

"He's the guy who fast-tracked my research. After I stumbled upon the dream you were making here, I found out he'd always wanted to meet the person who was making it. He really believes in the healing power of dreams. He wants to make a difference to the world and saw how you could help."

"Have you been into the orphanage?"

Maatje shook her head. "Not yet. But I want to interview some of the kids – if Hubert will let me."

Will chewed his lip. The knot that had been gnawing in his stomach ever since he'd arrived grew. Maatje didn't yet

"Will!" Maatje ran towards him. "Are you okay?"

He noted confusion in her concern as he gulped air back into his lungs, but all he could think about was Friedrich and the police . . . They were going to kill him.

Letting the horror of that notion flood through him, he pushed off the wall and ran.

know what she was getting herself mixed up in; heck, *he* didn't know what he was getting mixed up in. He shouldn't have come. Shouldn't have brought Friedrich here.

"Actually, Maatje, I'd prefer to work in your laboratory."

"Oh." Her face dropped. "I thought you might be more comfortable here. We can bring all the equipment over; we won't be disturbed . . ."

Will shook his head. "I can't. Not here. Thanks for my clothes though. Do send my apologies to the poor lady whose shoes I ruined. I'd like to get back to Friedrich now."

He turned for the door.

"What is it with this Friedrich?" Maatje hadn't moved. She crossed her arms. "I know you like to help people and all, but you can let him go now. Hubert will look after him."

Will wriggled. How could he tell her it was Hubert he was worried about? The man who had prevented him from seeing his sister, who had once wanted him arrested, and now wanted to work with him? How could he tell her the reason he made the dream for the kids in the first place was to stop Hubert from violating their sleep? The man was hidden behind years of rumours and messages from Rachel, so how could he explain his doubts to Maatje?

"I know," he said. "I'm just hungry."

Maatje snorted. "I'm so glad you said that. I could eat a horse." She took his arm and led him back down the corridor.

"How is Baggy?"

"Oh, I don't dream about him anymore." She waved a hand to brush her horse into the past, but the arm in his stiffened against him.

"Sorry."

Her hand slipped down into his. "You're warming up at last." She squeezed his fingers. "You haven't been sleeping outside, have you?"

"No, in a bar—" Will stopped by a window overlooking the main entrance to the manor. He could just about hear the crunch of gravel under the tyres of three police cars pulling up.

"It's too soon," Maatje whispered over his shoulder. "Hubert said . . . Do you think Friedrich tried something?"

The first officer got out of his vehicle, gun in hand, and Will felt as though a bullet had gone off in his head. He ran full pelt back down to where they'd left Friedrich and Hubert, his mind screaming.

Trap, trap, trap . . .

A butler bowed Will into the room and he sped straight for Friedrich, seizing his elbow and hoisting him off the chair. "Trap," he hissed into his ear.

"Is everything okay?" blinked Hubert.

In a heartbeat, Friedrich found his feet. He snatched up a butter knife and grabbed Hubert in a headlock.

"Hands above your heads, everyone, now!" Five policemen swarmed into the room, guns raised.

Will obliged. Maatje, who was by the doorway, squeaked in shock and put her hands up too. Even the butler was ushered into the room with his hands on show.

Friedrich ignored them, pressing the knife against Hubert's throat. It was too blunt to pierce skin, but Friedrich had more than enough strength to do some damage if he wanted. "You greedy, lying, scheming bastard!" he yelled at his prisoner, who was turning a deeper shade of red. "You want to tell them the truth, or should I?"

"Knife down and hands in the air!" the police barked. "Now!"

Will couldn't see how Friedrich would get out of this one. Why did he have to go on the offensive all the time? He wished Maatje wasn't there.

"Friedrich, please let him go," he begged.

Friedrich and the police trod a threatening circle around each other.

"We can shoot you much faster than it'll take to use that knife," an officer warned.

Hubert blustered and shook his head. Friedrich pressed harder. "You want to test that theory?"

Will had never felt so helpless in his life. "Don't shoot him." He stumbled into the officers' line of sight. A single gun turned in his direction.

"Don't move."

Will lifted his hands higher. "I won't – just please don't shoot him."

Hubert gaped like a petrified fish out of water. Friedrich inched towards the door.

Will shook his head. If he tried to run, they'd shoot.

"I said: don't move!" The police officer's voice was strained. Bad things happened when people felt as if they were losing control.

Friedrich gave Will a resigned smirk. "I think we're done here."

Will's body took over from thought. He lunged sideways, knocking the knife from Friedrich's hand as the air cracked with gunshots. In the same moment, Friedrich shoved Hubert forward, and Will found himself caught in a vortex of hard elbows and frantic motion as Friedrich fled through the door behind. A stampede of uniformed bodies followed in h wake.

"Wait!" Will wedged himself in the doorway, bloc the police from leaving. "Don't hurt him. He's innocent. just angry and scared—"

The force of two large shoulders careened him i hallway wall. The officers swarmed past.

NOW: FRIEDRICH

Get out, get out, get out!

The front door was blocked by the two beefy guys from last night, straining their ears to the commotion. Friedrich wasn't up for taking two men on at once.

He dashed along the corridor, hobbling, but barely noticing his ankle's complaints. A door was ajar further up. He fell inside and a lady with bright red lipstick looked up from her computer. There was a window behind her. He didn't have time to check if it opened. He snatched up a chair and ran towards it.

The lady screamed and shot back from her desk as he launched the chair through the glass.

Friedrich leapt through the flying shards after it.

The nearest tree cover was a fifty-metre sprint across the icy lawn. If he could make it in time. The police's shouts gained behind him. The gravel skidded underneath his feet; a gunshot and a wodge of turf exploded in front of him.

Go, go, go!

He could only hope he wouldn't be hit.

A whizz and more grass flew. Another bullet. A police car bounced over the grass towards him, cutting him off.

Oh god! He froze.

Whack! Something hard hit him in the shoulder from behind, throwing him to the ground, but all he could see was that police car, stopping in front of him. Friedrich pulled himself to his knees. Blood splattered the snow-peppered grass.

The car door opened, and two feet appeared.

Get up. Everything spun, ground and sky one grey mass.

The feet ran towards him.

"Friedrich!"

He looked up. "Will?"

Will grabbed him under the arms and heaved him up. For a moment, Friedrich couldn't remember how to stand. He clutched Will's jumper, searching for the right muscles to engage as the man half carried, half pulled him to the car.

A bullet thudded into the metal door as Friedrich hauled it open. He hurled himself inside and Will slid into the driver's seat next to him. The car jerked forward, spluttering.

"Put it in first!" Friedrich yelled.

Will fumbled with the gearstick to no avail.

"Clutch down!"

Will grimaced. "Oh yeah."

The police were almost on top of them. A bullet sparked off the bonnet. A hand reached out for the handle of the driver's door.

Friedrich slammed his fist down onto the central lock and the doors clicked. At the same moment, the car moved off again, slowly, then faster.

"Second gear!"

"How—"

"Put the clutch down and I'll do it." Friedrich seized the gearstick and yanked it back into second. "Now accelerate!"

The car roared and shot forward, up onto the driveway towards the gate. Sprinting behind, the police couldn't keep up. One more shot ricocheted off the boot and they turned back to the house. No doubt to get their other cars.

"Faster – the gate's closing."

Up at the top of the drive, their escape route was rapidly shrinking. The thick, heavy iron gate wasn't the sort that would succumb to ramming.

The engine screamed. It needed to go into third, but Friedrich wasn't risking any mishaps until they were through.

"Come on, come on, come on," he urged the car.

Will's knuckles clenched white against the wheel. "We're not going to fit."

"Keep going!"

"I'm flat to the floor."

The wing mirror cracked as the metal jaws of the gate closed in and the rear bumper crunched, pushing the car off course.

"Whoa!" Will fought the wheel.

They skidded left and straightened out. Back on the main road.

Friedrich laughed.

They'd made it.

Something hard and sharp dug into his backside. He slid his hand underneath him and pulled out two sets of car keys.

"Are these . . . ?"

"Can't have them following us." Will's clammy face was as white as the snow falling ever thicker onto the road in front. He looked completely out of his depth.

"The other police cars?" Friedrich couldn't believe what Will had done. The man was a genius. He slumped back in his seat and laughed harder still.

"Might be a good idea to put your seatbelt on," Will wheezed.

Wise advice since he obviously didn't know how to drive.

"Want to try going into third gear first? The car will thank you for it."

"All right." Will looked down and the car swerved.

"Keep your eyes on the road!" Friedrich stopped him.

"So it was clutch down . . ."

"And – without looking – pull the stick back into the middle and push it forward."

"Like this?"

"And as you take your foot off the clutch, add more power to the accelerator."

The car revved and jerked as the clutch came up, but then quietened and smoothed out.

"It worked."

"Now we can hear ourselves think again," Friedrich muttered and let his head fall back against the headrest.

Will glanced over at him.

"Eyes on the road."

"You need to bandage that up."

Friedrich lifted his head and eyed his shoulder. It was soaked with blood. The bullet had gone straight through.

"Shit."

"You okay?"

Friedrich shook himself. "Yeah, for now. Just drive." He leant forward and opened the glove compartment with his left hand. Now he'd comprehended his injury, it hurt too much to use the right. Perfect – a first aid kit. He unzipped it with his teeth and rummaged inside.

The car radio crackled.

"Four nine two on North Side, do you copy?"

"What does that mean?" Will cocked his head.

Another voice replied. "Four nine two requesting back up. Stolen police vehicle three six seven on Bonn Street."

"That's us," Friedrich registered.

"Tracking now – sending three units."

"Copy."

"Great, they can see us?" Friedrich studied the dials in front of him. "Is there any way of turning off our GPS?"

"Our what?" The car swerved again.

"No, no, it's okay. I'll look. You keep us alive."

"Sorry, I haven't done this since I was thirteen."

"What, drive?"

Will nodded. "My dad taught me. Never been on the road before though."

"It shows."

Friedrich couldn't see anything to help block their signal. It was likely the box was fixed to the car exterior and he wasn't sure they could afford the time to locate and disable it. Especially with Will's driving. And with Friedrich's shoulder, they certainly couldn't swap.

He busied himself with antiseptic and vast swathes of dressings and gauze. It was difficult to manage a burning hole that dripped blood everywhere with only one hand. His head spun and he was beginning to feel sick. He swallowed.

"Four nine two, this is four six five, approaching three six seven from west on Alm Street—"

"Will turn left here – left!" Friedrich cried.

The car rocketed around the corner, throwing Friedrich against his injured shoulder. He hissed.

"Sorry, sorry," Will muttered.

"No, it's fine. They're trying to block us off." He brought up a map on the dashboard. The green dot that was them blinked away from a blue dot labelled 465, which was approaching from the next street up.

"Okay, turn left at the end of the road here and then right at the far end of town."

"Where are we going?"

"Anywhere they're not."

"We don't want to head towards the highway though."

"Why not . . . ? Left!"

Another shoulder bash.

"Sorry. I thought I'd already gone left."

"Another police car. Our route is up for diversions," Friedrich groaned.

"I really don't think I'm ready to drive on a highway. I'm going to hit something if I'm not careful."

"You won't if you concentrate."

But the odds were stacking against them. The sky was almost dark and the snow fell heavier still.

"Okay," Friedrich decided. "We'll head to the old road and the mountain pass."

"In this weather?" cried Will. "We need to get you to a hospital."

Friedrich shook his head. "We'll be caught. We have to lay low somewhere."

"Friedrich, being caught isn't a problem. Your shoulder is. Everything will have calmed down by the time we get there."

"Right."

"I'm glad you agree."

"No *right* – turn right here."

Tyres screeched and Friedrich squeezed his eyes shut as fire shot down his arm. "Please, Will," he gasped. "I'll be fine. We need to find somewhere safe for the night, and a hospital isn't. I'm not going to jail."

Will grimaced. "Okay. Okay. I have some friends who live in the mountains. They have medical knowledge . . . I think. They might be able to help."

"Good." Friedrich swallowed. "What's their address?"

THEN: RACHEL

The summer stretched hot and relentless. Days merged into one sticky mass, punctuated only by sweaty nights of infinite black. Rachel couldn't concentrate on anything anymore. Friends let her wander about in her private daze, not wanting to be dragged down with her, and teachers noticed enough to scold her for poor work and lack of focus.

"It doesn't matter to me if you don't care about your grades," her chemistry teacher said after everyone else had left class. "But if your silly answers are going to disrupt the rest of my lesson—"

"I'm sorry, miss." Rachel bowed her head: the quickest way to get out of an awkward situation.

"Don't interrupt me," the teacher snapped. "I want two pages written on why we use moles in equations by next lesson." She leant in. "And any mention of the furry animal and there will be consequences."

"What about the product mass homework you just set?"

"What about it? That's due Wednesday too. Now scoot."

Rachel was too tired to fight. She drifted out of the room,

not even sure where she was going, let alone what a mole was. Was it lunch now or did they have another lesson?

Louis came from the opposite direction. He slowed when he saw her and she pushed herself against the wall, pretending to find the panelling inherently interesting so he could pass without issue.

"Rach?"

She stopped. He was talking to her? She was too afraid to look at him in case she'd imagined it.

"Rach, can we talk?"

She wasn't hearing things. Louis had addressed her of his own accord. She blinked at him.

"Is now okay?" he pressed.

"Yes, yes." Rachel shook herself back to the present.

"How long do you think you can stay awake for?"

"What?"

Louis's eyes gleamed. "Hubert's away on business for a week."

Rachel shrugged. "I know." It made no difference to her whether or not she saw his horrible red face anymore. There was nothing she could do about it.

"Well, we've got a plan – Lawrence, Mathieu and I. We're gonna escape. Wanna come?"

"What do you mean?" Rachel frowned. "You're all going to be sixteen and out of here soon. Why do you want to run away?"

"Because –" Louis looked about the empty corridor – "they're not gonna let you go when you turn sixteen next year, are they? And we're not leaving you behind."

Rachel blinked hard. Louis still cared? He smiled at her, almost as though nothing had happened between them. If it hadn't been impossible, she would have thought she was dreaming.

"Bu-but now you've told me, Esther will know."

"That's why I asked how long you can stay awake for. And why we couldn't tell you before. The plan's in place, your brother's helping too. All you've got to do is stay awake so she can't stop us."

"Will's helping?" Rachel's heart felt as if it might bubble over.

Louis nodded. "He's made this femme fatale dream for the guard on CCTV watch. Idiot's gonna meet 'her' there at exactly the time we'll be leaving. He got all the alarm codes out of matron last week by giving her a prison-break dream. Mathieu's memorised them, and Lawrence has mapped our safest route out and the location of all the keys. Course, we don't need to worry about anybody waking up either; your brother's got an irresistible dream to keep everyone riveted in their beds. All you've got to do is not fall asleep until we come and get you."

Rachel fizzed. "Wh-when? Tonight?"

"No time like the present."

She leapt on Louis and smothered him in the biggest hug she'd ever mustered. To her joy, his arms snaked around her and gently hugged her back.

NOW: FRIEDRICH

"Do you have any money?"

Friedrich patted down his pockets with his good hand. "No. Why?"

"We're running out of petrol."

Friedrich leant forward slowly and opened the glove compartment again. No money in there. There were a couple of police jackets on the back seat, just out of reach. He twisted round, trying to grab hold of a sleeve, but his shoulder blared at him and he hissed in pain.

"Are you all right?" Will wasn't looking at the road again.

"Yes, look ahead," Friedrich snapped.

For over an hour they'd managed to keep ahead of the police. Putting enough space in front of them to risk pulling over and disabling the GPS, which had been lurking under the car. Friedrich had almost passed out when he stood up again. Will insisted on retying his bandage when he fell back inside, stuffing more pads in and pulling the gauze so tight Friedrich felt as though he'd severed his arm.

They were heading up the pass into the mountains now. As well as the red fuel light on the dashboard, Friedrich could also just about see the gauge that showed the tank was empty. The car could die on them at any point.

He rested his head on the headrest, feeling sick and sluggish. "How far to your friends' place?"

"I don't know." Thankfully Will kept his eyes firmly on the white night outside the windscreen, crawling along in fear of skidding over the edge of the mountain. Without the GPS, Friedrich couldn't be sure how close the police were getting. At this speed, it was a wonder they hadn't been caught yet . . . Perhaps the police knew they hadn't much fuel left and so had no need to risk a chase in adverse weather.

"If you go up a gear, it'll be more efficient on fuel."

Will shook his head. "I can't go any faster than this. It's—"

The car spluttered and began to bounce up and down like a kangaroo.

"What's happen—?"

"Brake, brake!" Friedrich seized the handbrake with his bad arm in his panic. Pain, white-hot and vicious, shot through him and he yelled.

Will pulled the brake for him just as the engine stuttered and stopped. "I guess we're out." He turned to Friedrich. "We'll have to continue by foot. Can you stand?"

Friedrich nodded, screwing up his face as he tried to collect himself. "Just give me a moment."

Who knew if they even had a moment? Friedrich felt for the door handle with the fingers of his good arm and pulled. Even that hurt now. He slid off the seat, out into the fat snowflakes swarming the darkness. Pinpricks of light far below showed the nearest town, accompanied by flashing blue. The police. Still some way down the mountain, but moving fast.

Will eased himself out of the car and gripped the top for support. His front was saturated in what looked like oil in the snow-lit night, but Friedrich knew it was blood. Crikey, was he bleeding that badly? He looked down at himself. Slick metallic liquid covered his clothes too. Had the bullet nicked an artery? No. He'd have died in minutes. It was a clean shot, straight through. Lucky. But he'd lost a lot of blood. No wonder he felt so dizzy.

"Here." Will held out one of the police jackets from the back of the car. Thick, plump, black coats. A welcome layer in the bitter terrain.

Will helped him into it, but hard as he tried, Friedrich couldn't get his injured arm through the sleeve. Will gave up and tied the loose arm out of the way, before pulling on a coat too.

"We need to leave the road," Friedrich said.

"Are you crazy?"

"Those lights are going to catch up pretty quick." Friedrich stumbled towards the side of the road, searching for a route. "Can we get to your friends' place by going cross-country?"

Will caught up and wrapped an arm around him: an instant relief to his lurching senses. "I don't like it," he whispered. "It's a long walk and I don't even know if they're still there."

"We have to risk it. Better that than playing target practice."

"In a snowstorm?"

"Snow's good. It'll cover our tracks," Friedrich replied. Distant sirens wailed beneath them. The police were getting closer. "Which way?"

Will pointed. "Up."

THEN: RACHEL

It was late. Very late. Exactly how late, Rachel didn't know, but it must have been at least the early hours of the next morning. Surely the boys should have come for her by now? Something must have happened. She prayed they hadn't been caught. Maybe Lawrence hadn't been able to get all the keys and they had no choice but to hold the escape off for a night . . .

Telling herself this didn't ease the worry, so she indulged in her anxieties, knowing fear would chase sleep away. Even then, staying awake all night was harder than it sounded, despite the enticing promise of escape. The biggest killer was being tucked up in bed, in the dark, listening to the gentle breathing of her fellow prisoners. There wasn't much else that could have relaxed her more.

The night was cooler than it had been in recent weeks, so she kicked off the soft and comfortable blanket in an attempt to chill herself into awakedness. She had already pinched and poked herself until her body tingled all over, so it was time for a new tactic.

It would have been so much easier if she'd been able to get

up and run around, sing at the top of her voice or clap or dance or anything other than lie here. She sat up and shoved her hands under her bum to stop them automatically reaching for the blanket. She wanted to be warm and cosy and succumb to sleep. That was the second thing she wanted most in the world. The first was to defy Esther, escape this cursed place and see her brother again. It had been nearly three years, but not a day went by when she didn't think about him. She'd changed a lot since then. She was becoming a proper woman now, or so she felt. Breasts, hips – although not as curvy as she would have liked – and she was almost as old as Will had been when she'd last seen him. Her big brother. What if she didn't recognise him? What if he didn't recognise her?

She released her hands as they were getting pins and needles, and began to braid her hair into tiny plaits. That would kill a good hour. She was proud of her hair. Thick and slightly wavy, reaching halfway down her back. And it was golden, the warmest colour in this miserable place, so she always let it hang by the corners of her eyes so to frame everything with sunshine. Esther didn't have hair like that. Hers was dead straight and more white than blonde, like the icicles that made up her soul. They shared the same nose, thin and straight, and nothing else. For that she was glad; Rachel didn't want anything else to do with her.

Her head bobbed.

No!

She clambered down the bunk ladder and tiptoed over to the sink in the far corner of the room. She ran the tap until the water refused to get any colder and splashed it all over her face, dribbling it down her back and front with a shudder. Just to pass the time, she pretended to paint her finger and toenails with it.

A groan came from a nearby bed and a pair of socks hit

her on the head. "Knock it off." A head flopped back onto its pillow.

What Rachel would give for her pillow now.

She crept back to bed, missing all the squeaky floorboards. Never had the lumpy mattress looked so welcoming. She lay down on the floor and slid herself under the bunk. Hard wood dug into her bones. Perfect.

She unrolled the socks that had hit her and played puppets with them, just as she'd done when she was younger, creating faces and personalities until she could see them as real as any person she'd met. When she eventually grew tired of playing, she went back to plaiting the rest of her hair. It was trickier in the cramped space under the bed, but the challenge would keep her awake. She just had to keep herself entertained until either Louis came to set her free or matron unlocked the door for breakfast . . .

"God, you look awful."

"What happened?" Rachel flopped down next to Louis, Mathieu and Lawrence in the dining hall the next morning.

"Sorry, Rach. The stupid CCTV guy didn't show. A temporary setback. We've sorted it if he don't turn up tonight." Louis eyes were full of pity. "I take it you haven't slept?"

"Not a wink." Rachel yawned. She felt quite pleased with herself.

"With the bags to prove it. It looks as if someone punched you." Mathieu waved his toast at her.

"It's not that bad," Louis said. But he was probably just being kind to make up for the months of ignoring her.

"Well, I won't be able to make another night, so please, please say it's happening tonight."

Louis nodded. "It's happening."

But despite his smile and assurances, Rachel was sure something else would go wrong. It had all happened too suddenly; all too good to be true.

"What can I do to help?" she asked.

"Stay awake if it's the last thing you do," whispered Louis, his face flickering with the fearful expression he'd worn over the months he'd avoided her. "We can't get caught. Not this time."

Esther never did tell Rachel what she'd said or done to Louis, but perhaps it was best she didn't know. The guilt already ate away at her.

Tonight she would stay awake. Tonight she would be free.

NOW: WILL

Will had never been so cold in his life. The wind whipped straight through the police jacket and his jumper as though they weren't there, and icy shards of snow hurled in his face. He could barely catch a breath, and he was so, so tired.

They had miraculously found a bike headlight in Friedrich's pocket, and Will kept flashing it at him. He plodded alongside as if he were rusting up, his weight resting heavier and heavier against Will with each step. He wouldn't last much longer.

Will blinked through the blinding snow, scanning for a barn or cave in which to shelter. They'd been lucky not to step off a cliff yet. Why had he agreed to head through the mountains in weather like this? It was insane. He hadn't been thinking straight. He still wasn't. His head was a scrambled, frozen mess and it took all his energy to drag the bitter air into his reluctant lungs. They had never been the same since the fire, and resented being tortured in this manner.

It must have been late evening by now. Someone nearby would surely be asleep? Someone who could get to them fast.

A doctor. Mountain rescue. He'd reach out to their dreams as soon as he found somewhere out of the snow.

Will shifted Friedrich's arm higher up his shoulder and the man gave a grunt. Though skin and bone, Friedrich was a lot taller and heavier than Will. He coughed and took the strain. Their routine had become his being: one step forward, wait for Friedrich, catch him before he slipped over, then repeat. But this time Friedrich didn't step. He swayed, head bent against the elements.

Keep focused, Will. Keep moving.

"Anja," he blurted. "That's your daughter, right?"

Another grunt.

"She's quite an artist."

Friedrich took the step, his foot not quite finding the ground. Will held him up until he had, trying not to let the man see just how much effort it took.

"Has she always drawn bugs? She's got a wonderful eye for detail."

"Cats," grimaced Friedrich.

"Yes, the cats I've seen." Will tried to laugh, but it turned into a cough. "You'll have to ask her to show you the bugs next time you see her. Spiders, earwigs, woodlice . . . They really are something."

Friedrich turned his head slowly and stared at him, eyes glazed with pain and exhaustion.

"Are all your family so artistic?"

Half a grunt. Will might not have heard it if the wind hadn't dropped just then.

He looked about as a thin slither of moonlight pierced through the snow clouds. "I think the weather might be clearing up a bit." He shivered, too cold for it to make any difference. Though at least he was still shivering. He wasn't hypothermic yet. Unlike Friedrich.

The moon broke through the clouds completely and the

mountain glowed an eerie extra-terrestrial blue. Friedrich's face almost matched it for colour, his eyes now closed.

"Wow, it's magical." Will felt as though he was talking to himself. "Take a look."

Friedrich stepped forward again, but this time lost his footing completely. His entire weight took Will with it, crushing the smaller man beneath him into the thick, suffocating snow.

He made no move to get off.

"Friedrich?"

Panic rose when there was no reply. Pain lanced through Will's chest. He couldn't breathe . . .

"Stop now," a muffled voice sounded somewhere near his elbow.

Will tasted metal in his throat and coughed. Stopping sounded good.

He couldn't breathe . . .

His head sunk deeper into the snow.

No. He wrenched it back up. If they stopped, Anja and Milo would have no father. It had been his stupid idea to go and find his friends' hut, so it was his responsibility to get them there alive.

But Will couldn't breathe.

He wriggled out from under Friedrich's smothering form.

NOW: FRIEDRICH

W ill tugged at his arm. Not his injured one, but it still sent shockwaves through his body. The wound he'd almost forgotten about seared back into existence.

Friedrich tried to pull away. Let him sleep. He was so tired. He couldn't really feel the cold anymore, just heavenly soft snow. "Rest . . ." he murmured to Will's pleas, ". . . a bit."

"There's no 'bit' my friend," Will's breath gasped hot against his ear; a beautiful warmth Friedrich's body no longer had. "If you rest now, it'll be forever. We have to keep going."

Will was being overdramatic. Friedrich wasn't going to bleed out; he was too cold. He just had to get some energy back. His ankle needed time to heal . . .

"If you won't do it for me, do it for your children. Come on. Get up!"

Ugh, the man was persistent. But he was right: Anja and Milo couldn't wait. Friedrich rolled over, but his legs were lead. Will tried to help, a tugging, swaying silhouette above him – or was that Friedrich's head spinning? He closed his eyes. Will's knees hit the snow.

"No, no, stay awake." Will shook him again, coughing. "If

we're going to stop, we have to at least shelter under those pines over there."

He had to be kidding. Friedrich was already quite comfortable. He didn't need any shelter. But Will grabbed him under the arms and started pulling anyway.

"Argh!" Friedrich had forgotten what heat felt like, but there it was: a thousand suns burning in his shoulder.

"Sorry, sorry," Will kept apologising, but he didn't let go until they were – Friedrich presumed – at the trees in question. He cracked open his eyes, hissing his discomfort at Will, who propped himself against a trunk and gasped wet, heavy breaths, Friedrich in his lap.

He could smell blood. The idiot must have compromised his bandage whilst dragging him. Not that it mattered. There was nothing they could do now.

"Friedrich." Hands scrabbled to keep him close. Another cough. "I'm going to dream for help."

"Mmm."

"But you have to promise me you'll be here when I wake up."

"Mmm."

Something dark speckled Will's chin, like painted-on stubble. When he coughed, more speckles appeared. A pathetic attempt at a beard from a kid who'd missed his last growth spurt. He wasn't fooling Friedrich.

"Friedrich?"

"Mmm."

"Promise?"

Friedrich didn't know if he replied this time or not, but Will squeezed his hand and leant his head back against the tree, so he guessed so. His ragged breaths evened out. The hand holding Friedrich's went slack and Friedrich suddenly felt very alone. He grasped Will's hand as tight as he could manage. He couldn't die alone. He wouldn't die alone.

THEN: RACHEL

The second night's attempt of the plan was one of the hardest of Rachel's life. Her head nodded constantly, and in those split seconds between consciousness and sleep, she felt Esther pull her deeper down. But she couldn't let her succeed. Rachel wrenched herself out of the tempting arms of blissful oblivion, urged on by the satisfaction of finally being able to trump her mother. She couldn't fail now.

She splashed water on herself again, lay under the bed, pinched, poked and plaited her hair – until she was stopped by a soft scratching. The sound of a key sliding under the door into the dormitory. Rachel tiptoed over, dropped to her hands and knees, and fumbled for the key in the dark. The metal was warm from being held in someone's palm. She slid it as quietly as she could into the lock. The door opened; nobody in the room stirred.

Louis's figure stood in the dark corridor, swimming in her vision. Was he actually there? Could this really be happening? In a daze, Rachel clicked the door shut behind her and locked it again.

Stage one of the great escape complete.

They crept down the corridor, past the boy's dormitory and the night watch. They met no one as they tiptoed down the stairs to the ground floor. The whole world lurched and spun blearily as Rachel walked. She kept a firm grip on Louis's arm, the only thing that remained steady.

"It's us."

Rachel jumped as Mathieu and Lawrence slipped out of the shadows, both with broad smiles on their faces.

"CCTV guy is snoring like a dream," Mathieu whispered. "Heard him as we passed his cupboard."

Lawrence and Louis smothered amused snorts with their hands. An unannounced pang of jealously flared through Rachel. Even the CCTV guy, shared Will's dreams, whilst she – his own sister – hadn't seen one speck of him for years.

Tonight that would change.

"We shouldn't laugh though," Louis murmured. "What if someone hears him?"

"We'd better keep going," Mathieu agreed.

"All the alarms off?" Louis asked.

"Every one we had noted." Lawrence nodded.

"Okay." Louis took out a key and brandished it for them all to see. "To freedom."

At the staff room, Lawrence unlocked the door and the four of them slid inside. Waning moonlight shone through the massive glass conservatory, turning the coffee-odoured room a humming grey. Louis stepped forward, but Lawrence put his arm out, raising a finger to wait. He shone his torch at each of the armchairs in the room: tall, tatty, fabric and leather, every one of them empty. Rachel didn't know what she'd do if someone was sitting in one. If Hubert was there. Or Esther . . .

No, Esther couldn't be there. Lack of sleep told her otherwise.

Lawrence nodded and they ran towards the conservatory door. Louis in front, holding the key outstretched.

What if it was the wrong key? Everything had gone too well so far. What if Rachel had fallen asleep and this was just a cruel dream Esther had invented to punish her? She'd wake up back in bed. Trapped for the rest of her life.

No, Esther couldn't create dreams, only manipulate them. This was real. It had to be real.

The door opened and the four ran out onto the open grass and up towards the gate.

A security light flared into existence. Rachel stumbled, stunned by its brightness. There was a shout from inside.

"Go, go!" Louis shouted, grabbing her hand.

"To the wall!" Lawrence, leading, leapt left. The wall was closer than the gate and the gate code could be overridden from the house. But the wall was high. To Rachel's knowledge, no one had ever got over it before. Then again, no one had ever made it outside the front of the house before. It was just a view from a window on the way back from the comfortable room. The wall was lower here . . . or so it looked.

"Come on, Rach!" Louis pulled her into the trees where the wall towered before them. Adrenaline surged through her system, forcing the tiredness aside and leaving only a lingering unrealness to the whole affair. It made her feel invincible.

She lunged at the wall as Louis heaved her leg up. Lawrence, already on top, pulled her the rest of the way.

"Ow!" A hot pain seared across her hand. Glass shards poked out of the top of the wall. There was no time to worry about it; Mathieu was coming up next and she had to get out of the way.

She slithered over the wall, cutting her knees and shins, and half climbed, half fell down the other side.

Mathieu dropped next to her, followed by Lawrence and finally Louis.

"Where's the taxi?" Mathieu hissed.

"End of the road," Louis gasped, clenching his bleeding fingers. "Run."

And Rachel did. Faster than she'd ever run before, fuelled by the fear of the shouting and the revving of engines on the other side of the wall. Despite it all, her footsteps felt lighter than ever. Not from exhaustion, but a new sense of freedom. She was out. And every step she took was further away from the manor she had loathed for so many years. She wouldn't go back now . . .

"Taxi for Rachel Macher and friends?" A window rolled down as a car pulled up next to them, a voice enquiring from within.

"That's us," Louis gasped and yanked open the back door. "Thank you, Will."

They packed inside, Mathieu sticky and sweaty on Rachel's left, Louis's elbow sticking into her ribs on her right.

"You still off to the mountains? At this hour?" The taxi driver looked over his shoulder.

"Yeah, yeah," Louis replied.

"There's space for one of you in the front, if you like?"

Rachel looked at the others. She was squashed, but the thought of being separated from one of the boys terrified her, even by a short distance. The same expression spread across the faces of Louis, Mathieu and Lawrence too.

"Nah, we're good," Louis replied, glancing out of the back window to see if anyone from the orphanage had caught up. Rachel looked too. The road was empty.

"You in a rush?" The driver raised his eyebrows at the panting kids.

They nodded.

The driver shrugged and turned back to the front, and the taxi pulled off.

It wasn't long before the thrum of the car engine and the vibration of the road lulled Rachel's racing heart and reminded her of her desperate need to sleep. The excitement of being in a car for the first time in three years quickly wore off. The motion was strange and the world moved past too fast to make sense of it. Her head dropped onto Louis's shoulder.

He nudged her. "Not yet. Wait until we get there."

She left her head there, but picked up his hand and rubbed the blood off his fingers with the bottom of her pyjama top. "To the mountains?"

"Our safe house," he murmured. "There's a hut that belonged to my dad. I think it's still in the family, but no one ever uses it. It's miles from anywhere and everyone – the perfect place to keep Esther contained. You can sleep then."

"How do you know it's empty?"

"Will checked it out. He'll meet us there when everything's calmed down."

Will. In a way she was glad he was tied up creating dreams tonight. She wanted to see him so badly, but she was too tired to properly enjoy a reunion. Tomorrow would be best, after a good night's sleep. Oh, Esther would be furious.

"Rachel!" Mathieu slapped her leg with the back of his hand. "What are you doing?" He eyed Rachel's attempt to clean Louis's fingers as though she were trying to saw them off. "Your top's filthy." He asked the taxi driver for a first aid kit and took out some gauze. "Try this."

She took the gauze and began tying bits of it around Louis's hand. Glass was nasty; as soon as she wiped them, Louis's fingers started bleeding again.

"Let me see yours?" Mathieu took Rachel's hand and studied her palm. "I hope this hut has clean water," he mumbled.

Rachel's eyes began to droop again not long after the car turned off the highway and headed up into the hills. There were no lights to distract her – no passing cars or jazzy billboards, just inky black countryside.

Lawrence started singing. He had a rough earthy voice that made pleasant listening. Mathieu and Louis quickly joined in, Mathieu screechy and high, Louis out of tune. Rachel put her hands over her ears.

"Oy, this is for your benefit." Louis pulled her hands down. "Now join in."

Goodness knew what the taxi driver thought as he drove four raucous voices up into the peaceful wilderness, but by the third song Rachel began enjoying herself. They put on silly voices, did the actions and before she realised it, they were slowing down.

"Which house are you?" the driver asked.

"Just drop us here mate, thanks," Louis replied.

They rolled out, stiff-legged and laughing, onto a deathly quiet lane. Shadowy bulks of houses lined the roadside.

"Do I owe you anything?" Louis bent down next to the driver's window.

A hand dismissed him. "Already taken care of. Goodnight."

The taxi rolled away and the remaining quietness drew a seriousness to the group.

"Which way?" whispered Lawrence.

"To the footpath at the end of the lane," Louis recited and strode forward.

The end of the lane wasn't far. Five houses and then a dark expanse of blackness. Rachel followed Louis up the uneven mountain path. Every step felt as though she were getting onto a boat, the ground lurching up and down, her brain unable to decide how far away it was. All she could think about was sleeping.

They must have walked for four or five miles when eventually Louis stopped.

"You okay?" Lawrence's gruff voice came from the back.

"I found it." Louis sounded surprised. "I can't believe I found it!"

"We're here?" That was Mathieu.

"Yeah!" Louis spun round, beaming in the torchlight. "Welcome to our new home, everyone."

All Rachel could see of the hut was a bit of dark, stained pine. She'd be happy about it tomorrow. What she wanted now was a bed.

Inside was musty and dusty. Cobwebs laced her face as she walked through the main living area.

"Two mattresses," Mathieu announced coming out of a bedroom. "Probably full of mites and bedbugs."

"I don't care." Rachel wouldn't have cared if there hadn't been a mattress at all. She shuffled, zombie-like, to the nearest bunk, built into the bedroom wall: thick, wooden and solid. No creaking springs and swaying bedframes.

Louis threw a scratchy, stale blanket over her. "We'll catch up in the morning once Esther's packed away."

Rachel hummed. Sleep, sleep; finally. Away from the squeezing, smothering walls of the orphanage.

Free at last.

She closed her eyes and welcomed Esther's waiting fury.

NOW: FRIEDRICH

Friedrich felt as though he'd been hit by a train. Everything ached. If it wasn't for the constant *thud, thud, thud* of footsteps on wood, he might have slept for the rest of eternity.

"Oh, hello." The footsteps stopped. Friedrich didn't recognise the voice.

Where was he?

He blinked, stirring his fuzzy eyes into wakefulness. A wooden ceiling greeted him. There was a strong smell of wood.

How did he get here?

The pointed face of a teenager with thick dark hair and big teeth popped into sight. "Welcome to the land of the living."

Friedrich wanted to ask him who he was. He opened his mouth but only a croak came out.

The teenager didn't seem to notice. He was talking to someone Friedrich couldn't see. He didn't like that. He felt very vulnerable, lying there.

"How's that for skills, eh?" the teenager said. "Told you I knew what I was doing."

Something came flying through the air. Friedrich raised his hands to protect himself and instantly cried out. His shoulder.

Memories came flooding back. Being shot. The snow. Pain. Cold.

"Don't do that!" The teenager grabbed Friedrich's hands and lowered them. "You'll ruin all my hard work." He took the towel that had been thrown at him and put it to one side.

Just a towel.

"Time for some proper doctor questions to check your memory. Name?"

"Frie—" Friedrich cleared his throat and tried again. "Friedrich."

"Hello, Friedrich, I'm Mathieu. Age?"

Friedrich glared. He wasn't in the mood for silly questions. "Twenty-five."

"Okay, that'll do," Mathieu wisely surmised. "Just rest now. You lost quite a bit of blood and you've been in and out of consciousness for a few days."

"A few days?" That couldn't be right. Surely it had only been last night he'd been freezing his arse off in the snow?

Mathieu gave Friedrich a wry smile. "Let me get you some water."

His head disappeared from view and Friedrich heard two pairs of footsteps leave the room. All that remained was a deep rhythmic gurgle that sounded like someone blowing bubbles into a fish tank with a straw.

Friedrich slowly sat himself upright, leaning heavily on the wall behind him. Every movement pained his shoulder, and his head spun wildly, but lying down made him too defenceless.

It looked as if he was in a mountain hut. The floor,

232

ceiling and walls were all an orangey varnished pine and accounted for the smell, and the small window was drawn with thin red curtains. He had no idea whether it was day or night.

The bubbling originated from a bucket on the floor. A pink-tinged tube snaked up from it into a bundle of propped-up blankets on the bunk opposite. Wrapped inside the blankets, pale and still, lay Will.

Friedrich's heart reared and thudded. What had he missed?

He swung his legs over the side of the bunk; they had wasted to metal rods beneath the pyjamas he was wearing.

"Will?" he called huskily as he probed the floorboards with his feet.

No reply.

Friedrich grasped the bunk post with his uninjured hand and pushed himself up. Another wave of dizziness washed over him and he rested his head against it, resisting the urge to sit down again or be sick. He swallowed and closed his eyes, the sound of the slow rise and fall of bubbling focusing his mind.

He leant across and grabbed hold of the other bunk. His confused legs scattered as he stepped forward, sending him slithering painfully down to land next to the bucket.

"Oy." He touched Will's hand. It was like ice. His lips were a bruised purple, lashes dark against colourless cheeks.

What had happened?

"Come on, buddy, wake up."

"Whoa! What are you doing?"

Friedrich spun around and nearly passed out. Mathieu clattered to his side and caught him.

"You all right?"

Another stupid question. Even saying it brought to mind every single reason why Friedrich was not all right.

"Just breathe for me, okay? I need to save the oxygen for Will."

Friedrich's head fell back against the bunk, breathing long enough to catch enough air to speak. "What's wrong . . . with him?"

Mathieu refused to answer until he had tucked Friedrich back under his blankets and he'd taken a couple of sips of water.

"Tell me what happened."

Mathieu frowned. "You don't remember?"

"Not to me – to him," Friedrich growled.

Mathieu looked over his shoulder. "The bullet punctured his lung. I'm draining the blood and air, but it's tricky without an X-ray to work with."

"What?"

"It's a simple procedure. I've helped do them tons of times. Try not to worry."

That was easier said than done when concern was etched into Mathieu's face.

"When?"

Mathieu winced. "Okay – not tons of times, but enough. I'm a healthcare assistant at the hospital, but I know more about medicine than half the junior doctors. They lend me their textbooks."

That wasn't what Friedrich meant. He wanted to know when Will had been shot. It couldn't have been back at the manor. Surely he would have said something. Surely Friedrich would have noticed—

"You'd better rest." Mathieu's voice jolted him from his thoughts. He squeezed Friedrich's knee through the blankets, then strode out with the empty glass, leaving Friedrich to be lulled into an uneasy sleep by Will's bubbling, broken lungs.

NOW: FRIEDRICH

For the first time since his escape from the SDRC, Friedrich dreamt lucidly. He was back in his firewall prison. It used to be a safe space; he often dreamt about it when he was stressed or angry and eager to shut out the rest of the world. Now it felt more as though it were trapping him. The SDRC had made sure of that.

He was standing knee high in water, which slurped and steamed noisily out through a missing brick in the wall. A table stood near him with two fluffy ducklings waddling across the top, cheeping for their mother. Friedrich couldn't see her anywhere, and their cries were growing increasingly desperate, so he waded over. But before he could reach them, the ducklings gave up their tabletop search and plopped one at a time into the water, stumpy wings flapping uselessly. At first they bobbed like little corks, but their feathers were too new; they needed their mother's waterproof preening and quickly became waterlogged.

Friedrich scooped his hands in to help them, but it was like trying to fish drowning flies out of a bath. They washed through his fingers, cheeping and squirming to stay afloat as they drifted towards the hole in the wall, little legs whirring against the current. Friedrich plunged his hands into the water again.

Got you!

With a sound like a sock going up a vacuum cleaner, the duckling he hadn't caught was sucked through the hole.

At least he'd saved one. Though it wriggled as if he were the danger and *plop* – back in the water it fell. Seconds later, the rescued duckling shot through the hole too.

"No!" Friedrich slammed a fist against the wall. Water sloshed around his thighs. Somehow it was getting higher.

"Come on, Milo!"

Friedrich froze. That was Anja's voice – on the other side of the wall. He pressed his ear against the hot bricks.

"Anja!" he yelled back.

Anja called out to her brother again as if she hadn't heard Friedrich.

No, no, Friedrich calmed himself. *This is a dream. She's not real.* But even the possibility of seeing his children made up of memories pulled at his aching heart.

He looked about; there was no gate, nor ladder, nor anything else he could use to get to the other side. But never one to wait around for a miracle, he stuck his hands deep into the code and pulled. Numbers and letters showered into the water with a hiss, blistering his fingers with their heat. A deep grating of rock on rock came from somewhere inside the wall and it began leaning outwards. Bricks plummeted into the gushing water and Friedrich jumped back.

When the steam cleared, a jagged gap with a stairway of rubble had appeared in the wall. Friedrich's stomach twisted. What the hell was he doing? He'd just destroyed his dream defences over the notion of seeing some illusion of his kids.

Never mind; he could build them again.

He stepped up over the bricks and looked out.

Nothing. There was nothing outside. The escaping water was instantly swallowed up by a floor of hungry grey dust, like volcanic sand spread before him, as far as he could see. And he knew that out there wasn't his dream anymore.

A white-hot bolt of fear, more terrible than any bullet, sliced through Friedrich. Anja's voice hadn't come from him. It had been a trick, coaxing him to break down his wall, make him defenceless. But he hadn't felt any other minds, no one was attacking him, and there were no other dreams beyond the wall. What he saw before him had the empty feeling of space: a no man's land. Maybe it was still his head then – the perimeter between his dreams and whatever came next. But what was Anja doing out there?

"Anja? Milo?"

Silence echoed eerily after the crashing bricks. Friedrich was sure nothing existed beyond his wall except him. So how was he supposed to find them? What had they even been?

The dust sand plumed around his feet as he strode deeper into the empty grey desert. The ground was hot and grumbled like an overfilled belly. Smoke started hissing like fumaroles from bottomless cracks. With each step grew a feeling of being infinitely exposed. What was he doing out here? He needed to go back.

Suddenly, a shadow inside a plume of smoke swung out at him like a heavy weight on a pendulum, a flash of black in the corner of his eye. He ducked and heard a child's laughter. Milo.

When he looked up again, there was nothing there. Just billowing smoke and the sound of his racing heart.

"Milo!" Friedrich roared into the emptiness.

And then he noticed the ground was bulging and swelling like a rising cake. The grey sand trickled then poured down the climbing slope, revealing jagged stone and a giant ribcage of petrified wood that crumbled into ash upon meeting the air, leaving strange shapes and belching smoke in the dust.

"You're it!"

There was Anja's voice again. More laughter. She sounded as though she was playing chase. A flicker of a shadow raced behind Friedrich, but as before, when he turned around, it was only smoke.

"Show yourself, whoever you are!" Fear rose in Friedrich's throat. He couldn't feel anybody reaching in and scrambling his mind, but there had to be. He knew his own head and it didn't act like this. He turned on his heel and started downhill. No more. Time to get back to familiar territory; he had a wall to rebuild.

But the ground continued to swell up. Dust and smoke clouded the air into a hot, suffocating mass. He had no idea which direction he'd come from.

"What is this – some kind of test? I've no interest in it, so bloody well let me go back!" His temper rose quickly; that was how he coped nowadays. "And leave my kids out of it!"

The grumbling turned into a grating, groaning pressure. More voices – not just Anja's and Milo's – and shadows leapt in the smoke, whispering, laughing just out of reach. A bouncing ball. A shrieking swing. More smoke spiralled and clung, the horizon growing an ominous red tinge . . .

Friedrich roared. He yelled louder than he had ever before.

"STOP!"

And suddenly the air cleared and there was empty grey silence again. The only smoke came from a crater on top of the bulging hill, where a figure frantically swept it back inside with an oversized broom.

Will.

In a frenzy of fear and rage, Friedrich launched himself at him.

"GET OUT!" He seized Will by the collar until his knuckles shone around the fabric and shook him like a doll.

How dare he meddle with his mind! Will of all people should have known better.

It took Will a moment to realise what was going on. "Friedrich?"

Friedrich yelled again. Just noise. He needed control back. He'd destroy anyone who'd dare take advantage of his vulnerability.

Fight me!

But Will didn't fight. Friedrich hurled him down into the dust.

"GET OUT OF MY HEAD!"

Will lay on his back, trying and failing to take a breath, fingers clutching for the fallen broom.

Friedrich kicked it into the crater. The blazing red maw swallowed it in a lick of flame.

Will rolled over in panic, a silent "no" on his lips, until air gushed back between them. He coughed and spluttered, strangling tendrils of smoke coiling from his mouth, reaching for Friedrich. Will furiously swiped them away.

Friedrich reeled back. "What is this place? What did you do to my dreams?"

Will frowned distractedly, searching through his pockets. He pulled out a bobbin, and began spooling the smoke streaming from his lungs. "You're in my dream."

Friedrich flinched. "What?"

He had never gone into someone's dream before. That would be despicable, and he'd be a hypocrite.

"No, I can't be. I wouldn't," Friedrich said. "I heard my children."

Will paused his spooling, eyes widening. "Memories. You are searching for them, so my head tried to give them to you.

239

I'm sorry. I didn't realise. It's a bit of a mess in here at the moment."

Friedrich raised a hand to stop him as he tried to understand what he'd just heard. "Memories from the dreams you made for them at the orphanage – or my memories?"

"Both, I think . . ." Will coughed the last bit of smoke onto the bobbin and threw it into the crater. "Would you like to see them for real?"

What?

Will acknowledged his confusion with a careful smile.

Friedrich's mouth tried a variety of shapes before finding the right ones for the words he wanted to say. "Your dreams can reach them all the way out here?"

"Just about."

For a blissful second, Friedrich was about to reply with a resounding selfish "yes". Everything but the thought of seeing his children again vanished from his mind. Then he remembered himself and shook his head.

"Like you said: you're a mess." He shook off a wisp of smoke coiling up his leg. It seeped out of the crater like fog across the sea. "You need to stay away from other people's dreams. And I should leave too."

"They're too far away to be reached by anything other than dreams with complete stability," Will assured him, taking out another bobbin and spooling the writhing ribbon of smoke before it could reattach to Friedrich's leg. "Please – I owe you this at least."

"Owe me?" Friedrich couldn't believe what he was hearing. How could Will owe him anything? "No, I tell you what you do owe me. An explanation. Were you ever planning on telling me the police had shot you too?"

Will's face dropped. "I didn't realise."

"Even in the car? You could have waited there. A jail term for stealing a vehicle is much shorter than mine for murder."

"You would have died."

"What does it matter to you?" Friedrich clenched a fist, nails digging deep into the skin of his palm. People weren't supposed to do things like that for strangers. Did Will care so little about his own life? Didn't he have his own problems?

Will pressed his lips together and dropped his gaze. "They're too young to lose both parents."

They. Anja and Milo.

Friedrich couldn't reply harshly to that. Was that what they thought? That he and Brenda had abandoned them? The idea sickened him. They needed to know he was coming for them.

Before he could change his mind, he nodded at Will. "Okay, we can go and see them." He clenched his teeth, seething at himself for giving in to temptation. But this wasn't for him, he reminded himself. It was for his children.

Will came alive at that moment, bouncing up onto the balls of his feet. He threw the new bobbin into the crater and pointed behind Friedrich. He turned to see a door with red flaking paint standing alone on the grey slope. Will opened it, waving him through, but Friedrich held back. Here was someone else's dream, clear as day, and indeed daylight was streaming through that door. This went against everything he'd ever believed in . . .

He took a deep breath and stepped through.

NOW: FRIEDRICH

F riedrich had imagined playgrounds when he was young
– in the damp tarmacked corners of the children's home,
or in some overgrown field with a rusted slide and a swing
with no seat. He and the other kids had no trouble pretending
they were in paradise, building human catapults out of odds
and ends, or a cart to put the slip back into the slide. Sometimes all they'd had were each other's backs and an inventive
theme. A human pyramid reaching into space, a piggyback
rodeo, flying spin-arounds. Never had they come close to
imagining a playground like the one through the flaking red
door.

Climbing frames webbed the sky like ship's rigging;
swings hung high in the trees; a sorbet stand glistened
rainbow delights. There were sand tunnels, cliffs, Tarzan
ropes, hammocks, a giant fish belching out bubbles the size of
tractor wheels, and that was to name a few. The boy inside
him kicked and screamed to be let loose.

Children's laughter grew louder throughout the empty
place, until between the trees a little freckled face arrived.

"You'd better turn into something," Will said. "Adults aren't particularly welcome here."

"What do you mean?" Friedrich turned to him, but Will was no longer there. Instead, a blackbird hopped along the grass next to him.

"Anything you like; what do you fancy?" the bird tweeted.

Friedrich frowned. He wanted to see his children as himself.

More bodies appeared out of the trees, kids racing to their favourite attractions as fast as they could go. It wouldn't be fair to frighten them for the sake of his own. Okay, so what should he be? Anja loved cats, so . . .

The moment the thought crossed his mind, the world shot up towards him. Friedrich fell forward onto his hands, only they weren't hands anymore but paws. And, whoa, the sounds he could hear. Why did dogs get such a good reputation in the ear department? His cat ears could almost count every child's rushing footstep from where he was standing, though his feline nature disapproved of such mathematical challenges.

His heart stopped. Anja and little Milo skipped out of the trees, Milo leading Anja over to a massive boulder. They both looked so happy – skinnier, but happy.

He couldn't move. *Come on, legs.* What was holding him back? They were his children; he needed to be near them. But it all felt too good to be true. What if they vanished?

The blackbird fluttered up into a nearby tree. He was alone.

And then Anja saw him. She pointed straight at Friedrich, her face lighting up in delight, and pulled her brother in his direction instead.

"A cat, a cat," she cried as they came over.

What should he do? The cat in him wanted to run away.

Children generally weren't gentle animal petters. But the closer they came, the more love filled his heart. He had found them; they were okay. A deep rumbling vibrated through his body.

Anja laughed as she crouched down next to him. "He's happy to see us!" She ran her hand along his back.

Friedrich purred and purred.

"Cat," Milo cheered and stuck his thumb in Friedrich's ear.

Friedrich pulled his head away and instead rubbed the side of his face against his son's finger. Much better. Ooh, actually, that felt really good. He did it again. Milo crowed with joy.

A few of the other children had noticed him too and were coming over. The blackbird fluttered down from his tree and tweeted something Friedrich couldn't quite make out. They turned away.

His skin began to prickle. Milo was stroking him backwards. He could feel his fur sticking up in all directions. "Please stroke the other way."

His children froze.

"You can speak?" Anja gasped. How he loved her smile and the little dimple on her left cheek.

"I can? I can. Of course I can." Should he tell them it was him? No. What if they didn't believe him? What if they thought he was taking them home right away? How he wished he could. He wanted to sweep them up in his arms and hug them so tightly. But if he did that now, he'd never let them go again.

He jumped up onto Anja's knee and rubbed himself against her shoulder. Then he hopped onto Milo's back and rubbed the back of the boy's head.

The blackbird still sat on the grass. A feeble attempt at a wing flap caught Friedrich's eye. He was grounded, unable to get back up into his tree. Friedrich couldn't stay much longer. He jumped back to the ground.

"Your dad sent me," he purred to his kids.

"Papa?" they chorused.

"He's coming to take you home. No matter how long it takes, he's going to find a way."

"Where is he?" asked Anja.

"Making a plan. There are bad people who want to stop him, so he has to be prepared. But he's coming."

"I want Papa," Milo told his sister. Anja put her arm around him.

A cat heart wasn't big enough to hold all the love that welled in Friedrich. He licked Milo's knee.

Behind him, a boy picked the blackbird up and peered closely at him in his cupped hands.

Friedrich had to go.

"Look after each other." He trotted towards the bird and boy before saying goodbye could hurt too much.

"Hello, puss." The boy had muddy knees and twigs in his hair.

Friedrich meowed up at him.

The boy's face grew stern and he lifted the blackbird higher. "No, you can't eat him."

A little yellow beak peered out of the boy's hands. In a flurry of feathers, the blackbird flapped down onto Friedrich's shoulder.

Time to get out of here.

Friedrich marched back to the red door, bird on his back. He could feel the grubby-kneed boy's eyes on the pair of them as they went, until a peel of laughter came from behind. Friedrich stuck his tail in the air.

THEN: WILL

"Willem!"

Will woke with a start as his bedroom door slammed open. Papa stood there, dark, tall and very, very cross. He swept towards Will and yanked him out of bed.

"Papa?" Will blinked in the hall light, half asleep as his father dragged him into his own bedroom.

She was there. The blonde lady who didn't like him. Who wanted him to treat her like Mama. She was dressed ready for bed.

"What is this?" Papa let him go by the bedside. Mama's bedside. He threw back the covers.

Will stepped back. The sheets were covered in fat, juicy slugs. He would have laughed if he hadn't been so tired. Maybe the slugs had got cold. Papa looked at him, waiting for an answer.

"Slugs?" he replied. Surely Papa knew that though.

"Don't get smart," Papa growled. "What are they doing in the bed?"

Will shrugged. His father never used to get this cross. What was the problem?

"I will not have behaviour like this in my house, do you understand?" Papa yelled. "How old do you think you are – two?"

"Four."

"Then start acting like it. I told you to make Esther feel welcome here. It's very difficult for her to join a new family. What about that book she bought you? Is this any way to say thank you?"

Will shook his head, too afraid to say anything. Did Papa think *he* put the slugs in the bed?

"Go and get a tub from the kitchen and take them outside this instant!"

Will ran downstairs and returned with a plastic container. Silently, he scooped up the slugs – six in total, cold and slimy – and placed them in the tub. As soon as he finished, his father pulled the sheets off the bed and began to put new ones on. Will took the slugs downstairs and Esther followed. It was probably a good idea to put them at the end of the garden, in case they decided to come back. He slipped on his shoes and marched out into the night. He was only a little bit afraid of the dark, if he didn't think about it. The light from the doorway was bright enough to show the way. Will crouched down and popped the slugs one at a time into the flowerbed. Lots of leaves for them to munch on there.

Suddenly, the light vanished with a slam. Will whirled around. The door had closed. Now it was too dark. He ran as fast as he could back to the door and stretched up for the handle. He could just about reach it with the tips of his fingers, but he wasn't tall enough to grab hold.

He slapped his hands against the wood and cried out. But there was no sound from inside.

He tried again, more desperately. "Let me in!"

More silence.

Then the door creaked open and Esther stood there with raised eyebrows. "Where's the tub?"

He'd left it at the bottom of the garden in his fright. He pointed back to it.

Esther cocked her head. "Well, you'd better go and get it."

Tears spilt down Will's cheeks. It was too dark.

"It's just a suggestion, sweetie." Esther shrugged. "You don't want to make your father even angrier, do you?"

Will shook his head and raced across the grass, seized the tub and ran back again. Esther stayed in the doorway, blocking the entrance. She was looking at him as if he were a slug too. "Nobody likes a naughty little boy," she told him and went back upstairs to bed.

The next morning, Esther was down late for breakfast. Will had almost finished his toast and Papa was on his third cup of tea. Apparently, the baby inside Esther was making her feel unwell. But she looked okay when she pulled up the chair where Mama used to sit.

"OUCH!" Esther screamed and jumped off her seat.

In a flash, Papa was on his feet. Will dropped his last slice of toast into his orange juice.

"What's the matter? Are you okay?" Papa took her hands.

Esther looked down at the chair and rubbed her backside.

Will rescued his toast and climbed off his chair to look. Esther carefully lifted the cushion, gasped and removed two thumb tacks from the bottom of it.

"What is this?" She sounded astonished and looked at Will.

Papa turned black. His jaw clenched and his temple throbbed. Will had never seen him look like that before. Like a storm, he fell upon Will, chest heaving and arm raised.

NOW: WILL

Will screwed up his eyes against the light. It was only a table lamp, but its glare was intense and he hadn't the energy to turn his head away.

A hand shot out and grabbed it. "Sorry about that," came a voice, and with a clunk the lamp was placed on the floor.

A head peered over him. Louis's head. The real Louis, older than he remembered. For the first time, he wasn't in a dream. A year late, Will had made it to their hut. The corner of his mouth twitched.

Louis beamed. "Nice to meet you in the flesh at last."

Will opened his mouth to convey his thanks, but nothing came out. His chest felt as though someone were sitting on it. He reverted to smiling, eyes heavy.

"How're you feeling?"

He attempted a nod. It came out more like a spasm.

"Ah, and Rachel sends her greetings. She, uh . . ."

Will snapped to attention.

Louis turned red, wriggling in his shoes. "Oh, what the hell." He leant forward and kissed him on the cheek. "That's from her," he blustered.

Rachel...

He drifted back to sleep.

When he woke up again, Mathieu was there too, but still no Rachel.

"Rach . . . ?" he tried his voice.

Louis shook his head. "She's working down in the city hospital. Healthcare assistant. She wants to train as a nurse."

"She got us all the supplies we needed to treat you guys here." Mathieu beamed.

Will tilted his head slowly in acknowledgement. "Esther?"

"Bloody annoying," Louis replied.

"And getting stronger," added Mathieu. "Hello, by the way."

Will managed a smile for him. "Thank you."

Mathieu waved his hand. "Oh, no worries. It's the least we could do. Lawrence wants to say hi too; he's out chopping firewood at the moment."

Will felt himself falling asleep again, but he fought against it. "Stronger how?"

Louis sighed. "That's for another time. You gotta get better first."

"Is that why . . . she doesn't want to see me?"

"Who? Rach?" Mathieu blinked.

Will winced, afraid of the answer, but he had to know. Three nights after Rachel had first moved to the hut, he had contacted Louis's dream to arrange to join them, only to be told that Rachel had asked him to stay away, at least for a while. At first he was happy to. His sister had spent three years without him and had been through a lot. It wouldn't be right to push a reunion and all his emotions onto her as well.

But as time passed he wondered if maybe in those three years she had grown happier living without him. That was okay too – he respected her wishes – but he couldn't deny the rejection had hurt. He wasn't sure if he wanted to hear it confirmed.

Louis shook his head quickly, eyes wide as though he saw exactly what Will was thinking. "She wants to see you," he said. Mathieu moved away to give them some privacy as Louis knelt closer. "And wanted to. That first night, Esther vowed to make your life hell if you ever came near her. Like proper hell. Rachel thought it would be better this way. There's some serious stuff going on that she won't tell us about."

An unapproved laugh of either relief or sadness forced its way up Will's throat, turning into a cough that brought Mathieu running back. "She already was hell." He held a palm up to Mathieu to show he was okay.

But what could Esther have said or done to Rachel to make her change her mind about him coming to join them? Rachel knew he'd do anything for her. Why hadn't she spoken to him about it?

"Tell her . . . to come," he whispered. "Please."

Both Louis and Mathieu shook their heads furiously.

"No way are you strong enough," Louis said. "You want Esther using your head to contact Hubert? Tell him where to find you and your friend?"

Mathieu nodded. "You know they've got this plan they've been wanting to set in motion for years. Involving you."

Louis elbowed Mathieu sharply in the ribs.

"What," Mathieu hissed. "You think he's safer *not* knowing?"

"Rachel just wants to protect you," Louis said.

Protect him? No, that was all wrong. Esther was trying to protect herself. She had always been weaker when they had been together. Before Rachel had been forced to live in that orphanage, she'd started being able to dream. For short periods they could lock Esther away – sometimes keep her out entirely. That was why she had got Hubert to keep Will away for all these years. Didn't Rachel remember? What was Esther holding to her now?

But Louis was right. Esther would probably be too much to handle at the moment. "Just don't let her sleep whilst she's here . . ."

Louis hesitated. "That don't work anymore."

Will felt as though Louis had pushed a shard of glass into his abdomen. He shook his head as Louis blustered to put lightly what he'd implied. Was that what they meant by Esther getting stronger? She could come out in the day now too? Force Rachel to fall asleep?

"I'm sorry." Louis looked away. "You don't need no more stress. Rest."

"No." Will's breaths came painfully. "Please, I can help."

"Maybe so," Louis countered. "And maybe she can come up when you're better, but not now. I'm not gonna tempt Esther."

Will closed his eyes, too tired to argue. He felt so useless. A pathetic lump on a bed. And now, when his sister needed him more than ever, he was incapable of offering any assistance . . .

NOW: MAATJE

"El, who are you going to invite over for your birthday?"

"What?" Elinor spun in the kitchen doorway to face Maatje.

"Your birthday on Friday." Maatje waved the kiwi she was slicing at her sister, "Who would you like to invite? I'm planning a delicious meal with all your favourite things."

"I'm working." Elinor turned away again.

"Yeah, but only until seven, right?" Maatje wasn't giving up. "I'll have everyone come at eight – it'll be great."

Elinor wasn't listening, calling back to Maatje as she went down the hall. "Where are my black socks?"

"By the ironing board."

Elinor stuck her face into the kitchen again. "You ironed my socks?"

Maatje shrugged. "Yeah."

Elinor made a disgruntled noise and rolled her eyes before disappearing again. "You're worse than Aunt Marjorie."

Maatje had thought she was doing her sister a favour. The day she moved in last week was the first time she'd ever been in Elinor's flat and quite honestly she was worse than Dad at leaving things all over the place unwashed and gathering dust. The recycling bin had been full of old ready-meal trays, and the sink was more limescale than ceramic. Not a place any human could enjoy living in, let alone the two children Hubert had asked her to look after until Friedrich was brought to justice.

She'd been surprised Elinor had agreed to let her come at all. But after telling her the story of Friedrich, and his kids needing a place where he wouldn't be able to find them, Elinor almost demanded they come. She'd even given up her bed to Maatje and was sleeping on the sofa. Anja and Milo had the guest room, which had just been another dumping room, since Elinor had never had guests before. Maatje had done her best to make it a little more child-friendly and had taken the kids shopping to choose a few things they liked. A cuddly cat for Anja, a stuffed bear for Milo, and glow in the dark stars for the ceiling. Even Elinor joined them that night for their first stargazing session.

Elinor seemed to enjoy having Anja and Milo there. She worked more than she was at home, but made an effort when she was there to join in with a board game, read them a bedtime story, or if she was on a night shift, to watch a cartoon with them in the morning before crashing.

The kids had dealt with the upheaval well too. They were very quiet for two days, but Maatje was determined to make them feel as if it was a holiday to come to the city, and they'd responded. Today she was going to take them to the science museum, her favourite place when she was growing up. They now had a hands-on section where you could do your own experiments, partake in optical illusions and weigh yourself on all the planets in the solar system.

Though underneath it all, Maatje was just as worried and as confused as they were. But where they were waiting for their father – who for some reason they were sure was coming to take them home – she was waiting for news of Will. Nearly two weeks had passed and there had been nothing. She'd no idea where they'd got to. The police had found their stolen car near the top of a pass in the mountains, and she knew Friedrich had been shot – Hubert had told her about the blood out front. But every hospital had been checked and no one matching Friedrich's description had been admitted. This was another reason Hubert had been keen for Maatje to temporarily relocate to her sister's place. Elinor was in a prime position to hear any news on Friedrich. She worked at the biggest hospital in the country.

Maatje hoped his nonappearance meant the wound was superficial. As much as she blamed Friedrich for this mess, she was growing increasingly fond of his children. Like Will had said, they didn't deserve to spend the rest of their childhood in an orphanage.

"Maatje, Milo's tummy hurts." Anja came in, still in her pyjamas. The two of them had spent the last half an hour watching their daily dose of cartoons.

"That's probably because he hasn't had his breakfast yet," Maatje replied. "Are you coming to eat?"

Anja pondered her words before replying, "Okay." She went to fetch Milo.

Elinor came back in and snatched her badge from the worktop.

"You didn't answer my question," Maatje reminded her.

"What question?"

"Who you're going to invite—"

"For my birthday, yeah, yeah . . . I'll think about it."

"Ask them today," Maatje called after her as she waved goodbye. "I just need to know numbers."

"Bye, El," Anja and Milo chorused as they passed each other in the hall.

"Goodbye, goodbye."

The door slammed and Maatje dried her hands on a tea towel.

"Right then," she said as Anja and Milo sat themselves at the table. "Let's try and fix that tummy of yours, shall we?"

NOW: FRIEDRICH

Friedrich had slept fitfully for a few nights now. At first he thought it'd been because of Mathieu's infernal snoring and Louis's all night fidgeting. So he'd dragged the mattress off his bunk and into the main living area for a bit of peace. But still he found it hard to drift off, and when he did, it was the same dream he'd had for the past four nights: paddling a bed across a canopy of trees.

The wind howled the bare branches into grabbing, ripping fingers, seizing his oar and pulling him into their reaching grasp.

"No!" He battered the branches back. He couldn't let them win.

A human hand struggled amongst the twigs, stretching helplessly up. Will's hand. Suffocating somewhere beneath the writhing wood. Friedrich battered the hand back too. There was no time to stop.

He paddled on. The wind grew stronger. Pushing him back, calling with Mathieu's voice . . .

"Hey . . . hey!" Mathieu was poking him with the broom handle and a loud whisper.

The first night Friedrich had been awoken by Mathieu for his pain medication, he'd lashed out, convinced for a moment he was back in the SDRC. Ever since, all three of the boys had been wary around him, and Mathieu now used the broom to prevent himself receiving another bloody nose. Friedrich pushed the handle away with a growl.

"It's your watch."

Friedrich shook his head. He couldn't face another three hours of sitting and watching Will struggle to breathe. They'd taken the chest tube out a week ago, but he was still too ill to leave unattended. Mathieu was worried he might have caught an infection.

"What antibiotics do you need?" Friedrich sat up.

"Huh? He already took some tonight," Mathieu replied.

Friedrich tried not to lose his temper. "I meant the stronger ones you talked about. He's not getting better."

Mathieu shook his head. "Louis can get them tomorrow – he's a cleaner in the hospital. You can't go anywhere; the police are still after you."

Friedrich gritted his teeth. The dream still lingered. Along with a desperation to go. He'd been cooped up in this hut for weeks. He needed to do something useful. "I'll blend in perfectly with my arm in a sling. I'll just feign a temperature and get them to give me the drugs we need."

Mathieu snorted. "You're on their database. Got a nice picture in A&E reception too. But sure, go if you want to, just don't lead them back here – at least let's keep Will safe."

"Will's not safe," Friedrich snapped. "He needs proper medical attention, not your DIY botch job."

"I saved his life!"

Friedrich sneered. "Not good enough! You're a smart kid; I can see it when you look at him. You know it's not good enough either. What is it that's so important to protect him from that you're willing to risk his life?"

"Jail, for starters – for saving your skinny arse!"

"I didn't ask for that!" Friedrich shouted back. "And if you don't have a better reason—"

"What on earth is going on?" Louis blinked in the doorway. Lawrence yawned behind.

"Freddie here wants to expose us all by getting himself caught."

"Don't call me that."

"You're no use to no one caught," said Louis.

Friedrich sighed, not about to start explaining himself. He elbowed past them.

"Where are you going?" asked Mathieu.

"To start my watch," he retorted, and vanished into Will's room.

He went straight to the window. Not because there was anything to see – it was dark as pitch outside – but because he didn't want to talk to anyone else. He could see Will in the reflection: a pillow propping him up against the wall of his bunk; those too-bright, glazed eyes considering him thoughtfully. At least he didn't have to meet them. Friedrich was too much of a coward to turn around.

This wasn't his fault. Will was an adult. He'd chosen to follow him on his suicide escape.

But Will wouldn't be trapped in the middle of nowhere whilst some nutter kids played doctors if Friedrich had just agreed to turn himself in at the hospital, or surrendered to the police at the manor . . . Maybe he still could? Take Will with him whilst the boys were asleep?

It was a ridiculous idea. There was no way he could drag Will through the snow with his injured shoulder. And the cold would only make Will's lungs worse.

As if on cue, Will gave a wet cough. The suddenness of it

must have surprised him; he put a hand out against the bedcovers to balance himself.

Back came the dream. The drowning hand he'd struck aside.

Friedrich flinched.

He wanted to leave him. He needed to get back to finding his kids. The sicker Will was, the less chance he'd tag along for the ride.

Friedrich adjusted his eyes to look through the window again. Perhaps he was imagining he could make out the mountaintops. How soon would it be until sunrise?

"Wait until you're healed, my friend." Will's voice was low and coarse with misuse.

Did he read minds now as well?

Friedrich didn't have a plan though. Only a massive feat of kidnap would get Anja and Milo back now, especially as the orphanage would probably be guarded by the police.

Will shivered, coughed again and let his head fall back onto the pillow, eyes closing.

"Hey!" Friedrich spun around.

Will lifted his head once more and opened his eyes, but it took time for them to focus. Dark hair clung to his damp forehead.

"It's getting worse, isn't it?" Friedrich had nursed a feverish Anja and Milo enough times to know the signs.

"May I have another blanket please?" Will breathed.

Friedrich's palm didn't need to reach the man's forehead to feel the heat radiating from him. "Will, you're burning up. Does Mathieu know?"

Will was silent.

"I'm getting him." Friedrich left the room before he said anything he might regret.

NOW: RACHEL

"Rachel, Louis, come in." Elinor stepped back to let them inside her apartment.

"Happy birthday!" Rachel handed her a bouquet of deep purple and cream flowers that she'd spent the entire journey trying not to squash.

"Oh my gosh, they're gorgeous!" Elinor exclaimed and promptly buried her nose into the flowers.

They wiped their feet and followed Elinor into the kitchen. Ben, another student doctor, built like a brick, but with the face of a gentle beaver, was already there talking with a woman Rachel didn't know. By her looks she had to be some sort of relation to Elinor.

"Hello, hello," the woman greeted.

Elinor introduced them. "This is my sister, Maatje, who nominated us all this evening to be the guinea pigs for her sudden Master Chef urges. Maatje, this is Rachel and her boyfriend Louis, who work with me at the hospital."

Maatje smiled and shook their hands warmly. "It's great to meet you both. What can I get you to drink?"

Rachel liked Maatje at once. She had a genuity that

verged on the edge of dottiness. She leapt about the kitchen grabbing glasses as if there was nowhere on earth she'd rather be, no past to dwell on, no future to worry about; she was completely there to enjoy Elinor's party. Rachel felt a little envious. How she longed to be so free. Ben looked equally infatuated, watching Maatje with a smile on his face.

"Will your parents mind if you have a glass of something?" Elinor asked.

Louis shook his head. "I'd better not – I'm driving."

Rachel already had enough to deal with, having Esther messing in her mind. "Do you have any juice?"

Maatje beamed over the countertop. "I've made smoothies!"

As soon as they were all partnered with drinks and Louis's cheek had been pecked by Elinor when he'd slipped her a bottle of her favourite amaretto, Maatje ushered them all over to the table. Rachel sat sandwiched between Louis and Elinor on a narrow bench strewn with cushions in an attempt to make it more comfortable.

Elinor winked at her. "Thanks for coming."

One of the things Rachel loved about Elinor was that she constantly let people know she saw what they were doing and appreciated it. At work, she had the wonderful ability to acknowledge her patients fear or pain and empower it back to them, letting them own their recoveries and apprehensions, rather than feeling victim to the hospital machine. For someone who had always hated the victim inside herself, Rachel found this support invaluable. She wondered who Elinor's support was. Maatje, perhaps.

"I didn't know you had kids," Ben laughed, nodding at the paintings magneted to the fridge door.

Elinor laughed too. "I don't. They're Maatje's charges and asleep across the hall – so no drunken singing later on please."

"You work with many children, or just these ones?" Ben looked pleased to have a topic he could ask Maatje about.

"Just these." Maatje breezed from across the room. "Everyone ready for starters?"

The reply was a lot of nodding and murmurs of agreement.

The meal tasted divine and was devoured almost to the last crumb. The stunning strawberry birthday gateau earnt Maatje a hug from Elinor. Rachel held Louis's hand throughout. It was nice to spend time with him after weeks of having to live apart. Since Will had arrived, she'd been residing in a renovated garden shed in the foothills, far enough away from civilisation to keep Esther contained. She was spending most of her wages on rent and a taxi to and from work. She'd stopped taking the bus ever since Esther had pushed out one evening. Rachel had been shaken awake at the end of the route, miles from the city, terrified Esther might have found a trail of dreams back to Hubert. She wouldn't let Esther have her brother. She'd spend every penny she ever earnt for the rest of her life ensuring that.

No, stop it. She'd promised herself she wouldn't think about any of this tonight.

"So *are* you a chef?" Ben was asking Maatje, red-faced with wine.

"Oh no. It's just nice to have people to cook for," Maatje replied. "I'm not going to all the trouble of presenting strawberries like that for myself now, am I?"

"You're not seeing anyone then?"

Louis snorted and Rachel elbowed him as she barely suppressed a laugh. Poor Ben – he'd been at it all night, and the drunker he'd become, the less he realised Maatje just wasn't interested.

"A toast!" Maatje got to her feet and raised her glass. "To twenty-one years of the best sister in the world."

Rachel quickly raised her own glass, and Elinor hid behind her hand, smiling.

"Cheers."

"Louis, would you like some more cake?" Maatje continued, refusing to sit down.

"God, no, I'm fit to burst. Thanks tho—" His mobile cut him off. "Excuse me." He glanced briefly at the number. It was Mathieu's. "Better take this." And he went out into the hall.

What did Mathieu want? Knowing him, it could be he'd run out of cereal, but Rachel's thoughts automatically went to her brother and her chest tightened.

"Rachel?" The cake slice waved in front of her. "Hello?"

Rachel blinked. "Sorry, what?"

"Cake? Would you like some more?"

She shook her head. "No. Thanks." She glanced once more at the door before smiling at Maatje.

"Ben?"

"It was divine, but I must decline."

"Go on, El . . ."

Elinor plucked a strawberry off the top, popped it into her mouth and grinned. "I'm good."

Maatje sank back into her chair with a contented smile and again Rachel felt envious.

Just enjoy the moment, Rachel, she told herself. *That's all you have to do. Everything's fine. You're overthinking again.*

And then Louis came back in, looking as though somebody had died.

Rachel leapt to her feet, blood draining to her toes. She rushed over to him.

"What is it?" she breathed.

The rest of the party stared. Louis smiled at them and pulled her into the hall. He shut the door with a click.

"Will's fever is worse."

Rachel had been expecting him to say this, but her stomach still dropped. "Wh-what are we going to do?"

Louis shook his head. "We've gotta take him to the hospital."

"No – they'll find him!" Rachel tried to shush Louis, in a futile attempt to stop Esther hearing.

"Rach, we haven't got a choice. Mathieu's really worried. The antibiotics aren't working, and we all knew the risks of trying to treat them ourselves. We're lucky it was only Will who picked up an infection."

Rachel shook her head. "There has to be something else."

Louis took her shoulders. "Rachel, I know you haven't told me about all of your mum's threats, but you gotta trust me. He goes down, and you come back up to the hut. She won't be able to tell anyone nor do anything to him, okay?"

Rachel felt panic rising inside. And Esther. Esther was pressing against her consciousness. Not to drag her to sleep, but like an ear to a wall, listening intently. She shook her head again. "Elinor. We'll ask Elinor to look at him. She'll be able to tell if he needs to go to the hospital or not. If we can help him at home, isn't it better not to move him?"

Louis shook his head, but she knew it wasn't because he disagreed with her. The journey on that bumpy mountain road in a rickety 4x4 wouldn't be good for Will. He'd have to be carried for a mile first too. No, Louis was shaking his head because she wanted to bring Elinor into it; because Rachel was fixed on a hope that everything would be okay if they just held out. She could see in his eyes he didn't think it would, but he wouldn't say it aloud. He was trying to protect her.

"She'll keep the secret," Rachel assured him.

Louis sighed. "Okay, let's get her."

Relief washed over Rachel like a cold bath, misplaced though it was.

Concerned, Elinor joined them in the hallway. Maatje

and Ben thankfully didn't say anything, giving only a couple of anxious glances. Ben went back to trying to impress Maatje with a magic trick.

"Is everything all right?"

Rachel trembled, not sure she could trust herself to speak. "No . . . I . . . We . . ."

"Her brother was badly injured," Louis took over. "A friend of ours thought he could take care of it, but he's picked up an infection or something and it's getting worse. We were wondering if you'd come and take a look?"

"Me? You should take him—"

"There are people looking for him," Louis stopped Elinor. "Hospital has to be the last resort."

Elinor stared at him, first in surprise, then her eyes narrowed as though trying to work out his intentions through his gaze.

Please, please, please.

"Okay." She broke the tension. "Let me get my things."

"Thank you." Rachel let out all her breath.

Elinor stopped. "If you're in trouble, you should call the police, you know?"

Rachel and Louis nodded in unison and Elinor left to get her bag.

NOW: WILL

Will could hear people in the room with him, somewhat distantly, beyond a haze he could not shake. There was a voice he did not recognise.

"Hello, Will." The new voice came over to his bed. "I'm erm . . . almost Doctor Finkel. I've come to help."

Will lifted his heavy eyelids to take in the face of the gentle-voiced woman with Maatje's surname. He smiled. She looked like Maatje too; the same smattering of freckles across a slightly turned-up nose. Her eyes were smaller though and her hair blonde, but it had to be her sister. Was this the Elinor he'd so often heard about? Small world.

"Don't look too pleased to see me. I've been out in the snow for half an hour; my hands are going to be pretty cold."

"We were meant to meet . . . before," Will whispered, trying to wriggle back from the invisible force gripping his chest.

"Oh yeah?" Almost Doctor Finkel pulled up a chair and began rummaging through her bag. She pulled out a stethoscope and hung it around her neck. "Now, Will, if you don't mind, I'm going to take a look at this injury of yours."

Will made what he hoped was an affirmative noise and Almost Doctor Finkel got to work. She was right: her hands were cold. But his skin was so warm even a hot-water bottle would have made him shiver.

"You want to tell me what you were doing at the receiving end of a gun?" Almost Doctor Finkel asked conversationally.

Will wanted to laugh, but gave a cough instead. Only a Finkel would phrase a question like that. "Got in the way."

"Mmm." Almost Doctor Finkel disapproved. Heck, he disapproved. It hurt a lot.

The cough returned with a vengeance. Almost Doctor Finkel pulled back her hands as Will hacked. From the corner of the room, Mathieu hurried over with a plastic tub. Out of Will's throat came a thick creamy yellow mucus splattered with dark red flakes. It looked almost as horrible as he felt. He crashed back against his pillow, aching and exhausted.

Almost Doctor Finkel peered into the tub before Mathieu took it away. Both were spinning in his vision as if he were on a roundabout. She was saying something to Mathieu, but he couldn't quite make sense of it.

"Elinor," he gasped.

Almost Doctor Finkel placed a cool hand on his burning brow. "You're okay. What is it?"

"Hard to . . . breathe."

"I know – it's going to be." She brushed her thumb over his hair then put her stethoscope into her ears. "I'm going to listen to your lungs now, okay? Just take slow breaths; don't force anything." Her voice was calm. She wasn't worried, so why should he be?

But it was gradually getting worse. He couldn't get enough air to allow for any exertion. He hoped he wouldn't have another coughing fit.

"I'm going to lean you forward so I can listen around the back, okay?"

He gave her a tiny nod.

The whole world lurched again, hot and heavy, as Mathieu moved him so Almost Doctor Finkel could reach his back. He closed his eyes and waited for it to pass.

Breathe in. Breathe out.

"That's it. Well done," Almost Doctor Finkel said. Will felt himself tilting back again. "But we're going to get you to a hospital I think. You're going to need an X-ray and to get some of that pus drained off."

Will cracked his eyes open. She was looking at Mathieu, whose expression was serious. He nodded.

"You did great, doc," Will assured him.

Mathieu twitched a smile. "Not great enough, mate. Sorry." Then to Almost Doctor Finkel: "I'll get the guys ready to help move him."

She nodded and he left.

"Thank you," Will breathed.

Almost Doctor Finkel gave a half-smile and took off her stethoscope. "Tell me – how did you know my name?"

Will swallowed a cough. "We were meant to meet . . . before."

"Ah yes – you said." She laughed. "Meet when, exactly?"

"Years ago. Hotel." He struggled to stay awake.

"A hotel?" Almost Doctor Finkel's eyebrows shot up, then she laughed again. "Louis must have said it when I first came in, right?"

Will felt himself falling down into sleep. Almost Doctor Finkel's hand squeezed his and he heard the door open again. Louis's voice.

"If we're gonna take him to the hospital, we can get him in under a different name, right?"

Almost Doctor Finkel's hand tensed. "What?"

"Please," Louis said. "No one can know he's there."

"Because of those people looking for him?" Almost Doctor Finkel sounded irritated. "Who are they exactly?"

"I'll tell you everything, doc, I promise, just not yet. Not now. Can you do it?"

She sighed. "This is crazy. I'll see what I can do."

"Thank you. You're a legend. We won't be a minute." Louis left again.

Will pressed her fingers gently. An apology. "Your sister asked . . ." he murmured. "Take you . . . surfing with horses."

NOW: MAATJE

Maatje was in bed when Elinor returned home, and was woken by the sound of the shower next door. A quick look at her phone told her it was past one in the morning. She lay there listening to the water spray against the glass, wondering what the emergency had been. Now she was awake, the question wasn't going to let her go back to sleep again, so she listened for the shower to stop, a towel to fold open and the sound of toothbrush on teeth to begin before she slipped out of bed and knocked gently on the bathroom door.

Elinor looked around as she came in then spat in the sink. "Did I wake you?"

Maatje shrugged. "Is everything okay?"

Elinor wiped her mouth on her towel and nodded. "Yeah."

"What happened?"

"Can I dry in peace?" Elinor pulled her towel tighter around herself and waved her sister out of the room.

"Happy birthday!" Maatje grinned as she disappeared, wandering back to bed and burying her face in the pillow.

She lay there awhile, thinking only about how long she

could lie like that before her brain decided it needed more oxygen than she was supplying. Turned out it was about two minutes. She heard the door open and turned over to breathe.

"Hey, El." Maatje jerked up in surprise.

Elinor shut the door quietly and came over to the other side of the bed.

"What time are you working tomorrow?"

"Not until two," Elinor replied, pulling back the covers. "There's an animal sanctuary about six miles from here having an open day tomorrow. I was thinking of taking the kids there in the morning. Give you a chance to catch up on some work."

Maatje raised her eyebrows. She hadn't realised Elinor had grown fond enough of Anja and Milo to offer to take them out during her time off. "You'd like to do that?"

Elinor nodded and clambered into bed next to Maatje. "They'd love it. And to be honest, I've been wanting to check out the place for years."

Maatje laughed, though more in amazement than anything else. Her sister had just climbed into bed with her. She hadn't done that since they'd been kids. She refrained from pointing it out, in case it scared her off, but then wasn't sure what to say instead.

"Thank you for such a lovely evening. I had a really nice time," Elinor said.

"Good, that was the point."

"Sorry I had to rush off. I didn't think I'd be so long, but they lived at the arse end of nowhere. Did Ben stay much later?"

"Not really." Maatje grimaced. "Though he tried to."

Elinor chuckled. "He liked you."

"Hmm," Maatje made a noncommittal noise.

"And he's a decent chap."

"I'm sure he is, but he's not . . ." He's not what? Her

272

teenage crush she'd just discovered was real after years of believing he was a dream? *Yeah, keep on dreaming Maatje.* "I'm not interested."

Unlike Mum and Aunt Marjorie would, Elinor didn't press her. Instead, she considered her curiously in the hope she might expand on her answer. Once, Maatje would have shared everything with her sister. But she didn't want Will to come between them again. Not when it seemed things might finally be improving.

"Well, you're in good company." Elinor snuggled down into the duvet. "I think I got asked out by a patient today. Though he was so out of it he sounded as if I'd stood him up."

Maatje giggled and lay down too. "It's the gratitude. You saving lives. You must get asked out a lot."

"Not seriously, no."

"This one was serious?" teased Maatje.

"No, it was odd. I was supposed to meet him – and you actually – at some hotel to go surfing with horses."

"How do you go surfing with—" Maatje stopped. "Wait. Meet me?"

Elinor shrugged. "It was a little strange that he knew I liked horses, right?"

Maatje flapped her hands at her sister to stop her. "El . . . me?" Her heart was suddenly hammering.

The hotel.

Sure, it could be any hotel, but . . .

"Well, he said sister, so I guess that'd be you," Elinor chuckled. "Maybe he was hoping for a double date."

Maatje almost choked on her voice box as she tried to talk. "What . . . what did he look like?"

"You can't go on a date with one of my patients!" Elinor half laughed. "But he's okay-looking, actually. Even if he looked like death warmed up. Has the bluest eyes . . ."

Maatje felt sick. "He's in hospital?"

"I had him sent there, yes. His friends were trying to home-treat him." Elinor rolled her eyes.

"Home-treat him for what?"

Elinor opened her mouth, but then stopped and looked at her. "Are you okay?"

Maatje nodded. She swallowed. "I'm being silly, and I know you can't tell me his name because of patient confidentiality, but is his . . . does it begin with a W?"

Elinor shifted back in the bed and stiffened. Maatje closed her eyes. That was all the answer she needed.

"You know him?"

Maatje nodded. "Will, right? Dark hair, about my height?"

"Yes." Elinor breathed.

"He wasn't asking you out. And you didn't stand him up. That hotel was the dream hotel I wanted to take you to. We had a surprise planned for you."

"It's that Will?" Elinor sounded less confused than she looked. "But you told me he wasn't real."

"I didn't think he was. Turns out he was the Manager all along."

"A boy?"

"El, please tell me, why is he in hospital?"

"Damn!" Elinor sat up. "Maatje, you have to promise you won't tell anyone about this."

"What? Why?" Maatje sat up too.

"Apparently, there are some people looking for him. I didn't ask any more; I was just there to treat the patient."

"Yeah, *I'm* looking for him," Maatje replied. "And the police."

"What?"

"I'll tell you all about it, I promise. Just tell me he's okay? What happened to him?"

274

Elinor set her chin. "As long as *no one* comes looking for him and he stays and gets the treatment he needs, he should be fine."

Maatje shot a glare her sister's way. Was that a warning? "I'm not going to take him out of hospital. Not if he needs it. So why does he need it?"

Elinor shook her head. "I've told you too much already, especially since they asked me not to say anything. I'm sorry. I didn't think you'd actually know the guy."

"I'm your sister!"

"He's my patient!" Elinor snapped.

"He's my friend!"

Elinor got out of bed. Cold air wafted under the sheets and Maatje snatched the covers back over herself.

"I need to go to sleep. You can explain this whole thing to me tomorrow – when I get back with the kids. In the meantime . . ." She pointed at Maatje. "Don't go looking for him."

In reply, Maatje flicked off the bedside light and dived underneath the duvet. How dare Elinor tell her what to do. Especially when she knew nothing about it.

If the police found Will now, he'd go to prison, no questions asked. She wondered if Hubert knew of a private hospital where he'd be safe. Hubert had promised Maatje that if they found Will before the police did, he'd protect him from them. They both understood the situation he'd been in and why he'd taken the car. Just as long as Friedrich wasn't there too.

She waited until the door clicked shut and Elinor's footsteps padded down the hall, then reached for her phone and tapped in Hubert's number.

NOW: FRIEDRICH

F riedrich was stretching in front of the log burner when another strange blonde girl walked through the door. Exercising to get his shoulder and strength back was the only thing he had to do whilst trapped in this hut, and with all the fuss of getting Will to hospital a few hours earlier, he was feeling too hyped to sleep.

The newcomer glowered at him as he got to his feet and pulled on his top. Louis stood next to her, looking pleased with himself.

"Who's this now?" Friedrich grunted, jutting his jaw in the girl's direction.

"Rachel," Louis said. "Rachel, this is—"

"Friedrich, yeah, I know." Rachel eyed him as though sizing him up.

"Your girlfriend Rachel?" Friedrich couldn't believe it. "Anyone else you'd care to invite?"

"It's my house – I'll invite who I like," Louis replied. "Besides, Rachel lives here; she knows everything. She got stuff from the hospital for you both."

Rachel gave him a smile that was somewhere between a

sneer and a grimace. "You're welcome." She pulled off her coat, strode past him into the kitchenette and filled up the kettle.

Friedrich blinked. He was getting used to people disliking him, but Rachel's instant aversion set a new record.

Completely ignoring Friedrich, she went over to the burner, put the kettle on top and slumped into one of the four beanbags that were the hut's substitute for sofas.

"Rach?" Louis asked tentatively.

Rachel didn't look at him. "Please, I don't want to think about it."

Uh oh. Friedrich didn't fancy being in the middle of a domestic. He wiped the sweat from his forehead with his sleeve and headed for the bedroom, nodding at Louis as he went.

"You know you're still welcome here, right?" Louis told him. "As long as you need."

Friedrich was surprised. He knew they had only been sheltering him for Will's sake. "I'll be out of your hair tomorrow."

"We can help. You don't have to go it alone."

"*No*, we can't." Rachel spun around sharply, summing up Friedrich's thoughts exactly.

"I don't need your help," he replied. "And your girl-friend's right. You don't want to end up like the last idiot who jumped into my business."

Rachel leapt off the beanbag, turning a violent shade of purple. "He saved your arse!"

"My arse is my responsibility!" Friedrich scowled before the guilt could rear its ugly head again.

"And my brother is mine. So I'm warning you: don't go near him again. Don't even speak of him. You don't deserve to."

Brother?

Friedrich raised his eyebrows. "That's a lot of don'ts from someone who wasn't around whilst said brother was fighting for his life."

Rachel flinched as if she'd been slapped.

Louis stepped between them. Friedrich had never seen him look threatening before. "Maybe you should zip in for the night. You can leave in the morning."

It was a stupid argument anyway. Friedrich turned and continued towards the bedroom.

"Friedrich?"

Friedrich looked back. All the toughness had vanished from Louis's face. He looked like the scared teenager he was. "Don't say where Will is – if they catch you again, okay? They can't know."

Friedrich grunted. "How big of a jerk do you think I am?"

Louis shook his head as if Friedrich had misheard him. "I mean it. They find him – by your lips or from others – and your dreams will never be your own again."

Rachel stiffened. "Louis . . ."

Friedrich leered towards him. "Is that a threat?"

Despite the fear, Louis met a steady gaze. "A fact. They've been studying Will from afar for years – to build a machine to hijack and expand those dreams he creates. Hubert wants to control the dreams of the entire country."

Friedrich took a moment to process this and then snorted. "Yeah."

But Louis and Rachel weren't laughing.

Did they really believe themselves? Was this why they'd been so reluctant to get Will the help he needed?

"Yeah," he said again and made for his bunk.

Deluded idiots.

Friedrich dreamt he was paddling on the bunkbed again, battling wind and branches. He tried to ignore the struggling fingers of Will's hand. But it followed him no matter how hard he paddled. Eventually he could bear the pathetic sight no longer and reached down to pull Will onto the bed with him.

His hand went straight through.

He battered back the branches twisting around Will's fingers, and tried again.

But it was as if he wasn't even there.

"Come on, Will." Friedrich spun the oar around and shoved the shaft into Will's palm. "Grab hold."

But the oar slipped between Will's twitching, disappearing fingertips, until the branches covered him like hungry worms.

Friedrich bashed them with the oar again and again, yelling into the roaring wind and clattering trees.

It wasn't his fault! It wasn't!

"Not the prettiest birdsong in the forest, is it, darling?" a voice mused, cool and glassy.

Friedrich whirled round. A blonde woman sat at the end of the bed, so white and icy she might have been an illusion.

"Who are you?"

He must have conjured some sort of warped version of Rachel to make him feel worse about himself.

The woman dipped a pale hand into the writhing tendrils of tree and fished out Will's limp wrist between two manicured nails as if it were a dirty sock. "This what you want, is it, sweetie?"

Friedrich lunged, but again his hand swiped straight through Will's. Only the icy, older Rachel could touch him. He hated her even more.

"Pull him up," he demanded.

"Say please," she purred, a semi-seductive smirk on her

face. Then she tutted. "Honey, look at all that guilt eating away at you."

Friedrich narrowed his eyes. "I said, *pull him up*."

"But could you bear to see it?" she challenged. "His corpse at your hands."

The part of him that believed in the dream reeled in horror. "It's not as bad as that," he said. But the hand hung pale between her fingers. Friedrich didn't want to see the rest of him.

"Oh, sugar, you mustn't fret. It could have been a whole lot worse . . ."

How could it be worse?

"Oh, say you had rescued your children that night – whose arms would we be fishing out instead?"

As she spoke, Will's hand began to shrink and peel in two. The woman caught a toddler's hand in her other as it fell away from the first – slightly larger – arm, fingertips smudged with felt-tip stains.

Anja. Milo.

He dived towards his children, legs tangling in the bunk sheets.

"It's okay – I'm here. Papa's here." His hands passed through theirs. He couldn't touch them, couldn't save them from the smothering sea of knurled wood. "Pull them up!"

The woman's lips curled at the demand snarled in her face. "Honey, you really have to work on your manners."

Friedrich caught himself before he could disgrace himself by begging. This woman was playing him. He couldn't bear that she was touching his children. But they weren't really his children, were they? *It's just a dream.*

"Yes, it is," the woman sighed.

Friedrich balked. She could hear his thoughts?

She showed her sparkling teeth. "Does that frighten you?"

Friedrich glared. "No."

"How about this?" She opened her fingers wide and Anja's and Milo's tiny hands flopped into the sea of reaching wood, instantly swallowed.

"NO!" Friedrich lunged, but he was helpless, hopeless, useless.

"But they're just a dream, sugar. Wouldn't you prefer it if I told you where your children really are?"

Friedrich shoved the anguish down and made a noise he hoped sounded scornful. "I already know where they are."

The woman raised her eyebrows. "Oh, they're not there anymore. Why would they still be kept at the first place you'd come looking for them? No – they've been moved to a far more hidden, yet far more accessible place. Do you want me to tell you?"

"If I don't know, how can you know?" Friedrich retorted.

"Unless . . ." The woman's smile grew wider.

"Unless . . . unless you're not from my head, but . . ." Friedrich snatched up the oar.

"Whoa, slow down there, sugar."

Too late. Friedrich swung. The oar sliced straight through the woman, splintering against the bed-post at the bottom of the bunk.

The woman shrugged, untouched. "I did try to warn you."

"Get out of my dream!" Friedrich yelled. "How'd you get in without me realising?"

The woman cocked her head. "Should I leave first and then answer your question?" she smirked. "Freddie, darling, you're forgetting I can see right through you. You can't kick me out because you oh so desperately want to know where your two little life joys are being held. Am I right? Of course I'm right."

"GET OUT!" Friedrich bellowed, swinging again. Again he hit the bed-post, smashing the oar into a mangled stick.

"Sugar, don't you know it's very impolite to wave things through a lady?" The woman shook her glossy hair out. "You're scared, I know. You want so badly to find out where they are, but you know if you do, you'll be on the run for the rest of your life – for their lives. You'll be endangering them just for your own selfish desire to see them again." The woman tapped her porcelain finger against her cheek in mock thought. "And maybe they'd be happier without you? Look how violent you've become."

With a roar, Friedrich started forward, hands splayed, teeth bared, ready to rip and destroy. Real or not real, he would tear this intruder to shreds. "THEY'RE *MY* KIDS. THEY DESERVE TO BE WITH ME!"

He fell through her, almost tumbling head first off the end of the bunk. He snatched at the damaged bed-post and lurched to a stop, inches above the canopy of clawing branches.

The woman looked bored. "The quicker you answer my question, the quicker I can go. Would you or would you not like to know? You're giving me very mixed signals here."

Friedrich clung to the bed-post, panting. Yes, yes, he wanted to know . . . needed to know. But he couldn't—

The woman clicked her tongue disapprovingly. "Honey, that's no way to ask. I've come all this way; a little politeness wouldn't go amiss."

A low growl vibrated in his throat, but he swallowed it.

"Please . . ." He seethed internally as his lips betrayed him. "Tell me."

NOW: MAATJE

"What's he in for?" The receptionist's face already held the expression that her time was being wasted. She had a glazed, slack look and annoyance tinged her voice.

"Actually, I'm not sure. I was only told he was taken here in a bit of an emergency."

The receptionist blinked. "Well, either it was an emergency or it wasn't – there's no 'bit'."

"Then yes, it was an emergency," Maatje guessed. She'd already dug a huge hole for herself. All that was left was for the receptionist to push her inside it.

The receptionist shook her head. "Well, if you can't tell me what he's in for—"

"I can tell you what he looks like," Maatje offered.

"Look." The receptionist's voice was getting firmer. "If we have no one by the name of Willem Macher, I'm afraid he isn't here. Come back when you have more information."

Maatje groaned internally and cursed her sister. But she wasn't ready to give up yet. "Please – he definitely came here sometime yesterday. He's a close friend. If I could just—"

"Madam." That was it: the final voice. The receptionist

had drawn the line. "We have thousands of patients at this hospital and dozens of different units all over the city. I can't help you. Good day."

"Okay." Maatje raised a hand in defeat and turned away, dodging a very wobbly woman on crutches as she left the building. That had been a waste of time. If only she'd been able to get more information out of Elinor. Had Will been admitted under a false name?

Pushing open the door to Elinor's flat, she was greeted by the pleasant smell of the cooling scones she'd prepared for lunch – ready for when Elinor and the kids got back from the animal sanctuary. They'd be a couple of hours yet. Enough time to catch up on some of Paul's reports.

The front door closed behind her and she turned to hang her coat on the hook next to it.

"Where are they?" Friedrich stood in the hall as if he were made of stone.

Maatje yelled and leapt backwards. What the hell was he doing there? She swung her bag, wishing she'd bought the nice, heavy glass jar of peanut butter as well as the bananas, but Friedrich snatched it out of mid-air and yanked it towards him. Immediately Maatje let go; the man was a lot less skeletal than the last time she had seen him and she had no intention of being dragged closer. She threw her jacket at his head and sprinted for the kitchen.

Frying pan, frying pan, frying pan . . . There was no time to get it out of the cupboard so she snatched up a wooden spoon and the baking tray the scones had been on.

"WHERE ARE THEY?" Friedrich bellowed, marching into the room, her bag still in his hand.

Maatje swung the baking tray at him. He punched straight into it, metal crumpling. She careened backwards into the worktop.

"I know they're staying with you. So I'll give you one chance to tell me where they are."

How had he found out?

"Those children don't deserve a monster like you for a father," she spat.

Friedrich's face darkened. *Oh god.* She only had a wooden spoon to protect herself with.

He ran at her, all his weight crushing her against the cupboards. She gasped for air, and dropped the spoon.

No!

She clawed with her fingers, digging them deep into his shoulder. He howled in agony and elbowed her in the face. Colours she never knew existed exploded before her eyes, and she slid, dazed, to the floor.

A corny twinkling sound floated through the fear and disorientation. Her phone! It was still in her bag. She dived in its direction, but Friedrich slammed her back with his arm against her throat, and answered the call.

"Maatje," came Elinor's voice. She opened her mouth to call to her, but nothing came out. She couldn't make a sound. She couldn't breathe either. "Your friend Will isn't at the hospital anymore. I just had a call to say he was discharged against the doctor's wishes. It wasn't Rachel. I rung her. She mentioned the name of your boss."

Maatje tried to call out again. Rachel from the party? How did she know him? At least Will was safe with Hubert. Maybe that was why the receptionist hadn't been able to find him.

"Maatje, do you know where he is? He needs medical care. He shouldn't have been moved."

Maatje wanted to tell her not to worry, Hubert would have it all sorted for him.

Hell, no – more importantly she needed to keep Elinor and the kids away from the flat.

"Where are my children?" As Friedrich leant towards the phone, his arm pulled away enough for Maatje to grate a breath.

"HIDE THEM, ELINOR, DON'T COME BACK—"

The pressure on her throat returned. Elinor's frightened voice squeaked, "Maati?"

"You bring them right here," Friedrich snarled. "Any games and I snap her neck." He hung up before Elinor could reply and tossed the phone aside like a Frisbee.

His arm let up and Maatje fell forward, coughing and rasping. "My . . ." Using her voice felt like passing it through a cheese grater. "My sister's not a pushover. She's won't bring Anja and Milo back to a mad man. The police will be here any minute."

"Then she will just have made things very difficult for you," Friedrich replied. "I came for my kids. That's all I've ever asked from you. You had no right to take them from me." He ripped her bag strap off and tested its tautness. Strong enough to strangle her with.

"Have you seen yourself?" A rush of terror flooded through her. "I won't let you use those kids as leverage."

Friedrich snorted. "What leverage? They're my children." He snatched up her hands and lashed them tightly together with the strap. Maatje watched, shocked and relieved that he didn't yet mean to end her. By the time she pulled herself together, she was bound fast to the table leg.

"You're still on the run, aren't you? So you need them to protect your arse. First Will; now me . . . at least he's safe from you."

"Don't talk as if you care about him."

Maatje gaped. "I care more than you!"

"Yeah?" Friedrich leered. "Making him slave to a machine so Hubert can play with the dreams of the entire country is a much more comfortable situation to be in, is it?"

"What on earth are you talking about?"

"Don't pretend you don't know."

Maatje glared. "Is that why you hate shared dreaming so much? Because you think we just take people randomly off the streets and force our way into their dreams?"

"Yes, actually – that's exactly what I think."

From the corner of the kitchen came the twinkling of Maatje's phone again. Friedrich stood up and went over to it.

"Anyone important?" Maatje mocked.

Friedrich grinned. "Just the guy we need to speak to. I think it's time we found out the truth. You might want to hold your tongue."

"I will bloody well—"

"Maatje!" Hubert's voice blared from the loudspeaker.

"I'm afraid Miss Finkel is unable to take your call at this time," Friedrich's voice was smooth.

"Mr Reinhardt?"

"Surprise."

"Not really. You got our little message, I see."

Friedrich pulled back, obviously not expecting that answer. Maatje had been about to call out to him, but snapped her mouth shut. Hubert sent Friedrich here?

"You like the pretty ladies," Friedrich's voice continued in monotone, none of the surprise on his face showing in his words.

"Oh, she's the best. My Esther." Hubert cleared his throat. "I'd been meaning to let Maatje know, but I guess it will please you to hear instead, that Will is safe and sound back here with me, and in return I'm sure you've found your children. I expect not to hear from you again. What you do from now on is your own problem."

"Actually, there is a problem," Friedrich cut in. "My children aren't currently here, so we don't have a deal yet. And as a passionate activist against your research centre, I don't like what you plan to do with Will."

"All lies, I'm sure." Maatje could almost hear Hubert grinning. "Though I do suggest you and your children go far away from here if shared dreaming isn't your thing, because the range on this kid is pretty top notch. May I ask whether Miss Finkel will be returning to work any time soon?"

Friedrich looked over at Maatje and raised his eyebrows. She realised then that she was gaping like a fish.

"I think perhaps she might not," Friedrich replied.

"That's a pity." Hubert didn't sound in the least bit concerned. "She was a pretty one too."

Friedrich hung up with an exaggerated press and smirked almost drunkenly at Maatje.

"What the hell was that all about?" she demanded.

"I think you just left your job."

Maatje shook her throbbing head. Too many thoughts raced through it. Did Hubert think Friedrich had killed her? And he didn't care? No, he'd arranged it. He didn't need her anymore. He didn't care about her research. He just wanted Will. She'd done her job.

The blood drained to her toes. "Wh-what exactly does he want Will for?"

"Apparently, he's been taking note of Will for years. Built himself a machine to amplify Will's dreaming abilities and allow him to take them for himself. Or something like that."

Maatje was still shaking her head. "Impossible."

"That's what I thought. Now I'm not so sure."

"What does he need to do that for?"

Friedrich gave an exasperated snort. "Come on – thousands of miles, millions of minds and total control? Dreams aren't just for fun; they're a fundamental part of our psyche. Whatever he wants, it's going to involve screwing up a lot of people, not least of all your precious Will."

"But he's strong. Hubert can't just take control."

"He's not strong at the moment." Friedrich began to pace the room, fists clenched. Was he remembering what had happened to him in that lab? She was relieved for once that the anger wasn't directed at her.

But it should have been. She was the one who had rung Hubert. She'd handed Will over on a silver platter.

"It's my fault," she whispered.

Friedrich stopped pacing.

"I have to stop this. I have to . . ." Maatje cleared her aching throat and looked Friedrich in the eye. "If he's in trouble, it's my fault and I need you to let me go so I can sort it all out."

Friedrich narrowed his eyes. He was studying her carefully. He did care too. Whatever Will had seen in him under the anger, it'd rubbed off.

After an age, Friedrich bent down and began untying her wrists. "On one condition. The machine is destroyed."

Maatje nodded.

"Blueprints, coding, all traces of it," Friedrich continued as he worked the knots.

Maatje shook her head. "That's our evidence." God, she needed a plan. "But I don't know how to access all that anyway."

"You need a tech guy."

"There's plenty at the SDRC. I know none of them will endorse what Hubert's doing . . ." But what if some did? What if they didn't believe her?

"Or you could take me." Friedrich pulled the strap away. She was free. But she sat there staring at him and massaging her throat.

Her, work with him? He was having a laugh.

"Okay."

NOW: RACHEL

Rachel took a deep breath and pressed the buzzer.

"The Kröte residence. How may I help you?" came a prim voice through the speaker.

The wind had picked up and the heavy clouds behind Rachel threatened more snow. She had to press against the gate pillar to hear properly.

"I'm here to speak to Mr Kröte."

"Name please."

"Rachel Macher."

Silence, then, "Do you have an appointment?"

"No, but he'll want to see me."

"One moment."

Rachel shivered and rubbed her gloved hands together for warmth. The sun was about to disappear beneath the horizon; the tall gate separating her from her childhood prison stretched long, barred shadows down the drive towards the house. Oh, to be anywhere but here.

"If you'd like to make your way to the front please, Miss Macher," the voice from the speaker said.

With a clang, the gates began to part inwards. As soon as

there was a gap wide enough, she slipped through and strode down the drive. What was there to be afraid of? This was home – the only place she'd grown up in that was still standing. Inside was her only living family member.

The others had been planning since they first got the news from Elinor. Plotting, gathering supplies; it all took time. Will couldn't wait. He'd been waiting so long for her because she had wanted to stop exactly this from happening. And now it had, there was no point wasting any more time. Her brother needed her, so she was coming. Who cared about Hubert? Who cared about Esther? She wasn't going down without a fight.

Hubert was waiting for her in the hallway. He opened his arms. "Welcome back."

Rachel ignored the gesture. "Where is he?"

Hubert's hands dropped to his side and his lips formed a froggy smile. "You know you'll have to stay in the manor now. I can't let you go again."

Rachel was beyond caring. "I'll be here as long as Will is."

Hubert shrugged and took her arm. Rachel quickly shook him off.

"Don't you want to see your brother?"

"I'm quite capable of walking myself," she snapped.

Hubert's lips crinkled up towards his nose. "Miss Independent of course. Follow me then."

He led her down into the bowels of the building, two floors lower than she'd known existed. If it had been cold outside, it was even colder here, far below ground. It was dark, damp and the walls felt as if they were pressing in.

They stopped outside a thick metal door to some sort of bunker. Was he expecting a nuclear war? With some effort, Hubert hauled open the door. It was the same thickness as her.

"Don't want him wasting his energy dreaming for help before the grand unveiling now, do we?"

Rachel wanted to stuff his smile so far back in his throat he'd never be able to find it. Instead, she just grimaced back. "I want to be alone with him."

"Oh, absolutely," Hubert conceded. "As long as we all get what we want in the end."

"I'm sure you'll get your reunion tonight," Rachel muttered, stepping through the door.

Hubert beamed. "I'm glad." He puffed up and started heaving the door shut again. "You have two hours."

It was warmer inside the bunker. Rachel pulled off her gloves as she tiptoed through a dimly lit kitchenette towards the only source of light, coming from the next area: a hazy orange glow. Her heart picked up. She was moments away from seeing him again. Yet, through the excitement came the strangest urge to run away.

Four years was a long time. They couldn't just pick up where they'd left off; things were different now and it was her old brother she missed so much. What if he didn't like her anymore?

At the far end of the bunker was a single bed. Obviously, Hubert wasn't planning on saving anyone else in a nuclear emergency. In front of the bed stood a shadow, stiff and defensive.

Rachel blinked rapidly to adjust her eyes to the light, and slowly Will came into view. At first glance, he hadn't changed much at all, just a bit older. And sicker. But though he was physically Will, his expression was not. His face was tight and held no recognition of her. A closed, empty look. And as he stood there, blue-lipped and swaying, she realised his tense body was telling her something far worse – it viewed her as a threat.

She couldn't bear it; gasping, she took a step back.

His eyes flickered and suddenly softened. "Rachel?" He seemed to shrink to half the size.

A noise escaped from her. A sob, laughter, a cry? She wasn't sure. She ran and wrapped her arms around him. He deflated underneath her, hands brushing up over her coat until he held her gently too. She buried her nose into his shoulder and breathed her brother deeply.

Safe.

Home.

A younger Rachel – timid and scared – bubbled back and she crushed herself into his embrace a little bit more, allowing herself to be swamped by him. His knuckles dug deep into her back as he clung to her just as tightly. Nothing could reach her here. Not Esther; not Papa's rage; not Hubert.

"I'm . . . so sorry," Will gasped. Heat radiated from him like the pavement on a summer's day.

Rachel couldn't help it; tears began to roll down her cheeks.

No. She was going to be the strong one today. She rubbed them against his jumper and kept her face smothered until she'd gathered herself. More of his weight drooped into her arms, and they began to ache under the strain. But she refused to let go. When his legs finally gave way, she sank to the floor with him, grabbing the front of his jumper and holding him upright. His head nodded distantly.

"Are you really here?" he murmured.

"I'm going to get you out." Rachel cupped her hand against his burning cheek. "I don't know how yet, but I will."

Will smiled and coughed. Happily dreaming with his eyes open.

"Let's get you into bed." She slipped her arm under his shoulders and helped him onto the bed.

She propped him up on the lumpy mattress with a pillow as thin as a doormat and tucked him in with well-practised motions from the hospital. By the sound of his shallow rattling breaths, Will needed to be back in hospital. Had they even had a chance to start treating him before he was taken?

"Are you thirsty? Can I get you a drink?" She noticed an empty glass on the table by the bed next to a packet of pills. She peered at them. Antibiotics. "Have you taken any of these?" She rattled them at him.

Will shifted away from her, wedging himself in the corner of the bed. He placed a hand on the space he'd created beside him. "Sit."

His fingernails matched the blue of his lips.

"Have you been left any oxygen at least?"

"Please."

Rachel humphed like some of the senior nurses did to hide their worry. "I need to make Hubert a list." She clambered carefully onto the mattress and snuggled against him. His cheek dropped against the top of her head, solid and comforting.

"Remember when I was sick and you used to cut my toast into pictures?" she murmured, then lifted her head. "Would you like some toast?"

"Just sit."

Rachel lowered her head again, listening to the crackling and bubbling gunk in Will's lungs. "I don't know what to do."

"You don't have to do anything."

"But I do." Rachel sat up once more. "Do you know what he's going to do to you? To the whole country?"

"Yes."

"Then you know why we have to get out of here."

"How long have you known?"

"About the machine? Half a year before we escaped the orphanage."

"You couldn't tell me?"

Rachel hung her head. "I thought I could keep you away."

"What about the police?"

"We had no proof. The machine wasn't even built then. And what chance did four teenagers have against him? He practically owns the police."

"And now?"

"What is this – an inquisition?"

Will chuckled, which turned into a cough. His hot fingers found her hand and squeezed. "I should have come."

"What?"

"To the hut," Will clarified. "I should have just come."

"No." Rachel didn't want to think about it. About her. "Please . . . no."

Will coughed again. Rachel slid out of the bed and filled the empty glass from the tap in the kitchen. Will coughed and sipped until he exhausted himself. Rachel set the glass back on the table and took her coat off, folding it as small as she could and slipping it between Will's head and the wall.

"Thank you."

And then she sat. Just as he had asked. For two blissful hours. When Will wasn't dozing, they chatted and reminisced about a time before everything got so complicated. Rachel lost herself in the moment, relishing a contentedness she hadn't felt for so long. It wasn't until the door to the bunker swung open and a stranger in a white coat poked his head around that reality came crashing down about her.

No.

Their fingers tightened together.

Then Esther was there, pushing at the back of Rachel's mind, tempting her towards a sleep she couldn't avoid.

"No!" She shook her head.

"Rach?" her brother rasped.

"Leave me alone!" She jumped to her feet. She was going to stay with Will. She was going to get him out. There was no place for Esther anymore.

Rachel stumbled as Esther pushed harder in response. "NO!" Rachel screamed and threw the bedside table across the room. The whitecoat hastily retreated out of the door, no doubt to get backup. "NO!" She stuffed her hands into her hair and pulled as hard as she could.

Stay awake; stay awake!

"Rachel." Will was up, breath hot against her ear as he took her hands and lowered them away from her head.

She clutched at him, his image swimming before her. "She's coming. I can't stop her."

"It's okay," he assured, guiding Rachel back to the bed and settling her onto it. "Lie down."

"No, no – she'll come. She's too strong."

Will shook his head. "No, she's not." He brushed the hair from her eyes as she dropped onto the pillow. They were so heavy.

He sank to his knees beside her, hands cradling her head. "We'll meet her together, okay?"

Rachel nodded and let her eyes close, feeling Will tug at the corners of her consciousness and guide her towards him. The part of her that was still awake heard the door to the bunker open again.

"Just a moment, please." Will's voice. Distant.

The rest of her was running, hand clasped in Will's. In front of them stood the tree den they had made as kids to hide from Papa's worst days. They could hide from Esther there too. If they were quick enough.

A bitter wind blew across their backs, icy fingers reaching to claim Rachel back.

"Do you have your leaves?" asked Will, putting on an extra burst of speed.

Rachel hadn't collected leaves for years. "No, I . . ."

Will held out a bright red maple leaf and grinned. "I've got a spare."

Heart in her throat, Rachel took the leaf. It dropped heavy in her fingers as it grew to the size of a cloak. A protective wrapper from the hungry winter. She tried to put it on, but it snagged and pulled, as if someone were trying to snatch it away again.

"No, wait." Will's voice. She couldn't see him under all the flapping red cloak. He sounded panicked. Where had his hand gone?

The wind caught up and whipped its tendrils around her, tearing the cloak clean in two. Pulling her back; back into her own head.

"NO!" Rachel fought against it. She was so close. She couldn't lose now.

Will's hands slipped from her face. It felt cold. They'd taken him.

"Will!"

He couldn't hear her. She was alone. Back in her inky black prison.

NOW: MAATJE

Whatever Friedrich was doing, it looked complicated. Codes and text boxes flashed across the computer screen as his fingers danced across the keyboard, revelling in whatever conversation he was having with her computer.

They'd waited until the main SDRC working hours were over before she'd sneaked him into her office. Wearing one of Elinor's thickest coats, scarf up to his eyes, hat, gloves – the works. No one had batted an eyelid as he strode through the main doors.

The gloves had been the first things to come off, so he could type. But one by one, in the heat of the office, every extra layer had been removed. Hanna or Paul had better not make a surprise appearance.

"I can't access anything from here; you don't have permission." Friedrich's furrowed brow appeared above the screen. "Who's the head honcho?"

Maatje had been swinging her legs anxiously from her perch on Hanna's desk, pondering the pile of discarded clothes. She pointed to Paul's desk.

"Higher. CEO, president, the top dog."

Maatje suddenly had a thought. What if Friedrich wasn't helping at all? What if she was facilitating access to all the SDRC's documents for his little protest group to use?

"Can't you just give my computer permission?"

Friedrich looked impatient. "Yes, but that will take time, plus if we're not successful, it will lead a direct trace back to you."

"Oh."

"Yes, oh. CEO's office now."

"But I don't have a key. I think it's . . . we need a pass number to get in."

Friedrich smiled, but it was far from reassuring. "Already got it."

Maatje pursed her lips.

"What's the problem now? We need to hurry. People are going to start falling asleep soon."

"Why do you care so much?"

Friedrich's shoulders dropped and he stared at her in disbelief. "I have spent my entire life campaigning for idiots like you to stop your so-called research so that something exactly like this doesn't happen. My wife lost her life, and I lost my children, just because I believe all this is wrong. A man's mind is his and his alone; nobody should be venturing there, least of all forcing their way in." He stood up and glowered as if to test her. "So ask me again if I care, why don't you?"

Maatje swallowed. "Okay." She nodded to the pile of clothes. "Put your clothes back on."

They didn't meet anyone on their way to Rufus's office. The fifteenth floor was deserted. Friedrich marched up to the glass-fronted office and punched in the code he had scribbled on the back of his hand.

As soon as they were in, Friedrich threw himself in front of the computer, hammering the keyboard more furiously than ever. After a few minutes of grinding his teeth and a lot of delete button pressing, he sat back in the chair looking stumped.

"There's nothing here."

"Nothing?" Maatje peered over his shoulder.

"There's a whole host of other documents I'm sure are just as bad, but this dream machine isn't on the SDRC radar."

"Or maybe it doesn't exist?" Maatje was hopeful.

Friedrich stuffed his gloves back on. "Or maybe your friend Hubert doesn't want anyone to know about it, lest they stop him or take it for themselves."

"What, so we're just going to pop over to the manor and poke around in all a hundred rooms until we find this thing?"

Friedrich pulled the scarf back over his nose. "Unless you have a better idea?"

Maatje had just about had enough of him. "Actually, I do." She pulled out her mobile and typed in the number for the manor. The secretary picked up.

"Brigitte, hello. It's Maatje Finkel here."

"Good evening." The vacant greeting was a sure sign the woman didn't remember Maatje at all.

"I've been trying to get hold of Hubert on his mobile for a while now and can't get through. I have to speak to him quite urgently – would you know his whereabouts at all?"

"And what would this be regarding?"

"The research he and I have just begun together. I'm not really supposed to discuss it, but it's imperative I talk to him tonight."

"He's not to be disturbed tonight, Miss Finkel."

"I know, I know, but he's working on our project right now. There's a development that could jeopardise everything."

"He's not working tonight." Brigitte sounded wary. "He's gone stargazing."

"Oh, well, no – that's part of it. We have to check the planets' alignment in relation to what our subjects are dreaming about." Maatje cringed at her own lie. "But if he's stargazing he must be . . ." She left her sentence open, hoping Brigitte would fill the gap.

She didn't.

"In his observatory." Maatje guessed. Did Hubert even have one?

Brigitte sighed. "Himmel Hill, yes, but don't tell him I told you. No one is allowed to disturb him there."

"Himmel Hill." Maatje nodded to Friedrich and his eyes grew wide above his scarf. "Thank you. It'll be a disturbance you'll be happy you caused, believe me."

Maatje hung up and gave Friedrich a smug smile. "Shall we go?"

She turned to the door and froze. Behind the glass stood a team of four police officers and three SDRC security staff. All seven had their guns locked on them.

NOW: WILL

"You can't stay awake forever," Hubert's voice, tinged with annoyance, pierced Will's hot and hazy fog. His red face appeared over him, thin hair flopping over his eyes. Hubert tucked it carefully into place again.

Will gave the best grin he could muster. "I believe the alternative is worse."

Hubert tutted. "We've been through this already. You're the future of shared dreaming and our knowledge of it. How can that be a bad thing? Show us what you can do."

Will looked away, watching from his bed amidst the machinery, as two scientists in their spotless lab coats fiddled with monitors and checked and rechecked the computer. They seemed keen to keep their heads down and refused to make eye contact with him. A man and a woman, who kept fiddling with her earring. Will hadn't seen them before. They must have swapped with the two scientists who were in here earlier. Did that mean it was nearly morning? He'd survived the night. Good.

"You will comply eventually." Hubert shrugged, face

disappearing from view. Clacking footsteps looped around Will's head, circling like a shark.

Will coughed. Breathing had become increasingly difficult lying down like this. He needed to sit up, but had been too tired to fight the heavy probes and wires. Now the discomfort was too great not to try.

The scientists had him by the shoulders before he'd so much as wedged an elbow underneath himself, and pushed him back down.

"Not so fast – you'll pull out all your wires." Hubert stood by the door, arms folded.

"I have to sit up . . . please."

The scientists looked to Hubert for direction.

"Please."

"All you need is a decent sleep," Hubert replied.

Will couldn't fight them, dropping back down to the mattress. He rolled over as much as the wires would allow, to at least shift the building mucus to one side.

A mini victory. He tasted something foul and slimy in his mouth and swallowed it quickly.

Yuck.

He gasped – there was a lot of gunk in there, but the scientists were trying to turn him back again.

"Don't make us tie you down," Hubert warned.

Oh, goodness, no. Will closed his eyes.

Don't go to sleep.

He forced his lids open. He felt terrible. Why couldn't they just leave him alone? And what had they done with Rachel? How could Esther have taken so much control over her? He needed to see her. He needed to sit up. He needed to sleep. He needed to—

"Argh!" He slammed his head back against the pillow. The world felt like a jumping, jerking paused image on an old TV. It didn't feel real. He'd never hated reality more. It brought nothing but pain and confusion. He wanted out. Back to where he was free, where he could run, jump, dance – be anything or anywhere he wanted . . . But now this man was trying to take that away from him too, and worse, use it to hurt and control others.

Why? Why him? Surely he wasn't the only person with big dreams. Couldn't they find someone else?

The first time Will had realised the power of his dreams was after the accident at the lake, when his mother had spent a year in a coma. It was the only way he could reach her – the only way anyone could. She was so distressed being locked in her own head; his visits were the only thing he could do to make her smile again.

She'd had so many plans for the future. Starting a hotel with his father, travelling to distant lands, reading every book in the library . . .

Will could feel her hands now, brushing through his hair as they watched the stags rut in an eternal dusk, and her warm legs, wrapped around him on the beach, with the sea washing over their toes. His dream memories of her were stronger than any from reality. Maybe that was why he spent so much time there, hoping he might find her again; that somehow she'd stayed, like Esther had with Rachel.

No, Will.

She had faded from him, into a dream he could not follow. There was no use dwelling.

Damn, he'd closed his eyes again. He shook his head and blinked back into his predicament.

As Hubert let out a disappointed whoosh of air, Will heard the sound of the door opening.

"Let me know when he slips. I'm going for breakfast."

The door slammed.

Will lay as still as he could. How much longer could he

last? A cough forced its way through his throat and he rolled over to ease it.

In an instant, the scientists who wouldn't look at him were pushing him back again. This time they seized his wrists and tied them to the sides of the bed.

"No," he gargled, half swallowing, half choking on the foul-tasting mucus.

They ignored him and went back to checking their instruments.

Exhausted, Will lay back and stared at the ceiling.

Please, someone, help.

NOW: MAATJE

As the clock on the wall opposite reached nine o'clock, Maatje cheered in twenty-four hours in a police holding cell no bigger than a disabled toilet. She was on show to everyone, including the officer on guard and Friedrich, who was sitting on his bed in the cell next door, knees curled up and head bowed. He wasn't much company. He'd barely said a word since they arrived.

Arrested for aiding and abetting a fugitive. Apparently, because the fugitive was suspected of murder, it meant they could keep Maatje without charge for more than the usual twenty-four hours. She'd turned down their offer of a phone call. It was all very embarrassing and she didn't want Hubert to discover she was privy to his plan. The sceptic in her was still suspicious of Friedrich's tale of the machine. She had spent last night peacefully in her own head, surrounded by a jigsaw of circuit boards she didn't understand, keeping as far away as possible from the red-hot wall in the distance protecting Friedrich's mind. There had been no sign of Will or Hubert anywhere.

But how else could she explain Hubert's phone call back at Elinor's? What was he so desperate to achieve with this machine that he'd resort to kidnap, ransom and prefer she was removed from the equation permanently? She had to hold off telling the police anything until she had proof. As Hubert had told her before, he had good lawyers. Only something irrefutable could get her out of this mess. If it all turned out to be some elaborate plan concocted by Friedrich, she'd just have to tell the truth and pay the price for letting herself be used by him.

She lay back on her lumpy mattress and closed her eyes. Sleep didn't come easily after a day of boredom. She'd tried climbing up the bars of her cell, just to get a bit of exercise, but the officer on duty had fixed her a menacing glare and his hand had tightened on the hilt of his truncheon, so she'd quickly stopped. Just because society had labelled her a bad person didn't mean she deserved bad things to happen to her. Power-tripping prick. She'd done some stretches on the floor instead.

After lying there some time, staring at the back of her eyelids, Maatje gave in to her legs' aching desire to move about and sat up again. She had two options: walk around in circles or do the world's silliest dance. Whatever she chose would probably get her yelled at by the officer standing guard.

Wait . . . where was the officer? His seat was empty. They couldn't be changing over, because they did that in front of her. She looked around in case he was lurking in another corner of the room. He wasn't. And worse, Friedrich had disappeared too.

Maatje's heart started racing then. What had she missed? Maybe she had fallen asleep for a bit. Where had they taken Friedrich?

Then she noticed there was no padlock on her cell.

Oh.

Her heart leapt into her mouth. Should she open it? Where had it gone? Were they letting her go?

"Hello?" she called.

No answer, so she pulled back the bolt and slipped out.

She wandered down an empty corridor and through the squeaky door to the main reception. Deserted too, and – the biggest shock of all – sunlight was streaming through the window. Not just any sunlight, but the sunlight of summer. The two birch trees by the station door waved rich green confetti leaves in the breeze.

Maatje ran outside, staring in disbelief around her. Hot rays upon her cheeks.

It was summer. How was it summer? This was January. She had to be dreaming . . .

Maatje checked herself. She *had* to be dreaming. She was asleep. But it all felt so real.

People opened their doors and windows in the houses around the police station, blinking up at the warm blue sky in confusion before joining Maatje on the street to murmur amongst themselves.

"What's happening?"

"Am I dreaming?"

"Is this your dream?"

Everything looked and felt exactly the same as it did in reality. Every detail, down to the missing "a" on the bakery sign. Maatje walked towards the town centre. Also the same, only instead of a fountain, there was a tall statue of three arched metal stars. A circle of benches surrounded it, stacked at one end with newspapers. People began to help themselves to the papers, their murmuring turning to excitement and smiles. Maatje picked up a newspaper too.

Ever thought there weren't enough hours in the day?

Now there are.

Time to work on that invention, write that novel, get that promotion.

Carry on living whilst you sleep. Progress twice as fast as the rest of the world.

Do more. See more. Be more.

This is not just a dream; this is your new extension of reality.

"Oh my god." Maatje stopped reading.

"It's bloody brilliant," said a man next to her who was looking at a paper. Maatje grimaced at him.

This was the machine? What for? Though it sounded tempting to be able to live an extended life, she couldn't help thinking of who was powering it.

Flicking through the newspaper, she found a map of the country, highlighting the limits of this new reality. Nearly the entire nation. Did that include everyone in it? But that was millions of people. How could Will fit them all in his head? Or was the machine acting like some sort of external hard drive?

The back page contained the small print:

As an extension of reality, your body believes it. Please do not attempt anything you wouldn't do in your waking hours. For your protection, we will remove anyone who threatens the safety of themselves or others.

Thank you and enjoy.

Great. Basically that meant: if you die, you die.

She needed to find Will.

She ran up to the red door of the hostel Will lived in and banged on the door. The landlady, Adella, opened it wide-eyed.

"I dream? I right – I dream?"

Maatje nodded and shoved the newspaper into her hands. "Where's Will?"

"Guillermo? I have not see him in weeks."

"Sorry, ladies, but I'm going to have to break up the conversation." A policeman strolled up to them, beaming as if it were Christmas all over again. "There's a lot to discover out here – come and take a look."

Maatje blinked. Break up the conversation – why? She offered him her best fake smile and headed in the direction he was pointing – away from the SDRC. As soon as the policeman turned his back, she sneaked around behind him and slipped inside the hostel.

Maybe it was because she'd been paranoid since arriving in this dream, but she couldn't believe that the policeman's interruption was a friendly pointer in the direction of something fulfilling. He was trying to stop them talking about Will. Will was the machine, and had to be protected at all costs.

Could they hurt her here? Did they know what she was thinking?

A lamp sat in the corner of the hallway. Maatje headed straight for it.

She had to wake up. If by "remove", the newspaper had meant permanently, she had to get out of here. She didn't want to find out the hard way if you truly could die in this place.

It's not real.

She switched on the lamp. Lights were her dream fail-safe. If ever a dream got too much, all she had to do was switch a light on. In a dream, bulbs never lit up, which prompted her brain out of its trance and woke her.

But this bulb bloomed yellow.

Shaking, she tried the main light switch. It flicked on too.

No, no, no. What was she going to do?

Back out in the street, people had calmed down; they chattered excitedly, flipping through the newspapers. New puzzled faces were swept up to be initiated into their new world.

Maatje pinched herself sharply on the arm.

Ow!

That was going to bruise. Then again, how could it? It wasn't real.

She slapped herself across the face.

Oh god, please, Maatje, just wake up.

She hit herself again. Harder.

"Oy, oy." The policeman again. He wrapped his arms around Maatje, pinning her arms to her sides. "Don't do that – you'll hurt yourself."

"Let go of me!" Maatje wriggled against him. "I have to wake up."

But the policeman didn't let go. "Have you read the paper yet, miss? It explains everything. You have nothing to fear."

Maatje writhed like a snake, refusing to listen.

Just then the sun went in and rain started splattering from the sky. The policeman vanished, but the rain grew increasingly intense, as if someone had thrown a bucket of water over her . . .

Maatje sat up with a gasp, soaked to the skin. Friedrich stood in his cell opposite, an empty chamber pot dripping in his hands.

"Urgh!"

"Hey!" The officer on guard came running over.

"It's water." Friedrich looked at him as though he were panicking over a pin dropping. He put the pot down as Maatje got to her feet and shook herself off. "It's started, hasn't it?"

NOW: MAATJE

Maatje left her clothes in a sopping pile in the corner of the cell and shivered under the blanket in only her underwear. The officer had been less than helpful when she'd asked for a towel and something dry to wear. She'd have to wait until tomorrow, he'd said. She'd fancied calling him a lot of things, but held her tongue. She had to keep the police on side.

Friedrich watched her, arms crossed.

Maatje sighed. "Yes, the machine is active."

Friedrich ground his teeth and glanced over at the officer. He'd dismissed her attempts to tell him about the dream. "How bad?"

Maatje recounted everything that had happened. Her arm and face still ached where she'd hit herself, but they hadn't bruised.

"And everyone just accepted being yanked into a dream like that?" Friedrich exclaimed at the end of her tale.

Maatje shrugged. "It's a dream; your context is all thrown off. I have to say, if I hadn't known what was going on, it would have been pretty enticing for me too."

"What – being forced into somebody else's dream from which you can't wake up?"

Maatje shook her head. "No, but just think: the whole country to explore. All that extra time to learn new skills, meet with family, try new foods, make new friends . . . I don't know, but part of it had me."

"Do that in real life then." Friedrich scowled. "Prioritise."

"Yes but . . ." She realised what she was saying and stopped. "Do you think the dream is built to make you feel that way?"

Friedrich shrugged. Maatje pulled the blanket tighter around herself and bit her lip.

"Thanks, by the way, for waking me up."

Friedrich twitched, which seemed the closest he'd get to saying she was welcome. "We need to get out of here."

"Bozo over there isn't going to listen," Maatje said. "We'll have to tell someone about it first thing tomorrow."

"Can't wait that long," Friedrich grunted. "Where are they?"

"They?"

With a knock on the door from the corridor outside, in walked a young police officer. He had sandy-coloured hair and a strut that told the room he thought he was in charge.

"Hey, mate, how are you?" The new officer embraced the surprised officer on guard.

"Who the . . . ? I don't know you!"

"Me? Your old pal from riot training? You must be tired out or something. You should take a nap."

"But I don't . . . oh." The officer on guard wobbled and put a hand out to balance himself against the wall. "Maybe I—"

He crashed to the floor. Maatje jumped to her feet.

The new officer turned and grinned at them, revealing a needle up his sleeve.

"Tranquil," he said. "Courtesy of our friend Hubert."

"Who the hell are you?" Maatje blurted.

The sandy haired officer bent over his collapsed colleague and stood up with a bunch of keys. "The name's Lawrence, and I'll be your rescuer for the day. Any idea which key is yours?"

———

"Unlike you, I did use my phone call," Friedrich told Maatje later. He, she, Lawrence, Louis from Elinor's birthday party and another boy were crouching in the dark shadow of a slide in a freezing children's playground.

"We were actually going to leave you there," the other boy said.

"Mathieu," Louis warned.

"Well, we were," Mathieu said. "Until we realised we needed you." He looked at Maatje.

"Me?"

"Friedrich told us about Himmel Hill," Louis told her. "So we paid it a visit and found it empty."

"Empty?" That didn't sound good. Maatje pulled up the trousers she'd taken from the knocked-out officer. Even with a belt they were far too big.

"Shh." Louis ducked down. "The observatory was empty, but they'd been there. Looked like a struggle, with debris all over the floor   that's how we got our supply of Tranquil; there was tons of the stuff, and enough in used needles to knock out a small army."

"So Hubert, Will and the machine have been kidnapped?" Maatje asked. This was getting all so complicated.

"Along with however many scientists he had with him."

"They're not scientists," Friedrich scowled.

"Shut up," said Mathieu.

"So why do you need me? And how do you three fit into this?"

"Friends of Will and Rachel," Mathieu said.

"And enemies of Hubert," added Lawrence.

Louis gave a strained smile. "And Hubert trusts you, don't he? You were his partner on this?"

"Yes, but I didn't know about the machine, I swear."

"Don't matter; you know Hubert. You got contacts. We need you to get us to the machine."

"But I don't know where it is."

"We'll start in the manor and work out from there. You can get us in."

Maatje grimaced. "How? They'll have heard I've been arrested, surely?"

Louis shook his head. "Tell them it was a mistake."

"What about when the police realise we're missing?"

"Then let's make tonight count. You'll be back in prison by tomorrow."

Reality hit her. God, she'd broken out of jail. She was a fugitive like Friedrich. What the hell had she been thinking?

She had the most terrible feeling she hadn't woken up at all.

"Please tell me I'm not dreaming?"

Louis blinked. "What's tha—?"

"She was in the machine's dream earlier," Friedrich interrupted. "Hubert's called it his alternative reality."

"It's active?"

Mathieu gulped.

"It feels super-real," Maatje added. She told them about it.

"God."

"We need to shut that thing down."

"No, hang on a minute," Maatje stopped them. "If the

machine was stolen from Hubert, it's not his dream anymore."
She racked her brain trying to think who else could possibly
know about the machine. Who had the ability to take it and
the motivation to do so?

"It doesn't matter whose dream it is; we have to get Will
out," Mathieu said.

"And find Rachel," Louis added.

"It does matter if it'll tell us where he is," Maatje said. Just
as she wondered what had happened to Rachel, it hit her like
lightning. The three arched stars in the dream's town centre.
She'd seen them before: in Rufus's office. She jumped to her
feet and her head collided with the slide above her. Wincing
in pain, she announced to the rest of the group, "I know who's
taken them."

NOW: RACHEL

"**B**itch!"

Rachel spun around. She wasn't alone in her dark prison any longer. Hubert had joined her and he trembled with red-faced fury.

"Leave me alone." Rachel wasn't in the mood for gloating. She hadn't woken up since she'd last seen Will. How long ago was that? A day? A week? She'd long given up trying to get out.

Hubert blinked as if only just noticing she was there.

"Leave you? Your bitch of a mother dumped me here!"

"Finding it difficult sharing my brother out between you?"

Hubert snarled, his red face deepening to beetroot. "You knew all along, didn't you? She was seeing somebody else."

Rachel smothered a smile. She hadn't, but it wasn't a surprise. "He's probably better-looking."

Hubert roared and swung a meaty hand at her. She kicked him in the stomach and he stumbled back, dazed.

"You keep away from me," she warned.

Floppy blonde hair fell over Hubert's eyes as he got to his

feet, panting. "I have to get out. They've got my machine. My life's work. My passport into true greatness."

Rachel shrugged. "There's no way out of here, believe me."

Hubert smiled and a sort of mania danced in his eyes. "Oh, there is a way. You're connected to Esther, right? All I have to do is kill you and this nightmare will end."

Rachel stepped back.

"Don't worry; you'll just wake up. That's what you want, isn't it? She'll probably put you straight back under again, but at least I'll have a chance to escape." He took a step towards her and Rachel balled her hands into fists, lifting them in front of her.

"Don't come any closer."

"Or what?" Hubert smiled. "You're just a vessel. You've never been up to much."

It was possible Rachel had finally found someone she hated more than her mother.

NOW: FRIEDRICH

The lift pinged and opened into the SDRC basement. Crammed inside lab coats that were at least two sizes too big, Friedrich and the rabble of gangly teens were about as prepared as they could be. Friedrich and Lawrence had taken care of the CCTV, Maatje had made and handed out keys for every lab, Louis had delivered the pep talk, and Mathieu had only given Friedrich one cause to practise self-restraint.

Friedrich strode up to the first door – lab twenty-two – with adrenalin pulsing through his body, focusing him on the task at hand. The door bleeped green as he passed the key over it and he pushed it open.

It was dark inside, punctuated with the red pinpricks of machines on standby. He clenched his jaw. The last time he had been here he'd been wired to one of those things, his privacy and dignity violated. If he had time later, he'd come back and smash them all up; for now Will took priority.

The rest of his keys opened doors into similar surroundings. Friedrich met Maatje walking back from the end of the corridor. She was shaking her head, face pinched.

"Nothing."

They headed towards the others: Louis, Lawrence and Mathieu. All the labs were empty.

"Where is everyone? There's usually at least one lab in use all night." Maatje had that look about her again – the one that meant she was questioning whether she was awake or not. Friedrich cursed the machine under his breath.

"Maybe Rufus cleared the building?" Louis suggested. "Wouldn't want anyone stumbling across his new toy, would he?"

Maatje looked relieved at this. "Well, they must be up in his office then."

"We didn't do the cameras for up there," Lawrence pointed out.

"We'll sort it on the way." Louis clapped him on the shoulder and jumped into the lift.

Maatje pressed the button for the ground floor. The glowing red circle brought back memories of escaping this godforsaken place not so long ago.

Friedrich stepped between the lift doors to stop them from closing.

"What are you doing?" Maatje's nerves radiated from her like fire. Her eyes pleaded with him to help her get this over and done with as fast as possible.

Friedrich stuck his hand into his pocket and pulled out his penknife. Everyone stepped back. He smothered a laugh and flipped out the blade.

"What you doing, man?" asked Louis.

Ignoring him until he was sure himself, Friedrich jammed the knife into a join around a small metal panel under the basement button. He ran it all the way around, wiggling as if it were the lid of a paint tin until it sprang out. He smiled. Inside was another button.

"Hold the doors!" cried Louis.

Lawrence's foot shot into the gap before they could close again.

"When we were looking for the blueprints the other day, I saw the layout of the building. I was sure there was one more floor."

"A lower basement," Maatje breathed and punched the button.

Smugly, Friedrich flicked the knife back into his pocket. Louis gave an appreciative nod.

The corridor was dark when the doors pinged open again, but lights flickered on automatically as soon as they stepped out of the lift.

There were three doors. Friedrich pressed his ear against the first. Maatje ran to the second and did the same.

Silence.

"In here," whispered Louis, pointing at the last door. "But we don't have the passcode."

Maatje adjusted her lab coat and knocked.

"Hi, we're the replace— Hanna?" Her face dropped at the blonde whitecoat who opened it.

The woman frowned. "Maatje? What are you doing here?"

Maatje caught herself quickly. "Rufus asked me to join the team. Is Paul here too?"

The whitecoat shook her head, and flushed almost shyly. "I got a transfer to calibrations. Robbie wanted me to work on this project with him. I thought you were working for Hubert now?"

Maatje shrugged. "Turns out I'm a really good dream monitor." She motioned back to the rest of the group. "We've all been keeping check on the dream itself, rather than on the front line like you."

Friedrich was rather impressed with Maatje's lies. None of her nerves from earlier showed.

"Is there something wrong with it?"

"Oh no," Maatje exclaimed. "On the contrary – it's fantastic. You're doing a grand job."

The whitecoat laughed. "Cut the flattery, Finkel. What's it like?"

"Unbelievable," Maatje assured. "I can tell you over a cuppa whilst the boys get to work if you like?"

A little hesitantly, the whitecoat let them into the lab. "I have to admit, we weren't expecting anyone so soon. What needs doing exactly?"

This lab was about twice the size of the ones upstairs, and needed to be, because the machine was huge. A great mass of wires, monitors and lights, focusing around two beds. On the closer bed lay a man Friedrich didn't recognise with thick, wavy, well-groomed hair, gleaming underneath a metal head-dress of yet more wires and sensors. More sensor pads patterned the temples of his chiselled face and a smile lingered on his lips. Friedrich could barely see the man on the bed further away, as he was hidden behind the machine's bulk, but a tuft of dark hair and a white cheek told him it was Will. Maatje had spotted him too, but turned her back.

"System needs a clean-down," she chattered, "so I brought a couple of extra hands to hold everything level."

The whitecoat frowned. "What?"

"You can watch if you like, or go and have a peek at the dream. Rufus is about to hold a party to celebrate everyone who helped make this happen – nice to see you again, Robbie – and you're both invited, of course."

The other whitecoat in the room came over. There were only two of them. Good. Louis and Lawrence circled behind.

"What about Doctor Marco and Felicity?" The male whitecoat looked suspicious.

"What about them?" Maatje blinked. "They'll be there too."

Needles of Tranquil sunk straight into the top of the whitecoats' arms simultaneously. They shouted and hit out, but Louis and Lawrence jumped out of reach. They swung back to Maatje, but wobbled and sunk to the floor with shocked expressions.

Maatje looked down at them and gulped, all bravado slipping away again. "They'll thank us later."

As soon as both whitecoats were out cold, Friedrich raced around to Will's bed. He looked awful. Pale as the stark lab walls and glossy with sweat, his eyes darted about under his eyelids. There was a lot more machinery stuck to him than the other man. Heavy pieces of whirring, bleeping metal – smothering, suffocating . . . Underneath the noise, Friedrich could hear the wet, rasping breaths that had tormented him for weeks in the hut. The bastards hadn't even waited for Will to get better.

He wrenched the wires from around Will's head, relishing the popping and sucking of pads and the screeching of the metal headdress.

"NO!" Maatje yelled, running over.

Will gasped like a surfacing swimmer, back arching as he tried and failed to sit up.

Friedrich grabbed him. "Hey, buddy – it's okay, it's me."

Will's gaze didn't quite focus. He stared beyond at something that wasn't there, lips gaping silent words. Without warning, his eyes rolled back into his head and he was gone again.

"Will . . . don't . . . stay with me, Will!"

No response.

"YOU IDIOT!" Maatje hurled him away from the bed and grabbed the wires bouncing unattached around her. "You don't just yank someone out of their dream – especially not one like this. Not with that many people in his mind. Do you want to pull them out of their bodies?"

You could do that?

Friedrich froze until the last wire was back in place, then slowly he approached the bed again. Fearing what he'd done.

Maatje threw out a warning hand. "Stay back."

"Is . . . what . . . ?"

"He was just protecting them," she said, her fingers tracing the line of Will's arm. "We have to wake him up slowly. Give people time to get out, to sever those connections." She frowned and tugged up Will's sleeve. A cable tie bound his bruised wrist to the bed rail.

Friedrich immediately flipped out his penknife. *The bastards.*

Maatje's face hardened as she marched around to the main computer and sat in the chair. "Lawrence, can we make sure Rufus is appropriately restrained when he wakes up?"

Ah, so Mr Perfect on the other bed was the CEO. Friedrich couldn't wait to make that smile vanish from his impeccable face.

With a careful flick of his knife, he freed Will's other wrist then folded his arms and slumped against the wall, watching, waiting.

Maatje tapped at the keyboard, then got up and hovered over the two sleeping men, tutting, scratching her head and adjusting instruments. Lawrence and Louis lumped the two sleeping whitecoats onto the sofa in the corner of the room – which was more than they deserved. Mathieu used the sofa cushions to carefully prop up Will so he could breathe better, whilst eying Friedrich as if he'd be stupid enough to touch the machine again.

Later he would. When he was through, the machine wouldn't even be good for scrap.

Mathieu stiffened. "What's happening?"

In a heartbeat, Friedrich joined him at Will's bedside.

Will's eyes had started flashing under his lids as though

he were trying to count the windows on a passing train. His breathing rasped louder and his whole body began to tremor.

"Here too," called out Lawrence. The same thing was happening to Rufus.

"It's not the machine," Maatje called out. "Something's happening inside the dream."

"What?" asked Mathieu.

"Can we wake them up?" Lawrence added.

Maatje stood up; she was trembling too. "The machine is set as low as I can get it. The dream should be retreating back to Will's normal range, releasing people as it goes, but everyone within that radius will still be trapped. I don't know how to get it to let them go without . . ." She swallowed. "I have to go in and see what's going on."

"You'd go into that dream again?" Friedrich had seen the terror in her eyes after the first time.

Maatje nodded. "I'll use the observation room next door." She swept towards a door next to a big window, through which Friedrich spied two sofas and a coffee table.

"And me." The words were out of Friedrich's mouth before he realised what he was saying. But he was fed up of standing around idly. It was time to take action. "I'm coming too."

NOW: MAATJE

Fear kept the sleep away. Fear of the dream; fear for Will; fear of getting sent back to prison. Instead of sleep, Maatje found herself repeatedly trying to pinpoint the last time she'd gone to bed when life made sense. Was it possible she hadn't woken up yet?

She huffed out a surge of panic before it could overwhelm her and sat up. "I'm going to need some Tran—"

The lab was empty. She hadn't even noticed the machine stopping its whirring. In its place was a vast, vacant space. Will was gone too. Rufus and the boys. Just ringing silence.

She was back in the dream.

"Right – what are we doing?"

Maatje screamed and shot to her feet.

Friedrich raised placating hands from the sofa opposite, then probed one of the cushions thoughtfully. "Pretty realistic, this place."

Maatje gathered her wits and nodded. Definitely the dream. "We find where they're keeping Will. And get him out."

They took the lift back to the ground floor; the SDRC

atrium was flooded with the light of a cloudless summer's day. Warm air breezed across Maatje's face as the doors wheezed open onto the rest of the town.

It was all so real: the jumble of town houses, the plumy trees, the birds singing their hearts out. Even the crack in the pavement that always reminded her of an electrocuted starfish.

But it wasn't real. And she couldn't let it fool her. She strode down the empty road.

"Do you have any idea where they might be keeping him?" asked Friedrich.

Maatje didn't. She'd hoped that by turning the machine down as low as it would go, Will might have been able to fight back some sort of control. But the dream was still massive, and there were thousands of people in his head.

Speaking of people . . . where was everyone?

She spun back towards the SDRC, then froze.

"Friedrich, are you seeing that?"

"Back up slowly," he hissed.

A raptor – those nippy little dinosaurs she had on her Top Trump cards as a kid – was snuffling like a fox around the dustbins. It hadn't seen them yet.

Maatje stumbled blindly backwards, tripping over her shaking legs and only barely catching herself.

The raptor looked up and its nostrils flared.

"Run!" yelled Friedrich.

Maatje didn't need telling twice. She sprinted after Friedrich. Raptors were fast. Faster than them. Could you still die in this dream?

Friedrich shimmied up a pole that propped up someone's porch roof and reached out a hand to Maatje. She scrambled up – just before the raptor's jaws snapped shut around her ankle. She screamed, scrabbling towards the building wall, and clung to it. The raptor stretched up, but couldn't reach them.

"What is *that* doing here?" she gasped.

"It's a dream," Friedrich replied, as if it explained everything.

The raptor quickly lost interest in them and continued down the road towards an oblivious pigeon that was pecking about under a tree warbling a familiar melody. Maatje didn't know why it sounded so familiar; she'd never heard a pigeon sing a tune quite like it.

"Get off the street!" a terrified face yelled at them from a window opposite, ducking back inside as a flying saucer zoomed between the buildings and blasted pot holes into the road.

Maatje shielded her face against the showering rubble. "It's as if the dream's under attack!"

Friedrich scoffed. "What, by children?"

The flying saucer drew the pigeon's attention to the stalking raptor, but instead of flying off, it cocked its head and sang to its predator instead.

The dinosaur ducked its head and vanished.

"Whoa!"

Friedrich hadn't seen. He was watching a giant teddy bear amble across the road, arms stretched wide and eyes glowing red. "These are kids' dreams," he said again.

"More like nightmares. Look at the pigeon."

It hopped towards the teddy bear, singing its pretty song. The bear stopped to listen, then vanished too.

Suddenly, Maatje knew where she'd heard the song before. She leapt off the porch roof and dashed towards the bird.

"What are you doing?" Friedrich yelled. "Get back here!"

But it was the tune Will's violin had played every night to build the hotel. He was here. "Will!"

The pigeon opened its beak and Maatje felt the music wrap her like a blanket. She fell into it, cushioned by the sofa in the lab. Back in reality. She was waking up. The bird was helping people wake up.

Crunch.

Maatje snapped back into the dream like a backfiring catapult as a massive warty foot crushed the pigeon into the tarmac, missing Maatje by the length of the beach ball nobble on the end of its toe.

"ESTHER!" the owner of the foot bellowed from a toady head that was high above the tops of the houses. It crawled on, unaware of what it had just done. There was no sign of the bird ever having existed. But the song continued. All the birds were singing it.

"ESTHER!"

Maatje recognised the toad's voice too. Hubert.

"Mr Kröte, be careful!" She scrambled after him. "This dream can hurt people."

The toad stopped and a giant watery eye blinked down at her, his throat swelling like a bubble in a giant vat of custard. "Well, well, if it isn't Miss Finkel. Come up here where I can see you." Great toady fingers wrapped around her middle, and the ground shot away faster than Maatje could gasp. Hubert placed her on a roof and she clung to the nearest hold – a round, acorn-shaped finial – as her feet slid on the steep slate either side.

Oh, she was high. Though not as high as the SDRC building opposite, and there was someone clinging to that roof too, hanging over the edge by their fingertips, scrabbling to climb back onto the flat top. She squinted. It was Rufus.

Hubert reached out a warty finger and pushed Rufus back down. "What's the matter, old pal? A reality dream holding you back, is it?"

"Stop!" Maatje screamed. Rufus was going to fall. "You'll kill him!"

Hubert laughed a strange vibrating purr like a smothered alarm clock. "And doesn't he know it. Made a dream he could die in and doesn't even have the power to save himself." Hubert laughed again. "She got you good, Rufus, old pal. And now, so have I."

Rufus tried again to get back onto the roof. Again, Hubert pushed him back.

"How long can you hold on for? You're a patient man, I know. Waited years to get your hands on my machine and dreamer, didn't you? Forgot I still had the prototypes." Hubert purred self-contentedly. "Quite a few prototypes actually. And some very imaginative hosts to run it for me."

"You *are* using kids!" Maatje gasped.

"And why not?" His eye, as big as a pond, bulged at her. "No one else wanted them. Who'd have thought that hook enough up to me and I could take over such a wonderfully constructed dream. What's the point in an extended reality, anyway? I have far grander plans."

"They're having nightmares," said Maatje.

The toad gave what might have been a shrug. "Can't be helped. Young minds are not designed to run my machine."

Maatje gaped at his callousness. "They designed you right though," she scowled. "Made you into a big fat toad."

Hubert tutted. "Miss Finkel, what brought this on? It'll all stop when I get back what's mine. Since you did such an excellent job before, maybe you can find Master Willem for me?"

"Will isn't yours. And neither are those kids. You need to wake up and leave them in peace, and Rufus needs to end this dream before people get hurt."

"The only thing Rufus is ending is his life." Hubert turned back to the dangling Rufus, who no longer had the strength to try to climb to safety. A little speckled bird settled on the railing above him and started singing.

Hubert launched a fat, pink python of a tongue at the bird and snatched it into his gaping mouth. "Pesky birds. How are you hanging there, Ruf? Want to tell me where Esther is? She took all your power and left you hanging high and dry. She doesn't care what happens to you."

"Hubert . . . please,' Rufus gasped.

"Just let him up!" Maatje pleaded. "I'll help you find Will."

Hubert ignored her. "I don't think you're going to last much longer."

"Sh-she's by the moors. The white cottage on the west border . . . Let's sort this out like men, yeah? Just help me up!"

"Old pal, you ceased to be a man when you stabbed me in the back. Think of this as retribution."

"Hubert!" Rufus's hand slipped. He frantically snatched for purchase again, but his other hand went too.

In silent shock, he plummeted towards the street below.

NOW: FRIEDRICH

Friedrich threw open the skylight with such force that roof slates cracked and slid down into the gutter. He could only see Maatje's foot, so pushed himself through the window and waved up at the frozen woman, clamped to a finial like a terrified koala. There was no sign of the toad, but the air ground with the sound of it crawling off out of town.

"Maatje, in here."

She was looking down at the street below, wide-eyed.

"Maatje!"

She turned. "He vanished. That means he woke up, yeah?"

Friedrich didn't know what she was talking about. "Yeah. Probably."

Maatje shook her head. "But he hit . . . he hit the ground." She swallowed hard and swayed.

"It's just a dream." Friedrich grimaced as he said the words he hated. It was the worst argument people raised when they encountered anti-shared dreaming placards in the street. There was nothing "just" about dreams, but Maatje looked again as if she was confusing this one with reality. "Come inside."

Trembling, Maatje edged along the top of the roof and Friedrich helped her through the skylight. Her legs crumpled as she jumped down into the dusty attic room, and she gushed out what had happened, words damming the threatening tears in her eyes. As she finished, she looked up at Friedrich hopefully. As if he was going to tell her Rufus had woken up safe and well in the lab.

"Well, Hubert was right about one thing," he said instead. "Rufus is gone but the dream is still here. He wasn't in control."

"Then we have to find this Esther person. Who is she?"

The icy woman who'd manipulated his dreams? He thought she'd been working for Hubert. He shrugged. "If we get to her before the toad, maybe we'll find out."

<hr>

They stole the car belonging to the owners of the house with the skylight, and drove towards the moors. Friedrich had taken Anja and Milo kite-flying there a couple of times, and it wasn't more than a twenty-minute drive to the west border.

They caught up with the toad and his entourage of nightmares a couple of minutes in – skeletons, clowns, some sort of dripping bog monster and the black maw of an open wardrobe. They were all proceeding down the middle of the road sending traffic hooting and making screeching U-turns to get away. Friedrich bumped the car over the verge and pressed hard on the accelerator as a tornado wove menacingly towards them. But its interest was only cursory. All the nightmares seemed more occupied with accompanying Hubert to his destination than chasing them.

Friedrich and Maatje found the white cottage at the edge

of a village. There was something too pretty about it, like a touched-up photograph. The fence was a freshly painted pale blue and every bush in the garden had been clipped into round conforming bubbles.

"Right," said Friedrich, slamming the car door and marching around to Maatje. "Let's do this."

Maatje put her hand on his arm. "Does that look odd to you?" She pointed into the moors beyond the cottage. Desolate and miserable, even on a sunny day.

"The moors always look like that."

Maatje shook her head and walked towards them, frowning.

Friedrich looked behind before following. "We don't have much time before Hubert gets here."

"I know, but . . . do you think Will's in there?"

"Why would Will be in there?"

Maatje stopped at the edge of the moors and stared. Friedrich checked backwards again. "What's the problem?"

Maatje flicked the air by her waist. "A fence. 'Danger, keep out' signs? And the birds have stopped singing. Listen."

Friedrich couldn't care less about the birds. "What fence and danger signs?"

Maatje took hold of the air in front of her with both hands and gave it a shake as if it were solid. "This fence."

Friedrich laughed, but most of it stuck in his throat. "There's no fence."

Maatje glared at him as though she thought he were joking.

"Seriously. There's nothing there. Just plain old boring moors. We need to get Esther to stop the dream. Come on."

"No, hang on. If you can't see it, surely we need to investigate?" Maatje countered. She stepped up into the air as if a fence really were there and slid herself over and out of existence.

Friedrich started. "Where'd you go?"

"Here. You've disappeared too."

"You'd better come back." He liked the moors less and less the more he looked at them. They seemed to be whispering, "Stay away," and for once he was happy to oblige.

"I have to find Will," Maatje replied. "I know he's in here."

"Better to find him by stopping the dream."

"And what if this Esther doesn't stop it?" asked Maatje. "Whoever she is, she's using Will and keeping him hostage in his own head. Somehow, I don't think asking nicely is going to work."

"We don't have to ask nicely," replied Friedrich.

Maatje was silent for a long while. "You go and ask," she said eventually. "I'll look for Will. That'll double our chances."

The cloud-sucking top of the tornado began to darken the horizon. Splitting up was a bad idea, but they were out of time. Hubert was close.

"Okay."

He charged towards the house, leaping over the perfect picket gate, and barged shoulder first through the front door.

NOW: MAATJE

In the moors, it wasn't just the birds that had stopped singing; everything else had halted too. The sun hung dimly behind the not-quite clouds pressing against the grey grass. Water lay like glass in pools of peat. The wind held its breath at each of Maatje's footsteps. She was too loud. Though what she was disturbing, she wasn't sure.

"Will?" she whispered. Then feeling silly because she was quite clearly alone, she called a little louder. "Will, are you here?"

Silence.

On she squelched towards an unusually steep hill, mud splattering up her legs, straining her ears for any sound that wasn't her. Baggy would have been excellent to have about now. He'd have found Will, no problem.

The rumble was so low at first she didn't hear it. Just the tiniest tremor in the bog water.

And then it stopped.

Maatje peered at the bog, wondering if she'd imagined it.

Then the ripples came back. Faint vibrations buzzed up

her legs, as if the ground itself were growling. She continued on.

"Will!"

The rumbling deepened as she approached the hill. *Rumble.* Stop. *Rumble.* Stop. It warped the ground and clattered her teeth in her skull.

The hill rose before her, a rusty red as if autumn had come early, jagged rocks lining its spine. Now she was closer she saw it was too smooth to be a hill; but it was too large to comprehend as anything else.

"Will?"

The hill moved – a twitch like a rabbit in the grass – and opened a great yellow eye, its pupil like a slit of night seeping through the crack in the curtains. Maatje staggered back and a long neck, slated with scales of hardened flame, stretched into the heavy sky, not-cloud pouring from its cavernous nostrils. Its reaching jaws that Maatje had once seen swallow an entire hotel were now large enough to pluck the sun out of the smothering sky like a berry and plunge the world into a glowing red night.

The wind returned with the darkening of the moors, and the beast's throat caught like embers, spurting a flare to the end of the universe.

This was the dragon that had destroyed the hotel. Had it been waiting on the moors all these years?

Now it had another dream to end; a rotten parody of reality that could kill . . . and there were still too many people trapped in it.

Maatje ran.

NOW: FRIEDRICH

"Friedrich, honey, the doorbell is to your left," a voice that raised goosebumps purred as he elbowed his way into the cottage.

Esther rocked a baby gently in her arms at the far end of an immaculate living room. Pale blue curtains wafted gently in the breeze of the open windows, a cooling cake on the table.

"End this dream now."

"Sweetie, you looked quite washed out," she crooned. "Why don't you take a minute? I've made some elderflower cordial."

Friedrich picked up a little wicker chair with a strawberry on the cushion and slammed it into shards against the wall. "No games!"

Esther covered the baby's head. "You can't even contain yourself in front of the children, can you?" she said.

"When Hubert arrives, my containment will be the least of your worries. End the dream."

Esther jiggled and shushed the baby's complaints away. "Do you know how long I've waited for a life like this?"

Friedrich pushed his finger hard against the back of another chair. "I don't want a sob story. I want you to let all these people go. Whatever life you want, that's what reality is for; you don't risk other minds."

"But wouldn't you if you could?" asked Esther. "Your beautiful wife, with her future so horribly snatched. Wouldn't you risk everything to create a world for her consciousness to live in? A world where your children could still have their mother?"

Friedrich bristled. "Don't you dare talk about Brenda."

"I chose to stay. I deserved more. I found myself a man who would bend the world for me and now I get to live. Start again. Isn't he beautiful?" She half held out the baby, who clutched tiny fingers to the blue blanket wrapped around him. Friedrich could remember when Anja and Milo had been that small. He'd never known how teeny humans could be. How incredible his exhausted Brenda was to have grown and delivered him such creatures. How lucky he was to be given charge of such wonder.

And he'd lost them all.

He gasped a winded breath. "You're dead?"

"Not here."

"Yes, here. You're dead. You have no business playing with the living."

Esther placed an offended palm against her throat. He couldn't tell if she was mocking him. "Would you be saying that if I were her?"

Her voice was different, and when Friedrich met her eyes again, the beautiful black of Brenda gazed back at him.

Alive.

But cold.

Brenda had never been cold.

Friedrich destroyed another chair against the wall. "DO NOT MOCK MY WIFE!"

"Sweetie." Esther flickered back, pale eyed and blonde. "I'm just trying to get you to see it from my side."

"End the dream!"

Esther tucked the baby closer to her and tapped thoughtfully at her lips. "I think probably not."

Friedrich reached for another chair, but this one wouldn't leave the floor. The wicker strands wove up and out of the back of it like a vine on steroids, wrapping around his wrist. Friedrich pulled, but the chair had bound his wrist fast.

"You see, sugar, you're really not in the position to be making demands. I'd have thought you'd be a little more careful considering the fact that I can . . . Oh, there they are." Esther's gaze lost focus, and she smiled. "Little souls. Hiding under the bed. Scared that the bird tapping on their window to wake them up is something more nefarious."

Friedrich's face dropped. Anja and Milo. They were trapped in the dream too?

"Well," she continued in a no-nonsense sort of tone. "We don't really need birds here scaring everyone, do we? That boy needs to learn when to stop interfering."

All of a sudden, the sky outside fell silent. Friedrich hadn't even noticed the singing. But he noticed its absence. Without the song, he fell heavier into his body, the detail of the room became clearer, and for a disorientating moment he felt as if he had woken up and found out the nightmare was really happening.

No. The cooling cake on the table – delicious though it looked – was odourless. There was never anything to smell in a dream. He was still asleep. Will had been reaching out, helping people escape. Now the doors had been resealed.

"That's better," said Esther. "Now what shall I send to rap on your little joys' window instead?"

Friedrich's roar of objection was swallowed by a great toad crashing through the front door. It was a lot smaller than it had been in town – maybe the size of an elephant – but, unable to fit through the pretty entrance, it forced its way in through stone and plaster.

Esther barely blinked. "What is it with men and doorbells?"

"ESTHER!" Hubert's bellowing croak rattled the delicate china in the dresser.

"I see you've had work done," she replied. "It's no improvement."

Hubert crawled into the room, smashing furniture and splitting walls. Friedrich pulled with renewed desperation at his trapped wrist as a plume of debris from the collapsing table exploded all over the room.

"Any final words?" asked the Hubert toad. "Before I destroy every last trace of you, you treacherous witch?"

Turned out Friedrich and Hubert did have some sentiments in common. Friedrich felt discreetly into his pocket for his penknife.

Esther only laughed. "Honey, you don't have the guts."

Hubert's swelling throat near filled the room. "No? Well, I hope you weren't expecting your man Rufus for tea tonight."

Friedrich's heart jumped in relief as his fingers found the knife handle. Esther's attention was away with another glazed look. Though she kept smiling at Hubert, he saw the flickering moment she couldn't find Rufus.

"So he's had to wake up for a bit. He'll be back." Esther shrugged.

"He fell actually," Hubert corrected. "A long way. So I don't think he'll be anywhere again. Dangerous thing reality."

And fair play to her, the only thing that dropped on Esther's face were her eyes – to the child in her arms.

"Aw, Daddy's not coming home," oozed Hubert, then his voice turned sharp. "You've been dead for years. If you're not going to leave of your own volition, I'll be doing the world a favour."

Friedrich slipped the knife between his wrist and its wicker bonds and began to saw.

Esther raised her chin. "And how do you propose to do that? This world's rather fond of me."

"I think you'll find I am not bound to it like all these other minds. I can wake up when I wish, and you have no power in reality." One of Hubert's massive eyes swivelled onto Friedrich. He stopped sawing and bared his teeth. "Little Rachel is lying right next to me – so innocent. I'd hate for anything to happen to her for your sake." His swollen throat whirred with apparent amusement. "But if you don't cooperate, it will."

"Oh, please." Esther rolled her eyes and scoffed, but Friedrich could see the strain. A piece of wicker binding pinged loose.

"But not to worry. I'm betting my chances here. You're only as powerful as the dream maker, and I'm pretty sure it won't be long until my colleague pulls him out of your sticky web and destabilises everything . . . so shall we have tea whilst we wait?" Hubert launched a tongue like a vomited up intestine and rocketed the remains of the cake into his mouth, plate and all. "I didn't know you could cook."

Another piece of wicker went. Friedrich tugged experimentally, but the remaining strands looped tight. Through the windows, Hubert's nightmares slunk closer, circling the house. The clown stared in, straight at Friedrich. It had no proper eyes, just crosses, which watched as if it were waiting for him to run. As if it craved the chase. Friedrich tore his eyes away and concentrated on not cutting himself with his shaking hand.

"It's best for everyone if the boy is left alone," Esther said gravely, and nodded to the creatures collecting outside the window. "You're not the only one with nightmares."

As if to prove her words, the air split with an almighty roar that shook not just the remaining plates from the dresser, but toppled the entire dresser as well. The sky outside flicked off like a switch, and the horizon took on a steaming red glow.

Friedrich sliced through the remaining wicker so fast he cut into his palm. There was no time to feel the pain. The darkness outside lit up with a blaze of fire, illuminating the colossus bulk of a dragon, wings stretched wide enough to smother the world. Maatje half fell out of the air in front of it, as if she'd clambered over a fence that wasn't there. She stumbled, and ran towards the cottage. He'd never seen anyone move so fast.

"You idiot!" Esther said to Hubert.

Friedrich sprinted outside. No one tried to stop him, not even the nightmares. There were bigger things to worry about. Gigantic, horrific things to worry about. One puff of flame from that mouth and the whole village would go up, and everyone in it. People were already running and screaming. They wouldn't be fast enough.

Maybe Maatje realised it too. The terror in her face slackened when she saw him and she turned sharply on her heel, opening her arms wide to the oncoming dragon in a pathetic attempt to stop it.

The dragon swallowed Maatje without breaking pace. Then it scooped up the white cottage – nightmares and all – and swallowed that too. Thunderous wings cracked, as it continued on towards the village, tearing turf and tarmac from the ground, blasting Friedrich, the stolen car and a nearby stunted tree into its tumbling under-draft.

"Wake me up!" yelled Friedrich as he spun through the air. "Mathieu! Louis! Wake me up now!"

NOW: FRIEDRICH

Friedrich sat up on the lab sofa gasping and coughing and collecting his soaking limbs in a furious clamour. Louis jumped back, holding the dripping washing-up bowl from the sink as he tore off the probes that had allowed Louis to read when Friedrich wanted to get out.

"You all right?"

"Wake Maatje up," Friedrich spluttered, and dashed into the room next door.

CRACK!

Sparks shot out of torn wires as Friedrich yanked them free from around Will's bed, severing him and his dragon nightmare from the machine in one violent thrust.

Mathieu yelled as he pumped the chest of the grey, not-smiling-anymore Rufus. It only fuelled Friedrich further.

This dream had killed. And if Friedrich didn't stop it, the dragon would kill so many more.

He stripped, slashed and snapped sensors, praying that without the machine the dragon would only be a terrible nightmare. Praying that without the machine he wasn't killing everyone himself instead – ripping them from their heads with no way back.

"You hold them!" he yelled as blood ran from Will's nose across his cheek. "You hold them and get everyone out if it's the last thing you do!" Then Friedrich rammed his elbow into flashing buttons and blaring screens.

Someone was shouting at him, and jumped onto his back. They got an elbow in the face too. Then he dropped to his knees, swiping through wires to the sockets that powered the machine. He yanked the plugs out one by one and, at last, the lab whirred down into an awful silence.

What had he done?

The enormity of it hit him. The dragon might have killed everybody, but that wouldn't have been his fault. This was. How many minds had he forced into Will's head unsupported? The brain was just a computer, they said. He'd seen what happened to overloaded computers.

"I'm sorry," he gasped to the floor in front of him. "I'm sorry."

Hands grabbed his legs and pulled, cracking his chin into the floor. Dazed, Friedrich was dragged out and flipped onto his back by Louis and Lawrence.

"What the hell, man!" Louis yelled at him.

"Is Maatje awake?" Friedrich slurred, struggling up. Louis and Lawrence slammed him back.

"She won't wake up. Her vitals are coma-low. What did you do to her?"

"No . . . no . . ." Friedrich pressed his hands against his face and let out a helpless groan. "There was no fail-safe." He slammed a fist into the floor. "Why was there no fail-safe?"

"What are you talking about?"

Friedrich told them what had happened. When he got to the part where Hubert threatened to kill Rachel if he woke up, Louis swore and grabbed his coat, Lawrence not far behind. At least they seemed to understand the connection between Esther and Rachel.

"Where's Rachel? At the manor?" Louis demanded.

Friedrich shrugged. "I guess. Hubert said she was lying right next to him."

Louis swore again, running to the door.

"Guys!" panted Mathieu, still pounding on Rufus, but staring over at Will. Without the sound of the machine, his breaths could be heard, gurgling like a straw at the bottom of a cup. "I need someone here . . . not him."

Friedrich let the comment slide. He wanted to escape from the consequences of his destruction. Just for a bit. Whilst he still might be able to do right by someone.

His children had been in that dream . . .

Lawrence threw his coat back onto the sleeping white-coats on the sofa. "You guys go."

Louis was already halfway up the corridor. Friedrich fled after.

NOW: MAATJE

Maatje sat up, nearly knocking her head on a charred wooden beam.

She was alive!

Though she had no idea where she was. The soot-blackened remains of a fire-gutted building. With a jolt, she remembered being swallowed by the dragon. Was she inside it?

Grilled floorboards creaked threateningly as she stood. The room was more like a collapsed bonfire. Smoke trailed from glowing timbers, and charcoal clinked as she picked through the ruins. She coughed more on instinct than necessity. The smoke tasted like hot heavy air.

Only a small bookshelf stood untouched by the fire. It was full of dusty glass bottles containing flickers of colour that moved and glowed in the corner of her vision, but never when she looked directly at them.

"Wishes," said a voice.

Maatje jumped backwards into a burnt desk, causing a cloud of shrivelled grey paper fragments to burst around her, confetti that crumbled to ash against her skin.

"Who the heck are you?"

The voice belonged to a balding man whose familiar face tugged disconcertingly at her mind. The thick arms of his glasses made his ears stick out, and he held an empty bottle as if he'd just slipped it from the last space on the shelf. The peeling label read "Original Dry Gin".

"I'm a jinn," said the man. "And you're my last wish to bottle."

Maatje backed around the remains of the desk, hands outstretched. "Whoa, hang on a second – I thought jinns were supposed to grant wishes, not bottle them."

"No, no – you're confusing me with a jinn. I'm a gin." He tapped the "gin" on the bottle label with a stubby finger.

"Huh?" Suddenly, Maatje remembered where she'd seen him before. "You're the man who runs the off-licence in the village back home."

Aunt Marjorie always bought the brandy for her Christmas cake from that shop. Said it was her secret ingredient. Not much of a secret though; she told everyone who asked.

"Fascinating, I'm sure," said the gin, stepping closer, bottle outstretched. "Now if you could just hold still – don't want to miss any bits of you."

Maatje's back hit what was left of the wall, showering dust and plaster. "But I'm not a wish, I'm a person."

"Well, someone wished for you."

"Who?" Maatje wondered, then stopped herself because it made her heart flutter stupidly to think it could have been Will, and a stupid heart was the last thing she needed right now.

"Well, he's not getting you, is he? Not getting anything. Keep all of that in here; quite a collection, don't you think?"

Maatje peered inside the bottles: a slug, a tree den, a weird shifting yellow light. And a violin.

"I have to say, it's been a while since I last got a wish. The others are so old and dull now."

"Then why don't you let them go?"

The gin chuckled. "Boring old wishes are better than none. And you will brighten the shelf tremendously for a while."

A wind came from the bottle in his hand, sucking at the air like the nozzle of a vacuum cleaner. Maatje's hair whipped about her face, and her fingers lifted without her consent, out towards the rim of the bottle.

She didn't want to be a trapped wish. Her mind raced at the speed of the pounding fear in her chest. "Would you do a trade?" she yelled.

The wind died a little, but her hand stayed outstretched and she couldn't pull it away, no matter how hard she tried.

"A word to my liking," said the gin. "What are you offering?"

"My wishes," she gasped. "You're bored of Will's, so why not trade them for some of mine instead? I have loads of wishes."

The wind died completely and Maatje snatched her hand close.

"All right – what have you got?"

Maatje wrinkled her nose as she thought. If the gin stole wishes for himself, it had to be things she didn't mind losing. "Okay, first I wish to be a millionaire."

The gin laughed; the kind of laugh she'd only ever seen in movies. He threw back his head and shrieked glee into the smoky air. "You're confusing me with my brethren again, who take the fanciful whims mortals think to be wishes and twist them to their advantage. I can't feed off a whim, young lady. I need a proper wish – one with a sticky piece of soul still attached."

Maatje bit her lip. Okay, so this would be harder. What did she really want, but didn't mind losing?

"I wish I wasn't scared of horses."

"Better," mused the gin. "But it's not a soul wish."

"Well, what do you mean then?" Maatje snapped, and pointed at the bottle with the violin in it. "I wouldn't say that learning to play the violin was a soul wish either."

The gin picked up the violin bottle and rubbed the dust off on his shirt. "That's because the violin is not the wish, only a symbol of the wish."

"What's the wish?"

"None of your business," said the gin. "If you want reality, ask the real world. We deal with images in here."

But there were so many images that Maatje didn't know where to start. She was chatting to a gin inside a dragon, the same dragon that had appeared the night of the fire, but bigger. A nightmare, not just lingering, but growing. She remembered the newspaper article about the fire. Will's father had died that night too. He had been a violinist . . . and an alcoholic. Will had made his image manager of the hotel, built it out of the music from his father's violin, then hid himself away as one of the staff, with no one thinking twice about him. The look he'd sometimes given Maatje, as if she reminded him that he existed . . .

And suddenly Maatje knew what the violin symbolised: a boy reaching for his father. But in doing so, he had lost himself along the way.

She pressed fingers against her temples. She'd been so naive. So envious of Will's dreams and hungry to sample every wonder they brought. She thought his creations were the revolution of dream science – they'd helped so many people, were going to help Elinor – but they were only the perfect hiding place from himself. Where everyone saw him just in relation to themselves.

351

She'd done that with Elinor too. For so many years, Maatje had viewed her as something to fix. Ever since moving in with her, she'd begun reacquainting herself with the real Elinor, not the science project. The one who existed outside of being Maatje's sister.

And with that, she knew her first wish.

Maatje took a deep breath, but her lips struggled to let it go. "I-I wish I could fix my sister."

The gin beamed. "Now that's more like it!" He held out the empty bottle and the wind started sucking again, but this time it pulled at her insides, stealing the very breath from her throat, though her heart tried so desperately to cling to it. Tears came, and the bottle drank those too.

The gin screwed on the cap and there it was, her wish with her sister's smile, beaming behind the glass. It was just how she'd imagined it for all these years, if only she'd tried hard enough to make Elinor happy again.

Maatje wiped her eyes. "Okay, let the violin go," she said, hoping the payment was worth it.

The gin put Elinor's smile on the shelf. "No can do; that wish was in place of you. I have to fill my last bottle first."

"That's not fair!" cried Maatje.

He pushed his glasses firmly up his nose. "What's not fair? I'm a gin of my word and you wanted to trade wishes . . . unless you'd prefer I let the violin go and bottle you instead? But then I wouldn't get any more wishes, would I?"

"I don't want any more wishes," scowled Maatje. She didn't think she could go through losing a piece of herself like that again. She was still shaking.

The gin shook his head. "The deal was *wishes* – plural. So get wishing."

But what else did she want besides fixing Elinor? Her stupid fluttering heart knew, especially now it knew he liked her too. It didn't care that he had tried to stuff her into a bottle instead of admitting it to himself.

And then she had a brilliant idea. The kind of brilliant idea that could backfire horribly, but she was already trapped inside the deepest corner of Will's mind, so how much worse could it really get?

The gin leant forward hungrily. "You've got a good one, girl, I can tell. Come on – spit it out."

"I-I wish, for Will."

The gin drew back, smacking his lips as if he could taste her deception on them. "Which part of him? The wondrous hotel that eased your loneliness? Or how about his generous heart all to yourself, to beat beside your jealous one?"

"Now whose confusing wishes with whims?" she replied, but her soul yanked with his words because she was lonely and jealous – yet dreams wouldn't ease it. "I wish for all of him. His generous heart, his wondrous dreams, and his darkest nightmares too. I want everything."

The gin's eyes rounded like golf balls behind his glasses with the enormity of such a wish. He shook the bottle with the violin in it out onto the floor.

The sucking wind began again, stronger than before, pulling and pulling, until the room itself was being tugged inside out. Pieces of Will whipped through the cracks in the walls: silver, glimmering thoughts, burning grief and speckles of laughter. The gin uncapped another couple of bottles and chucked out the contents to try to fit it all in, but the wind sucked faster and stronger than he could keep up with, whipping bottles off the shelf and smashing them on the floor.

"No, no!" The gin scrabbled as all the wishes he'd thrown away were sucked back up again too. They were all pieces of Will. All part of Maatje's wish.

She braced herself against the wind and hurtling debris

under the desk that was so far too heavy to be sucked up. Instead it leapt and slid in jerks across the floor.

"Stop it!" yelled the gin as a nearby bottle began to swallow him too. "Take back your wish!"

With a *floop*, the bottle slurped him up. And the wind stopped as if it had been corked.

Maatje fell out from under the desk, breathing hard. What was left of the room was strewn with ceiling, charred pieces of crockery and long twisted branches. A punctured beach ball flopped to a stop next to her, and a confused deer scrambled to its feet and hopped away through a gap in a collapsed wall. Every bottle on the shelf had smashed, the shelf itself splinters in the sparkling shards.

And lying in the centre of it all, curled into a ball, was Will.

NOW: WILL

Everything. That was how it felt.

His head wasn't just splitting, it had cracked like continents of moon rock streaking a spectacular sky into extinction. Burning fire raged through the crevasses with boiling, hissing pressure, building into taut silence like a held breath the moment before a firework blew.

A last breath.

He'd never know another. It became everything too. Too much. Too awful; too beautiful to hold.

And in that silence, everything screamed, because it wasn't supposed to be everything; it was supposed to be one.

One.

One.

One . . .

A thousand individuals. Each with a dream crying for them in a there that existed beyond.

With that last breath, he blew them back towards their dreams, with the power only a breath containing everything could. And like little rockets pockmarking the collapsing sky, they left.

With each hole, the everything became less; his head began to hurt like a head, and he remembered a name that was his.

"Will."

Someone whispered it. A jarring jerk that stopped him falling out of his name as well.

He stoppered those final precious wisps of breath, uncurled tight fists from his hair and found her knees pressed close. She shouldn't be here. Why hadn't she gone with the others?

Her fingers released their grip on the back of his jumper and gently lifted his chin. A constellation speckled across her nose. And for a crazy moment, it seemed to him like a whole new universe: messy and painful, but solid and real. A world that wasn't collapsing like his sky of dreams, but one that blossomed with life.

He stretched out his fingers. He wanted life so badly, but somewhere beyond this dream, his ribs shuddered into exhausted, suffocated stillness; lungs drowned in their own sickness. Only a moment remained on his lips.

"Maatje . . ." Her cheeks warmed his fingertips. "Everyone's gone. You . . ." He couldn't hold onto the thought long enough to speak it.

She steadied him. "You got everyone out?"

Not everyone. There were two others apart from Maatje still here, sunk deep into his psyche.

And then he realised. She couldn't go home because she was too far down. Snagged by his collapsing mind, his death pulling her with him.

As much as he feared facing the end alone, he couldn't let that happen.

Hold it together, Will. Just a bit longer.

He still had a moment more to give. The moment was hers.

Will pushed himself shakily to his feet, and half fell against a wall. He squinted through the pain in his head, and the ache in his heart. "I've got something to show you."

He led her over the rubble, sliding across slanted floorboards and staggering over smouldering beams.

"Will, shouldn't we be looking for a way out?" Maatje's voice was hesitant. Her hand stiff in his. "Y-you don't look so good."

Without the energy to laugh, he choked and stumbled. "Getting . . . you out."

They came eventually into a gutted but once grand hall where the collapsed concertina of floors looked like layers on a burnt cake. The stairs were ash and the once heavy front door little more than a melted knocker and handle. The front desk had survived best, its warped keys on rusted flame-licked hooks on the wall behind.

Maatje gasped. "This is the hotel!"

Instead of replying, Will concentrated on not leading them through a hole in the crumbling floor and out of existence entirely. *A little longer.*

The door he was looking for lay flat and singed in the ash. It sang to him in a way it never had before. As if it knew the words that came after the end. With an effort that made his vision swim black, he propped the door up against the wall.

"Will, this isn't the way out – this is . . ."

All that remained of the peeling letters on the front of the vanishing room was the word "ish". It blurred in his vision as if it were about to disappear too. He grabbed hold of the handle for balance. "You wanted to see what was inside."

"What? Nothing?" Maatje sounded miffed at the explanation he'd once given her.

"Yes."

She gave an unimpressed snort. "Yes? You know you could have come up with a better . . ." She stopped and narrowed her eyes suspiciously, but the old curiosity gleamed too. "Hang on – did you actually mean nothing?"

"Yes."

"Actual, actual nothing?"

His lips tugged. "Yes."

Her eyebrows lifted so high, for a moment her eyes became perfect circles. "Oh. In that case . . ." She took an eager step forward.

He swallowed. The moment was nearly over. His last wisps of saved breath pressed heavy against his lips.

With a small bow, he pulled open the door.

To nothing.

NOW: MAATJE

Inside the vanishing room was dark and cold, yet at the same time neither. It wasn't even a room, more a feeling – like the bottom dropping out of her stomach. And across that feeling stretched a rickety wooden jetty, on either side nothing but utter incomprehensible, out-of-ideas absence.

"Whoa!" Maatje creaked along the jetty, trying to work out what it could be made of. "It's not really nothing, is it? It can't be."

She crouched at the end, which finished not with some incredible boat or magical chasm like the hotel of old, but the same lapping emptiness. Almost like liquid. She reached out her fingers and they disappeared into it as if they'd never been.

"Where did it come from?" Dark vapour shadowed her fingertips when she lifted them out, and wouldn't waft away.

"It was always here." Will sat down heavily beside her. He had a dazed air about him, as if someone had taken a cleaver to his skull. In a way, this was exactly what had happened. He was doing pretty well considering.

He wove his fingers through hers, catching the lingering

darkness like cobwebs. "I found it after my mother died. Dived from a jetty into the lake and never resurfaced." He swirled the vapour into the shape of an arching swimmer as it plunged back into the abyss.

"I'm sorry."

"Don't be. Sometimes things get swallowed up, and we can't reach them anymore." He stared at the spot into which the vapour had vanished. "But that's okay, because everything eventually must succumb to nothing. If it didn't, everything wouldn't be possible. Possibility is beyond time." His lips quirked a hopeful half-smile. "That's where dreams begin."

"You build dreams from this?"

Will shook his head carefully. "Not directly. But they wouldn't exist without it."

He swayed where he sat, and Maatje shifted closer to offer a supporting shoulder. She wanted to ask so much more, but they needed to wake up so she could unplug him from the machine and get him some real rest.

"The things we lose aren't gone forever," he continued. "We already have them, or we wouldn't be missing them. And that means in the end, when we fall out of time and go back to being pure possibility, they'll be there to welcome us . . ." His drawn face lit up. "Do you see her?"

He pointed into the darkness, reaching for it, but Maatje couldn't see anything. She suddenly had the awful feeling he was saying goodbye.

She snatched his hand back. "Will, we should go now."

"Can't," he whispered.

"Can. Look at me." His entire body dipped forward. Maatje leapt to her feet and yanked him back by his collar. "Tell me how we get out."

He pointed clumsily over his shoulder. "Every dream has a door to here; go back through it and you shall return to yours."

"You mean this door?" came an icy voice behind them.

Maatje spun around. A beautiful, pale lady holding a terrified toad in her hand slammed the door of the vanishing room shut behind her.

Will's head rolled forward with a groan. "Esther."

She strode along the jetty towards them and lifted her palm to address the toad. "Is this your colleague? I wouldn't have been so complacent if I'd known. She was always very good at letting the monsters out."

She stopped in front of Maatje and Will, so stunning it was nearly impossible to read the ugly way malice turned her lips.

Maatje recognised her then: the ghost locked in the ice sculpture, though this time there was no door to hold her back.

Esther crouched in front of Will. "Oh, sweetie, you look a frightful mess. Not long now, I shouldn't think. Do us a favour and take this revolting thing with you." She passed him the toad.

Too spaced out to object, Will blinked down at the creature.

She pinched his cheek in a manner that made a mockery of fondness. "I'd say it was a pleasure, but it really wasn't." She twinkled her fingertips and strode back to the door. "Toodles."

Will lifted his head. "You won't be able to get back without him."

Esther waved a dismissive hand. "Why, because I don't have a dream of my own to lead me? The machine should have copied from you what I need to sustain my new world. Biological components are too fragile to rely on long-term, aren't they, sugar?"

As if he were pulling his limbs out of hardened treacle,

Will climbed to his feet. "I won't do it." He took a lurching step back up the jetty towards the door.

Esther turned, blocking his way. "Oh, I think you will. If you let him through that door, there'll be no stopping him. He has a direct machine link to his body. A body lying right next to your sister. A body he said he'll use to kill her to get revenge on me." She stepped aside and offered a clear route to the door. "But if you still want to open it . . ."

Will didn't move.

Esther smiled. "I didn't think so."

"I won't," the toad cried desperately. "I promise I won't – just let me go!"

"Play me another one, honey. I know exactly where you bury your problematic little bones. You've marked a space for her already."

Will made a noise Maatje had never heard a human make. He curled over himself as if he'd been punched.

Maatje raced to his side. "It's okay," she said, even though it wasn't. "You don't have to open the door." She was struggling to follow what was happening, but if Hubert was going to kill someone – his sister – then Will couldn't let him go.

But Will pulled away and staggered past Esther towards the door.

"Will!"

"Listen to your girlfriend, sweetie. You don't have any other choice."

Will's face twisted as he tried to run thoughts through his ravaged head. "No choice. None at all. Just kindness."

"Kindness?" Esther scoffed.

Maatje was inclined to agree with her as she hurried after him. She felt like ripping Hubert out of his hands and hurling him into the nothingness herself. "Will, wait. You can't let him go. Just hold him until—"

Will swung back in front of the door. "I'm dying, Maatje.

I can't hold him because I'll die with him. And I can't die with him because there are too many cracks." His hand quivered against his head. "He might get hurt, or get lost, but his machine will pull him back to himself eventually. All I can do is let him go and ask for mercy in kind." A sudden panic filled his gaze. "I can't help her. I'm done, but there's still so much to do."

Maatje shook her head, forcing back the tears that had been gathering behind denial since Will's strange speech at the end of the jetty. "Will, you're not done."

"I can't wake up."

"Then I will wake you."

Will shook his head. The strain, the fear and the end were clear in his desperate eyes.

Maatje took a shuddering breath. She took his cheeks between her palms. "And if I can't, I'll call the police and I'll make sure they get your sister out of there."

A little of his panic faded. "And if they can't?"

"Then I will make sure she's the last."

Will's mouth gaped for words that wouldn't come. He nodded.

"For goodness' sake." Esther marched over, snatched the toad from Will's grasp and threw it out into the nothingness. The toad shrieked like a tortured rabbit, but didn't leave her hands. It hung upside down, stuck to her palms. Esther shook and flicked her wrists, but still it stuck. Her face turned glacier grey. "You little . . ."

"I'm letting him go," Will said. It was barely a whisper, but it carried like a sergeant's order. "It is not your place to kill him, nor mine."

"Even to have her die cursing you?" Esther asked in disbelief. "You have one last chance to protect her. You've dedicated your miserable little life to it, and you're going to let him win at the final hurdle?"

"Yes." Will's trembling fingers pushed Maatje's hand around the doorknob. "Please, please don't hurt Rachel, Mr Kröte. This is all I can give you to spare her. Please."

Maatje's fingers tightened as Will's touch vanished. Suddenly this was it. She had to go. Had to save him if she could; had to help his sister; had to stop Hubert.

Blinding, bright whiteness assaulted her eyes from the other side of the door as she pushed it open. The lab back in reality. The sofa. Her body was draped across it, asleep.

She turned to Will. Not a single strip of the radiating light reached his face.

"See you around," she said, pretending she could be brave enough to leave him here as if she'd be back.

He leant forward and gently pressed his lips against hers.

Oh.

Oh!

For a moment the world dropped away and she kissed him back. A soft *you're welcome* to his wordless thanks; a delighted *me too* to his *I've always wanted to do this*. A lingering *goodbye* to his last whisper of breath escaping across her face.

From somewhere, the toad pulled itself and the helplessly attached Esther towards the gaping, irresistible reality.

"You're a snivelling excuse for a brother! I'll make sure you rot in her hatred!" Esther was snarling. "And don't think I'm finished with you either, you disgusting amphibian!"

Maatje had to go. She'd made a promise.

She pulled away and stepped through the door.

NOW: FRIEDRICH

A lot of Tranquil and a couple of knockout punches later, Friedrich and Louis burst into a small dormitory near the top of the manor. There were six beds in this room. The five around the edge held boys, none of whom could have been older than thirteen, all attached to machines of various sizes, shapes and flashing lights. All five of them were joined by a long wire to the bed in the middle, where Hubert lay.

"Hey!" Two whitecoats amidst a wall of monitors in the corner stood up in alarm as they entered.

Friedrich and Louis marched up to them, the last of their Tranquil raised in gleaming needles. "We can do this the easy way or the hard way," Louis told them.

One of the whitecoats snatched a gun from the desk.

What the hell?

Friedrich charged at him. The man's aim was all off. He didn't know how to use the thing. He'd be just as likely to hit one of the kids as them.

"Stay back!" the whitecoat yelled, swinging the gun to point directly at Friedrich. He was too close to miss.

Bowling him over, Friedrich pinned him down with an

elbow to the throat and seized the gun. "You forgot something," he smirked and cocked the gun. "There." He aimed it into his face. The man froze and Friedrich emptied the syringe of Tranquil into his arm.

The man quickly lost consciousness and Friedrich moved away. He snarled at the other whitecoat, who put his hands in the air at once.

"Wake the kids up," he growled.

Obediently, the man got to work at the first machine. One by one, the boys began to stir. Friedrich followed the whitecoat closely and yanked out the wire connecting them to Hubert, trying not to think of the mess he'd left of Will.

"Rachel's not here," Louis said in a low voice, as he came over.

"Oy!" Friedrich shouted at the whitecoat, who jumped as though he'd been shot. "Where's the girl?"

"Wh-wh-what girl?" the man stammered. The last boy beside him began to wake.

Instantly, Hubert sat up with a howl. Friedrich and Louis turned and launched towards him at the same moment the man tore out the wires connecting him to his own machine, and thundered to the door. Their heads collided, sending them sprawling to the floor.

Precious seconds were lost as they struggled up again. Friedrich recovered first and rammed his elbow into the fire alarm. A shrill ringing echoed around the room.

"Up, everyone! Get up," he yelled.

The boys groaned, clutching their heads, still half asleep, all trying to orientate themselves.

Hubert was already out of the door. Friedrich and Louis sprinted after him.

Next door was a storeroom, shelves stacked to the roof with cases and chests and boxes. Hubert slammed the door as he raced inside, accompanied by the sound of a key fumbling in the lock.

Like one enraged beast, Louis and Friedrich hurled themselves against the door.

With a *crash*, they fell inside. Hubert scrabbled away from them, down the long line of shelves, hurling crates to the floor to block their way. Friedrich stumbled over the rolling wine glasses from one splintered box, and Louis received a faceful of stationery.

Hubert grabbed a pair of scissors like a knife as he fled deeper into the storeroom. He looked deranged, like a provoked bull, hair on end and blood trickling down his nose.

"There's nowhere to run!" Friedrich yelled after him, pulling a shard of glass out of his knee.

But there was. Rachel was curled up at the far end of the room, like a cat under a blanket. Hubert charged straight for her.

Louis roared and put on an extra burst of speed. Friedrich limped behind. They wouldn't make it. Hubert was too far in front. Friedrich grabbed an ornate vase and hurled it against the wall, inches from Hubert's head.

Before he could get something else to throw, Rachel suddenly sat bolt upright and in one fluid movement punched Hubert with a neat right hook. He skidded across the floor, blood from his nose spraying everywhere.

Louis threw himself in front of Rachel, shielding her, but Hubert lay still.

Friedrich kicked the scissors under the nearest shelf and Louis cupped Rachel's face in his hands.

"Are you okay? Are you hurt?"

She laughed and gasped at the same time. "She's gone. She left me."

Friedrich checked Hubert's pulse. It was weak, but still

there. A red, fist-shaped mark throbbed on the side of his face, but it didn't account for the blood from his nose.

"What happened to him?" he asked Rachel.

She didn't even look at Hubert. "She called me her beautiful little girl and then let herself die inside his head," she told Louis, who nodded as though he understood what she was talking about. "She wanted to take him with her." Then to Friedrich she asked, "Is he . . . ?"

"No." But he was in a bad way. Friedrich considered finishing the job.

Rachel burst into tears and Louis pulled her close.

Friedrich got to his feet. "I'll get an ambulance."

NOW: FRIEDRICH

For nearly a week, no one would tell him if he was a murderer after all. He was kept in by the police and questioned for charge after charge – damages, breaking and entering, violent assault – the list was endless. And they wanted witness statements for everything else.

"Did anyone die?" Friedrich kept asking.

"Yes," came the eventual answer. But they wouldn't say who or how many.

His kids had been in that dream, and he'd ripped it to shreds.

It was Mathieu who turned up to release him on bail. He'd saved Rufus's life and was now quite a hero. It seemed Rufus's lawyers wanted Friedrich on-side before the media turned up. But Friedrich was on no one's side.

As soon as they left the police station doors, they were hit by a wall of cheering, waving people. It turned out Friedrich was an even bigger hero. No one else in the dream had died. Will had got them back to their heads, though many suffered severe migraines and a handful had been hospitalised.

"I hope you don't mind us telling everyone what you did," said Mathieu. "Seemed like the best way to get the charges against you dropped."

Friedrich didn't care if they charged him for all the wars in the world – his children were alive. Relief gushed from his twisted, knotted insides. Mathieu clapped him on the shoulder.

"But they said people died." Friedrich reined in his celebration.

Mathieu's face dropped. "Yeah. Hubert didn't make it. Haemorrhagic stroke. But that wasn't your fault."

"And Will?"

"Went into respiratory arrest as Maatje was coming around. He's in a coma. Doctors think it's more because of the untreated pneumonia than your trick with the machine though."

Friedrich's insides reknitted. "But it didn't help."

Mathieu shook his head. "That's on all of us, mate. Want to go and see him?"

By the end of the week, Friedrich was still a free man, sitting in intensive care, listening to Rachel jabber to her brother about the things she wanted to show him in the mountains when he woke. If he woke. Today, however, even that thought couldn't bring Friedrich down. Today they were coming.

He shifted on the hard plastic chair, his anticipation uncontainable. As soon as two o'clock arrived, he got to his feet, heart pounding.

"Friedrich's off," Rachel said without pausing for breath. "I think he wants to say goodbye."

The hospital staff had encouraged Will's visitors to talk to him, to which Rachel had eagerly taken. But Friedrich hadn't been able to say a word. There hadn't seemed much point, and his throat was so tight.

But today he had to try. Today wouldn't have happened without Will.

He squeezed Will's hand. "Thank you—" His voice seized. Words that weren't anger were hard to express. "I won't forget . . . what you did." Then he went out into the corridor.

Maatje was coming up it, another lady with a similar face walking next to her. In between them, holding hands, were Anja and Milo.

"Papa!" They flew towards him like two pebbles from a catapult.

Friedrich thought he would burst as he dropped to his knees and opened his arms. He had never known love like it. He felt as though he had become love itself as he pulled them close and breathed them in. He was love; that was what he was. That was what he would always be.

"Thank you for looking after them," he said, standing up again with one child on each hip.

"We'll miss them," the lady said. "I'm Elinor."

"Friedrich." He nodded back. "Sorry about, erm . . . the phone call."

Elinor pursed her lips. "That wasn't the way to get them back." She nodded to his children. "I'd watch yourself, if I were you."

"El." Maatje nudged her sister with a pointed look.

"No, she's right," Friedrich said. "I'll be careful. And . . . I'm sorry for attacking you."

Maatje nodded, absently rubbing her throat. "It's okay."

But it wasn't. He'd let out a beast; a beast that had saved people, but also caused so much damage. It needed containing. He looked at Anja and Milo. "Shall we go home now?"

The two little faces either side of him beamed.

"Where's Mama?" Anja asked.

Friedrich went rigid. Her beetle-black eyes were so earnest, and Milo wriggled excitedly at the mention of his mother's name. He didn't know what to say. So he drew them in and held them tight.

NOW: MAATJE

That night, Maatje dreamt she was back in her bedroom at Mum and Aunt Marjorie's B&B. A bedsheet acting as a makeshift curtain flapped in the breeze of the open window. She couldn't bring herself to look outside; she slid down the wall under the sill and drew her knees up to her chest. Ever since that night with the machine, the moors in her dreams throbbed with darkness like the nothingness. A gaping hole that churned all her dreams violent and completely consuming, trapped in a loop of not quite waking up and thinking it was real life, again and again.

A polite knock came on her bedroom door.

"Come in."

It was Will.

Immediately, she sat up straight. The hospital had told them to keep an eye on their dreams. A coma patient's consciousness appearing was the first sign they might be waking, but Maatje couldn't trust that her dreams hadn't just made him up.

With a soft smile, he crawled over to join her.

"It's not really you, is it?"

He studied her with the sort of care that made her want to burst into tears. She blinked them back furiously. How she wanted him to be real, but he didn't deny her words.

"I hurt you."

Maatje scoffed. "No, you didn't."

"I took away your trust in dreams."

She quickly rubbed her eyes before a traitorous tear could escape. "It's not your fault . . . I just need some time to sort through everything."

Will nodded.

"Do you think . . . are we wrong to be studying dreams?"

"If we are, we're wrong to be studying anything."

Maatje pressed her lips together. "My boss wants me back at work on Monday. I don't know if I should go." After they arrested Rufus, the protests outside the SDRC had grown so big they'd had to close off half the street. And the police had started making excavations at Hubert's manor. Maatje shivered. "He would have killed you too, and I didn't see it. I helped him. I don't want to mess with anyone's dreams anymore."

Will gently cupped her cheek and turned her head towards him. "I'm glad you messed with mine. They . . . feel lighter now."

Maatje pulled away. "No. You don't get to say that if you're not really Will."

For a flicker of a moment, he looked as though he doubted his reality too, then he smiled. "I am. It's me. I promise."

Down fell the treacherous tears. Maatje shook her head. "Don't lie. I don't want to hear any more lies."

"I'm not." He took her face with both hands this time. "Look at me. I'm not lying. See. It's Will."

She could have made him up. She knew his features by heart. Those big blue eyes and lashes like a girl. But the way he looked at her – as though she were the final gleaming note

374

from his violin; beautifully his, ready to set it dancing across the moors – Maatje couldn't make up a look like that. Not in a million years. It was too Will.

She gasped. "You came back."

"Working on it."

She threw herself over his outstretched legs and pulled him close, breathless with joyous disbelief. "You came back."

Gentle fingers traced her face, her nose, her lips, so close she could feel the artificial rhythm of the ventilator in his rising breaths.

She sat back and Will's fingers curled back to himself as if they'd overstepped their mark.

She shook her head reassuringly. "When you're better. It's a hundred percent more amazing in reality." She kissed his fingers and slid off his lap.

Will twitched a smile. "In that case . . ." He got to his feet.

"Hey," she objected. "I didn't mean you should go." The dread of her dreams rushed back.

Will hovered at the door. "If I've got a date with reality, I need to rest."

Maatje laughed despite herself, then nodded. "Don't be too long."

He tilted his chin towards her window. "Three's a crowd anyway."

Three? Who else was here?

Maatje jumped up before the fear of what might be waiting for her outside could take hold. In the paddock down below, Elinor waved up at her.

Elinor, in her dream?

"I'm glad it wasn't a creepy old man you were crushing over in that hotel," Elinor called.

"Shh!" Maatje swung around, but Will had already gone.

Elinor dropped her hand. "I'm sorry I told on you to Mum."

Maatje raised her eyebrows. "You were probably right to, thinking about it."

Elinor nodded. "But I'm sorry it upset you. Do you . . . would you like to join me tonight?"

Maatje realised then that the carnivorous moors of her recent nightmares no longer lay beyond the paddock; instead was a meadow, full of buzzing flowers in every shade. A herd of wild horses stamped their hooves excitedly against the grass, impatient to be off.

She pushed away from the window and thundered down the stairs.

WANT TO READ MORE?

The Little Cloak of Leaves
Winter's knocking . . .

A fairy tale based on characters in *The Dream Maker*.
Plus other tales, competitions and news.

Sign up for the *Once Upon a Nixe* Substack.

onceuponanixe.substack.com

ACKNOWLEDGMENTS

Thanks to my sister Harriet. There is no language text can translate to convey how much you deserve my gratitude. I'd need to write an essay to even begin scratching the surface. Maybe one day I will.

Thanks also to my mother, who took very well the explanation why I needed to turn my back on a well-paid career to become a starving artist.

Thanks to my father for the laptop. I'm taking our bargain seriously. Get working on that album.

Thanks to my brother Nicholas for your belief and your drive. I needed both. Here's the result.

A huge thank you to Write MAGIC, the world's most incredible writer's group who have put up with me living on Zoom sprints for many years. You taught me the true value of support and I love you all.

Thank you especially to Caroline Serpell, Carolyn Nicholson and Ian Hunter for the feedback and enthusiasm, and to Karen Bultiauw for her meticulous eye.

Thanks to my editor Catherine Coe. If you understood any of the previous pages, you may thank her as well.

Thanks to Raph Biss. We never sussed out shared dreaming that voyage, but as you can see I've been working on it since.

And thank you reader, for lending your soul to these words and bringing them to life. I will strive to nurture such a precious gift and treat it with the respect and sustenance it deserves. The adventure has only just begun. The world is wonderous and light, and heavy and dark. But all will be well in the end.

All will be well.

ABOUT THE AUTHOR

Kiera Nixon has always been fascinated by the ways words can be used to twist insanity into perfect sense, and thought she better take some responsibility and twist some of it back again.

She can be found at the bottom of any clear body of water and tempted out with a decent story or sandwich.

facebook.com/onceuponanixe

instagram.com/onceuponanixe